SHOCKWAVES CIRCLED THE GLOBE. . . .

Countless millions were awed by the inexplicable events that had taken place in Jerusalem. Yet at the center of the maelstrom stood . . .

MOSHE EITAN—Israeli chief of staff of the armed forces. His country was his life, yet his soul had died when his wife and children were mown down by Arab gunfire.

LEON HALCOMB—An English journalist with a reputation for anti-Semitism. A cynic with his career in shreds, he would do anything for an exclusive story on the event that had shaken the world.

KATE HIRSCHFIELD—An American psychiatrist. Daughter of an eminent Zionist, Kate was emotionally and spiritually drained by the violence she witnessed daily . . .

. . . obsessed by the man who had emerged from the tomb—the man who stood at the very heart of . . .

REVELATION

REVELATION

W. A. Harbinson

Copyright © , 19 by W. A. Harbinson

All rights reserved. No part of this book may be reproduced, transmitted in any form or by any means, electronic or mechanical, including photocopying, recording or by any information storage and retrieval system, without the written permission of the Publisher, except where permitted by law.

Dell ™ 681510, Dell Publishing Co., Inc.

Dell ® TM 681510

Printed in the United States of America

First U.S.A. printing—May 19

A DELL BOOK

Published by
Dell Publishing Co., Inc.
1 Dag Hammarskjold Plaza
New York, New York 10017

A slightly different edition of this book was
published in Great Britain by Corgi Books.

Dell ® TM 681510, Dell Publishing Co., Inc.

ISBN: 0-440-17216-0

Printed in the United States of America
First U.S.A. printing—May 1983

Verily, I swear by the day of resurrection; and I swear by the soul which accuseth *itself:* doth man think that we will not gather his bones together? Yea: *we are* able to put together the *smallest* bones of his fingers. But man chooseth to be wicked, *for the time which is* before him. He asketh, When *will* the day of resurrection *be*? But when the sun shall be dazzled, and the moon shall be eclipsed, and the sun and the moon shall be in conjunction; on that day man shall say, Where *is* a place of refuge?

—The Koran

With the footprints of the Messiah, insolence will increase and dearth reach its height; the vine will yield its fruit but the wine will be costly. There will be none to offer reproof, and the whole empire will be converted to heresy. The meeting place of the scholars will be laid waste and Golan will be made desolate and the people of the frontier will go about from city to city with none to take pity on them. The wisdom of the scribes will become foolish, and they that shun sin will be despised. The young will insult their elders, and the great will wait upon the insignificant . . . The face of this generation is as the face of a dog; and a son does not feel ashamed before his father. On whom then can we rely? On our Father who is in heaven.

—Sanhedrin 79a (Quoted from *The Messianic Idea in Israel,* J. Klausner)

Armageddon (From the Hebrew words *har* = "mountain" and Megiddo, place name.) The place where all the nations of the world will meet for a final battle, followed by universal peace. Mount Megiddo is in the northern Galilee, not far from Lebanon, Syria, Jerusalem, and the West Bank.

—*The Jewish Almanac*,
Richard Siegel and Carl Rheins

Woe to you who desire the day of the Lord!
Why would you have the day of the Lord?
It is darkness, and not light; as if a man fled from
 a lion, and a bear met him;
or went into the house and leaned with his hand
 against a wall, and a serpent bit him.
Is not the day of the Lord darkness, and not
 light?
and gloom with no brightness in it?
                    —Amos 5:18–20; also, Isa. 2:11

For my one and only
Tanya

PART ONE:

Annunciation

. . . and lo, the star, which they saw in the east, went before them, till it came and stood over where the young child was.

—Matthew, 2:9

1

The fear limned the edge of the experience and the Whole drew her in. The Whole was a white hole, a burning sun expanding, the light spreading out all around her and dissolving the darkness. The fear receded with the darkness. The sun climbed above the mountains. A line of white crosses dominated a breast of earth, and beyond were more hills, a shimmering haze, the desolate plains of the desert.

She knew it was a dream. The light shone on her father's grave. Each mourner added a shovelful of dirt and stepped back with head bowed. Someone chanted the mourner's kaddish. God's greatness was affirmed. "Beyond all the blessings and hymns . . ." A voice rising and falling.

The rabbi was disenchanted, touching his skullcap with one hand, a mild wind tugging the dark cloth of his suit as he tried not to look at her. No tears. You won't bend. *Only the rabbi could have made her cry. She ignored his silent reprimand and looked away, surveying the parched, ancient Holy Land.* I do not belong here; I resist and it destroys me. *The pain, which was greater than that caused by her father's death, now forced her to rise up and glance down upon herself on the windswept hill.*

I'm a woman: I bleed. *All women bleed, the rabbi said. You must accept the bleeding as a sign that life constantly renews itself.* I'm a victim of my body. *You err in thinking so; the body is the temple of your spirit and you chose to defile it. She refused to accept this. The open grave was her truth: her father's corpse in a plain wooden box, now buried deep in the earth.*

More dirt was shoveled in, the sun flashing off the spades, and the cantor stepped back to make way for the man offering the eulogy. He was flesh and no more. An old man, he is no more. My father, a stranger, a memory: already swallowed by history.

Leon's tired eyes examined her. She looked down and surveyed herself. The Valley of Kidron filled her eyes, grassy slopes strewn with rubble, the ghosts of Solomon, Hezekiah, and Absalom permeating the air. Leon knew what she was thinking: I will not give in to this. . . . Her confusion was greater than her grief and made the pain more unbearable. I won't bend, she insisted. That's your dilemma, the rabbi accused. She glanced up and was blinded by the sun and then she fell to her knees.

The Pool of Siloam was filled with water. The brilliant sun flashed around Him. He stretched out His hands to the blind man and restored the man's sight. The man called out and wept, kissed the feet in the sandals. The wind tugged at the white robes of Christ and made the red water ripple. Then He turned toward her. His radiant eyes filled her with shame. She lowered her gaze and saw the blood illuminating the Pool of Siloam in which, with a rank, shocking foulness, a fetus was drifting. Someone's child. Her child. The butchered flesh of the unborn. She sobbed and felt a terrible loss as the breath of Christ touched her. Flowing white robes and dark hair, His hands outstretched in beckoning . . . she sobbed for the loss of her child and fell down at His feet.

—Blessed child.

—God forgive me.

Her grief made her cry aloud. She opened her eyes and saw the grave. The fear returned and filled her whole being as the ground roared and parted. The dirt fell away, a fierce wind lashed the hill, and she dissolved and became a silent scream as the grave opened out. The dark earth was forced aside and the wooden box was pushed back up; her father's fingers curled around the splintered edges as white light filled the darkness.

The blinding radiance of His presence. Exultation and terror. The bloody fetus in swirling water, the marble sheen of her father's face, the rabbi with his gentle accusations, Leon's tired, jaded gaze. The confusion increased her terror as the wind roared around her, and she fearfully turned away—from His radiance, His resurrection—as the arms in the white robes in the white light were raised to embrace her.

She cried aloud and awakened.

Kate jerked onto her back, ripping the sheet from her naked body, opening her eyes and glancing wildly around her, gasping harshly, her heart pounding. Silence. Something else. The silent screaming of the dream. She saw the white walls of the bedroom, the window open, the curtains fluttering, a light breeze chilling the sweat on the tanned skin of her trembling limbs.

"Damn," she muttered, rubbing her face with a sweating palm. "I should never sleep alone."

She sat up, wrapped her arms around her bent knees, and studied the quiet room. White walls, a few paintings, some framed diplomas, scattered clothes, functional furniture, and numerous books on psychology; little else of real value. She glanced around her and shivered. The night's silence was unreal. The phantasmagoria of the dream was still with her, cobwebbing her thoughts.

Her father's room was next door, but he had died a week ago. She remembered him lying on his bed, his body cold, his face white, an unrecognizable, alabaster mask, her fingers pressed on his sightless eyes. Death: the inevitable. Death: the unforgettable. Kate shivered and removed her hands from her knees and then stretched her long legs. *Physician, heal thyself*. Kate tried to ignore the thought. She reached out to the bedside cabinet, lit a cigarette, and inhaled; then with a sigh, her body cool, swung her legs off the bed.

The darkness was not comforting, the silence was strangely threatening, and bewildered that the fear should still be present, Kate stood up and stretched herself. Naked, she was alive, her flesh releasing her from her mind. A cool breeze came through the window, touched her skin, and made her yearn for oblivion. Not mere pleasure —oblivion, the ephemeral drowning in sensuality. Kate thought about sex, about blood, the dream's fetus; and the fear, which for a brief moment had left, now returned to take hold of her.

"Damn," she murmured. "I'm *still* dreaming."

The words were no comfort, sounding ethereal in the empty house, echoing in the depths of her head as if spoken by someone else. She shivered again, inhaling deeply on her cigarette, her uncombed hair caressing her shoulders and the blade of her spine. The fear was insidious and could not be explained; in trying to explain it, she returned to the dream and that merely increased the fear.

Silence. Shifting shadows. A faint light fell through the window. Out there, beyond the window, was the night and its dark, treacherous deserts. Kate stared at the window. The light seemed to be calling to her. Shivering, she took a step forward, then stopped again, feeling nervous. She inhaled on her cigarette and let the smoke out slowly, took a deep breath, and then walked up to the window.

She saw the star immediately, very large, very bright, dominating the glittering mosaic all around it with a pulsating brilliance.

A star. What star? She had never seen it before. Unfamiliar with astronomy, she nevertheless knew the sky by sight and understood that that star should not have been there. She blinked and looked again, but the star remained there, pulsating yet unreal.

She saw little else. Her eyes were fixed on the heavens. The large star was at the vortex of an immense web of smaller stars and black sky, the pale moon wreathed in thin clouds, streaks of blue light around it: the great tapestry of the cosmos, infinite, impenetrable, stretching over the sleeping hills and plains, the night's conspiracy of silence. Kate was drawn to the star; it drew her in and then dissolved her. She blinked, shook her head, looked again, and saw its hard, glittering brilliance.

"This is stupid," she murmured. "You're being foolish. It's just a damned star."

Her own voice sounded strange, disembodied, and unreal, lingering like an echo in her head before fading away.

The star was large and pulsating and unnaturally bright, dominating the glittering sky. That same sky had colored her dream, that same moon had shone down; the pool of blood and the drifting fetus had been drawn from her past, but the star, which she had never seen before, had no place in her history. She inhaled on her cigarette, blew the smoke out, and shivered, her lean body framed by the window and licked by the breeze.

"Five o'clock in the morning," she said ruefully. "I'm still drunk . . . or still dreaming."

Still dreaming of nameless fears, of a past that refused to die, of the physician who could not heal herself and instead let her work rule her life. She did not belong here. This land was not her land. No longer young, now alone in a passionate country, she, who viewed passion as an irrational impulse, passed her days in a desperate fight against despair and could not sleep at night. Also her dreams were haunting, colored with guilt and confusion, the contradictions of the spirit and flesh resurrecting her lost hopes. A child in a woman's body, a frightened being with a defensive tongue, a physician who healed wounded minds but could not soothe her own fears.

Kate Hirschfield was naked. Her eyes reflected an unknown star. She looked up, unable to believe what she was seeing, wishing that daybreak would come.

"Go away, damn you! *Go!*"

A star. *What star?* It did not belong there. She inhaled on her cigarette, exhaled slowly, licked her dry lips, hung over, half asleep and confused, the fear slipping around her. She shivered and shook her head, trying to break free from the dream, thinking of Leon and the rabbi and her father's death, and feeling defenseless. She had drunk too much last night and was drinking too much in general; between Leon and her own sense of desolation she was losing touch with herself.

"I need sex," she said.

She walked back to the bed, sat down and crossed her legs, stubbed her cigarette out in the ashtray, and then reached for the telephone. Her hand wavered in the air, a pale web in the darkness, fingers outspread and curving down slightly, hesitating, retreating. No, not at this time . . . not at five in the morning. She shook her head wearily, crossed her hands and held her shoulders, rocked her body slowly from side to side, and then lay down on the bed.

"He's dead," she said. "My father is dead. I'm thirty-five years of age."

The confession was no comfort and did not dispel the fear that continued to coldly drape itself over her. She tried to rationalize the feeling, putting it down to the dream, but her eyes, roaming restlessly around the silent, moonlit room, were drawn inexorably back to the window and the darkness beyond. Kate felt disoriented. She couldn't shake the dream off. Now, blending in with the pervasive images of the dream, was the image of a large, brilliant star that should not have been there.

"Kate Hirschfield," she said aloud, "you're imagining things . . . or you simply never *saw* that star before."

The silence mocked her words. Shivering with cold, she was also sweating. She wanted someone beside her, on top of her, inside her, obliterating the fevers of the night and the fear clinging to her. She closed her eyes and touched her body to confirm her own being, touched her breasts and nipples, ran her fingers along her stomach, slid both hands along her smooth thighs, felt inside, then gasped softly. She kept her eyes closed and explored herself and drifted out toward freedom.

Darkness and silence. She surrendered to sensation. The prison of her body disappeared and left her adrift. Her eyes were still closed. The moon and stars filled the void. . . . Leon running his tongue slowly down her throat and filling his mouth with her breast. Last night, about midnight. Then more whiskey and a taxi home. Not kosher, but good for sleepless nights before the dreams resurrected her. . . . The dark, upturned earth, her father's grave washed in white haze; the cantor and the rabbi and Leon, the murmured grief of the mourners. Fierce heat. Dazzling light. The sun climbing in the sky. Darkness falling with abrupt, startling speed and bringing with it the moon and stars. . . . The stars. *What stars?* The large star should not have been there. What sky is it? Where am I? I am here. It must have been there before. . . . The large star was unnaturally bright. She looked up and the fear returned. The star expanded and became a blinding light that spread out and engulfed her.

Kate gasped and opened her eyes, heard the rumbling, felt the shaking, saw the paintings swinging crazily on the walls as the light filled the room. The fear shook her awake, but she didn't know what was happening: the rumbling was a muffled sound all around her, both outside and inside. The room continued shaking, ornaments rattling, the paintings swinging, and Kate groaned and rolled onto her hip and grabbed the side of the bed. Then she blinked, disbelieving, taking in the brilliant light, crying out as her whole body shook and the panic whipped through her.

The room was brilliantly illuminated; the floors were shaking and rumbling. The fierce white light was pouring in through the window and turning the night into day. Kate couldn't believe her senses. She heard the low, muffled rumbling. The room shook even worse than before and then the bright light transfixed her.

"Oh, my God!" she exclaimed.

The muffled rumbling continued, cups and saucers were rattling, and then the bright light started flickering on and off with dazzling rapidity. Kate gasped and gripped the bed, felt it shaking beneath her, fixed her eyes on the paintings on the walls as they swung back and forth. The light and darkness formed a jigsaw of brilliant chiaroscuro, the stark black and white creating bizarre shapes that were constantly changing. Kate opened her mouth to scream, felt the breath drawn from her lungs, choked and somehow managed a groan, and then rolled onto her stomach, her face turned to the side.

"No more!" she hissed.

The room was plunged back into darkness, the harsh rumbling faded away, and Kate lay there, too frightened to move, as the bed stopped its shaking. Silence. And darkness. She couldn't believe what had happened. Her heart was pounding and she felt very cold and yet her sweat stained the bedsheet. She licked her parched lips and let her pounding heart slow down. The paintings on the walls had stopped swinging and the silence was absolute.

Kate lay there for some time, covering her face with her hands, too weak and frightened to move, wondering what had occurred.

Perhaps it had been an earthquake. What else could it have been? Yet an earthquake would not explain the light that had poured in through the window. She lay there, still trembling, closed her eyes and saw the star. . . . Then, retreating from the edge of the impossible, she opened her eyes again.

Her eyes were fixed on the open window. She could not get off the bed. Still naked, she lay there on her belly and wondered what was outside. She breathed deeply and evenly, still looking across the room, and saw the window framing a crimson light that bled weakly from darkness.

Eventually she stood up, feeling weak, her skin cold, and stepped forward as if in a trance and then stopped at the window. Shivering, she pressed against it, her flat stomach touching wood. She felt her body, the naked skin, the hard nipples, reaching out toward the night. Where was she? She wasn't sure. What had happened? The inexplicable. And so fearful, hypnotized, a child startled by the unknown, she leaned against the window frame, licked her lips, took a deep breath, and then, not too sure of what she would see out there, glanced up at the bloody sky, heaved a sigh of relief, then looked down at the golden domes and spangled minarets as they emerged from the quietly retreating darkness and took shape in the crimson haze.

Dawn light.

Over Jerusalem.

2

Major General Moshe Eitan, chief of staff of the Israeli armed forces, walked into the VIP lounge of Ben-Gurion International Airport, twelve miles from Tel Aviv, just as the self-propelled passenger steps came to rest against the side of the El Al 747 beyond the light-reflecting, bulletproof, plate-glass windows. Lieutenant Paul Frankel, standing in front of the windows, nodded at the soldiers outside, watched them march in two well-armed lines toward the parked aircraft, and then turned around and stepped forward to greet his superior.

"He's arrived?"

"Yes, Major General. They've just put the steps up. I've posted men all around the terminal, at every entrance and exit."

"Any more phone calls?"

"No."

"Very good. They're clever bastards."

Standing in front of the slim, neat, delicately handsome Lieutenant Frankel, Major General Moshe Eitan looked even larger and more disheveled than he actually was, his tanned face—with its lined skin, broken nose, and cold gray eyes—a parchment of singularly harsh experiences, made more intimidating by its tightly controlled tension and by the body, all muscle and bone, that strained against a tight uniform. Now Moshe stepped forward, running his fingers through his tangled brown hair, and stopped when he reached the plate-glass window, placing one hand upon it.

"Any more on this morning's earth tremor?"

"I'm afraid not. It was totally unexpected. There would normally be signs; in this case there weren't. So far we can't explain it at all."

"I really can't accept that."

"Nor can our geologists. They were still debating the matter when I left them—almost tearing their hair out."

"They were probably just upset at being pulled out of their damned beds."

"I don't think so, Major General. On the contrary, they seemed excited. There was no indication of such a tremor, and now it has them intrigued."

" 'Sweet of voice, short of brains,' " Moshe quoted. "Still," he added, "I thought it was some sort of an explosion."

"So did I, Major General, but it wasn't. It's an absolute mystery."

"Both mysteries," Moshe replied. "The earth tremor and the phone call. This is shaping up as a potentially bad day."

With his fingers still pressed to the plate glass, Moshe glanced quickly around the empty lounge, automatically searching for something amiss. Seeing nothing, he was nonetheless still worried. The telephone call had been made direct to the air traffic controller at 4:30 that same morning, the unknown caller stating that there would be an attempt on the prime minister's life when he disembarked at Ben-Gurion Airport. The air traffic controller had immediately notified airport security, and the message, relayed to Moshe through Shin Beth, had forced him to leave his bed and organize the temporary closing and thorough searching of the whole airport terminal. Neither a bomb nor a would-be assassin had been uncovered, and although it now seemed that the call had merely been one of harassment, Moshe had good reason still to be very anxious.

"You're sure you've checked everything?" he said to Lieutenant Frankel, without looking over his shoulder.

"Everything," the lieutenant replied rather testily. "We've turned the place upside down."

"And the call was untraceable?"

"We only know that it came from the Yafo area. It was too brief for a more detailed check."

"Damn them," Moshe said.

The lieutenant walked up to his side and they both stared through the plate-glass windows as the soldiers fanned out around the aircraft. It was just after dawn and the sky beyond the plane was a cloudless, dazzling crimson, streaked here and there with yellow sunlight and silvery striations. The rear passenger door of the aircraft had been opened, and two men wearing the uniform of the IDF emerged and took up positions at either side of the door, their eyes scanning the highest points of the terminal and the shadowed ground of the apron area. The special task force, commanded by two veterans of the last

Arab-Israeli war, had now formed a protective triangle around the passenger steps; and at the top of the steps one of the two uniformed men, obviously satisfied with the security arrangements, turned to glance back into the plane and then nodded his head.

"What a way to arrive home," Moshe said quietly. "Will we ever know peace?"

"I doubt it," the lieutenant replied. "It's getting worse every year. We'll only know peace when either the Jews or the Arabs are obliterated."

"Hopefully the Arabs, Lieutenant?"

"Naturally, Major General."

"Ah, yes . . . naturally." Moshe dropped the words dryly, his voice softly cutting, glancing quickly at the lieutenant, noting the blush on his cheeks, grinning slightly, mockingly, before turning away to focus his cool gray eyes on the airstrip.

"There he is," he said, nodding.

The Israeli prime minister, wearing only a pair of rumpled gray slacks and white, open-necked shirt, and with his jacket draped informally over one arm, had emerged from the interior of the aircraft and was carefully making his way down the steep passenger steps to the tarmac. When he reached the bottom, the soldiers of the special task force closed in around him, and then, when the prime minister had shaken hands with his personal secretary, the whole group began to head toward the terminal building.

The sun was rising behind the aircraft, an enormous, incandescent globe, yellow blending into gold, its shape distorted in the shimmering air, spreading out through the haze like a stream of molten iron, the surrounding sky streaked with blue and crimson, setting the few clouds on fire. On the tarmac the soldiers were colorless, holding their rifles at the ready, their shadows stretching grotesquely in front of them, elongated and jittery. The prime minister was walking casually, glancing around at the heavy guard detail, mopping the sweat on his balding head with a handkerchief—a small man, deceptively insignificant, almost lost in the larger group.

"He looks tired," Lieutenant Frankel said.

Moshe didn't reply, but merely stood where he was, leaning forward, fingers outspread on the glass, his head turned to the right, his cool eyes following the prime minister as he reached the side door of the VIP lounge and disappeared into the corridor at the other side of the wall. The soldiers, forming a protective path stretching from both sides of the door, snapped to attention and then performed an about-face, while Moshe, offering a sigh, running his fingers through his hair, turned back toward the lounge, his body silhouetted in the exotic crimson dawn that was framed by the windows.

"So far, so good," he said quietly.

The prime minister, followed by his immaculately suited secretary, came into the lounge, blinked his eyes and then rubbed them, looked up at Moshe and Lieutenant Frankel, and offered a weary smile. "I'm too old for all this traveling," he said. "I could sleep for a month."

The two soldiers in charge of the task force entered the lounge behind him, closed the door after them, and then stood close to the urbane, gray-haired secretary, their Uzi guns slung over their shoulders. Moshe nodded at them both, offering a flickering smile, and then returned his attention to the prime minister.

"So," the prime minister said. "Do we, or do we not, meet the famed Rashid Idriss?"

"Yes, Shlomo, we do. He's having breakfast in one of your offices in the Knesset right this minute."

"I don't believe this," the prime minister said, shaking his balding head from side to side, a bemused smile on his face. "The dreaded PLO leader right there in the Knesset . . . It's ridiculous. Impossible."

Moshe grinned laconically, the humor absent from his gray eyes. "Well, he's there all right. He arrived just before I left. He's being entertained by the undersecretary—and is breathless to talk to you."

"If word of this leaked out, we'd *all* be in trouble."

"The word won't leak out, Shlomo. We've only informed Mossad and Shin Beth. And Rashid is in the same boat as us: what would *his* people think if they knew he had actually stepped foot in the Knesset?"

The prime minister nodded, scratched his nose, and glanced around him. "So, Moshe, how did you get him here?"

Moshe smiled, tilting his head to the right in a kind of salute, his eyes fixed on his old friend. The prime minister was a small, rather stocky figure whose sixty-three-year-old face still retained a deceptively childish innocence, his hazel eyes a bit too large, displaying constant surprise, his face finely boned and moon-shaped, his smile advertising the openness of a peasant. More than one man had made the mistake of judging Shlomo Ben Eliezer by that immature countenance, forgetting that behind the carefully cultivated peasant's simplicity lay a life of harsh military experience and cunning, frequently ruthless political intrigues. What made Moshe smile, as he stared obliquely at his old friend, was the knowledge that he, too, even knowing what he knew, had fallen more than once for the prime minister's quietly theatrical air of naiveté.

"He traveled incognito from Cairo to Suez," Moshe said, "took a hired boat across the Canal to El Shatt, was met there by our men, and flown to the airstrip at Hakirya, then driven from there, in an escorted convoy, direct to the Knesset, arriving about an hour ago and being slipped in through a side door that was guarded by selected members of Shin Beth. So very few on either side know that he's here. . . . Lieutenant Frankel arranged it."

"Very good, Lieutenant. I am reassured."

Perhaps understanding that the compliment was automatic rather than heartfelt, Lieutenant Frankel nevertheless blushed with muted pleasure and stroked the mustache on his dark, delicate face with a pianist's long finger. Moshe noticed the gesture, sensed the lieutenant's suppressed nervousness, smiled slightly, and turned his head away to stare out at the rising sun.

"So, Prime Minister, shall we go?"

"Yes, Moshe, let's do that."

At a curt nod from Moshe the two army officers removed their Uzi guns from their shoulders, held them at the ready, and led the whole group out of the VIP lounge, down a private corridor that bypassed customs, and out into an underground garage. Construction of the corridor and special diplomat's garage had been completed four months ago after some PLO terrorists had, remarkably, managed to get into the airport terminal and attempted the assassination of the prime minister; now the enormous garage, with its walls of thick concrete and electronically controlled doors, had the appearance of some ghastly, futuristic bomb shelter, the air cold, footsteps echoing. Moshe, who did not like enclosed spaces and was also now reminded of this morning's mysterious telephone call about another possible assassination attempt, was glad when they were all seated in the armored limousine and it was bouncing over the top of the ramp onto the road that would lead them eventually to Jerusalem. The sun, now much higher in the sky, was filling the air with a pearly gray light.

"And how was New York, Shlomo?"

"Need you ask, Moshe? You've obviously read about my lamentable faux pas—it's already sold lots of newspapers."

Moshe grinned laconically, pulled a cigarette from his tunic pocket, held it up before the nonsmoking prime minister, and received a nod of consent. "Yes," he said, lighting the cigarette with the lighter in the back of the limousine. "Whatever possessed you, Shlomo?"

The prime minister groaned, put his head back, and rubbed his eyes with his small hands. "I shudder to think about it. I just stupidly lost my temper. We're not popular in the United Nations, and I think it just finally got to me. . . . But what a thing to say . . . so *stupid* . . . I behaved like a klutz."

"Not like you," Moshe intervened.

"No, Moshe, not like me." The prime minister removed his hands from his head, looked up, and shrugged, smiling sardonically. "Well, you know what the General Assembly is like: sanctimonious morality and mock outrage. . . . The Russian delegate was assuring the Assembly that so long as Israel continued to pursue her expansionist policies, they, the Soviets, would continue to supply arms to the United Arab Republic—and at that, very foolishly, I found myself loudly proclaiming that should the need arise we would be prepared to use our atomic weapons. . . . So, you can imagine . . . Before I even got into my bed that night, my outburst had been eagerly seized upon and news-flashed around the world as—"

"Israel's own Final Solution."

"Please, Moshe, don't remind me." The prime minister offered a rabbinical groan of despair, covering his lowered face with his hands and then removing them and glancing wearily around him. He and Moshe were sitting side by side in the rear seats facing the front of the car; Lieutenant Frankel, neat and handsome, nervously stroking his thin mustache, was sitting in the seat opposite, his back to the driver, his dark eyes fixed on them both. Up front, beside the driver, was a commando with an Uzi gun; and two trucks filled with armed soldiers, one in front of the limousine, one behind it, were churning up clouds of dust that were blotting out the exotic brilliance of the sunrise over the hills and plains around Ramla.

"Why not?" Lieutenant Frankel said, his dark eyes flashing with suppressed anger. "Use our atomic weapons and put an end to it. Let the world complain later."

Moshe glanced at the prime minister, saw a hint of amusement, then turned his cool gaze on the young lieutenant.

"I admire your enthusiasm," he said quietly. "What you lack is discretion."

The lieutenant blushed, looked down at his feet, then nervously stroked his mustache with one finger. Twenty-eight years of age, an Orthodox Jew, graduate of the National Defense Academy, Frankel was a relatively inexperienced but highly promising member of Shin Beth, the security service responsible for internal security and counterintelligence within Israel. Moshe also knew that the young lieutenant was a fanatical Zionist who saw in the present government and its leading members the possible weakening of true Zionist ideals in the face of increasingly antagonistic worldwide opinion. Now, studying the young man with his cool gray eyes, taking note of his embarrassment and suppressed anger, Moshe understood but feared Frankel's feelings, because though rooted in a passion for Israel, they left no room for compromise.

"Why all the guards?" the prime minister asked.

"We had another anonymous phone call."

"A threat?"

"Yes. Though it appears to have been simply harassment."

"Arabs?"

"No, Shlomo." Moshe took a deep breath. "We think it was Jews."

An uncomfortable silence followed Moshe's remark, causing them all to stare through the windows of the speeding limousine and dwell on the implications of what they had heard. The land here was flat, no longer green, parched by the sun; and as they passed the wrecked tanks and trucks, left as monuments to the war of 1967, the irony of the scene was not lost on them. Moshe sighed and inhaled on his cigarette, feeling terribly weary.

"I find it hard to accept that it was Jews, Moshe."

"I *refuse* to believe it," Lieutenant Frankel said.

Moshe pursed his lips, let the cigarette smoke out, watched it drifting lazily in front of him, and then rubbed his eyes.

"Our young lieutenant is shocked," he said quietly, "but unfortunately the facts speak for themselves."

"What facts, Moshe?"

"Four months ago, Shlomo, two PLO assassins managed to get into the airport and hide themselves there all night. How they managed to do it, we never found out, but we know that they couldn't have done it without the assistance of Jews, since only Jews are allowed to work in the airport. An anonymous phone call put paid to the attempted assassination, but since the caller obviously knew exactly where the assassins were hiding, we have to assume that he was involved in getting them in there, but wanted to scare us rather than actually kill you. However since only an airport worker could have gotten them in there, he had to be one of our own."

"And this morning?"

"Obviously a similar case—both harassment and a warning. However, the anonymous phone call was made direct to the air traffic controller, and that number, as you know, is classified. So it had to be someone who knew the airport, which means he is Jewish."

The prime minister did not reply and an uncomfortable silence prevailed as the western outskirts of the Golden City came into view. The prime minister pursed his lips, Lieutenant Frankel stared at his feet, and Moshe studied them both with his gray eyes, concealing his thoughts. . . . Jew against Jew. An unprecedented situation . . . Moshe felt a spasm of grief and outrage, an anguished incomprehension. What did Lieutenant Frankel know? His innocent world was not their world. Neither Orthodox Jews nor fanatical believers in Zion, Moshe and the prime minister were embroiled in international diplomacy and now had to accept that Israel was merely part of it. Lieutenant Frankel saw it differently, with young eyes, insular eyes, his view more emotional than realistic, rooted firmly in a devout, unyielding Judaism. Doubtless he had felt revulsion at bringing Rashid Idriss into Israel, had secretly felt like a traitor during every mile of the journey, convinced only that he was protecting an Arab murderer, a notorious PLO leader. Moshe knew what he was thinking and could understand his suppressed anger: what was Israel coming to that she could stoop to negotiating with terrorists? That she could vacillate about the West Bank to the point where Jew was ready to kill Jew for it? Yes, Moshe understood—he shared the young man's frustration—but he also realized, with the heavy heart of an older man, that compromise, that very bitter potion, could not be avoided.

"So, Moshe," the prime minister eventually said. "What do you think Rashid Idriss wants?"

"What he's *always* wanted," Lieutenant Frankel said, his bitterness obvious. "Some form of surrender."

"Hardly the correct word," Moshe admonished.

"It's the *only* word," Lieutenant Frankel said.

The prime minister sighed, waving his hands to silence them both, then leaned his head back against the seat, suddenly looking his age.

"We're not in a good position, gentlemen. We're out of favor in the West, the Arab Republic is almost united, and now the Neturei Karta zealots and the fanatics of Gush Emunim are turning the West Bank into a fortress and dividing the country, Jew against Jew. . . . No, gentlemen, not a very good position. In fact, it's never been worse."

Moshe cupped his large hands, lowered his face, wiped the sweat off, then removed his hands and glanced outside the car, displaying his secret despair.

"Jew against Jew," he said quietly. "Who would ever have thought . . . ?"

He didn't complete the sentence, but instead stared at Lieutenant Frankel, the veil dropping back over his eyes, leaving them cool and unreadable. The young lieutenant licked his lips, stroked his mustache with one finger, then studied his own feet as if disowning the issue. Moshe smiled, without happiness, feeling weary and haunted, trying to steel himself for the meeting to come, dreading what it might lead to.

The driver turned off the road, moving past wide green lawns, offering a panoramic view of the hills and valleys of Judea, sun-scorched and magnificent, before heading through dense trees and emerging in front of the Knesset, Israel's parliament house, while Moshe stared at the young lieutenant and the aging prime minister, their eyes meeting for a brief, embarrassed moment, trying to express the unspeakable.

Five minutes later, in the prime minister's office, they were informed that a bomb had exploded in Jerusalem.

3

The bomb had exploded at seven o'clock in the morning, destroying a synagogue and three houses in one of the densely populated streets of the Mea She'arim quarter. Thirty minutes after the explosion Kate Hirschfield was leaning against a wall of the Hadassah Medical Center and watching as the wounded and their shocked relatives and friends were brought into the reception area. The victims were all members of the unpopular Neturei Karta sect, the men wearing frock coats and dusty wide-brimmed hats, the women dressed in equally somber clothes, looking shabby and archaic. The women wailed and wrung their hands, their men were dazed and murmuring prayers, and the medics, carrying the wounded on the stretchers, had to push them aside. *"Gevalt!"* someone cried. *"Gottenyu,* all the blood!" The blood was bright on the wounded on the stretchers and stained the clothes of those walking. The reception hall was in chaos, the weeping and wailing making it worse; the medics in their smocks were pushing through with the stretchers while the walking wounded or those simply shocked stared around in confusion.

"How many were hurt?" Kate asked.

"Nine," the harassed doctor replied. "Four are dead and five are badly wounded. The rest are shocked. Some are deaf."

"Who planted the bomb?"

"We don't know yet, Kate. Either Arabs or fanatical Zionists . . . the Neturei Karta aren't popular."

Still shaken by her dream and the bizarre events of the early morning, Kate stepped forward and waved her hand at Nurse Jabotinsky. The patients on the stretchers were disappearing, but the other zealots remained, the women shaking and sobbing, the men groaning or murmuring prayers, eyes dark, cheeks hollow, beards gray and long, their frock coats covered in dust from the explosion, their wide-brimmed hats askew.

"Let's sort them out," Kate said. "Some are probably just dazed. I only want the really bad cases; we haven't beds for the others."

Nurse Jabotinsky nodded vigorously, her brown eyes big and bright, her worker's hands pressing the heavy thighs of her small, fleshy body. "Terrible!" she exclaimed dramatically. "What a terrible thing to do! For *this* we come to live in *Eretz*! We should all be committed!" She stepped toward the milling zealots, her face flushed, her lips firm, while Kate, feeling exhausted and fearful, pushed herself from the wall.

Another stretcher was carried in, the victim strapped down and groaning, both legs a ghastly mess of exposed bone and blood, the plasma jars swinging above his head, a medic holding the rubber tubes up. "Make way! Let us through!" Kate stepped aside to let them pass. A woman stared at the stretcher, her eyes widening, bright with horror, then she shrieked and staggered forward, one hand outstretched, trying to reach for the wounded man. Kate quickly grabbed her wrist, jerked her back, snapped in her ear, and the woman, shuddering with shock, turned away and covered her face with her hands. The stretcher was rushed away, the medics shouting at one another, and Kate walked up to the side of Nurse Jabotinsky and stared carefully around her.

The women were still wailing, wiping the tears from their eyes, burying their faces in handkerchiefs and scarves, holding on to each other. The men were less demonstrative, if just as shocked or outraged, some licking their lips or covering their faces, others kissing their prayer books. "Beasts!" someone said. "Who would do such a thing?" Kate reached out to the speaker, an old man, his eyes dazed, placed her hand on his shoulder, and shook him gently, whispering soothing inanities.

"It's all right," she said. "Quiet, now."

Blood, she was thinking. *This whole country is drenched in blood. I live in a country that's been built with love and death, and I dream about my own draining blood and the deaths of the young and old.* She looked at the man before her, a religious fanatic, an anachronism, his wide-brimmed hat shading the eyes that were glistening with tears. One of the Neturei Karta zealots, the guardians of the gate, an old man now resembling a child, his tears staining his cheeks. Kate felt sorry for him. She wanted to despise him, but she couldn't. Instead she felt the sort of despair that twists down into bitterness.

This land was not her land, these people not her people. They lived with a dream that had its roots in the past and was strangling in the thorns of its contradictions. Kate wanted no part of it. This impassioned land turned her cold. Her father dead, she was now on her own, and she wanted to leave.

"Medics!" she suddenly snapped, waving her right hand in the air. "Get your hands out of your pockets and let's do some work. Over here, you *luftmenshes*!" The medics jumped to attention, their indecision swept away, galvanized into awareness by the familiar sound of Kate's commanding voice. "Take these people to my clinic. Put those two women and that man in beds, the others into my waiting room. You understand? *Immediately!*" The medics did as they were told, moving amongst the dazed survivors, taking hold of the men and women, speaking softly as they led them away.

"Go with them," Kate said to the man before her.

The old Jew didn't move, towering over her, looking down at her, his eyes gleaming from the shadow of the wide brim of his hat, the tears rolling out of that shadow and draining into his gray beard. "A bomb," he said quietly, his voice cracked and dry, emerging from the depths of his dazed incomprehension like the sound of the wind across barbed wire. "Why us? We are nothing. . . ." Kate murmured soothing words but the man's gaze remained fixed, weeping eyes focused inward on a past that ran back to the Holocaust. An obsessed visionary, a religious zealot, an anachronism, he would watch the world go down in smoke and flames before renouncing his faith.

Kate could not share such faith and did not believe in resurrection. She believed in the reality of flesh and bone, dust to dust, no returning. Yet staring up at the old man, she suddenly remembered her recurrent dream, the strange, unknown star, the light pouring in from the rumbling darkness as the bedroom shook wildly. The recollection was a challenge, making her question her own beliefs, now wondering, with the sort of chill that springs from inchoate panic, if the bizarre event had actually occurred—and if so, what the dream and the extraordinary event had represented.

"—sorted out," Nurse Jabotinsky said. "We'll have to sedate the bed cases. I don't know about the others in your clinic, but no doubt you'll find out soon enough."

Kate tried to focus her thoughts, wondering what was happening to her, gradually forcing herself back to the reality of the more brutal present. The departing women were still wailing, their menfolk chanting prayers, the medics ushering them away with professional hands and whispered words that meant nothing. Kate started to follow them, but someone called her name, and she turned around to face Lieutenant Frankel as he stopped right in front of her.

"Filthy bastards," the lieutenant said. "Someone buys a loaf of bread from a shop and leaves a bomb by the door. What the hell are they proving?" The lieutenant's handsome face was grim, his eyes luminous with rage, and he stroked his thin mustache with a finger, beads of sweat on his dark skin. He glanced briefly at the old Jew who still stood in front of Kate, looked back at Kate, shook his head, and shrugged his shoulders despairingly. "His son was killed," he said, obviously referring to the old man. "At least three buildings were demolished. A few others are moderately damaged and the fire is still burning. Filthy bastards. Why *there*?"

Kate looked around as a medic approached, a young man, an Arab, moving over to place his hand on the old Jew's shoulder, keeping his eyes down. The lieutenant stared at him with hatred, obviously thinking of the bomb, and Kate, taking note of the lieutenant's eyes, offered the Arab a friendly nod.

"It might have been Zionists," she said. "They have fanatics as well. The Neturei Karta zealots are against the Zionist state, and a few of them *have* been murdered because of that."

"There's no proof that it was Zionists," Lieutenant Frankel replied coldly. "And you, Dr. Hirschfield, particularly given your standing here, should not be listening to subversive tales from the bazaars."

Kate smiled and stepped back, letting the Arab reach the old Jew, watching carefully as he shook the old man gently and said, "Please, sir, come with me." The old Jew didn't move, but continued to stare straight ahead, his tearful gaze fixed directly on Kate without really seeing her. "A bomb," he said. "Why?" He had stopped weeping, but his cheeks were wet. "Please, sir," the Arab medic said quietly. "This way . . . come with me." The lieutenant stared at the Arab medic and then returned his gaze to Kate. "I don't think the old man can hear; the explosion probably deafened him." The Arab led the Jew away, looking very small beside him, and Kate glanced down and saw blood on the floor where it had dripped from the stretchers.

"I think you're an Arab sympathizer," Lieutenant Frankel said stiffly.

"No," Kate said. "I'm not. I'm just sick to death of this damned country and its unreasonable hatreds."

She turned and walked away, brushing the hair back from her eyes, feeling weary, confused, and slightly feverish, the night's fears still pursuing her. Nurse Jabotinsky hurried up beside her, saying, "A rude one, that lieutenant," and they walked side by side along the corridor, following the Jew and Arab.

"He's all right," Kate said. "He's just a bit upset. It always hits them harder when they're young. Was that an earthquake last night?"

"Something like it," Nurse Jabotinsky said. "It shook most of Jerusalem. I thought it was an explosion—a big explosion, far away —but it went on too long to be that, and our whole street was wakened. Some sort of earth tremor that didn't do any damage, so we all went back to bed and said our prayers."

Kate was slightly relieved, but the feeling of foreboding remained with her, the memory of the unknown star and the frightening bright light keeping her in a state of nervous tension. They passed one of the emergency wards, glanced in, saw blood and bone, moved on toward the psychiatric wing, where Kate's patients were waiting. *Physician, heal thyself* . . . Kate found herself shivering. A sharp banging sound accompanied swinging doors as a stretcher was pushed out of a theater. Someone groaned, a medic cursed, light flashed off a plasma jar, rubber tubes swinging above the blood-soaked patient, the trolley's wheels making squeaking sounds.

"Did you see anything?" Kate asked, unable to let the matter rest. "I mean when you looked out after the earth tremor. Did you see anything strange?"

"Strange, Kate? No. A lot of my neighbors in their pajamas, I saw, all looking as though Judgment Day had come, none particularly attractive."

Kate managed to smile, but her good humor was fleeting, swept away on another tide of disbelief when she thought of the bright light. She wanted to rationalize her experience—to understand it and make it acceptable—but so far there was no explanation for what had occurred. Dwelling on this, feeling worse, a state of unreality invading her, she turned a corner at the end of the corridor, went through another door, and entered the small reception room outside the psychiatric ward.

She glanced around the ward, a small room with eight beds, sunlight pouring through barred windows onto white walls, making the steel bed rails shine. Two of the women were lying down, still fully dressed, wailing loudly, one of them having her forehead

stroked by a bearded zealot, the other surrounded by some friends and
a young Orthodox Jew who repeatedly kissed his prayer book and
rocked back and forth, his lips murmuring a repetitive litany. The
other survivors were less affected, though obviously not that well,
either wandering to and fro or staring around them in a daze,
sometimes reaching out to embrace one another, weeping quietly and
shaking.

"Make them all lie down," Kate said. "I don't want them walking
about. We'll probably need some chlordiazepoxide and mepro-
bamate. I'll be back in a minute."

She didn't know what was happening to her, feeling the need to
escape, wanting to rid herself of her patients and the demands they
would make upon her, and aware, as she walked toward her office,
that she was losing control of herself. Nurse Jabotinsky hurried after
her, always faithful, ever watchful, reaching out to touch her
encouragingly on the shoulder as they entered the office.

"I know," she said. "It's terrible. All these bombings are too much.
And you . . . just look at you, poor child, you've had far too much
work. . . . And now this . . . and your father."

Kate ignored the last remark, refusing to accept that it might be
true, still not knowing if she was shocked by her father's death or by
the possibility that she simply didn't care. What was grief, after all? It
was the disease she was supposed to cure. She sat down behind her
desk, covered her face with her hands, massaged her aching eyes with
uncertain fingers, and then looked up at the nurse.

"I don't care anymore," she said. "I think I might even despise
them. I'm tired of the sick and the maladjusted and the shocked. I feel
nothing but revulsion at the sight of them. I want to scream. I *don't
care* anymore!"

Nurse Jabotinsky smiled and nodded, obviously not believing a
word of it, putting it down to the emotional exhaustion wrought by the
recent spate of bombings and to the very recent death of Kate's father.

"You're drinking too much," she said. "It's the influence of that
Leon Halcomb. More vitamin C is what you need, and that man won't
provide it."

Kate had to smile at that, amused that Jerusalem had no secrets;
then she sighed and placed her hands on the cluttered desk, staring
down at the papers. "You attend to them," she said. "I'm sure you
know what to do. Sedate them if necessary, and I'll have a talk with
them when they're pacified. I'm not up to it right now." The nurse

nodded understandingly, unclasped her hands, and turned to leave, but before she reached the door, it swung open and Lieutenant Frankel walked in.

"Don't you know how to knock?" Kate said acidly, wanting someone to whip.

"My apologies," the lieutenant said, touching his mustache with a restless finger, his skin dark from the sun, his eyes darker, looking steadily at Kate. "I would remind you, however, that I have certain responsibilities in this matter."

"That sounds very pompous, Lieutenant. What do you want?"

"I have been sent personally by Major General Moshe Eitan—"

"I'm not interested in who sent you, Lieutenant. I want to know what you want."

The lieutenant, who was not used to being talked to in such a manner, least of all by a woman, flushed with anger and tried to keep his gaze steady.

"I want tape recordings of everything that is communicated between you and those survivors during their forthcoming psychiatric treatment."

"You sound like a tape recording yourself."

"I did not come here to be abused by your notoriously sharp tongue. I repeat: I want your tape recordings."

"You can't have them."

"I demand them."

"No," Kate said icily. "I'm entitled to protect the confidentiality of my patients."

"It's a matter of security," the lieutenant replied, contempt creeping into his voice. "We want to know who bombed those people. They might mention things that could be important, so we want to hear everything."

"Find out some other way."

"There *is* no other way. You'll be talking to those people when they're dazed or in shock, and what they might unwittingly reveal could be of great value."

"I'm not interested, Lieutenant. I won't betray the trust of my patients, and that's all there is to it."

"To save your precious American conscience I won't *ask* you, Dr. Hirschfield. Instead I will make it an order: You *will* pass on your tapes."

Kate suddenly exploded, almost rising out of her chair, all her

recent resentments and fears finding release when she banged her fist
hard on the desk and glared at the shocked Lieutenant Frankel.

"Damn you!" she yelled. "Get the hell out of this office! I can't
stand your pompous patriotism and devotion to duty. Those people
outside are *suffering*! I can't help them unless they *trust* me! I will not
abuse that trust by becoming a spy for the IDF, so go back to Shin
Beth, to your paranoid friends, and have me turned in as a traitor. You
understand, Lieutenant? I'm telling you to go to hell. If you want to
interrogate those people, you can do it when I discharge them—but
until then keep your nose out of here and don't bore me with
platitudes. Now get the hell out of this office and close the door when
you leave."

The lieutenant straightened his shoulders, took a deep breath and
glared at Kate, then turned and walked angrily out of the room,
pointedly leaving the door open behind him. Kate glared at the open
door, let her breath out, and sank back, shaking her head wearily from
side to side, letting the anger drain out of her. Nurse Jabotinsky
cleared her throat, her head nodding automatically, then a smile
illuminated her matronly face as she put her hands on her hips.

"You still care," she said.

"Perhaps," Kate replied. "Either way, the work has to be done, so
let's go see our patients."

They both walked out of the office and into the ward, where the
women were still weeping dementedly, the men murmuring prayers.
Kate stared at them, mesmerized, strangely shocked by the familiar:
the face of Israel, represented by stricken zealots.

The women had shaven heads and wore kerchiefs over their wigs,
having given up the right to retain their attractiveness when they
married their extremely pious men. The men were anachronisms:
beards and fringes untouched by scissors, their breeches tight around
the knees, their faces deathly white beneath their wide hats, framed in
long ringlets. The men lived for the Torah while their wives remained
invisible, only recognized in secular matters—birth, marriage, and
death. It both appalled and angered Kate, made her feel that here time
had stopped, and that this land, the Holy Land, drenched with blood
and mere dreams of freedom, was a land so totally devoted to its
menfolk that its women were ciphers. Kate couldn't take it much
longer—her American soul was in revolt—and as the women continued wailing and the men kissed their prayer books, she surrendered to
shame and outrage, feeling alien and ostracized.

"I'm still an American," she said obliquely. "I'm just beginning to realize that. This country and I don't belong together and should never have met."

"You're just tired," Nurse Jabotinsky replied.

"Maybe. I hope so. . . . But somehow I don't think it's true: I feel as if I'm drifting away and losing sight of these people."

"Innocent fools," Nurse Jabotinsky said, as if not quite hearing Kate. "They can't even accept Israel. They still wait for the coming of the Messiah and think we've denied Him. What can we say to them?"

"Nothing," Kate replied. "Just look at that old man. He's just lost his son and he's shocked, but his faith is intact."

Kate wanted to go up to him and console him in his loss, but the old man, an anti-Zionist, member of the Neturei Karta zealots, obviously stunned by the loss of his son, doubtless shocked beyond measure, nonetheless raised his head, touched his lips to his prayer book, and then, his eyes tearful, his hands shaking with flagrant emotion, placed the frontlet on his forehead, wound the *tefillin* around his left arm, and quietly buried his grief beneath the soil of his unyielding faith by praying fervently that the Messiah might come and establish the true Promised Land.

Kate was filled with despair.

4

"I came here to talk," Rashid said, his voice soft and his English precise. "Not to fight; just to talk." They were in the new guest chamber, an austere, modern room, enlivened only by the Chagall tapestries that dominated one wall, the three of them in chairs at the end of the long table, Rashid and Moshe Eitan face to face, the prime minister between them. "The situation is getting out of hand," Rashid continued, "and I don't think either of us wants it to get worse. That's why I'm here."

Moshe, leaning lazily back in his chair with one large hand stretched out on the table, tapping a pencil up and down on the polished wood, studied Rashid with cool, unfathomable gray eyes, neither friendly nor resentful. Rashid, knowing Moshe's history, was not fooled by the neutral look, if not certain at least willing to accept that it might conceal hatred. Likewise the prime minister, an old fox with a sweet face, now leaning forward casually, his elbows on the table, his shirt sleeves rolled up, the shirt unbuttoned to the neck, looking like a simple member of the *kibbutzim*, his gaze mild and inoffensive.

"The situation is getting out of hand," Moshe said, "because you, Rashid, and your terrorists are murdering more Jews each week."

Rashid imperceptibly tensed and then forced himself to remain calm. Replacing his brief flash of anger was a vision of a Palestinian refugee camp in south Lebanon: dogs barking at Land-Rovers with machine-gun mountings instead of seats; the young men in fatigues, carrying rifles and pistols, posing pathetically under posters of Yasser Arafat; the posters tattered and bleached by the sun that blazed down on the dispossessed . . . most of whom had originally fled from Galilee.

"I did not come here for talk of Arab terrorists and murderers," Rashid said. "You can try giving that to your Western newspapers

—though I doubt that even they, in their growing disillusionment with Zionism, would bother chopping wood to get it printed."

Moshe smiled at him, without warmth, with respect, while the prime minister, his elbows still on the table, nodded his head rather sleepily.

"Very good," the prime minister said. "Your reputation preceded you. We have heard of your excellent education and talent for oratory. . . . Now the proof has been offered."

Rashid leaned forward in his chair, placed his hands on the table, looked directly at the prime minister and Moshe, his calmness concealing his anger.

"I risked a great deal to come here," he said. "I'm sure you both understand that."

"We risked a great deal in letting you come," Moshe replied. "A fact I am sure *you* appreciate."

Rashid stared at Moshe and smiled, still suppressing his anger, keeping his head clear, silently saying thanks to Allah for his excellent education and what it had taught him about fighting words with words.

"My terrorist murderers," Rashid said, "are increasing their activities because the situation on the West Bank has become intolerable and their patience is running out."

"The West Bank?" the prime minister replied, his mild eyes histrionically surprised.

"Such innocence would be touching, Ben Eliezer, if it were also convincing."

The prime minister glanced at Moshe, smiled gently, then looked down at the table. "So, Rashid, what is this question about the West Bank?"

"You know about the West Bank, Shlomo Ben Eliezer. According to the Camp David peace agreement of 1979, Palestinians were to be granted a degree of self-government on the West Bank. For the past eight years, however, with the tacit agreement of Mr. Begin and the further connivance of every Zionist politician, the Jews of Kash, Gush Emunim, and Neturei Karta have taken over practically the whole of the West Bank. They are now systematically driving most of the remaining Arabs away, by violence as often as not, determined to remove every last Palestinian from the area. Since your own government has done nothing about this, it seems increasingly clear that your intention is to ensure that ultimately there will be no Arabs in

Palestine at all. . . . I cannot control my men much longer, Ben Eliezer. They will not sit back and watch as the Jews rob them of the little they have left in their own homeland."

"This is the *Jewish* homeland, my friend."

"The Balfour Declaration did not represent the word of God or Allah. You are here, Ben Eliezer, and I must accept that you will remain, but I cannot accept that the Palestinians can have no say in this land."

"Israel is open to those Arabs who accept Jewish rule."

"No, Ben Eliezer, it is not. You have your Wailing Wall, but it has not satisfied your greed; now you have the Temple of the Mount and soon you will have the whole of the West Bank. As for Arab freedoms, it has long been perfectly clear that the Arabs of the occupied territories are being deprived of their rights, robbed of their homes, and systematically driven out to rot in the refugee camps of Lebanon and Syria. That is as true today as it was back in 1917 when our fine British friends sold us out by kissing the feet of Chaim Weizmann. You stole from us then, and you continue to steal from us today—so don't tell me this land is open to the Arabs."

"Are you suggesting that we do nothing to defend ourselves against your assassins and bombs?"

Rashid stared at Moshe, examining his steely gray gaze, but finding nothing either there nor in the laconic lips to suggest the slightest weakness. "Freedom fighters are not necessarily assassins," he said quietly, "and your own bombs have not fallen unnoticed. What I am suggesting, Moshe Eitan, is that your so-called acts of reprisal are in reality but part of a systematic drive to rid this country of true Palestinians."

"Not true," Moshe replied levelly.

"I'm afraid it is, Major General."

"We could argue about this all afternoon," the prime minister said. "Alas, it will get us nowhere."

Moshe continued to lean back lazily in his chair, casually tapping his pencil on the table, his gaze cool and perceptive. This was not the first time that he and Rashid had met; nor was it the first time that Rashid had found himself wondering just what attitudes were concealed behind Moshe's hooded eyes and steely smile. It was no secret that Moshe believed completely in preserving Palestine for the Jews; what had never been ascertained, even by Arab security, was the actual extent of that commitment. On the one hand a man with good reason to hate the Arabs, he was, on the other, a man who more than once had displayed a certain understanding of the Arab grievances —one who had treaded a fine line between the dedicated Zionists and those who believed that Arab assimilation was essential to Jewish survival. Moshe was clever, and had eluded the spleen of successive governments, but Rashid was not alone in often wondering just where his sympathies really lay.

"Settlement of the West Bank," the prime minister said eventually, "has not been a deliberate policy of this government."

"But you sanction it."

"Not so. Settlement of the West Bank may have been encouraged by Menachem Begin, but it is desirable neither to the majority of Jews nor to myself. Settlement of the West Bank has been made, without our consent, by the members of Kash, Gush Emunim, and, recently, the more fanatical members of the Neturei Karta sect. Now, as you well know, most of those Jews are as unreasoning as the most pious of Muslims, and so nothing we can say to them will make them move. It is their belief that God gave Jews the right—or, as they are more likely to put it, the holy duty—to live on the West Bank, and successive attempts to persuade them to leave have proved to be fruitless."

The prime minister nodded and glanced briefly at Moshe, then returned his unrevealing gaze to Rashid. "We have a problem there," he said. "You understand that problem perfectly. Only removal by force would now clear those Jews off the West Bank—and neither politically nor morally can we afford to do that."

"Morally?" Rashid said. "And you think it is moral for the Arabs to be forcibly removed from their last foothold in Palestine?"

"They are not being forcibly removed," the prime minister said.

"They are being *forced out*, Ben Eliezer."

"I repeat: It is not government policy."

"And I repeat: You cannot let it continue. If you do, I will be unable to control my men."

"Let *me* repeat," Moshe Eitan said, "that you are hardly controlling your men now: they are crossing our borders in increasing numbers, planting bombs, ambushing soldiers, attacking innocent civilians, and then boasting about it from the safety of Lebanon or Cairo. The situation is, as you say, getting out of hand, but things will not get better until you still the activities of your so-called freedom fighters."

"Honor the Camp David agreement before asking me to cool the ardor of my men."

"Gentlemen! Gentlemen!" the prime minister exclaimed, waving his small, fine-boned hands. "We are at an *impasse!*"

Moshe lay his pencil on the table, took a cigarette from the packet in his tunic pocket, lit it from a soiled box of matches, then blew a cloud of smoke to the room, his cool eyes, now fixed on Rashid, glinting with what might have been anger.

Anger or hatred? Rashid couldn't be too sure. Eitan had good reason to hate him—to hate all Arabs on principle—and if such were the case, Rashid could certainly understand it. Yet even as he thought this, and felt a latent sympathy, he had a recollection of a similar case, one of a singularly intimate nature, frozen in a not so distant past and kept alive to sustain him. . . . An Arab child awakening in the cool dawn of south Lebanon, awakened by the droning of aircraft . . . then the droning as the shriek of jets, other catastrophic noises, his mother and father screaming, his sister weeping, all fleeing their beds . . . then mushrooming dust, fierce heat and flames, the walls collapsing around them with a roar. . . . More images: The village street, the gray light filled with smoke, the men and women racing to and fro as the bombs blew their homes apart. . . . Then silence. Swirling sand. The dust settling over the dead. And his father pointing up, his finger shaking, to the sand-covered ridge. . . . Fear. Unreality. A stunned disbelief . . . A long line of troop carriers, the soldiers spreading along the dunes, silhouetted against the sand's brilliant whiteness, moving down toward the village. . . . The child's father praying to Allah, the wind slapping his words back. The guns roaring and people shrieking and falling down—men, women, and children. . . . Death. Devastation. Another silence filled with sobbing. The child clinging to his mother, now dead, as was his father, the blood splashed on them both and on his sister, also spread-eagled. . . . This bleak vision dissolved, became a glaring white sun that then shrank and became the light bulb above Moshe Eitan's head. . . . Moshe Eitan: a Jew. And like Rashid: without a family. So many in Palestine, Jew and Arab alike, were forced to live with the loss by violent death of someone they had loved. In this, as in their passion for Palestine, they had something in common.

"So," the prime minister said, raising his hands in a desultory gesture, "you have come here to ask us to remove our most fanatical

Jews from the West Bank, if necessary by force. I tell you, Rashid Idriss, that we cannot do it. We cannot pit Jew against Jew."

Rashid glanced briefly at the silent Moshe Eitan and then, leaning forward and placing both hands on the table, fixed his gaze steadily on Ben Eliezer.

"I think you'll have to," he said.

"Oh? And *why* will we have to?"

"Because, Ben Eliezer, Jew is *already* fighting Jew—and it will get worse if you don't do something about it."

The prime minister glanced quickly at Moshe Eitan, received no visible response, and then looked back at Rashid, his mild eyes as innocent as a child's, concealing his tension.

"I don't know what you're talking about," he said.

Rashid couldn't resist smiling, his amusement briefly defeating his anger, now aware that he had struck a delicate nerve and must not let it go.

"You know what I'm talking about. Both of you—you know. The settlers of the West Bank, which they call Judea and Samaria, are doing what they want because they think that no Jewish government will use its conscript troops against fellow Jews who claim to be exercising their ancient biblical rights. So far this has been true, but since, in the last few years, settlement of the West Bank has become such a blatant violation of the Camp David agreement, it has outraged not only my people but the whole Western world, filling the majority of your Jews, conservative and anti-Zionist, with foreboding, and placing you in a very unpleasant dilemma. Yes, already aware that both Jewish and international opinion might force you to attempt to clear the West Bank with your troops, the settlers, prepared to die for their beliefs, have turned their towns into fortified camps, with bunkers, minefields, heavy machine guns, armored vehicles, and antitank missiles—and although they pretend that this extraordinary wealth of hardware is there merely to combat the odd Arab freedom fighter, one of their leaders has publicly proclaimed that the security of the West Bank is more important than the constitution. You are, in short, on the brink of civil war—with Jew prepared to kill Jew."

"That's not true," Ben Eliezer said.

Rashid knew that it was. While it was true that his Arabs had increased their raids into Palestine, it was equally true that they only came in small numbers, carrying no more than hand grenades, small explosives, or rifles for ambush. There was therefore no logical explanation for the fortified gates, heavy security, and massive arsenals of the West Bank other than the one Rashid had offered—and that explanation was original neither to Rashid nor the majority of conservative Jews of the occupied territories. The fortified towns of the West Bank, run by Jews, were designed to combat the potential threat of Jewish government forces. Rashid, studying Ben Eliezer and Moshe Eitan in turn, knew that they both understood this fact.

"It's true," Rashid said, "and you know it." He waited for a moment to let his words sink in, and then asked them the one question that he knew they both dreaded to hear: "Who planted the bomb in the Mea She'arim quarter?"

Neither Moshe Eitan nor the prime minister displayed the slightest physical reaction, but something almost imperceptible flashed between them, and Rashid knew that his question had struck home.

"Since you already know about the bombing," Moshe Eitan replied, "it was obviously planted by one of your own Arabs."

"Not so, Major General." Rashid kept his voice calm. "Some of your more fanatical Jews are now convinced that you will eventually have to try to force them off the West Bank, and they are willing to murder any prominent Jew who supports that idea. Indeed, even now, some of those Jews are trying to topple your government. The bomb that exploded in the Mea She'arim quarter was meant to kill Rabbi Nachman, a moderate Orthodox Jew who is concerned by the increasing number of Neturei Karta zealots who are disowning the Zionist state and consorting with Arabs. Ironically, that bomb, planted by a Neturei Karta zealot, merely killed some of his own kind."

"And the West Bank?"

"You know your options on the West Bank, Ben Eliezer. The West Bank is now controlled by fanatical Jews who fear and despise their own legitimately elected government. Sooner or later, due either to outside diplomatic pressure, negative reactions from your own electorate, or the threat of all-out war with my people, you will have to return autonomy to the Arabs. Your Jewish fanatics won't move, so you will have to use your own conscript troops—Jew against Jew."

"That's our problem. I still don't know what you're driving at."

"What I am saying, Shlomo Ben Eliezer, is that if you do not remove those Jews from the West Bank soon—when it would be fairly easy to do—you will have to do it later, when the fanatics will have increased dramatically and will be in a position to start a civil war. Once that happens—when Jew is busy killing Jew—it will be impossible to prevent my people from trying to exploit the situation; and then, Allah forbid, the Soviets and Americans will have their excuse for the so-called war of intervention that they both want so badly. In the name of world peace the Soviets and Americans will then police all of Palestine—and neither Arab nor Jew will have a say in it. I come here, then, for both our sakes: this problem has to be solved."

Now, while Rashid removed his hands from the table and sat back, much too casually, in his chair, it was the turn of Moshe Eitan to lean forward, his thick arms on the table, and stare at Rashid with his unrevealing, perceptive eyes. Rashid did not avert his gaze, but stared back, his lips tight, until Moshe, with a slow, heavy sigh, raised his hands in despair. Then Rashid glanced very quickly at the prime minister and saw his interlocked fingers.

Simply that—the white knuckles—an acknowledgment of what had happened here.

An Arab had come to the Knesset and voiced the unspeakable.

5

It was late in the afternoon when Kate walked into the Jerusalem Intercontinental Hotel on the summit of the Mount of Olives and saw Leon Halcomb at his usual table in the Seven Arches restaurant, drinking whiskey, smoking a cigar, and gazing vaguely down at the Old City. Walking up to the table, Kate noticed that Leon was, as always, very dapper in his pinstripe suit and white shirt and tie, his cuff links gleaming, his black hair neatly combed, his face flushed and looking healthier than he probably felt. When Kate reached the table, Leon glanced up and nodded, crow's-feet around his bloodshot, restless eyes, his lips, which were thin, overtly sensual, covertly ascetic, forming a quick but strangely self-mocking grin.

"Ah, my lovely Kate, my darling psychiatrist, did you have a good day?"

"Obviously you've already heard."

"An excellent day for journalists, Miss Hirschfield: bombs are always good copy."

"I can do without that sort of low joke."

"A mere slip of the tongue, Kate."

Kate smiled in acknowledgment of the patent lack of sincerity, then set her shoulder bag on the table and sat down facing Leon.

"I'm a very weary woman this evening."

"A gin and tonic?"

"Why not?"

A resident of the hotel, Leon had no trouble in finding a waiter and getting Kate her drink. Kate had an appreciative sip and then lit a cigarette and sat back in her chair, feeling exhausted, both physically and emotionally. Looking down the slopes of the Mount of Olives where the churches and graveyards were bathed in dimming light, she saw the archaic splendor of the Old City, the gold and silver domes still majestic. Then she slowly raised her eyes, unwillingly, almost fearfully, and saw the blue sky growing darker, streaked with drifting gray clouds. The stars were not out yet. Kate shivered, feeling relief. She dropped her gaze and stared at Leon who was holding up two tumblers, topping up his fresh whiskey with the remains of the previous one, his lips puckered, one eye focused on the rim, the cigar still in his right hand.

"How long have you been here?" Kate asked him.

"I'm *always* here, Kate. I am, as you know, more or less a permanent resident, treated with the required condescension by the excellent staff."

"I don't know how you stand it."

"Hotels are very pleasant, both spacious and anonymous, God's gift to the nondomesticated man who carries only a suitcase."

"Let me rephrase my question: What time did you get out of bed?"

"In time to cover the bombing in the Mea She'arim quarter and telex such information as was gathered to my superior beings in Washington, D.C.—but quite a long time after you left me." He finished topping up his fresh glass, then had a drink and licked his thin lips. "Naturally I could only write about the casualties," he added, "but perhaps you will now inform me about the survivors."

Kate smiled. "No."

"What a loyal Jew you are. I said it before and I stand by it: You're a real little *bubeleh*." He grinned and inhaled on his cigar, his restless eyes roaming around the restaurant, then exhaled a cloud of blue smoke and reached out for Kate's hand. "Seriously," he said, "you don't look too good."

"I'm just tired," Kate replied, remembering the events of the early morning, still uneasy but not wanting to discuss them, already doubting her senses. "Too much sex, too much drink. Then, after the chaos in the hospital, an old friend paid a visit. He informed me that you're a very bad influence—and that made me more weary."

"I won't ask you who said that about me—but of course he or she was quite right."

"It was Rabbi Latinavots."

"Ah," Leon said. "Our acting Ashkenazic chief rabbi. A nice man, but an old friend of your father's, so that could explain it. Also, of course, he has a few problems of his own—the usual quarrels with the Sephardic chief rabbi, the customary disagreements with the Council of Torah Sages, the day by day headaches of the Rabbinic Court of

Appeal—so it's possible that his nervous system has been shattered and he needs someone to horsewhip."

"His nervous system is fine—and he *does* have good reason to detest you."

"Me? But I'm not even Jewish. Hardly more than a *tourist*." Leon sipped some more whiskey, his public schoolboy face mocking, the cigar thrusting up from the fingers that stroked the back of Kate's wrist. "So, Kate, how did the rabbi describe me?"

"You want the brutal truth?"

"I'm a masochist."

"You're a cynic, a drunkard, and an anti-Semite."

"That sounds quite reasonable."

"He really doesn't like you."

"That's because I'm always proclaiming loudly in print that this country is being divided by religious bigotry and the demented ravings of the chief rabbis. This has not helped to make me the most popular gentile in Jerusalem, but it *has* made me a reasonably respected journalist."

"An unsavory breed."

"True."

"The word is out that if you continue to write your anti-Zionist articles, a certain Major General Moshe Eitan may have you thrown out of the country."

"I doubt it," Leon replied, inhaling on his cigar, exhaling blue smoke. "The venerable chief of staff is too aware of the negative shift in worldwide opinion."

"I've heard the very opposite: that Eitan is as stubborn as a mule, ruthlessly efficient, and doesn't give a damn what anyone thinks of him."

"Ruthless and stubborn he certainly can be—but he's also an astute diplomat. Bear in mind that Eitan is one of those legendary Israeli warrior-heroes with a history of personal tragedy and public glory. Born and raised on a kibbutz, noted fighter in three wars, wife and children murdered by Arab raiders, then leading light of the military command. . . . Not, then, a great lover of his restless Arab neighbors, he is, nonetheless, a politically aware military man who has more than once cooled the ardor of the more aggressive members of the IDF. Ergo, while it is true that Eitan detests my widely syndicated and extremely popular column—and please note the self-advertisement—it is also true that he is not the sort of fool to seal the lips of a foreign journalist and invite the wrath of the democratic countries."

"A situation you exploit to the hilt, being thoroughly devoid of normal scruples."

"Scruples are for the likes of Moshe Eitan. Israel's juicy hypocrisies are *my* game."

"What hypocrisies?"

"You may further your education, sweet lady, by simply reading my columns."

He grinned wickedly at Kate, removed his fingers from her wrist, then sat back in his chair and looked down at the walls of the Old City, after which he turned his gaze back on Kate. Studying his eyes which, though red with drink, were still bright with intelligence, Kate again found herself filled with a premonition of disaster, the feeling that Leon, hiding behind his cynical wit, was twisting slowly on the blade of self-contempt and unstated pain. He possibly judged what she was feeling—or at least sensed her lack of joy—for he now crooked his head, squinted at her with one eye, and offered her a bright, encouraging grin.

"The lovely lady is not herself tonight."

"No, I suppose not."

"The cries of the bereaved at the hospital?"

"Yes . . . I'm fed up with it."

"All psychiatrists go crazy in the end."

"I won't argue that point."

"Your father's dead, Kate. You have no one left here. Why don't you simply pack up and leave? Go back to America."

"I don't know . . . that's the question."

"Your Jewishness?"

"I don't think so. That's not what holds me here. In fact, I think it's the fanatical Jewishness of this damned country that's driving me crazy. I'm only Jewish by birth. My father's beliefs never touched me. I'm American and I feel it to my bones and this country defeats me. . . . No, I think I've just been here too long to ever go back. . . . I'm too old for a new life."

Yet that wasn't the truth, since recent events had confirmed the opposite: first the dreams, then the strange star, then the earth tremor and mysterious light, then the fear that had dogged her through this day and driven her out of the hospital. The buried shame of her past? A premonition of the future? Whatever their source or reason, the events had opened a chasm beneath her. An only child, she had missed her mother, who had died five years ago; but the death of her father, for whom she had felt no great affection, had torn her from the anchor of her past and then cast her adrift. Now more than ever she felt a foreigner in this country, isolated, confused, ostracized by its contradictions, wanting desperately to escape back to America, but too frightened to move. That fear, more than anything else, filled her long nights with shame.

"Too old," Leon said. "That explanation rings hollow. More likely the legendary magic of Judaism has rendered you senseless."

Kate couldn't resist smiling. "I don't think so, Mr. Halcomb. Your infamous disrespect is contagious and has turned me into a sinner."

"Is that what they say?"

"Gossip comes back to its subject. It's possible that I said it first, but now I'm branded for life: a thirty-five-year-old spinster, sharp-tongued, anti-Zionist, who drinks too much and sleeps with Leon Halcomb—a dissolute, English, anti-Semite."

"A very pretty picture that conjures up." Leon grinned and held his glass of whiskey high, as if offering Kate tribute. "But tell me, dear," he said, having a sip, putting his glass down, "why did a nice girl like you end up with this pagan?"

"That's another question I've often asked myself."

"But that isn't an answer."

Leon's eyes, blue and bright, streaked with red but still sharp, studied Kate with a thinly disguised intensity that made her uncomfortable. Perhaps that was the answer: Leon's mockery revealed the truth; Leon's cynicism, with its grasp of the ridiculous and hypocritical, was a knife that stripped the flesh from the bones to show the poison beneath. The poison was life itself, its private dreams and public dramas, just as much a part of Kate, with her need to bury her guilt in work, as it was a part of Israel with its dream of freedom drenched in blood and its faith in the Messiah kept alive by the roaring of guns. The ridiculous and the hypocritical, both in public and private: perhaps Kate was drawn to Leon because his lack of faith was comforting, his realistic view of life's horrors a rebuke to her own growing doubts.

"Yes," she said, "I want to leave. At least I *think* I want to leave. I no longer like my work, the woes of my patients now revolt me, and I keep thinking that I don't belong here, that my life is slipping away from me. Maybe it's just my age, my father's death, the empty house;

something stupid like the fact that I'm not married and don't want to be; but that I, the psychiatrist, in my supposed wisdom, secretly dread the thought of being alone. I don't know if that's true. If it is, it's detestable. Nonetheless I'm running scared, feeling desolate but keeping my distance, not wanting to be involved yet feeling hungry for some form of commitment. I'm in conflict with myself. I'm beginning to behave like my patients. The truth is that I'm no longer a good psychiatrist. I'm just a woman . . . and stupid."

Leon smiled and stubbed his cigar out. "You have the premature, middle-aged blues," he said. "Not the stuff of the Sabra."

"No, not a Sabra. Not even a good Jewish girl. I have strange dreams at night—about you and the rabbi, about my father and my past—and those dreams, perhaps more than anything else, make me want to leave Israel."

"Your past?"

"Various skeletons. Long buried in various closets. I'm sure a man with your low boredom threshold wouldn't want to discuss them."

Leon proved that point by turning his head and nodding at the waiter, who soon arrived with two further drinks and just as quickly departed. Leon raised his glass to Kate, then nodded and took a sip, while Kate, remembering the events of the early morning, looked out at the sky: velvet blue growing darker, streaked with faint lines of crimson, areolas of gray light around the clouds as the evening descended. There was nothing unusual there and Kate wondered if there ever had been. She shivered, feeling disoriented and nervous, then turned back to Leon. He was stretching himself and gazing around him, studying the tourists at a nearby table, a small, mocking smile on his lips, shadows under his eyes.

"And why a disreputable character like Leon Halcomb? That question hasn't been answered yet."

"I told you," Kate replied. "I'm just a woman . . . and stupid. Also, I'm trying to keep my distance—and you're helpful that way."

Leon's eyes, very alert, one eyebrow raised, turned back to fix on Kate's face. "*I'm* helpful? How come?"

Kate stubbed her cigarette out, lit another immediately, then glanced up at the darkening sky. It was, at least as far as she could see, devoid of unknown phenomena. "Because you're sweet," she said. "Because beneath it all, you're soft. Because for all of your cynicism, you're neither aggressive nor demanding and, believing in nothing, don't stand in judgment. I think that's what it is. You don't expect anything from me. I can come and go as I please and you never complain . . . because you don't give a damn."

Leon looked interested. "And that's what you like about me? The fact that I don't give a damn?"

"That's it. That's your answer."

Leon raised his right eyebrow, ran his finger around the rim of his glass, glanced quickly left and right, his grin bemused, then looked back at Kate.

"I'm not sure I understand, Kate."

"It's really not very complicated. I neither want to possess nor be possessed, and I feel safe with you. It's your inability to stake a claim on anyone that makes you attractive."

"My inability to stake a claim?"

"Come on, Leon, don't act innocent. . . . You're a married man, two children, separated from your wife, and, by your own admission, separated because you couldn't stand home life. Now you travel the globe, carrying no more than your suitcase, hopping in and out of beds in impersonal hotel rooms, feeling comfortable with no place to call your own, with no lasting relationships. You and me, we're both the same that way, which is why we get on so well. We're both wary of involvement, of more than superficial experience, and we both look at life from the distance of supposed objectivity. You have your journalism—the unprejudiced eye, the clear ear—and you pretend to take no sides, to report only what you see and hear, and in this way you deny your own involvement in life's irrational passions. Unfortunately it's a lie. Objectivity doesn't exist. What you see and hear are filtered through your own emotions—and it's this, the realization of your weakness, that you hide with your wit. That also explains your suitcase and hotels and Kate Hirschfields: they're all part of an impersonal world—a world of comfort, but twice removed—you can take them or leave them as you wish, but they won't draw you in. Your need for disengagement isn't threatened, and that helps you feel comfortable."

"And Miss Hirschfield?"

"Miss Hirschfield is in psychiatry, another supposedly objective field, but psychiatry, like the farce of journalism, weaves its own sly deceits. Miss Hirschfield also analyzes with her eyes, ears, and brain, breaking down the thoughts of her patients, often complex beyond imagining, into patterns of words that presume to define the psyche in logical terms. In doing this she must play a role—that of human objectivity—a pretense of reason and understanding which transcends psychic chaos. A transparent hoax? Possibly. Yet it often works with the patients. Unfortunately it also works with Miss Hirschfield, but in a negative way: like Mr. Halcomb, she fears involvement, seeks the safety of distance, and thus psychiatry, which insists on a so-called objectivity, becomes the wall behind which she can hide. . . . We are two of a kind, sir."

Kate picked up her glass, swallowed a mouthful of gin, put the glass down, and inhaled on her cigarette, breathing deeply and nervously. The restaurant was now more crowded, the conversations louder; and, outside, the first stars were appearing in a sky of dark velvet. Kate looked up, scanned the sky, saw nothing unusual, sighed with relief and lowered her gaze, and stared straight at Leon. He lit another cigar, exhaled a thin ribbon of smoke, then placed the cigar on the ashtray and leaned over the table.

"Why Miss Hirschfield's fear of involvement?"

"I will never discuss that."

"And what makes you think I'm not involved with you?"

"Don't even suggest it."

They stared at one another, their faces close, neither smiling, held together by the sealed doors of their past and the words still unspoken. Then Kate turned her head, wondering what she had said, and saw the darkened Valley of Kidron, the blackened domes of the Old City, the spotlights beaming up through the palm trees and illuminating the limestone walls. Down there were the twisting lanes and Oriental *souks* and covered passageways, the Orthodox Jews and Franciscan monks, the Muslims in flowing robes and *kaffiyehs*, the nuns in their habits, the Bedouin women in their embroidered dresses, the young soldiers with their machine guns on their shoulders, all the shops and bazaars. The Old City: a mirage. Kate's heart broke at the very thought of it. She looked up at the sky, saw the stars, all familiar, then stared back at Leon and saw his blue eyes and thin lips—no smile, not the trace of a grin as he leaned over toward her, his voice low and passionate.

"Come to bed, Kate! *Now!*"

They made love in the impersonal comfort of Leon's room on the top floor, high above the darkened Valley of Kidron and the illuminated walls of the Old City, locked together in silence and the moonlit chiaroscuro, the white sheets thrown back across their feet as their limbs intertwined. Kate lay beneath Leon, her legs raised, her arms around him, feeling herself dividing in two, one part surrendering to sensation, the other divorcing itself from the sweat and flesh and surveying the act from a distance. To touch and be touched, possess and be possessed: these were needs that could not be denied and sought to circumvent the void within. Desire howled like the wind, but like the wind it passed away, always leaving in its wake the great silence that had to be filled again. Kate dreaded that silence, feared the challenge of its emptiness, sought the brief obliteration of her Self in the thickets of singing nerves. To touch and be touched: the sensuality of the skin; her Self, which refused to be obliterated, split in two and broke free. One part of her surrendered, willingly gave in to sensation, but her other Self, more frightened, held in check by the past, drifted somewhere above the moonlit bed and gazed down in cool judgment. Kate turned her head aside, her hair streaming across her face, eyes wide, reflecting stars and pale moon, her arms and legs holding Leon, both breathing in spasms.

Breathing also in desperation. What was causing it in Leon? He had brought her to this room in urgent silence and now seemed to be lost in her. Not the Leon she knew, no smile, no stinging wit, he filled his mouth with her breast and thrust himself deep inside her with a voiceless intensity that repudiated what she had said to him. He bit her lips and swallowed her tongue, his breath sour with cigars and whiskey, and she turned her head aside and felt his eyelids on the stem of her neck. Not Leon, someone else, a faceless assailant in the darkness, someone trying to drain himself of despair in the well of her body. Kate looked down and saw the tableau, coiling limbs, sweating skin, then her divided Self became one again and she felt the cool air.

Leon made love like a stranger, with a fierce, demanding hunger, straining above her body, pressing down on her breasts and stomach, his eyes closed, his black hair disarrayed, his spine pale in the moonlight. She saw him and turned her head, raising her legs, pulling him in, feeling nothing but the urge to draw him out of his strange, throttled anger. She was crushed by his ferocity, some threat emanating from his pores, and she gasped and held him tighter with arms and legs and let him pour himself into her. He groaned and dropped his head, his body quivering like a reed, then just lay between her legs, breathing harshly, his cheek pressed to her breasts.

Kate sighed and stroked his head, stared at the window and saw the stars, shivered and closed her eyes and wondered whom she was addressing as the night, with its ominous silence, lay its dark hands upon her.

"You can't have me," she said.

6

"So," the prime minister said, "I've finally met Rashid Idriss. An interesting man, very calm . . . indeed, he seemed almost gentle."

"Don't be fooled by his beautiful brown eyes, Shlomo. That Lebanese gentleman is as sharp as any Arab alive."

The prime minister grinned and nodded, raised his glass and drank some beer, wiped his lips with the back of his left hand, and then glanced down through the darkness. They were sitting at a small table on the patio of Moshe's house on the summit of the hills of Talpiot, the lights of Jerusalem far below them, the Dome of the Rock and the El Aqsa mosque still visible as impressive black globes above the floodlit walls of the Old City. Moshe stared down but saw little, his thoughts focused elsewhere, then he looked back at the prime minister, small, almost gnomish, his eyes too large for his moon-shaped face, and watched him having another sip of beer, his lips pursed and moist.

"He seemed like a reasonable sort of chap, Moshe."

"A very British way of putting it, Shlomo."

The prime minister chuckled, perhaps remembering his English acquaintances, old enemies and friends of long ago, when he had fought with the Palmach.

"Rashid's astute," Moshe said. "That's why he seems reasonable. As he said himself: he has to accept that we'll remain here. What he resents is our greed."

"Ah, yes," the prime minister murmured. "Jewish greed . . ."

Moshe pulled another cigarette from his tunic pocket, lit it, inhaled, and then blew a thin stream of smoke to the air, thinking of what the prime minister had said. As both a Sabra and a military man, Moshe had lived for years with the belief that Israel, to survive, must retain Jewish autonomy and guarantee the security of her borders with constant military vigilance. What this meant, in effect, was that the country needed to be dominated by a military rather than a political consciousness, and that support for the military had to be constantly psychologically reinforced. However in recent years Moshe had begun to wonder just where this philosophy was leading: the need for constant alertness had led to conscription and censorship, an unconstitutional use of internal and external security organizations and, perhaps inexorably, the increasing withdrawal of legitimate Arab rights with a parallel increase in Jewish authoritarianism. Rashid had been right: the Jews were sowing the seeds of their own suspicions; and Israel, which had been founded on the principle of Jewish freedom, was now accepting that the end was justification for the means. Now, when Moshe thought of the Jews of the Holocaust, he also thought, with undeniable shame and guilt, of the Arabs of Palestine.

"Yet what can we do?" the prime minister said. "Only our so-called greed will protect us. If we give the Arabs an inch, they'll take a mile. . . . We must hold on to Israel."

"I don't like it, Shlomo; it disturbs me."

"What disturbs you?"

"What Rashid knows. The West Bank is our Achilles' heel—that's no secret anymore—but Rashid knows *too* much for my liking."

"He has people on the inside."

"*Jewish* people, Shlomo. We simply have to accept that it's happening and do something about it."

"We *can't* do anything about it. We can't use force against our own kind. Even now, if we tried to remove those fanatics from the West Bank, we would have fifty thousand of their supporters in the streets, probably armed to the teeth." The prime minister shrugged wearily, drumming his fingers on the table, a cool breeze sweeping over the patio and whipping his white shirt. "So, Moshe, what do we do? Do we invite a civil war? Do you want me to order you, my chief of staff, to use your conscript troops against fellow Jews? No, obviously you don't. We both know what would happen. And yet if we don't do something soon, the situation will worsen. There's no answer. *No* answer!"

Moshe sighed and stood up, glancing around at the dark hills, then walked to the low wall of the patio and stared across at Jerusalem. The land fell down through the darkness and swept back up to the Old City, sacred to the three great monotheistic religions—the world's spiritual center. Down there, cramped together within the limestone walls of the Old City, were the Wailing Wall, the golden-domed Mosque of Omar, and the Church of the Holy Sepulchre—the most sacred sites of all to Jew, Arab, and Christian respectively. Small wonder that for centuries Jerusalem had been ravaged by a succession of bloody wars and that that violence, which had started so long ago, was not finished yet. Moshe shook his head sadly, wondering where it would end, then turned back to face Ben Eliezer, feeling the trap closing in on him.

"Rashid Idriss was right," he said. "He has us whipped, and he knows it. World opinion has turned against us, the West Bank problem is becoming explosive, and if Jew should openly move against Jew, the Arabs will swoop in from all sides. That's all the Soviets and Americans need: a convenient war of intervention. And if that happens, Israel as we know it will cease to exist."

The prime minister looked up slowly, his large eyes unblinking, and Moshe, feeling cold, shivering slightly, knew at what cost his old friend was concealing his fears for the future.

"What we need is a miracle," Ben Eliezer said. "Nothing less will suffice." He smiled sardonically and raised his hands, slapped them lightly on the table, then pushed himself to his feet, rising slowly and wearily. "This wind is too cold for my liking. Let's continue inside."

Moshe nodded and waved one hand, letting Ben Eliezer enter first, then he followed and closed the sliding glass doors behind him. The central heating was off, but the living room was warm, and as Moshe faced the room, he felt both comfortable and desolated, surrounded by the bric-a-brac of his past and the tales they could tell. The furniture was functional, a careless collection of bits and pieces, obviously purchased without thought of compatibility or style—simply there to be used. There were a great many books, scattered as haphazardly as the furniture—Jewish and military histories, current affairs and foreign politics—on chairs, on the table, on the cluttered shelves, many open and marked. Most revealing were the numerous photographs, very few taken recently: an adolescent Moshe in the fields of a kibbutz, his hair tousled, his grin wide and charming; the same young man a few years later, dressed formally and looking grave, his arm linked with the arm of his new bride, both afraid of the camera; then a series of family snapshots—his wife a dark, quiet beauty, his son and daughter more outgoing—on vacation in Cyprus, camping out in the Negev, swimming in the sea at Eilat, a birthday party in someone's garden; then a much older Moshe, rarely smiling, eyes haunted, usually feigning amiability, socializing with Golda Meir and Menachem Begin and Teddy Kollek, acting the diplomat with Harold Wilson and Henry Kissinger and Rashid Idriss. Moshe's history was on those walls—as was the continuing history of Israel—but when he looked, when he examined his wife and children, he did not look for long.

"Another beer, Shlomo?"

"I'd prefer a vodka, Moshe. Another beer would put me to sleep, and I can't face my bad dreams."

Moshe went into the kitchen and returned with a bottle of Maccabee, a half full bottle of Keglevich vodka, and two glasses rattling with ice cubes. After pouring a considerable amount of vodka into one of the glasses, he passed the glass to the prime minister, opened his own bottle of beer, and then drank where he was standing, still close to the sliding glass doors that led to the patio. The prime minister, who had often been here before, sat in the chair behind Moshe's small desk and raised his glass high.

"*L'chaim!*"

"*L'chaim!*"

They both drank, and then the prime minister, after rubbing his tired eyes, grinned at Moshe and put his feet up on the desk. Moshe returned the grin and nodded understandingly, amused by the prime minister's informality.

"I don't think young Lieutenant Frankel was very pleased at having to escort our Arab friend back to the border."

"No, Shlomo, he wasn't."

"Well, he's had a busy day. First meeting me at the airport, then going to check on that bombing, then escorting Rashid back from whence he came. Nonetheless I have heard good things about him."

"He's good," Moshe said.

"And?"

"Lieutenant Frankel is an intensely serious young man who probably despises us both."

"A Zionist?"

"Yes."

"So are we."

"Not to that extent. Frankel is an Orthodox Jew with the Talmud in his hip pocket: there is no such place as Palestine, no such people as the Palestinians; the Holy Land belongs to the Jews and is no place for Arabs."

"The West Bank?"

"It's possible. He may sympathize with them. At the very least he doesn't see any problem there: he would solve the problem by simply removing all the Arabs and supporting the activities of Kash and Gush Emunim. I doubt that he has time for our procrastinations."

"A representative Sabra."

"That's it."

The prime minister sighed, poured himself another vodka, and continued to lie back in the chair, his feet on the desk.

"Do you think Rashid was right about the bombing in the Mea She'arim quarter? That the bomb was actually planted by a Jew?"

"I doubt that he'd invent it."

"And what do we know so far?"

"Not nearly as much as our good friend Rashid. Lieutenant Frankel was the first man on the scene, and he took the survivors straight to the Hadassah Medical Center. Naturally they were still in a state of shock, and according to Lieutenant Frankel, he was given a hard time by that psychiatrist, Hirschfield."

"Mayer Hirschfield's daughter?"

"Yes."

"An interesting woman. I knew her father and mother well. Her mother died some time ago, and her father's death, about ten days ago, was a considerable blow to the World Zionist Organization and the Foundation Fund in particular. That man did an enormous amount of work to bring funds into Israel; and his daughter, from what I gather, has performed remarkable psychiatric work at the medical center. Of course Hirschfield was a Zionist with the immigrant's dedication, and I believe his daughter quarrelled with him over that."

"Did you know she also sleeps with Leon Halcomb?"

"I *have* heard that rumor . . . but I don't believe her sex life should concern us."

"No, perhaps it shouldn't. But I do find it offensive that a woman whose father did so much for Israel should so blatantly sleep around with a drunken anti-Semite like Leon Halcomb. That man has done more to turn the world against us than any other single journalist enjoying the hospitality of this country. I shudder to think of what he's already written about your unfortunate remark to the General Assembly, but I don't doubt that he'll have made the worst possible use of it. And it angers me to think that that woman, with her background, could insult the memory of her father by openly flaunting her relationship with such a *momzer*."

"Americans have their own morality in these matters."

"Unfortunately that's so."

The prime minister chuckled sardonically and had another sip of vodka while Moshe, removing his glass from his mouth, wiped his lips with his hand. The land below was very dark, the lights of Jerusalem shining magically, the illuminated walls of the Old City dreamlike and entrancing. Moshe thought of his wife and children, of how much they had loved this land, and then, with the old pain whipping through him, put the glass to his lips again.

He was just about to turn away from the window when something in the distance caught his attention. Startled, not too sure of what he was seeing, he blinked and looked again, and saw a strange light in the dark sky just beyond the Old City. The light appeared to be pulsating, winked out, winked on again, moving too slowly to be an aircraft, and hazed in a dark cloud. Yet even as he saw this, there was an indistinct rumbling sound that seemed to emanate from below the house—and then, as the rumbling grew louder, the floor started vibrating.

Moshe jerked his head around, saw the prime minister in the chair, cursing as his vodka splashed on his shirt and kicking his feet off the desk. "What—?" the prime minister exclaimed, glancing up, his eyes startled, putting his glass down on the desk as the vibrating grew stronger and the rumbling down below seemed to spread out in no fixed direction. "Last night!" Moshe said quietly, remembering the unexplained earth tremor and turning his face back toward the window, his eyes fixed on Jerusalem.

"What on earth—?" he said, trailing off.

As the rumbling continued and the floor vibrated beneath his feet, Moshe stared through the darkness at the east side of Jerusalem and saw the strange, shapeless light spreading out through clouds of dust that were being picked up from the Valley of Kidron and then whipped into a dense, swirling mass. Amazed, Moshe reached out and placed his free hand on the window, his other hand shaking from the vibrations of the floor and splashing the beer over his wrist. Blinking, he tried to ascertain what the distant light was, saw it spreading out, shrinking, then spreading out again, diffused in the whirlwind of dust that rose higher and seemed to sweep across the summit of the Mount of Olives. The light in the middle was bizarre, expanding and contracting, moving forward through the sky now blotted out by the swirling dust, dropping lower and then spreading out again through the storm that appeared to have enveloped the Mount. Moshe felt the shaking window, the floor vibrating beneath his feet, heard the rumbling and then the sudden squeaking of a chair on the floor. "What is it? *What's happening?*" The prime minister's voice was shrill. Then, still looking down, Moshe saw the other lights winking out, first one, then another, as the swirling black cloud swallowed the houses on the Mount of Olives and raced on toward the walls of the Old City. Moshe kept staring, mesmerized, his fingers outspread on the glass, the floor vibrating beneath him, the rumbling filling his ears, watching as the diffused light shot out through the swirling dust, briefly illuminated the summit of the Mount, then shrank with startling speed and disappeared, leaving nothing but darkness.

The rumbling sound faded away, the floor stopped its vibrating, and then the ringing of the telephone on the desk shattered the silence. The prime minister cursed, grabbed the telephone, hissed his own name—but Moshe didn't turn around, his eyes fixed on Jerusalem, seeing the domes and minarets and lights disappearing as the swirling dust swept across the city and gradually swallowed it. Moshe stood there, disbelieving, transfixed by what he was seeing, as Jerusalem, the Golden City, the very heart of *Eretz Yisroel*, was devoured by an extraordinary storm and then simply disappeared.

Moshe broke free from his trance, turned away from the window, and saw the prime minister putting the phone down, looking up, his jaw slack, his eyes stunned as he started to speak with a strained, breaking voice.

"An unidentified object has disappeared below our radar's ground clutter, directly above the Chapel of the Ascension. It appears to have crashed."

7

Kate stubbed out her cigarette, swung her legs off the bed, and then, still naked, feeling cold, walked across the room, through the moonlight, and stopped at the window. She saw the darkened Valley of Kidron, the white stones of the Arab graveyard, the Old City, its ancient walls bathed in floodlights, the Dome of the Mount, and the El Aqsa mosque as black globes in the darkness. The air was cool and fresh, the breeze almost imperceptible, and she took a deep breath and looked up to where the mysterious star had been that morning.

The star was not there. That particular area was covered with dark cloud. It was a single, large cloud, almost circular, nearly black, surrounded by a clear, vitreous sky and a mosaic of normal stars. She stared at it, mesmerized, feeling inexplicably nervous, trying to still the speculations that filled her head with uncomfortable vibrancy. It was a cloud, a normal cloud, a single cloud in a clear sky, and her imagination, stirred by the early morning's events, was obviously running away with her. . . . Yes, that it was; put it down to imagination. . . . But the tension remained with her, and she knew that she would have to go out there and resolve the matter once and for all.

She looked up at the black cloud, a perfectly normal cloud, then shivered and turned away from the window and proceeded to dress herself. The room was very quiet, quiet enough to reveal her heartbeat, and she also heard Leon's even breathing, saw his pale form in darkness. His back was pressed to the bedrest, his head tilted to the right, his hands folded primly on the white sheet that covered his loins. Kate dressed quickly and automatically, combed her long, tangled hair, then slung her bag over her right shoulder and walked up to the bed. Leon was snoring softly, his chest rising and falling, and she leaned over and kissed him on the forehead and then left the hotel room.

She took a deep breath, raised her eyes, saw the black cloud . . . and then she saw the impossible.

The cloud was breaking apart, thinning out in the middle, gradually taking the shape of an enormous smoke ring, a hazy light beaming through it. She stared at it, amazed, unable to repudiate the ridiculous, as the cloud became a dark, ragged ring around a large, brilliant star. That star should not have been there, was too large to be real, and yet it beamed down on the summit of the Mount with remarkable clarity.

"Oh, my God," Kate said quietly.

She inhaled on her cigarette, held the smoke in her lungs, let it out very slowly, reluctantly, her eyes fixed on the brilliant star. It was there, large and bright, ringed impossibly with cloud, and much as she tried to will it away, it would not disappear. She felt her heart pounding, grew hot and claustrophobic, her reason slipping away in defeat before the incomprehensible. It was a star, had to be, could not be anything else . . . and yet as she stared at it, disbelieving, forced to accept it, the star, or what she thought was a star, seemed to suggest something magical.

She dropped her cigarette, ground it flat beneath her shoe, then turned right and started walking downhill, feeling tense and unreal. She looked down the dark path, looked up at the star, looked down and then looked up again, a silent prayer on her lips. The star was still there, big and brilliant, ringed with dark cloud—an unnatural sight, both ominous and beautiful, like an eye staring down at her. . . . An eye? What was she thinking? Was that a logical response? Yet as she walked the narrow road where it began curving uphill again, she could not shake off the feeling that the star was observing her, following her as her feet kicked up the stones.

Where was she going? She hardly thought about it. Now, thinking about it, confused but still walking, she wondered why she was moving in this direction for no obvious reason. She stopped and looked up, saw the star and moved forward again, her will dissolving, a strange instinct pushing her on. The dust drifted up around her, did not settle down again, and then she realized that the breeze had become a wind that was growing in strength.

The wind tugged at her clothing and then started to moan, sweeping across the dark Valley of Kidron and whipping up more dust. She glanced down the slopes of the Mount, saw scattered buildings, holy sites, domes, and minarets floating in the darkness, more black than the night. Something took hold of her heart—a feeling of grief and desolation, an inexplicable, overwhelming sense that she no longer had roots—and she almost stopped again, changed her mind, not knowing why, and tore her eyes from the valley below and kept moving uphill.

The wind was now much stronger, but hot, almost clammy, making her shield her eyes with her right hand as the dust swirled around her. At first she did this automatically, more annoyed than frightened, but then she suddenly wondered where the wind had come from, and the fear slithered through her. She passed the colonnaded courtyard of the Church of the Pater Noster, wondered again briefly just what she was doing here, and then glanced up at the unknown, cloud-ringed star and froze where she stood.

With the ring of cloud around it the star looked like an enormous eye, a dark eye with a silvery-bright iris, fierce and unblinking. It had that—stunning brilliance—but it also had something else: a strange, majestic stillness and splendor, a mysterious beauty. She looked at it and shivered, closed her eyes and looked again, judged the star against the mass of stars behind it, and then knew what was bothering her: The other stars were more distant, part and parcel of the dark sky, but the unknown star was different, much larger, too bright, separated distinctly from the sky as in a three-dimensional photograph. . . . Yes, that was it: It was too close to the Earth; it had not been obscured by the lone cloud but hidden *inside* the cloud. . . . She licked her dry lips, tried to reject her own analysis, blinked and looked up at the star again, and then felt her heart pounding. . . . No, she was not imagining it. There could be no doubt about it: the light of the star was illuminating the extraordinary ring of cloud surrounding it, its rays shining clearly through the cloud and beaming down on Jerusalem.

Kate took a step backward, letting out an involuntary groan, putting her hand up to her mouth and keeping it there, her eyes fixed on the brilliant star. She could not believe what she was seeing, kept looking, had to believe it, and then, faced with the impossible made actual, her reasoning started to falter. She groaned again and bit her lip, clamped her hand on her mouth, shook her head slowly from side to side, trying to hold down her panic. The moaning wind began to howl, unnaturally violent, much too warm, as her hand moved from her mouth to shield her eyes and she took a step forward.

The wind was beating against her body, howling around her, racing

on, whipping up clouds of dust and shaping the dust into dark streams
that moved in immense circular motions. Yet what she saw was
worse, more bizarre and inexplicable: an enormous cloud of dust,
swirling furiously and roaring, rising up from the Valley of Kidron,
spewing earth and stones, and moving slowly forward toward the
Garden of Gethsemane like some ravenous beast.

Kate stood there, scarcely breathing, the storm hammering at her,
her right hand shielding her eyes, her heart pounding, her sense of
reality crumbling. The spiraling column was awesome, dividing the
sky, obscuring the stars, even darker than the darkness of the night,
but glowing strangely within. Then Kate raised her head, trying to
find the unknown star, thought she saw it, then lost it, saw instead a
stream of dust—black, dense, swirling wildly—sweeping out from
the roaring column in the valley and hiding the unknown star from
view.

She started to run, hardly knowing where she was going, instinct
driving her to find a hiding place before the storm devoured the
summit of the Mount. She shielded her eyes with her hands, kept her
gaze fixed on the ground, her feet kicking up the stones on the road as
the storm lashed her body. The wind continued howling, the dust
hissed all around her, and the roaring, now coming toward her, grew
louder each minute. The sound was terrifying, encouraging her to
keep moving, yet forcing her to turn her head and look again at the
extraordinary phenomenon. The roaring column was rising higher,
mushrooming above the valley, spreading out to obliterate the sky and
devour the Old City. The southern wall disappeared, then the Dome
of the Rock; then the dust enveloped the Antonia Tower, swept across
the Muslim Quarter, and spread out until all of East Jerusalem was
totally obscured.

No stars. No Old City.

Kate sobbed and turned away, kept her head down, watched the
road, moving forward as the howling wind pummeled her and the
dust hissed and swirled. She saw some Arab houses beyond a strip of
waste ground, some Arabs hurrying through the violent storm,
waving hands, shouting desperately. Then she heard the snorting of
camels, was whiplashed as she looked ahead, shielded her eyes and
stumbled forward and saw the walls surrounding the Chapel of the
Ascension. The camels were in panic, tugging wildly against their
ropes, snorting loudly, looking enormous and strange in the dense,
swirling dust.

Kate stopped and glanced left, saw the houses beyond the waste ground, lights flickering on and off in the windows, the storm sweeping across them. Someone ran across the waste ground, white robes whipped by the wind, calling out, waving arms, disappearing, a ghost in the stricken night. Kate glanced across at the Old City, saw nothing but more dust, a dark mass spreading out and advancing toward her, blotting out the whole world. She gasped and clenched her fists, felt a blast of hot air, was enveloped in a hissing, smothering cloud and then pushed forward again. She let the wind carry her toward the braying camels, was lashed by flying branches and stones and heard the rattling of rolling cans. Then she passed the panicking animals, hugged the wall of the mosque, eventually reached the forecourt and rushed through the open steel door.

Now she knew what she was: a creature stripped of all pride, its only instinct that of survival, past and future superfluous. She thought of this briefly, experienced a spasm of shame, then lurched forward, fighting against the wind and dust, the darkness deepening around her. She saw the circular walls of the modest Chapel of the Ascension, and she wanted to go inside, to find peace and shelter, but the howling became a roaring, something crashed down nearby, and then the ground began to shake, started rumbling and cracking, and then long, jagged cracks appeared in front of her, crisscrossing the courtyard.

The earth rumbled and split, opened out at her feet, and she jumped back as the jagged crack grew wider and raced across the small courtyard. She gasped and turned around, sensing the danger she was in, heading back toward the entrance and the open road beyond, wanting to be clear of the walls of the mosque tower if the earthquake grew worse. Already the courtyard stones were cracking, groaning and spitting cement, while beyond, filling the sky above the area of Gethsemane, the column of dust had become an enormous swirling dark mass that filled her whole vision. A terrifying sight, extraordinary, unprecedented, it froze Kate where she stood, paralyzed her, drained her mind, until something out there, something different, made her focus again.

That dark mass contained a glowing, a shapeless, pulsating white core, striations of pale light that spread out from the murky depths and appeared to move forward with the swirling dust. Kate blinked and looked again, wondering if she was hallucinating, covering her eyes with her hands and looking up as the demented wind pummeled her.

No, she was not imagining it: there was light in that darkness; a pulsating core of light buried deep in the storm and emitting striations of weaker light in every direction. The light was in the sky, inside the vortex of the whirlwind moving forward with the fiercely swirling dust and illuminating the night.

"No!" Kate shrieked. *"No!"*

She moved forward and stopped again, no longer sure what she should do, terrified to move ahead into the roaring storm, no longer keen to take shelter in the chapel as she had originally intended. Then the ground snapped and split, shook violently and growled, and then a jagged crack shot across the courtyard, from one side to the other. Kate gasped and stepped back, stared at the wall surrounding her, heard it cracking and saw the jagged lines forming a dust-spitting jigsaw. She jerked her head back, glanced briefly at the circular chapel, saw the cracks darting down the dome-shaped roof, a Roman pillar collapsing. She returned her gaze to the front, saw the wall of the courtyard collapsing, the howling dark mass everywhere, raging across the road outside, and then the roaring wind reached her, slapped her back, dragged her forward, picked her up and slammed her down to the ground and sent her sliding across it.

She did not feel fear or pain, dissolving into the experience, hardly aware that she was choking in the dust and being torn by the debris. Just the noise, a shocking bedlam, all around her, inside her head spreading out and returning as the wind when she rolled onto her back. She rubbed her eyes and looked up, saw a dull light expanding, growing brighter and then suddenly flaring out with a blinding ferocity.

A shriek. Her own voice. She closed her eyes and jerked her head around. Her cheek pressed the rubble as the ground beneath her shook, then she opened her eyes, opened them wider, disbelieving, and watched the Chapel of the Ascension rising up, ballooning out, cracking apart and then collapsing with a catastrophic roaring, clouds of dust blowing wildly while the ground heaved and shuddered beneath her. Kate sobbed and clenched her fists, grief and anguish sweeping through her, then closed her eyes and saw streaming stars and drifted into the void.

Shalom, she thought. *Peace.*

8

The dust that swept around Kate's prostrate body also swept with extraordinary force around Moshe Eitan's jeep as the driver, wearing goggles, raced past the wall of the Old City, which, even this close, was obscured by the roaring dark mass that seemed to have originated in the Valley of Kidron, traveled up the slopes of the Mount of Olives, and was now coiling back in a great arc and racing over Jerusalem. Moshe was sitting beside the driver, a lieutenant and sergeant in the rear seat, all of them wearing protective goggles against the fine earth and stones. The jeep passed the Dung Gate, leading into the Jewish Quarter, but both the gate and the wall were nearly invisible in the heart of the storm.

"I don't believe this," Moshe muttered.

Nor could he believe it; too much had happened too quickly: first the unidentified object, which appeared to have crashed on the Mount of Olives, now this storm of unprecedented fierceness, so sudden, so inexplicable, springing up out of nowhere, following an unnatural course, and covering the Old City and the Mount of Olives as if trying to devour them. Moshe glanced up to his left, saw the towering mass of the Temple Mount, the Dome of the Rock now no more than a black globe soaring high above the obscured Turkish wall, the storm raging around it. Moshe didn't know what was happening, couldn't think of an explanation, and he felt the muscles tightening in his stomach as the tension took hold of him.

"It's getting worse!" the driver shouted.

"It doesn't matter," Moshe replied. "We've got to get to the summit of the Mount and find out what happened there."

They were now heading north, along the east wall of the Old City, the earth on their right sloping down to the Valley of Kidron, unnaturally dark, the clouds of dust still boiling skyward and sweeping over the Garden of Gethsemane and up the obscured slopes

of the Mount of Olives. Moshe glanced to his left, saw the Dome of
the Rock behind the wall, heard a subterranean rumbling, felt the jeep
shaking violently before careening sharply across the road. The men
in the rear bawled, their weapons clanging together, the driver cursing
and slamming his foot down, bringing the jeep to a screeching halt as
the ground growled and shook and became a jigsaw of gaping cracks
that ran out from the center of the road toward the low wall.

The driver cursed and smacked the steering wheel, licked his lips,
and glanced at Moshe, his eyes hidden behind the rubber-framed
goggles, beads of sweat on his face. Moshe pushed himself upright,
shook his head, and turned around, looking beyond the men in the
rear at the other two jeeps, which had also ground to a halt at the side
of the road. The men were shouting and gesticulating, pointing at the
jagged cracks in the road, and then the ground growled again, shook
and heaved in short, sharp spasms, and Moshe heard a roaring, a gasp
of horror from the driver, and he jerked his head back and looked up
through the dust just above him.

Even through the murk he could see the ugly cracks appearing
above the double arches of the magnificent Golden Gate; and then, as
he watched, hardly believing what he was seeing, the Byzantine
structure shook violently, spitting pulverized mortar, a web of jagged
cracks appearing, lumps of stone falling down, and then the whole
walled-in section collapsed, leaving the entrance to the Temple Mount
clear for the first time in centuries.

Moshe stared at the tumbling rubble, momentarily paralyzed, while
beside him the driver bowed his head and started murmuring a prayer.
Moshe was similarly affected, both shocked and outraged, watching
the rubble of the Golden Gate tumbling down the sloping earth, over
the wall below and onto the road. The sergeant in the rear cursed
loudly, the lieutenant answered with a throttled groan, and then
Moshe broke free from his reverie and turned to the driver, punching
him lightly on the shoulder and ordering him to start the jeep again.
The driver raised his head, his eyes hidden behind the goggles, then
licked his lips and opened his mouth to shout.

"The gate!"

"I said move!"

"But the gate . . . the Golden Gate!"

"Damn it!" Moshe bawled. "It's too late for that. *We've got to get
to the summit of the Mount of Olives!*"

The driver did as he was told and the jeep roared into life, churning up more clouds of dust and shooting off through the storm. Moshe turned to look back, saw the sergeant and lieutenant, both staring at the gaping hole in the Golden Gate, neither saying a word. Moshe raised his right hand, waving the other two jeeps forward, then he looked straight ahead as the jeep turned away from the Old City, passing the road that led up to St. Stephen's Gate and heading for the Garden of Gethsemane. They entered the Jericho Road, passed the Tomb of the Virgin, and then headed up the crude, narrow track on the lower slopes of the Mount.

Here the earthquake was stronger, the ground heaving relentlessly, splitting open in thin cracks that seemed to originate from the summit of the Mount and run back down toward the Old City. The jeep bounced over the cracks, its wheels squeaking in protest, throwing Moshe and his men from side to side, backward and forward. Also, the storm was worse, much louder, the dust thicker, rising up from the far end of the Valley of Kidron, sweeping over Silwan and up the slopes of the Mount of Olives, back down over the Garden of Gethsemane and on toward the Old City. The storm's course defied logic, as did its singular ferocity, and now the air was filled with uprooted cacti and bougainvillaea, the olive trees bending and shedding their greenery above the walls of the Basilica of the Agony. Moshe saw this through his goggles, through the distorting murk of the storm; he realized that he was sweating, that the wind was unnaturally hot, and as he wiped the sticky dust off his face, his bewilderment increased.

Higher up, the storm was terrible, appearing to be almost solid, a dark mass blotting out the moon and stars and streaming back down the slopes. Moshe saw the clouds of dust, a darker mass, perhaps more dust, then a light, a very faint pulsating glow, in the depths of the storm. The sergeant behind him bawled something, his hand dropping on Moshe's shoulder, shaking him, another hand passing his face, jabbing up at the sky. So, he was not alone—he was not hallucinating—and he kept looking up, saw the light passing over the road, high up, in the sky, in the eye of the storm, first dull, then growing brighter, striations wavering through the clouds of dust, then suddenly flaring out in a brief, blinding flash that swept over the whole area and just as suddenly winked out, leaving the original darkness.

"*Riboyne Shel O'Lem!*" the driver exclaimed.

"What was that?" the sergeant shouted.

"Don't stop!" Moshe bawled, hardly aware of his own voice. "Damn it, keep your hands on the steering wheel! Put your foot down! Let's move it!"

The jeep kept moving forward, bouncing wildly on the steep track, the ground heaving and splitting open in spasms, the dust still swirling furiously. Moshe kept scanning the black sky, wondering what the light had been, seeing nothing but the extraordinary storm, feeling a strange awe and fear. It was a different kind of fear—not the healthy fear of the soldier—and he cursed and tried to keep his wits about him as the storm raged and howled. The jeep kept grinding uphill, passing low limestone walls, then turned right past the Mount of Olives Hotel and screeched to a halt in front of the walls of the adjoining mosque. The jeeps behind did likewise, their engines coughing into silence, but Moshe remained where he was, as speechless as his men, staring beyond the ruins of the tower of the mosque to the remains of the Chapel of the Ascension: a dark hill of rubble.

There was nothing to say. What had stood for centuries had fallen. Moshe climbed out of the jeep, his body pummeled by the wind, hearing wails of despair from nearby houses, the camels braying in panic. The ground beneath his feet was steady, no longer rumbling and cracking, but the wind, which had diminished a little, was still too fierce for comfort. Moshe turned to the other men, saw them climbing out of the jeeps, their faces turned toward the ruins of the chapel, their heads shaking from side to side. Then they all gathered around him, perhaps instinctively seeking comfort, aware that what had happened would particularly affect the Arabs and Christians, but themselves extremely shocked by the event. Moshe studied them, looked away, stared at the ruins and shook his head, forcing himself back to reality and what had to be done.

"Okay," he said. "Let's go."

They clambered over the piled rubble, smacked by wind, whipped by dust, and then spread out and walked through the ruins. The walls of the courtyard had collapsed and the steel doors were buried in stones, so they simply marched across the scattered rubble into more devastation. Hulda's tomb and the chapel had both been destroyed completely, and were now merely two hills of debris, one large and one small. The men stopped between the two, looking around them, still stunned, lashed by the swirling storm, almost deafened by the howling wind, all of them temporarily forgetting just what they were there for.

"No wreckage," Moshe said, not bothering to shout against the wind, speaking more to himself than to his men. "No wreckage . . . no sign of an aircraft."

The remark drew their attention and made them look at him, but for a moment they seemed unsure of what to do, each locked in his private dream. Moshe felt it in himself—a hapless grief and disbelief —and he turned away from the rubble of the chapel to look down on Jerusalem. The storm seemed to be abating there, the dust thinning and settling down, the Dome of the Rock reappearing as a black globe in drifting cloud; then the El Aqsa mosque and the Church of the Holy Sepulchre with the lights of the New City behind it. The Old City had survived—for that he quietly said his thanks—but then the storm raging around him snapped him back to attention and he turned again to look at the rubble that towered above him and stretched across the dark, windswept courtyard. He sighed and wiped the dust from his goggles and then waved his men forward.

"Spread out," he said. "We're looking for metallic debris. Obviously it wasn't an aircraft, but it had to be something. If you see anything unusual, don't touch it; just tell me about it. Okay, let's go."

The men didn't move immediately, simply stood there indecisively, slightly stooped against the wind, their bodies rocking, the dust hissing around them. Moshe knew what they were feeling —being Jewish made little difference—but he turned his flashlight on and started walking, examining the ground at his feet. Eventually his men did the same, spreading out across the courtyard, moving around the cone-shaped rubble of the Chapel of the Ascension with their flashlights pointing down at the ground, searching for debris.

Moshe was not a religious Jew and sacred sites did not move him, but as he searched for the missing debris of whatever had crashed here, as the wind howled about him and swept the dust from the broken stones, as the broken stones, rolling, revealed nothing underneath, he felt something draining out of himself and leaving him hollow. These ruins brought back other ruins, another time, another place, the torn dress of a girl, the smashed toys of a boy, a tangled web of hair stained with blood, sightless eyes staring sunward. He felt a choking anguish, the resurrection of buried grief, and was shocked that this terrible night had opened up that old wound. The pain was like a fist clenched around his beating heart, more cruel than the howling wind and dust, draining the blood from his head. He stopped, feeling dizzy, blinked behind the dusty goggles, then cursed softly and started forward again, his flashlight shining on rubble. The other rubble had been different: not windswept but still; not hidden in the darkness of night, but bright and sun-scorched. The bloody hair had been dark, the eyes dark, drained of life, and her lips, when he touched them with his, had been cold and unyielding. Moshe remembered and closed his eyes, saw his children, opened his eyes again, retreating from the horror of that distant day and fixing his gaze on the windswept ground.

"Not a thing, sir," someone said.

"Pardon, Sergeant?"

"There's nothing here, sir. No aircraft could possibly have crashed here . . . nor anything else."

No, not a thing. The whole night was a mystery. Moshe nodded at the sergeant, hardly seeing him, scarcely hearing him, and then walked on, skirting the rubble of the collapsed chapel, his flashlight fixed on the ground. No memories, just the present, dissolving the pain with activity, the beam of his flashlight on the rubble, the rolling rubble revealing nothing, no indication of what it could have been that crashed down on the chapel. . . . The earthquake? Probably. No other possible explanation. Yet what had flown down beneath the radar's ground clutter and disappeared above the summit of the Mount? Moshe wiped sweat from his brow, spat the dust from his mouth, cursed the raging wind's demented howling, and wondered why he felt hot. . . . It was the wind that was hot, too hot, unnaturally so, and he suddenly felt haunted and claustrophobic, divorced from himself. What was happening to him? *The dead eyes staring sunward.* Moshe walked around the rubble, coming back to where he had started, saw the lights of the Old City rising out of the night, then heard one of his men shouting and looked around, facing into the beating wind.

"—here, sir! Over here!"

One of his men was kneeling down, his left hand raised and waving, his flashlight on the ground at his feet, beaming into the rubble. Moshe felt a pang of fear, something cold sliding through him, his mind filled with intimations of change that could not be defined. He licked his lips and stopped breathing, felt the pounding of his heart, listened intently to the howling wind, as if willing it to speak, and looked through the dust at that dark hand raised skyward, a snake's head waving to and fro, both seductive and dangerous. A mere moment passed this way, perhaps two or three seconds, but a distant time unfolded, revealed its horrors and passed on, and only then did he jerk himself free and force himself toward the kneeling man. The man stared up, teeth gleaming, his eyes hidden by the goggles, then lowered his head and pointed at the ground near his dust-covered boots.

"It's Kate Hirschfield. That doctor."

Moshe knelt down in the rubble, shone his flashlight on the woman's face, heard a groan, and saw her licking her lips and staring up, her eyes blinking. Large eyes, very brown, brown hair whipping across her face, long hair, thick with dust, her tanned face smeared with dust, her lips full and too wide, almost too wide for the face, at odds with the short nose, the nostrils slightly flared, framed by high cheekbones that emphasized the brown eyes and lent the face a taut, aggressive beauty. No, not beauty, at least not in the classical sense; but something else was there, certainly maturity and intelligence, and beneath that, behind the dark eyes, in the curve of the too wide lips, was a suppressed sensuality, a finely controlled tension, a strength of spirit made luminous by its own inhibitions: an attractiveness based on some part of her that was just out of reach.

Something took hold of Moshe and wrenched him out of himself, hurling him brutally into his past and then dragging him back again. He stared down at the woman, shining his flashlight beam on her face, feeling anguished, disoriented, dissolving into her being, and then he reached out, placed his free hand on her forehead, and brushed the hair from her face. The woman licked her lips, blinked her brown eyes, glanced around her, shook her head gently from side to side and then looked up at him.

"Am I all right?"

"Yes. You're all right. You can probably sit up now."

She sat up very slowly, pressing her hands to the ground, the wind whipping her long hair around her face as it howled all around them. The other men were moving toward them, shadowy forms in the dark night, and Kate blinked and stared at them, her head moving left and right, one hand brushing the hair back from her forehead, the other opening and closing. Sitting up, she looked slim, almost bony, her breasts small, her extremely long legs in loose slacks, the gray blouse hanging free. She turned her head to stare at Moshe, her gaze dark and direct, a quiet, sardonic smile at her lips as she pushed his flashlight from her eyes. Moshe thought of another time, another place, a skein of dark hair, and the recollection, conjured up by Kate Hirschfield's presence, invited pain and despair, the resurrection of buried grief, and filled him with an unutterable longing that cast him adrift.

"What happened?" he asked.

Kate blinked and opened her mouth, started to speak and then stopped, her brown eyes filming over with fear and confusion, glancing up, moving left and right, studying the dark forms all around her, then returning to Moshe, staring at him, hardly seeing him, a sort of blindness in the brown of her eyes as they reflected the flashlight beam. Moshe raised his right hand, saw it shaking in the wind, the wind fiercer, much louder, almost smacking them both sideways as the ground began to rumble, first shaking, then heaving, much worse than before, further jagged cracks crisscrossing the courtyard and making the rubble dance wildly.

"Another earthquake!" Kate hissed.

Moshe grabbed her right wrist, stood up and pulled her with him, saw large stones tumbling down the sloping rubble of the chapel as the ground shook with extraordinary violence and gave off a bass rumbling. The other men were already moving, racing back toward the road, when the rubble of the chapel started rolling across the courtyard, the ground cracking beneath the large mound, unleashing a terrible roar, then heaving upward through the center of the rubble and pushing it aside.

Moshe thought he saw light, couldn't believe it and turned away, his hand firmly on Kate's wrist as he pulled her with him, following his men toward the open road. The ground beneath them was shaking terribly, a harsh, rhythmic vibration, then the roar became deafening, a blast of hot air engulfed them, and Kate groaned as Moshe hauled her from the debris of the collapsed courtyard wall.

They stopped near the waste ground, neither looking at the other, both transfixed by the strange light that cut through the murk around them and illuminated the faces of the other men, all frozen, their goggles glinting, their jaws slack, saying nothing, simply staring in stunned silence beyond Kate and Moshe, their gaze obviously fixed on the source of the heat and noise that had turned the raging storm into something demonic.

Moshe and Kate both turned around, looking back where they had come from, and then stood there, just as frozen as the men around them, not believing their senses.

The center of the courtyard was erupting slowly, the ground roaring and breaking apart, heaving up through the middle of the collapsed rubble of the chapel and exuding striations of brilliant white light. Blocks of stone screeched and cracked, poured down the slopes of the parting rubble, rolling in waves of smashed rock and powdered cement across the devastated courtyard. The ground below continued heaving, roaring hideously and spitting light, the earth thrusting up through the rubble of the fallen chapel as if being forced up by a giant fist. The wind howled and the dust swirled, forming billowing black clouds, spreading out and rushing down to meet the light streaming up from the heaving earth. A fierce heat came from the courtyard, the brilliant radiance destroying the darkness—and in that stark chiaroscuro, in the unreal, dazzling clarity, the rubble of the chapel rolled away and another mound of earth appeared, the loose dirt emitting smoke and then also rolling away to reveal a large, glowing, rectangular object.

The downpouring light vanished, winking off like a light bulb, and simultaneously, miraculously, the wind ceased its demented howling and the silence rushed back to rule the night.

No one said a word. The event had made speech redundant. The ground had stopped its terrible shaking, the spiraling dust was settling down, the stars reappeared in a clear dark blue sky, and on a ragged mound of earth, where the Chapel of the Ascension had stood, obviously buried in the earth but rising above the upturned soil, a large object of unknown origin, rectangular, glowing brilliantly, filled the darkness with heat and white light, illuminating the witnesses.

Moshe reached out for Kate's hand.

9

They all stood there for some time, too stunned to think coherently, staring across the rubble at the extraordinary object that had emerged from the earth where the Chapel of the Ascension had stood for centuries. The storm had gone completely and now the night was calm and quiet, but eventually doors creaked open in the few houses beyond the waste ground and hesitant, fearful voices started calling to one another as the Arabs emerged from their homes to survey the devastation wreaked by the storm. Then a shout of surprise or horror, a woman's wail of fear or grief, as dazed eyes came to rest on the ruins of the chapel and that mysterious, awe-inspiring, glowing object.

Moshe, hardly aware that Kate's fingers were locked in his, stared through the subsiding dust and saw the stars reappearing in the starry sky beyond the high mound of rubble. He tried to focus on the large object but did not find it easy—his vision distorted by the brilliant light, his senses stripped by the evening's events—but eventually, forcing himself to remember just what he was here for, he was able to bring himself back down to earth and gather together his scattered thoughts.

The object was very large, perhaps fifty feet long, its straight sides and flat top surmounting the arched rim of the rubble and giving off the dazzling brightness of white-hot metal. The heat was intense, actually reaching as far as the waste ground, making the illuminated nocturnal air shimmer and distorting the stars beyond. Indeed the object could have been a mirage, a holographic photograph, its linear contours distorted by its own radiant heat, bending and wobbling like jelly, its edges hazed by the fierce silvery brightness. For this reason it was difficult to judge its true shape and size, but from where Moshe was standing, about two hundred yards away, the object appeared to be rectangular and was either sitting upon or buried in the upturned soil. If, as Moshe thought, the object was buried in the soil rather than sitting on top of it, it would not necessarily be rectangular; but either way it looked solid and was obviously white hot, made featureless by the radiance of that heat, its light illuminating the darkness.

Moshe turned to look at Kate, saw her dark eyes staring back at him, and then realized that he was holding her hand. Startled, strangely embarrassed, he released her hand and looked away, remembering other dark eyes, dulled by death, staring sunward, a skein of equally dark hair in the dust, a light breeze playing through it. His men were standing all around him, hardly aware of him, saying nothing, removing their goggles and squinting against the brilliant light pouring over the rubble. The Arabs were moving across the waste ground, shocked that their mosque had been destroyed, their dark faces very clear in the brilliance of the light, their shadows stretching out behind them to form bizarre, shivering shapes. Moshe studied them carefully—some pointing excitedly, some wailing with grief—then he looked again at Kate, felt a spasm of longing, turned away and smacked his left palm with his fist, stinging himself back to action.

"Lieutenant!"

"Yes, Major General."

"I want your men to move all civilians out of this area and then block off the road at both sides—there"—he pointed—"at the far end of the Mount of Olives Hotel; and there, in front of the Church of the Pater Noster. When you've done that, ring the central office, tell them we have an object of unknown origin and nature up here, and ask them to send us a physicist, a weaponry expert, a geologist, and anyone else who might have a specialized knowledge of what could have occurred here. I also want some representatives of Shin Beth and any information you can get from Meteorology and Air Defense about the earthquake and the reported unidentified. Also, we'll want a decontamination unit to check if the object is radioactive, and a bomb disposal unit at the ready should our weaponry expert decide that that thing is explosive."

"Right, Major General."

The lieutenant turned away and walked toward his sergeant, and Moshe, feeling as if he were dreaming, looked back at Kate. The fierce wind had been reduced to a constant light breeze that was brushing her dark hair from her neck. Her back was turned to Moshe, her slim form shivering slightly, silhouetted in the brilliant white light, her shadow touching his feet. Moshe wanted to go to his jeep and call through to the prime minister, but the sight of Kate Hirschfield magnetized him and made him feel helpless. He thought of his wife and children, of the grief he had suppressed, studied the woman, slim and silent, bathed in that unreal light, and felt himself dissolving all around her, melting into her being. Embarrassed even as he felt this, amazed that he could feel it at such a time, he had to will himself to tear his eyes away and concentrate on the object.

The object was still white hot, its edges hazed in the shimmering heat waves, but the edges seemed straight and beneath the brilliant whiteness was a dark sheen that suggested a solid surface. This possibility was staggering, since the intensity of the heat was enough to melt the toughest of metals. Rubbing his eyes, Moshe looked again at the object, trying to ascertain if it was shaped like an enormous plate or actually had a back and sides. He was convinced that it was box-shaped, something like a large room, but he couldn't be sure because the iridescent heat waves were diffusing the object and illuminating the rubble all around it.

As Moshe stared at her, Kate took a step forward, her right hand covering her eyes, the wind rippling her loose blouse and slacks, her shadow stretching out behind her. She took another step forward, stopped again, shook her head, then offered a muted groan and started walking as if in a trance.

Moshe was briefly startled, and just stood there, transfixed, as Kate brushed the dark hair from her eyes and hurried toward the ruins across the road. Then he came back to his senses, feeling the scorching waves of heat, and rushed forward to grab Kate by the elbow and jerk her back to him. She tripped on a stone and came toward him in a spin, and as he reached out to grab her with his free hand, she swung her fist at his face. He ducked just in time and the blow merely glanced off his cheek as Kate hissed something and then pulled away, trying to make her escape. She was surprisingly strong, leaning forward, her dark eyes gleaming, and Moshe pulled her toward him and slapped her face without thinking about it. Kate straightened up, shocked, raised her shaking right hand, touched her cheek, blinked and licked her lips, then lowered her hand again.

"You hit me," she said.

"Yes," Moshe replied. "I'm sorry. I didn't think you knew what you were doing, so I had to do something."

"Yes . . . of course."

"You were heading straight toward that thing on the rubble. It could have burned you . . . or blinded you."

"I didn't realize . . ."

"No."

"I'm sorry. I don't know what came over me."

The light pouring around her had a dazzling intensity that turned her face into a featureless mask and bathed Moshe in a suffocating heat. Aware that the heat was already burning his skin, he took Kate by the elbow and walked her toward his men, who were clearing the civilians, mostly Arabs, out of the area and blocking off the road at both ends of the devastation. Looking beyond the houses at the far end of the waste ground in front of the destroyed chapel, Moshe saw that the lights of the Old City had reappeared, the walls and domes clearly visible, the dark sky drenched with stars. This relieved him a little, but his thoughts were elsewhere, concentrated on the feel of Kate's flesh between his fingers, spread thinly on the bone of her elbow as he guided her forward. He noted that she was silent, her head down, her body shivering, the light breeze blowing her hair around her face in languorous motions. He flicked his eyes toward her, looked away, feeling guilty, remembering his wife's blood in the dust, the dust covering her brown hair. He felt disoriented, strangely removed from what was happening; thought of what he had said a few hours earlier about Kate Hirschfield and wondered what was happening to him now. The light of the object filled the road, fell across the emptied houses, and he saw his men holding the civilians back just beyond the parked jeeps.

"What happened?" he said.

"I'm not sure," Kate replied. "The ground was cracking open, then a noise, the roaring storm . . . another noise, a light in the storm, spreading out, all around me . . ."

"Around you?"

"Above me. It came out of the sky. I swear, it seemed to come from the sky and then spread out, or explode, all around me. . . . I fell down, was *thrown* down, heard a roaring, a terrible noise, then the chapel either exploded or collapsed, and after that I passed out."

"You just saw a light?"

"Just a light."

"Nothing else?"

"Nothing else."

Her voice was like an echo, strangely hollow, repeating his words, and then he saw her lifting her head, her dark eyes staring blindly. *The dead eyes staring sunward.* Moshe felt haunted and unreal, an old pain whipping through him as he reached the first jeep, which was parked beyond the range of the object's light. It was darker here, cooler, the breeze soothing scorched skin, and Lieutenant Gonen put the telephone down and turned around, looking weary.

"Everything's been arranged. The men are on their way already. I also asked them to send up some floodlights."

"Floodlights, Lieutenant? Are you serious? The light from that damned object is almost blinding."

"I don't think it's going to last very long. It's growing dimmer already."

This was true. Looking back at the mysterious object, Moshe noted that the white-hot glow was dimming, the brilliant light already fading from the middle of the road, darkness creeping back over the houses and deepening around the ruined courtyard of the chapel. The object itself was less dazzling, the air around it no longer shimmering, and the dark sheen of its surface was emerging like streaks of black paint on fluorescent glass. The top and sides still looked ragged beneath the distorting white-hot glowing, but it was now perfectly clear that the top and sides of the object were straight. Whether or not the object was shaped like an enormous plate or was merely one side of a three-dimensional object was still an issue of doubt; but since the rays of light were now mainly beaming upward, it was evident that the object was tilting backward a little and thus effectively hiding any possible further right-angled surface.

"Well, Lieutenant, what do you think it is?"

"I don't know, Major General. I just can't make it out. However, judging by the way that upturned soil has been pushed back, I'd say that it's as deep as it is long."

"Box-shaped."

"Yes."

"That's a pretty big box, Lieutenant."

"Precisely."

"What about the earthquake?"

"A member of the Weizmann Institute, helpfully a resident in Jerusalem, is coming to talk to you."

"And the unidentified?"

"A real mystery." The lieutenant shrugged his shoulders and rubbed his eyes with his hands, either weary or bewildered or both.

his jowls displaying his middle age. "They had an unidentified on the screens for no more than a few seconds and it disappeared below the radar's ground clutter right over here. Whatever it was, it didn't ascend again, and it certainly hasn't been seen since. However, that unidentified was picked up by the radar at precisely the same time as the first earth tremors were recorded on the seismometers, so it's thought that there may be a connection. Air Defense also pointed out that although the unidentified was the first and only one observed, there *has* been inexplicable interference on the radars throughout the past two nights."

"There was a tremor last night."

"That's right . . . with simultaneous radar interference."

Moshe sighed dejectedly, ran his fingers through his hair, then glanced over the lieutenant's shoulder at the men forming a barricade across the road. It was dark where the men were, and it made them look ominous, their rifles held high as they kept the jostling civilians from entering the area. The Arabs were unusually quiet, their eyes large, doubtless shocked, straining to see the object that had emerged from the earth and destroyed not only their mosque but one of the chapels most sacred to all Christians. Above the people were the stars, glittering brightly, perfectly normal, and Moshe looked up and then dropped his gaze and fixed his eyes on Kate Hirschfield. She was leaning against the jeep, biting her lower lip, her dark eyes gleaming, her brown hair fluttering gently against her face and its taut, repressed beauty.

"Are you all right?"

"Yes."

"Are you sure?"

"I'm a psychiatrist."

"That wouldn't necessarily help at the moment; you still seem distraught."

"I'm just confused, Major General. I'm not sure what's happening to me. I've been seeing things I just can't believe, but now I have to accept them."

"You mean that thing over there?"

"That—and something else. I heard you talking about the radar, about an unidentified flying object, and I think I might have seen that as well."

She offered a tentative, self-mocking smile, dropped her gaze to the ground, then, raising her face again, looked across at the glowing object, spread her hands in a gesture of bewilderment, and looked back at Moshe. He was drawn to her brown eyes, to their secretive depths, to something that was just out of reach and refused to reveal itself; and he felt that he was drowning, slowly losing his senses, his beating heart proclaiming his confusion and remembered despair. He rubbed his eyes with one hand, his head down, in retreat, then he looked up and saw the brown eyes and felt the strength draining out of him.

"Yes?" he said.

"It's crazy."

"You're a psychiatrist: you should know."

"It was a star, Major General. I saw it last night and tonight. It looked like a star—though it was too large and was obviously very low in the sky. I saw it first last night just before that minor earthquake; I saw it tonight just before that terrible storm started. Whatever it was, it fascinated me. In fact, it nearly hypnotized me. I was in the Intercontinental and then, for no reason, I found myself walking up to here with the star practically following me. Then the storm came up. It started directly below the star. When I reached here, and just before I passed out, I saw that light in the very heart of the storm, coming right down on top of me."

She stared directly at him, a steely light in her brown eyes, her brown hair fluttering across her high cheekbones and full, sensual lips. Moshe thought of Leon Halcomb, of this woman in his bed, and his revulsion, which came instantly, was made more complete because it was wedded to his own desire for her. His feelings astonished him, made him feel that he was going mad, more so because they were inseparable from the events of the whole evening. He had despised this woman on principle, without knowing her, on hearsay; but now, standing face-to-face with her, he was lost in her dark eyes. He tried to break free, to concentrate on what had happened, but the mysterious object, which grew dimmer with each second he stood here, seemed no more than the instrument that had brought him to this singular meeting.

"Major General?"

"Yes, Lieutenant?"

"I was wondering if we could send one of the men to walk around the courtyard to have a look at the other side of that object and possibly ascertain just what it is."

"No, Lieutenant, I don't think so. He would have to go too close to it. God knows what it is, but it just might be radioactive—and I don't think it's worth taking that chance. I don't want anyone to go near that thing without a lead suit on, so we'll just have to be patient and wait for the decontamination unit to arrive."

"It's really growing dim."

"Yes, it is. We might even be able to see what it is without going near it."

The blinding white light had now disappeared completely and the object had become a red-hot rectangle surrounded by darkness. No longer obscured by the fierce, shimmering heat waves, it was obviously very solid, its edges perfectly straight, its base clearly buried in the upturned soil and rubble, its surface dark beneath the dimming red-hot sheen. Judged from this distance, it appeared to be about fifty feet long and twenty feet high from the lowest point of the irregular rubble. The sky beyond it was now black, serene, drenched with stars, and the object, thrusting up to that sky, looked infinitely mysterious.

"I still can't see any sides, Major General."

"I think it has them, Lieutenant. As you just said yourself: the shape of the rubble suggests depth, so I think it might be as deep as it is long."

"If so, it's a pretty enormous box."

"Or a tomb," Kate said quietly.

Moshe and the lieutenant stared at her, wondering what she had meant, then the lieutenant glanced at Moshe and shrugged his shoulders and looked down at the ground. Moshe kept glancing at Kate, drawn again to her sheltered depths, but was distracted by the growling of trucks beyond the crowd of civilians. He looked across the jeep as the trucks ground to a halt, their headlamps beaming through the darkness and illuminating the spectators. The sergeant barked an order and some of his soldiers broke ranks, stepping forward to force the civilians aside and make way for the new men. The first to appear were members of the decontamination unit, all bulky and bizarre in their loose white lead suits, carrying their sealed masks in one hand, their Geiger counters in the other. Leading them was Professor Paul Madsen of the Weizmann Institute, a featureless silhouette in the glare of the headlamps, regaining his features when he stepped around the jeep and stood before Moshe. Wiping sweat from his pink face, his eyes widening in disbelief, he stared past Moshe at the enormous object thrusting up from the earth.

"Ai-ai-ai!" he exclaimed.

"That's it, Professor. Don't ask me what it is—I've no idea—and
I've let no one near it."

"Very good. But how did it get there?"

"We still haven't a clue. It appears to have been buried beneath the
chapel, but we can't be too sure of that."

"You're not too sure?"

"No. It's all very confusing. Something unidentified might have
come down over the chapel. That object either pushed itself up or was
drawn up by something else."

"Now you're confusing me."

"We'll discuss it later."

"Any noise from the object?"

"No, not a sound."

"Very good. We'll go over there."

The professor nodded to the three men behind him and they all put
on their sealed plastic helmets. Looking remarkably like astronauts
and walking just as awkwardly, they moved off and made their way
across the road toward the ruins of the courtyard. Turning his back to
the jeep, standing very close to Kate, Moshe followed the progress of
the men as they spread out through the ruins. He glanced once at
Kate, watched her shivering and folding her arms, leaning back
against the jeep, her spine curved, her long hair hanging down.
Moshe thought of another time, another place, a distant grief, then he
silently cursed and looked straight ahead, his eyes following the men
in white lead suits. They were moving forward carefully, holding
their Geiger counters in front of them, skirting around broken pillars
and smaller mounds of rubble and gradually closing in on the
enormous object that surmounted the remains of the chapel. The
object was cooling quickly, its red-hot sheen growing darker, now
reduced to a mosaic of dull red patches on a vitreous black surface.
Moshe watched, feeling strange, aware of Kate's proximity, suddenly
imagining that she and the object were somehow related. This thought
came and went as he studied the object, as he blinked and strained to
see through the darkness and surrendered to disbelief. The edges of
the rectangle had become invisible, merging in with the black sky,
and as the men clambered up the rubble, white suits gleaming in the
darkness, the red patches faded further, became pinpricks and

vanished; and then, to the amazement of Moshe and those around him, the men in white finally converged near the top of the rubble and were framed by a stark, total blackness.

The object had disappeared.

connected and then, to his amazement (it Moshe and those around him, there is no such thing of most incredible fog of his own lanu) which drifted by a small local Palestine.

The object was different lines

10

Lieutenant Gonen cursed loudly, Kate simply bit her lower lip, and Moshe felt himself falling down a dark well without any bottom. The unreal was now real, the impossible a fact, and he closed his eyes and tried to get a grip on his scattering senses. He was a practical man, quick-witted and highly adaptable, but nothing in the extremities of his experience had prepared him for this. He clenched his fists very tightly, shook his head and tried to think, then opened his eyes again and looked across at the men on the rubble.

"It's still there," the lieutenant said.

"No, it's not," Moshe replied.

"I can see it. It's even blacker than the sky. There are no stars where the object is resting—there's just a rectangular blackness."

The lieutenant was right: The men were obviously in front of something, moving carefully along the arched rim of the rubble, past a blackness devoid of stars. The object was still there, a blackness painted on black, a black rectangle blotting out the stars and stretched across the high rubble. Moshe heaved a sigh of relief, glanced briefly at Kate, noted the strange, remote glitter in her eyes, and then reached for the telephone.

He talked to the prime minister, leaning into the jeep, his elbows digging into the front seat, beads of sweat on his forehead. The situation defied description and left him short of words, and as he heard the prime minister's startled gasp, he glanced across at the Arab onlookers. They were exceptionally quiet, almost reverentially so, massed between the trucks and the jeeps, the soldiers pressing them back. Other men had arrived, two in plainclothes, some in uniforms, all looking left and right, shaking their heads, walking straight to the jeep. Moshe kept talking to the prime minister, trying to explain, answering questions, but he hardly heard the sound of his own voice, his thoughts circling elsewhere. Eventually he rang off, promising to keep the prime minister informed, then he straightened up slowly, glanced warily at Kate, and then turned to the plainclothesmen, both of whom were members of Shin Beth, the internal security service.

"I can't see any object," one of the men said. "All I see is the wreckage of the chapel and those men with the Geiger counters."

"It's there," Moshe replied. "Those men are standing right in front of it. You'll see it if you look a bit more carefully—it's blocking out the stars."

"He's right," the other man said. "I can see it . . . a very large, rectangular hole where the stars should be."

"Is it *invisible*?"

"It's very black."

"Nothing's *that* black, Moshe."

Moshe shrugged. "We'll know soon enough, Levi. Those men are checking it out."

They all looked at the distant men and saw them framed in a rectangular black hole, a space darker than the night, devoid of stars, like a doorway to eternity. Moshe shivered at the sight of it, feeling as if he were dreaming, then he noticed that Kate was shivering as well, her brown eyes glinting strangely. He wondered what she was thinking and how the experience had affected her, then he looked away, more disturbed than ever, and faced the men from Shin Beth.

"What about the earthquake?"

"Unaccountable," Levi Shapiro said. He was in his early thirties, had blond hair and blue eyes, and was wearing a white shirt and tie, his jacket over one arm. "It caused havoc on the Mount of Olives, seems to have destroyed a lot of buildings, and badly damaged parts of the wall of the Old City. We just don't understand it. There was no indication of it at all. It was more like an explosion than an earthquake—a subterranean explosion."

"That doesn't make sense."

"Nor does that thing over there. Something came down below the radar's ground clutter and then disappeared—that's impossible as well if, as you say, nothing crashed here." He suddenly looked at Kate, as if seeing her for the first time, let his gaze roam up and down her body, and then looked back at Moshe.

"Kate Hirschfield," Moshe explained. "From the Hadassah Medical Center. She was here when the chapel either collapsed or exploded, and she thinks she saw the unidentified object."

"Oh?" Levi said.

"Yes," Kate intervened. She moved back and sat sideways in the jeep and covered her face with her hands.

"What did it look like?" Levi said.

Kate didn't reply. She just sat there in the jeep, leaning forward, shivering slightly, hiding her face in her hands, the breeze brushing her long hair. Moshe stared at her, entranced, letting her presence filter through him, wanting to know what was going through her mind, what she saw with her closed eyes. Levi Shapiro also studied her, but more objectively, with professional interest, and Moshe, unable to tolerate his objectivity, looked across at the ruins.

"They're coming back," he said quietly.

The men were clambering back down the rubble, ghostly white in the darkness, the enormous black rectangle above them, a framed void in the starry sky. Moshe stared at that great space, could not believe that it was solid, kept looking and thought he saw a tunnel leading out to the infinite. His rational self was outraged, refusing to accept what it was seeing, but he searched the sky for a star that should not have been there. No such star was in the heavens. Moshe dropped his gaze to the men in white. They were walking back across the courtyard, moving slowly and laboriously, looking almost spectral in the darkness, their flashlights turned down.

Kate raised her head, brushing the hair back from her face, her eyes glinting with the light of obsession as the men walked toward her. She rubbed her cheeks and licked her lips, smoothed her hair down with one hand, then stood up and leaned against the jeep, a clenched fist to her mouth. Her eyes flicked toward Moshe, recognized him, slipped away, then settled on the men in the white lead suits as they crossed the dark road. Professor Madsen was in the lead, removing his helmet as he walked; he stopped in front of Moshe, threw his helmet in the jeep, wiped the sweat from his face with the palm of his hand, then shook his head slowly from side to side to express his bewilderment.

"You won't believe me," he said.

He didn't say anything else immediately, merely stood there looking around him, his white lead suit covered in dust and smeared with dark earth.

"What *is* it?" Kate said.

Moshe studied her carefully, noting the strange glint in her eyes, the moonlight falling over her face, one hand covering her lips. She seemed very distracted, locked in a private dream, her gaze fixed on the rectangular blackness that dominated the rubble. Perhaps, as with

Moshe, that perfect blackness had chilled her soul, making her think of a tunnel leading to the infinite and the ultimate unknowable. Moshe studied her, drank her in, was soothed by her proximity, then returned his attention to Professor Madsen, who seemed slightly dazed.

"It's a cube," the professor said. "There's no other way to describe it. It's about sixty-five feet long, about the same depth and height, and seems absolutely solid from top to bottom. Don't ask me what it's made of. It seems to be some kind of stone. It has a perfect matte-black, nonreflecting surface that makes it practically invisible in the dark. It was cold when we reached it—and obviously went cold incredibly fast. It was red hot in patches as we climbed up that rubble, but the last of the red patches disappeared just as we reached it. No heat. None at all. We couldn't see a damned thing. We hadn't bothered to use our flashlights because the red glowing was bright, but the instant the last red patch faded out, we were faced with pure darkness . . . not darkness: a total blackness. So black it pulled my eyes out of focus and destroyed my sense of direction. God, it was frightening. I've never seen anything like it. The blackness seemed to go on forever. Nothing solid. A void."

Moshe looked across the road, automatically, hardly aware of it, straining to see the surface of the object that was practically invisible. There was just a rectangular blackness framed perfectly by the stars, the edges of the rectangle defined by how they cut through the starlight—a large space, unreal and disorienting, mysterious and frightening.

"Then we turned on our flashlights. You could see it with the flashlights; you could see a perfect circle of stone where the beam of the flashlight fell on it; but you still couldn't see anything, not a hint, outside that circle of bright light. It definitely wasn't metal—though it's not remotely like any stone I've come across. . . . Then we walked around it, a weird experience, pretty frightening; we knew it was there, but it looked like a black hole and we were frightened to even lean against it in case we fell into it. . . . It's buried deep in earth and rubble. The whole thing is smeared with mud. That suggests that it's been pushed up from the ground, that it was buried down there. God knows for how long . . ."

He stopped talking and shook his head, looking at them one by one, almost embarrassed by what he was saying, hardly believing it himself. Moshe glanced again at Kate, saw her staring across the road, oblivious to the people around her, her thoughts circling elsewhere. The moonlight fell on her face, emphasizing her isolation, and Moshe, wondering what was happening to him, wanted to reach out and touch her.

"There's hardly any rubble at the back, so we checked that side carefully. The cube is tilting in that direction because there's no earth to support it, so at that point you can see near to the bottom. If it's stone, it's very smooth and would have to be man-made; I've never known stone that smooth before, so I can't work it out. Anyway, I examined it, hammered on it with a rock. I didn't make a dent—that stone was solid—but the cube had a hollow ring. So it might be hollow. I wouldn't swear to it, but it might be. Then I ran my fingers around the surface area and thought I felt some fine cracks. Two vertical, one horizontal, the size and shape of a large door. The cracks were *extremely* fine, very easy to miss, so there's no way I could check how deep they went."

"A *door?*" Levi queried.

"Perhaps a removable panel," the professor replied. "No hinges, no locks, no sign of a way of moving it, and those cracks were too fine to allow that section to swing in or out at an angle. If those cracks go right through, it would mean an incredibly precise fit and the panel would have to be pushed out or pulled in like a piece in a jigsaw. So it might be hollow and it might have an entrance, but don't ask me how we're actually going to open it."

"It's hollow," Kate said, almost hissing like a cat. "I know it! *Damn you, it's hollow!*"

They all looked at her, amazed, wondering why she was so convinced, were faintly embarrassed by the intensity of her gaze, and stared uneasily at each other. She looked at them and through them, as if not really seeing them, then shivered and turned away and once more stared across the road, her eyes fixed on the enormous, rectangular blackness. Moshe watched her for a moment, wondering if she was cracking, then Professor Madsen's voice broke the silence, sounding hoarse, not too steady.

"There's no radioactivity—no form of radiation—so you won't have any problems in examining that thing. However you're going to need a bulldozer to clear away that rubble—and the sooner you get those floodlights here the better, because that matte-black is completely disorienting and plays tricks with your vision."

"What I can't understand," Levi Shapiro said coolly, "is how that thing got there in the first place."

"Don't ask me," the professor said.

They all stared at one another, too bewildered to say more, not knowing what it was they were dealing with, hardly able to grasp it. Moshe felt very strange, far removed from himself, some part of him floating away in the darkness and embracing the object. It was blacker than the night, too black to be real, a solid with the features of a void: neither shape nor dimension. He shook himself from this reverie, glanced around him, trying to focus, saw the men in the moonlight, the soldiers beyond the jeeps, the civilians massed under the stars, their eyes wide, disbelieving. Then he looked at Kate, the brown hair and brown eyes, one fist in her mouth, her body shivering, her gaze fixed on the distance. Moshe studied her intently, wondering why he was drawn to her, knowing why, remembering his wife's hair in the dust, refusing to accept the truth of this. Then he heard a rumbling sound, saw Kate turning rigid, and he looked across the dark, destroyed courtyard as the ground shook beneath him.

The rumbling came from the distant object, from the rectangular blackness, and was accompanied by the sliding of rubble as the ground heaved again. The men around Moshe looked startled, were gasping and shouting, and the civilians beyond the soldiers moved back a little, their massed voices hysterical. The object remained invisible, but more stars disappeared as the dark line of its edge shifted slightly, moving up toward the sky. It had obviously tilted forward, its back edge lifting higher, the rubble along its front sliding away as it settled back down again. Then the rumbling suddenly stopped, the ground was still, there was silence; then a single, sharp explosion came from the far side of the object and Kate, letting out a peculiar cry, ran across the dark road.

Moshe was frozen for just a second, his soldier's instincts betraying him, hearing a voice bawling out Kate's name, his own voice, almost anguished. Kate did not respond but continued running across the road, her long hair dancing wildly around her shoulders as she reached the ruined courtyard. Moshe cursed and jumped forward, leaning into the jeep, grabbed a flashlight, straightened up and spun around, and then followed Kate. He saw her in the courtyard, wending her way through the rubble, a slim figure being swallowed by the darkness as she raced toward the object. He called her name again, flicking his flashlight on, beaming it down, but she didn't look back, refused to stop, and he had to keep chasing her.

He didn't know why he was doing it, but he felt a great fear, as if something in the object, or in the night's bizarre events, was a threat to the landmarks of his past and hopes for the future. His past was what sustained him, both in pleasure and in pain, but as the darkness devoured him, as that distant figure led him, he felt that his future was dependent on what they would both find. His boots ground the broken stones and kicked up the fine dry soil while Kate, now at the base of the remains of the chapel, stopped and looked up, scanning the enormous black rectangle, then turned right and made her way around the high mound, trying to get to the back of it.

Moshe cursed softly when she vanished, swallowed up by the darkness, but he raced on to the base of the high mound, the flashlight beaming ahead of him. Glancing up, he saw the object, a rectangular blackness directly above him, then he turned and followed the curved base of the rubble, his throat dry, his heart pounding. The rubble towered high above him, sloping down to his feet, but as he circled behind the ruins, as the darkness increased, the top of the rubble dropped lower, came level with his shoulders, disappeared, and left him staring at nothing: a complete, chilling blackness.

He stopped, disoriented, his senses streaming away from him, his eyes straining to adjust to a void defying shape and dimension. He felt disembodied, his mind adrift in the Nothing, black painted on black to infinity, all around him, above him. Then he clenched his left fist, raised the flashlight in his right hand, pointed it straight ahead, and saw black stone at the end of the yellow beam. He glanced up and saw more blackness, a dizzying Nothing high above him, its angled edge cutting through the stars that filled the sky sweeping over it. Moshe gasped and held his breath, let it out, lowered his gaze, moved the beam of the flashlight to the right, watched it bend and stretch farther. The beam now stretched out a long way, exposing black rock farther back, and Moshe sensed that he was seeing another wall set back deep in the base of the huge cube.

Kate was possibly inside.

Moshe put his left hand out, watched it disappearing in blackness, spread his fingers and felt a hard surface, very smooth, very cold. He kept his hand on this surface, moved it right, and then followed it, his flashlight beam traveling ahead of the moving hand to find the edge of the entrance. Then his foot kicked something. He looked down and felt dizzy. He was standing on the edge of a rectangular black hole, which made him lose all sense of direction. He raised his foot and dropped it gently, his heart pounding, feeling dizzy. His boot stopped on the blackness, on something solid, and he let his breath out. It was part of the matte-black stone, a panel-shaped block, and then he realized that the explosion, whatever its nature, had blown this section of stone off the object to expose its interior.

Moshe called out Kate's name, heard a cry from inside the blackness, kept his hand on the invisible surface, and shone his flashlight to the right. The beam bent and traveled farther, moving deeper into the object's interior, and Moshe moved on to where the beam of light was bending and found the edge of the opening. He moved on past the edge, put his hand out, felt nothing, then stepped forward into the cool, total blackness and lost all sense of direction.

"Where are you?"

"I'm here!"

There was no here nor there, no left nor right, and both their voices rang and ricocheted from no clear direction. Moshe was guided by his flashlight, a circle of light framing stone, then the light bent and traveled on farther and illuminated Kate's face. Large eyes, very brown, staring at him, wandering off, a choked sob as her face disappeared and she moved away from him. Moshe called her name again, heard his own voice ricocheting, heard the echo of her footsteps, her choked sobbing as she stumbled through darkness. He walked into a wall, cursed aloud, found the edge, moved around it and shone his flashlight on the back of Kate's head, then moved forward and grabbed her by the shoulder and pulled her close to him.

"Hold my hand, Kate. *Hold it!*"

She broke free and ran forward, moving out of the flashlight beam, was devoured immediately by the blackness, and cried out in despair. Moshe walked into another wall, pulled his head back, looked up, saw a blackness so deep it made him dizzy, slipped sideways, moved forward. One wall, then another, slipping sideways, stepping forward, passing through invisible chambers filled with darkness and a stark, chilling silence. No ceiling, no floor, none to see, just to touch: the interior of the enormous, frozen cube was honeycombed with empty rooms. Then he suddenly heard Kate breathing, shone his flashlight on her dark hair, felt her warmth as he stepped up beside her and took hold of her arm. She was standing very still, her eyes wide, looking ahead, and he followed her gaze and saw starlight pouring down through the blackness.

Moshe kept hold of Kate's wrist and stepped into the starlight, glanced up and saw the stars in a frame of black ceiling, then followed the starlight down, saw stone walls, a large chamber, a stone bed supporting the vision that would haunt him for the rest of his days:

A bearded man in a white shroud.

Kate returned to herself, sweeping back through the dream, hardly knowing where she was or how she had come here, only aware of falling light, swept by fear and exultation, hearing a sound, someone's voice, her own voice sobbing brokenly, seeing the man in white robes, his face pale and serene, ageless even beneath the beard, his hands folded on his chest, either unconscious or dead, not real, her only truth, as she looked and beheld him and turned away from his radiance, sobbing brokenly, triumphantly, her shaking hands clutching Moshe, her dark hair trailing across her trembling lips as he rocked her from side to side.

"Oh, my God!" she cried. "Help me!"

PART TWO:

Nativity

. . . And when she saw *him,* she was troubled at his saying, and cast in her mind what manner of salutation this should be.

—Luke, 1:29

11

"How long do you intend keeping me here?" Kate said, swinging her legs off the bed, straightening out her white smock, and lighting a cigarette with sharp, nervous movements, the smoke making her squint. There was a bed and small cabinet, a writing desk and chair; the walls were white and bare, there were bars on the window, and the door, also white, had a sliding grill that could only be opened from outside. "One of my own rooms, damn it. Locked up in my own ward! Your sense of occasion, if I may say so, is execrable—and now I've been here two days. When, if ever, Major General, will I get out of here?" She spoke with deliberate harshness, trying to get a response from Moshe, but sitting by the desk, his fingers motionless, he remained quite impassive.

"Just a few more days," he said. "It's for your own good, Kate. You were in a state of shock, you slept for twenty-four hours, and like me, you had burn marks on your face and hands."

"I didn't see any burn marks."

"They disappeared before you woke up. Nevertheless, although the inside of that object was very cold, we both had what appeared to be burn marks."

"They took skin scrapings?"

"Yes—and blood samples. In any event, both were perfectly normal—a fact that merely deepens our confusion." He stared steadily at her, his gray eyes unreadable; but something about him, perhaps his lack of movement, convinced her that he was a man who felt most comfortable when not expressing too much emotion. He was leaning slightly toward her, his uniform badly pressed, his hair carelessly combed, his large body all muscle and bone, thick arms covered in dark hairs. Very physical, Kate thought. Not your Jewish intellectual. She studied his face with some interest, noting the stone in his gray eyes, the small scar just below his left cheek, the broken nose and webbed lines. A face carved from granite, like the body; perhaps even the soul.

"So they want to run further tests on me?"

"Yes, Kate, on both of us."

"Radioactivity?"

"There was no radioactivity."

"Whether there was or wasn't, we're guinea pigs."

"That's one way of putting it."

Moshe offered a slight smile, but the humor didn't reach his eyes, which were, she noted, perpetually weary behind the cool gray. "We couldn't take any chances, Kate. We had to try further tests. We didn't know what that object was, nor where it had come from, so we had to cordon the whole area off and run instrument checks. The locals were placed in quarantine, you and I were brought here, and then our scientists moved into the area to check out the object."

"And?"

"I don't think you're going to believe this . . . the object disintegrated."

Kate stared at him, shocked, her aggression swept away, the hand holding the cigarette wavering as it went to her mouth. His face blurred and then changed, became another face, elsewhere, bearded and washed clean of experience, radiant with innocence. Not Moshe but the other, the face bathed in moonlight, the bearded man in the white shroud in that place which resembled the void. She closed her eyes and remembered, saw the dream within a dream, then shuddered and opened her eyes again and saw Moshe's gray eyes. The cigarette, which was wavering before her mouth, was now gratefully inhaled.

"Disintegrated?" she said, her exhalation like a sigh, the smoke drifting lazily before her eyes. "You mean it just—?"

"Disappeared." Moshe shrugged and lifted his left hand off the desk and then let it drop again, his fingers outspread. "We still can't explain it. There *is* no rational explanation. The object was hard as diamond—unquestionably solid—and yet it disintegrated. Apparently it happened quickly, about four hours from start to finish, and no one really knew it was happening until it was half gone. It was still dark at the time—about five hours before dawn—but because of the invisible effect of that matte-black surface, and the fact that the floodlights were a long time in coming, it must have been disintegrating for a couple of hours before someone noticed that the stars that had been blocked out by the object were gradually reappearing. Then the floodlights arrived, another half hour to set them up, and then, with the floodlights on, the scientists on the scene saw that the object was disintegrating, literally aging before their eyes, cracking apart into pieces so fine they were like flakes and which, when they fell off, turned to dust. What I mean, then, is that I mean just what I say: the object simply disintegrated."

"Nothing left?"

"Only dust."

"And?"

"No one in the Weizmann Institute has managed to get to bed yet, but so far their analysis has only produced perfectly normal Judean dust. The problem, of course, is that no known dust can be transformed into a solid, perfect matte-black material. Nonetheless, that's all we're left with: a handful of dust. Up there, on the Mount of Olives, where the Chapel of the Ascension and mosque stood, there is nothing but terrestrial rubble and dust—that, plus a great hole in the rubble: a hole filled with normal earth."

Kate shuddered again, inhaling smoke and closing her eyes, relived the evening with frightening clarity, saw the striations of moonlight pouring down from above and illuminating the white-shrouded, recumbent figure. That singular image: a bearded man in a white shroud, his face ageless and blank, as pure as the face of a newborn child, radiant with innocence.

"And that man—the man we found inside—was he really . . . ?" The question hung on her lips, uncompleted, frightened of answers, retreating from the incomprehensible and what it might represent.

"Human? Yes. Alive? More or less. He's still being examined, so I can't tell you too much, but I gather he's flesh and blood, about thirty years of age, yet has a face that's remarkably unlined. His heartbeat is too slow and sometimes erratic, his pulse is regular if practically undetectable, and his body temperature is quite a bit below normal. His EEG is recording a very slight but definite electrical flickering, just above a flat tracing—so his brain is obviously registering something, though not very much."

"You're describing a man just on the point of death."

"That's right . . . except that his temperature, though low, isn't dropping as it should; and the EEG reading, if almost flat, is not diminishing. In short, his condition, which by normal standards should be deteriorating, appears to be constant."

"That's impossible."

"It *should* be," Moshe said, "but that's what we've got here: that man, whoever he is, should be dying right this minute, but instead all his symptoms remain unchanged and he just keeps on living."

"It sounds like a form of suspended animation."

"Something like that. We still can't believe it ourselves, but the facts suggest a bit of a miracle."

His gray eyes were very steady, revealing little but oddly comforting, as if veiling an emotion, a warmth, that he was wary of offering. Kate stared back, confused, thinking of Moshe and the other, that bearded man lying on a stone bed, his white face serene. The confusion was in her mind, in her recollection of what had happened; she felt drawn to Moshe—a public figure, but a stranger to her —perhaps because he had shared that extraordinary experience with her and was therefore part of it.

"I'm trying to grasp it," she said, her struggle for words shaming her, "but it's just too incredible to be comprehended."

"You're not alone," Moshe replied. "We *all* feel that way."

"But the burn marks . . . ?"

"We're back with the impossible again. We were both covered in red patches and it should have been frostbite—but it wasn't . . . something definitely burned us."

"They faded too quickly to be burn marks."

"They were burn marks of *some* kind."

Kate closed her eyes for a moment, opened them again and stood up, went to the window and took hold of the iron bars and pulled herself to and fro as if exercising. She felt confused and frustrated, nervous yet strangely exultant, all her preconceptions of life, of reality and logic, swept away by the knowledge that none of this made sense, that the laws of man and nature were being defied with each fresh revelation.

"Go on," she said quietly, pulling her body to and fro, wanting to feel the logic of flesh and bone, the reality of blood. "Keep talking. I'm listening."

Moshe sighed, sounding weary. "The scientists and weapons experts went in after we left, wearing heavy protective clothing and carrying bright lamps. This was just before the object started to visibly decompose, so they were able to have a pretty good look at it. It was like a mausoleum, pitch-black and soundproof, with seven square-shaped chambers of various sizes. Six of the chambers were completely bare and had remarkably smooth stone walls—but no decorations nor markings nor windows; no hint of who had made them nor when. The seventh chamber—the one in which the bearded man was found—was similar to the others, but had a solid stone base on which the bearded man was lying, and a single, square opening in the ceiling—which was, of course, the top of the object."

"An opening or a window?"

"It appeared to be an opening. It was letting in fresh air. The object disintegrated before they managed to inspect the opening, but they suspect it was the same as the entrance: a block of stone, fitted with remarkable precision, possibly blown off by the same explosion that blew off the main door."

"Then it was man-made."

"It was certainly made by *someone*."

Kate stopped pulling herself to and fro, straightened up and shivered slightly, then ran her fingers through her luxurious hair and stared steadily at Moshe.

"What made that object finally surface?"

"We think that the unidentified—as represented by that light in the storm—was some form of energy that created the storm, drew the object out of the earth, then somehow or other vaporized. There's certainly no record of the unidentified having *ascended* again."

"Some form of *energy*?"

"Yes."

"Is that possible?"

"Theoretically *none* of this is possible . . . not even that man lying in the adjoining room."

Kate sat on the edge of the bed, lit another cigarette, inhaled deeply, and blew the smoke out, her face raised toward the ceiling. Again, when she closed her eyes, she saw the man in the white shroud, his face pale and serene, unlined, inexpressibly beautiful. It was the beauty of innocence, of a soul untouched by life; the face of a man still a child, before the wounds of experience. A vision of the impossible, of the dream offered and withdrawn at birth, the flesh too pure and smooth to be human, ridiculously unblemished. She thought this with grief and wonder, opened her eyes, and saw the ceiling, all white, painted by very human hands, then lowered her gaze to stare across at Moshe, feeling drawn to his silence. He was leaning forward in his chair, the shirt tight on his broad shoulders, his large hands folded together on the desk, his face webbed with the experience so lacking in the man in the white shroud.

"How do you feel?" he said.

"I'm not sure," Kate replied. "Frightened, dazed, disbelieving, overawed, almost childish. I think of him all the time, day and night, in my dreams, as an image that can't be shaken off and is larger than life. Who is he? Where did he come from? How could he survive down there? The questions swim like goldfish through my head, going round and round endlessly. I'm not used to this sort of thing. I feel that I'm dreaming, that I can't wake up, that if I don't wake up I'll go mad, locked inside my own skull. Did it happen? Yes, it did. He's actually lying next door. I keep thinking of him lying next door and I want to go in there. I want to see him and touch him."

"Your requests have been noted."

"But consistently ignored. Why won't you let me go in there? Why are you keeping me here?"

"I told you: we want to run more tests."

"That shouldn't prevent me from seeing him."

"We are, as you must realize, running tests on him as well, but as soon as we're finished, you can see him."

Kate stretched her spine, exhaled a stream of smoke, and tried to glean some facts from the unrevealing gray eyes staring at her. *Moshe Eitan*, she thought. *This is the man who despises Leon. This is the famous major general who has devoted his life to Israel and is reputed to be a man with few weaknesses*. She put her cigarette to her lips and gazed at him through the smoke, both repelled by and drawn to his remoteness and air of quiet strength. He was a strong, physical presence, his face a parchment of harsh experience, and she stared at him and imagined him changing and becoming the other: the man in the white shroud. *The other*, she thought. *That's all I can think to call him. And why, when I look at Moshe Eitan, do I think of the other?*

"You were with me," she said.

"What does that mean?"

"You were with me when I found him. I keep thinking there was a reason for us being there—and that, also, is irrational."

"Maybe," Moshe said. "Maybe not. Why did you go in there?"

"I can't remember. I just had to. I hardly knew I was doing it. I felt that I was dreaming—or that I was someone hypnotized—and something, some fierce conviction, just pushed me forward. Why do you ask?"

"Because that's what it seemed like at the time—as if you were hypnotized. How do you feel about the man in the white shroud?"

"I feel that he's mine."

She felt embarrassed as soon as she spoke, her blushing cheeks confirming the fact, and she glanced at Moshe and then looked away, shrugging her shoulders forlornly. She inhaled on her cigarette, wondering how she could become so foolish, then blew the smoke out and gave a sigh, trying to focus her thoughts. It was no longer easy; her concentration had gone; when she tried to apply logic to what had happened, her thoughts scattered and spun. Why had she said that? What had she meant by it? She looked at Moshe and thought of the man in the white shroud and felt enmeshed in them both.

"Don't ask me to explain that," she said, "but that's what I feel."

He nodded and smiled, the merest hint of amused acceptance, then raised his hands in a rabbinical gesture and pushed his chair back. Standing upright, he was very tall, very broad, all bone and muscle, and his face, lined and scarred, oddly handsome, was carefully composed.

"Do you mind staying here?" he asked.

"Just a few more days," Kate said.

"We'd like you to stay a bit longer—"

"I won't."

"—because we want you to look after that man next door."

Kate jerked her head up, wondering if she had heard right, saw the very serious gray of Moshe's eyes, and knew that she had.

"You want *me* to look after him?"

"Yes."

"Why?"

"Various reasons," Moshe said. "One: You're a psychiatrist and that could be useful should that man actually return to his senses."

"And you think that's possible?"

"Yes, Kate, we do. On the one hand, we can't explain that coma he's in; on the other, we can't find a thing wrong with him. By normal standards we would have to accept that he's close to death, but remarkably he's not degenerating: his condition is constant."

"That doesn't mean it will improve."

"It has to go one way or the other: either he dies, or he revives."

The thought of either possibility was shocking to Kate, making her shiver and blush, her heart pounding, as she inhaled on her cigarette. Her feelings were almost mystical in their intensity, yet she now had to accept that her whole being was surrounded by the presence of that man in the adjoining room. *He's mine*, she thought. *I know it. It's ridiculous, but I can't deny* it. She tried to cast the vanity aside, to confess to its transparent duplicity, but the beating of her heart, her charged emotions, defeated her efforts. To never discover who he was or where he had come from would be a loss akin to the loss of an unborn child, the crushing of overwhelming expectation, the fetus torn from a bleeding womb. She knew the feeling well, was still scourged and haunted by it, and now, as she thought of that serene, ageless face, she knew that his loss would make her future a void of despair.

She stubbed her cigarette out, lay back on the bed, covered her eyes with the palms of her hands, and saw his face in the darkness.

"Well," Moshe said eventually, his voice muted and strangely tense, almost desirous as it floated somewhere above her in a fine web of fear, "will you stay a bit longer?"

"Yes," Kate said. "He's mine."

12

Moshe left the room, trying to keep his face composed, closed the door quietly behind him, and then took a deep breath. He stood there for a moment, pressing his back to the door, thinking of Kate lying inside and letting the thought cleanse his secret wounds. Here the light was bright and harsh, the corridor bland in its tasteful tones, and Moshe looked at it and smiled and thought again of the woman behind him. *The sinner,* he thought. *The woman I condemned. The American with the morals of a whore has the soul of the lost.* He pursed his lips and shook his head, disbelieving his pain and joy, trying to separate what he felt for Kate from the events of the past few days. Unprecedented events, momentous and extraordinary, they should not, by the laws of common sense, have left him room for such sentiments. He shook his head again, his heart beating, his flesh alive, seeing her face in the darkness, illuminated by his flashlight, feeling the warmth of her body against his own, his ears filled with her haunted cry. The past and present merged. *The dead eyes staring sunward.* He felt fear, an onrushing love and grief, his beating heart gently breaking.

The two guards were at the other door, their Uzi guns across their shoulders, their sunburnt faces turned toward Moshe, both respectful and casual.

"Anything happening in there?"

"No, Major General. The men who were examining him have just left, and they said he was sleeping."

"Sleeping?"

"Unconscious. As dead as a doornail. They told us to report any movement—and the room's wired for sound."

"They don't want anyone to go in."

"But they want to hear if he moves. The sound is wired to a room in the doctors' quarters. It's our men in that room."

"Do you know who the patient is?"

"No, sir. We weren't told."

"But you were told how important this is?"

"*Ken*. We were told."

Moshe went to open the door and then stopped, undecided, remembering the black object, the total darkness inside, the image of a gateway that might have led to eternity, the illuminated face of a man who should not have existed. He shuddered, feeling haunted, not frightened but uneasy, cast adrift on the tide of disbelief that now constantly washed through him. So he just stood there, unable to open the door, wanting to go inside, wanting to avoid what was in there, thinking of the man in the white shroud, and of Kate, who had found him. He tried to reason and failed, not accepting his own deduction, remembering Kate on the dark road, her eyes fixed on the black object, her whole body straining toward it as if it possessed her. Yes, that tomb had possessed her . . . and now she possessed him.

"You're going in, Major General?"

"No. I've changed my mind. Maybe later."

He nodded and walked away, feeling guilty and disoriented, ashamed that what he felt was a weakness that had long been discarded. Turning left where the corridor ended, passing another two armed guards, he entered the high-ceilinged, rectangular reception room and there, to his dismay, was confronted by a smiling Leon Halcomb. The journalist was wearing a gray suit, his shirt and tie immaculate, his black hair neatly combed, his face flushed, his eyes bloodshot but sharp. He grinned mockingly as he stepped in front of Moshe, one hand raised in the air.

"*Shalom*, Major General!" he said. "A few words for the press!"

Moshe stopped walking, feeling angry, not bothering to conceal his distaste, his gaze steady and cold.

"How did you get in here?" he said.

"I'm a *journalist*, Major General."

"You might call it that, Leon Halcomb; I'd have other words for it."

Leon shrugged and grinned laconically. "Freedom of speech is all," he said. "However, not everyone shares your opinion—and I *do* have some friends left."

"One of whom let you in here."

"Correct."

"If I find out who he is, he'll be in trouble."

"I must protect my few sources."

Moshe never failed to be repelled by the extraordinary mixture of extended youthfulness and dissipation in Leon's face, but now, observing that very English expression of superiority, he felt like erasing it with the back of his hand.

"What do you want this time?" he said.

"I want to know what's happened to Kate."

"You mean you want to see her."

"Correct."

"You can't. She's still in a state of shock. As I told you at the press conference, she was there when the chapel collapsed; she was shocked and now she's under observation."

"You mean she's unconscious?"

"I didn't say that."

"Then just let me talk to her for a minute."

"No."

"Why not?"

"Because she's not in a fit condition to talk."

"I'm one of her most intimate friends, Major General."

"So I've heard."

"Do I sense disapproval in that remark?"

"Kate Hirschfield's private life is not my affair."

"Well, I'm glad to hear that. However, knowing Kate well, I can't imagine her being that shocked by the collapse of an ancient Christian chapel."

"She was caught in the eye of the storm and thrown around quite a bit. She was knocked unconscious and is still badly bruised. Believe me, she's in shock."

"No visitors at all?"

"No visitors."

"I just want to look in her room and check that she's there."

"Are you calling me a liar, Leon?"

"Alas, I lack such boldness. I merely suggest that you may have good reasons for keeping her locked up."

Leon made the last remark with his bloodshot eyes unblinking, his smile mischievous and mocking, advertising that he wasn't impressed by rank or authority. Like too many from the West, Leon had led a cushioned life, had not known the constant threat of extinction, thought of life as a game. But life could never be a mere game to those who lived in Israel; and Moshe, who devoted his life to the preservation of the Jewish homeland, despised Leon for his cheap mockery of Israel's hopeless task.

"Good reasons?" Moshe said, treading carefully. "Just what do you mean by that?"

Leon withdrew a small cigar from his breast pocket and then, glancing around at the nurses and milling patients, sighed forlornly and put it away again. "There's a rumor circulating to the effect that the chapel and mosque were not destroyed by that earthquake, but by something that actually crashed on the Mount of Olives."

"Nonsense. The chapel and mosque weren't the only buildings damaged by the earthquake—as a good look around Jerusalem will tell you. Most of the buildings on the Mount were severely damaged, and even parts of the Old City, including the Golden Gate."

"But the chapel and mosque were *completely destroyed*."

"The major turbulence happened to be in that area."

"Just the earthquake?"

"Yes."

"Then why is that whole area cordoned off? And why, Major General, before you suggest the hazards of falling rubble, have all the people in that area been evacuated?"

"The ground was badly cracked and the cracks remain: they're deep and too dangerous."

"Like the falling rubble, yes?"

"I'll answer your questions; I won't listen to your sarcasm."

"Sorry. Where are the evacuees now?"

"I gave that information during the press conference: they have to be rehoused."

"Admirable, certainly . . . but where are they at the moment?"

"You probably know that already."

"Correct. They're right here in the hospital. Why here, Major General?"

"Some are in shock and have to be treated, and we would rather not separate the families. Also, we happened to have that new ward still available, so it was convenient to house them here until such time as alternative accommodation becomes available."

"And where might that be?"

"We don't know yet."

"A refugee camp?"

"Definitely not."

Leon grinned. "You *do* realize, Major General, that the Arabs are already using this as yet another example of Israeli determination to remove all Arabs from this area? You are, after all, intending to rehouse Arabs whose homes were not damaged by the earthquake."

"The houses were directly opposite the chapel and were certainly damaged. I understand the Arab suspicions, but in this case they're wrong: those houses and the surrounding area are now dangerous."

"Certain Arabs would say otherwise."

"Which Arabs? All the Arabs from that area are in this hospital and have spoken to no one."

Moshe realized he had made a mistake when he saw Leon's tight smile, and he quietly cursed himself for his stupidity at falling into the trap. He glanced briefly around the reception hall, saw the polyglot citizens of Israel—the Arabs in flowing robes, pious Jews in black frock coats, others, culled from the four corners of the Earth, wearing more casual clothing—and then thought of the man in the white shroud and what he might mean to them. The possibilities were frightening, so he forced the thought aside and concentrated on Leon again, looking straight at his face.

"As you say," Leon said, smiling mockingly, "those Arabs have spoken to no one. . . . A lot of journalists would like to know why."

"I've just told you—"

"Shock."

"Correct."

Leon grinned at Moshe and shook his head from side to side, his disbelief clear in the gesture. "All right, Major General, we are at an impasse: I can't talk to Kate, I can't talk to the Arabs, and you insist that nothing crashed on the Mount of Olives. Would you therefore be willing to comment on the unidentified light which was observed by many people as it hovered inside the eye of the storm?"

"We have no record of any unidentified."

"Why, then, were there numerous landing and takeoff delays at Ben-Gurion Airport at approximately the same time that storm commenced?"

"As far as I can ascertain, the radars were temporarily malfunctioning due to electrical interference of the kind that often preludes a heavy storm."

"What kind of electrical interference?"

"Ionization of the atmosphere."

"A normal occurrence."

"Naturally." Moshe had had enough, and he glanced openly at his wristwatch, but Leon, who was familiar with such tactics, merely smiled in response. The smile angered Moshe again, but he held himself in check; instead he suddenly thought of Leon and Kate in bed together, and this image, which seemed to burn itself into his head, both shamed and revolted him. He felt himself flushing, with embarrassment as much as anger, and he realized, with a shock, that his normal contempt for Leon was now colored by jealousy. This realization was humiliating, sweeping through him and rocking him, making him despise not only Leon but his own lack of sense. Reeling inwardly, his emotions in collision, he tried to keep his voice steady:

"Any more questions before you leave?"

"I'm leaving?"

"That's right."

Leon shrugged and scratched his nose with his index finger, grinning slightly but more flushed than usual, as if concealing his anger. "All right," he said, "I'll go. But let me put this on record. I don't believe that Kate's in that ward because she's still shocked. Even if she were in a state of shock, that would hardly be a reason for refusing to let her friends go see her. I have, furthermore, been informed that there are two guards in constant attendance at the room adjoining Kate's, and that they are guarding someone else. I also have statements from a couple of witnesses who testify that they saw a light in the eye of that storm and that that light appeared to descend over the summit of the Mount of Olives. Finally I have unofficial verification that the flight delays at Ben-Gurion Airport were caused by an unidentified blip on the radar screens just before the storm's commencement, and that that blip, when it disappeared off the screens, was located over the vicinity of Jerusalem. I don't believe you, Major General. You're obviously covering something up. And believe me, I'm going to find out. Put *that* down in your records!"

He stared directly at Moshe, no longer smiling, his anger apparent, then he turned and walked along the crowded hall and disappeared through the front door. Moshe simply stood and watched him, expressionless, not moving, but inside he was boiling, his emotions in chaos, thinking of what Leon had said, of the man in the guarded room, of the terrifying possibilities in this whole situation—and then, helplessly, shamefully, his personal conflicts defying history, thinking of Kate and Leon in bed together, their limbs intertwined. This vision burned into his mind and remained there like a scar, making him realize that his logic, the very basis of his soldier's life, was now contaminated with possessiveness and childish jealousy.

No, he thought. *This can't happen.*

13

Leon drove down the Judean Hills toward the sun-baked Jordan Valley, his left hand on the steering wheel, a cigar in his right, the wind sweeping around the car and through the windows to whip his dark hair. He passed outcroppings of pale rock, lonely groups of olive trees, stone villages unchanged since biblical times, children shouting, goats braying. Such scenes hardly touched him, were mere shadows in his mind, his thoughts focused on what had happened on the summit of the Mount and on why Kate was apparently involved in it.

Moshe Eitan was hiding something and that meant it was serious —more serious than the destruction of an unimportant Arab mosque and one of the sites most sacred to all Christians. Also, Moshe was taking unusual chances. The loss of the chapel had appalled and shocked the whole Christian world, and already an international scandal was brewing because the Israeli government, offering vague generalities about danger, was refusing to let representatives of the Christian Church inspect the ruins of the chapel. Indeed that very morning Monsignor Pio Lazzari, the Papal See's apostolic delegate in Jerusalem, had lodged a formal complaint with the acting Ashkenazic chief rabbi of all Israel, Jozsef Latinavots (*Kate's very good friend*, Leon thought grimly, *and disapproving of me*), and, since no response had so far been forthcoming, Leon realized that something other than the destruction of the chapel, something truly extraordinary, was behind it.

Coming out of the hills and driving across the Jordan Valley, he surveyed the surrounding wilderness, its bizarre, barren beauty, then glanced up at the sky, his eyes protected by sunglasses, and saw the shimmering anvil of God, that merciless white void. That great emptiness offered nothing, no pity, no mercy, and Leon, in his secret, choked bitterness, thought it mirrored his life. He threw his cigar through the window, wiped the sweat from his brow, tried to work out what was happening to Kate and what Moshe was concealing. First an unidentified flying object, then rumors of a crash, then someone other than Kate in a guarded room, surrounded by secrecy. An object, a crash, someone brought down from the Mount, someone rescued from the destruction that Kate had been witness to, and Kate, like that someone, also guarded because of what she had seen. An aircraft? No, the destruction would have been greater. A satellite? No, the destruction even greater still. Only the chapel and mosque were gone. The explosion must have been minor. What explosion? That would have been heard for miles. No explosion . . . Then what?

Leon couldn't work it out. He glanced through the window, saw the huts of refugee camps, now derelict, the doors swinging in the wind, the blank earth all around them. The good old days, he thought. Rough justice and vengeance. The camps passed out of view and he looked straight ahead and saw the road cutting through the empty plain and leading to Jericho. The town soon came into view, a brilliant oasis in the desert, first the excavated remains, then the small, Arabic settlement, open-front shops and stalls, fruit piled high in the streets, tourists mingling with the Arabs in flowing robes, children begging and playing. He drove past citrus groves, parked the car beneath some palm trees, climbed out, and gratefully entered the shaded garden of the restaurant, smelling the orange blossom, seeing gardenias and bougainvillaea, then Lieutenant Frankel sitting at a table, dressed in gray slacks and white shirt. The lieutenant looked up when Leon approached the table, his dark eyes not surprised.

"Ah," he said, "you've arrived."

"What does that mean? Am I late?"

"No. I wasn't sure of the time, so I thought to come early. You want something to eat?"

Leon sat down, took a cigar from his tin, lit it, inhaled, and then sat back, glancing casually around him. The garden was cool and colorful, the Arab waiters in white robes, most of the tables crowded with tourists, all eating and drinking.

"I couldn't eat," Leon said. "It's too hot for food. I never eat lunch in this damned country. A chilled beer would be fine."

Lieutenant Frankel raised his right hand and called the waiter over, gave the order in Arabic and watched the waiter departing, then smiled at Leon and bit into his *falafel*. Some mashed chick-peas fell out of the pita bread and littered his plate.

"That snack looks like a challenge."

"It's very popular, Leon. Alas, as you say, it's a challenge and not good for the dignity."

"I believe you had some problems with Kate Hirschfield—that she, also, was not good for your dignity."

Paul removed the pita bread from his lips and looked up, his dark face flushed. "She told you?"

"No. A friend in the hospital told me. This friend told me that you wanted some information and that Kate wasn't helpful."

Paul put his bread down and sat back, dabbing his lips with a napkin. His dark face, thin-mustached and too solemn, looked decidedly uncomfortable. "That woman is more eager to bed anti-Semites than to help defend the country she lives in."

"I'm not an anti-Semite; I'm anti-Zionist. And Kate, if not sharing your uncommon zeal, does valuable work for this country."

Paul shrugged and put his hands out. "Forgive me," he said with irony. "I keep forgetting I'm a Jew. We Jews, as is well known, are all fanatical and offer mercy to no one."

"I'll accept that jibe as straight comment; it describes, if not all Jews, your own good self."

The Arab waiter returned, placed the glass of beer on the table, bowed slightly, and walked back to the bar. Leon picked the glass up, drank, then set the glass down again.

"So," Paul said. "What do you want this time?"

"You don't like dealing with me," Leon replied.

"Naturally I don't."

"Why? Because I'm anti-Zionist?"

"Yes, that's part of it. Unfortunately, in politics, we have to put our scruples aside."

"And that, of course, is the other part of it."

"Yes, you might say that."

Staring down at his plate, Paul had the look of a sulky boy, his feelings hurt, his pride outraged. Studying him, Leon wondered just what it was that made him talk, that made him shift from one side to the other, trading out of his left hand. Conviction, certainly; lack of faith in the old regime; the genuine belief that his elders had gone soft and would give up part of what they had earned to appease world opinion. Paul was an Orthodox Jew, a hard-line Zionist, a true believer; and his fear, patriotic in the extreme, was that his leaders —older men, men like Ben Eliezer and Moshe Eitan—would, in their acceptance of internationalism, betray the promise of Israel. So there was that—he wanted to bring the government down—but behind that, in some dark part of his nature, there was something less noble. Now, looking at him, studying his handsome, humorless face, Leon was certain that Paul's weakness was vanity, the need to be recognized. Religious, dedicated, he was nonetheless human; and unable to admit that this was so, he had excused it with politics. Leon smiled, having seen it all before, knowing that nothing was pure.

"Why did you want those tapes from Kate?" he asked.

"*I* didn't want the tapes; Shin Beth did."

"They wanted to find out who planted the bomb?"

"Naturally."

"And you already knew."

"I didn't say that."

"No, you didn't say that. But since what you say suggests you weren't interested, why get angry with Kate?"

"Because the woman's contemptible—and please forgive me if she's your mistress. Also, because I was ordered to get the tapes and her refusal made me look like a fool."

Leon chuckled and shook his head from side to side, not believing his ears. "You're priceless," he said. "You're willing to have fellow Jews murdered for your beliefs, but can't stand the slightest blow to your pride. I should frame you and hang you on the Wailing Wall."

Paul stared at him with anger—or the hatred of outraged pride —then spread the fingers of both hands on the table, his thumbs curling under it. "At least I believe," he said. "That makes me a human being. But you—what do you believe in, Leon? I think, nothing. You have nothing at all with which to sustain yourself."

"What is there to believe in? Love, honor, patriotism, eternal life? I have seen all those illusions at work and they're no more than crutches."

"And your nihilism has made you strong? No, Leon, it has not. You have discarded your wife and children, you can call no place home, and you drink to deaden the pain of your loss, disguising your desolation with cynicism. Show me it doesn't matter, Leon: stop drinking. Face yourself without *that* crutch."

Leon felt himself recoiling, deep inside, in his depths, and the shock of this retreat was unexpected, springing out of some buried faith. Certainly it was true: He had repudiated all belief; had discarded his wife and children, traveled the world as a voyeur, and gradually picked up a bad drinking habit that kept his tongue oiled. But had he ever believed in anything? Yes, long ago. And if now he truly believed in nothing, why the flurry of guilt? Pondering this, he thought of Kate, in the hotel, before the storm; remembered that she had accused him of experiencing life from a distance, safe in his supposed objectivity, shielded by wit. He had wanted her desperately then, and had taken her with blind ferocity, not making love but exacting vengeance, perhaps pleading for clemency. Now, analyzing it, recalling the intensity of his passion, he was struck by the sudden nakedness of his need to make her accept him. . . . *Accept* him? With what? With love instead of flesh? Leon wondered this and shivered, feeling a ghost pass over his shoulder; then he blinked and stared at Paul, at his handsome, humorless face, and grinned, picking up his glass of beer, avoiding the question.

"*Shalom,*" he said, drinking some beer and then setting his glass down. "By which I mean, peace. Now tell me what's happening."

Paul glanced down at the table and then looked up again, his brown eyes strangely embarrassed, his hands flat on the table. "I take it you're talking about Kate Hirschfield."

"Yes."

"She's being held in the hospital."

"I know that."

"Then you also know that she's connected with what happened on the Mount of Olives."

"I'd assumed that. Naturally. What I can't figure out is why they're holding her in that hospital and why there are guards on the room next door."

"I'm sorry," Paul said, "I can't help you there."

"You don't know?"

"I'm afraid not."

Leon leaned forward to examine Paul more closely, noting his faint look of embarrassment, his shifting eyes, his fingers rising and falling. The Arab waiter stepped toward them, seeing Leon's empty glass, but Leon shook his head and he walked away, mingling in with the tourists.

"They haven't told you?" Leon said.

"No," Paul replied.

"Why?"

"I'm not sure. I think very few people, *very* few, know just what's going on."

"If they didn't tell you, it must be something very special, something unusually delicate—or extraordinarily dangerous."

Paul shrugged his shoulders, raised his hands, and let them fall. "There are rumors—I can't call them more than that—but they come from strong sources."

His hurt pride was obvious, brightening his eyes, pulling his lips down, and Leon, observing it, understood him more fully, realizing just how dangerous he might be in the weakness of vanity. Resentment was in that face—perhaps the bitterness of rejection—and Leon, who knew ambition when he saw it, knew it could not be thwarted. Moshe Eitan and Ben Eliezer had left Paul out in the cold, and that slight, combined with Paul's lack of faith in their sense of purpose, could only intensify his need to bring them down. The irony was superb and filled Leon with grim humor: this dedicated Zionist would destroy his fellow Jews to prevent them from betraying their ideals. . . . What he wanted was Judgment Day.

"Okay," Leon said, "I'll settle for rumors."

Paul picked up his glass of arak, had a sip, and set the glass down, dabbed at his lips with his napkin, then spread his hands on the table. "The following facts are known," he said quietly, his eyes flitting from left to right. He then reviewed the facts that Leon already knew, finishing with his belief that the Chapel of the Ascension had either collapsed or somehow been crushed.

"The earthquake could explain the collapse of the chapel. Why do you think it might have been crushed? That word suggests that something *crashed down* on it."

Paul shook his head from side to side, obviously confused. "The stories get mixed up," he said. "They conflict and confuse. . . . No, nothing crashed; there was only an explosion of brilliant light. A crash, *any* crash, would have caused wider devastation, and reportedly that isn't the case here. But the stories agree on one thing—that brilliant light was the unidentified—and assuming that this was so, and that it was picked up by the radar, we can surmise that it was some kind of unknown force—a force that could have either crushed the chapel or pulled it apart. One suggestion is that the light, by somehow burning up the atmosphere, created a very brief but powerful vacuum which, to put it crudely, *sucked* the chapel out of the earth and then spat it back down again."

Leon slumped back in his chair, experiencing a trickle of fear, his brain swirling with infinite possibilities beyond the believable.

"So," he said, "Kate was there when it happened."

"Correct."

"And where *was* she when it happened? I mean, precisely."

"She told Moshe Eitan—this conversation was overheard—that she was standing inside the circular courtyard, close to the door by the tower of the mosque."

"That's not very far from the chapel."

"No."

"Accepting your hypothesis of a brief but powerful vacuum, could Kate have survived such an experience?"

"Yes. It would depend on where the vacuum was localized and how widespread it was. Try to imagine the vacuum as the beam of a flashlight, emanating from the broader light that covered the whole area and only focusing on the chapel itself. If such were the case—if the vacuum was like a funnel which fitted only over the chapel—then Kate, outside that area, well away from the edge of the vacuum, would have been badly hammered by the air swirling around it, but otherwise, theoretically speaking, could have survived."

"Which, of course, she did." Leon looked at his cigar, which had been resting, unsmoked, in the ashtray, stubbed out the charred butt, and then leaned forward, propping his chin in his cupped hands. "What about the hospital? Why are Kate and the local residents locked up there? And who's in that guarded room?"

Paul shrugged, letting his hands rise and fall, his brown eyes soft and wounded. "When Moshe Eitan and his men arrived at the Chapel of the Ascension—trying to locate what they then thought was an object that had crashed—they found Kate lying in the rubble and brought her back down. However, an unusually long period elapsed between when Kate was found and when she was actually brought into the hospital. While I don't know exactly what caused the delay, I *do* know that Moshe Eitan was also brought back with Kate and that both of them, for at least the next two days, were under intense observation. More interestingly, a source at the hospital claimed that an hour or so after Kate and Moshe arrived at the hospital, *another* ambulance, surrounded by a remarkably heavy guard detail, also came down from the Mount and went around to the back door. Whoever—or whatever—was inside that ambulance was taken to the room beside Kate's room. Now that room is under guard twenty-four hours each day; it's wired for sound and under surveillance, with no less than Moshe Eitan personally responsible for it. As for Kate, I can only assume she saw something—but what she saw, I don't know."

"Do you know why they're still guarding that whole area?"

Paul shrugged again, dropping his eyes, glancing sideways, his hands rising and falling in that gesture that signified his bewilderment. "All the soldiers on that detail are sworn to secrecy, so we're talking in whispers now. Whispers are confusing, more so when they're passed on—so, I'm not sure about this; it could just be some nonsense."

"Tell me."

"There's nothing up there now. The bulldozers are shifting the rubble. But when I say they are shifting the rubble, I mean more than that . . . apparently they are filling in a very large hole where the Chapel of the Ascension originally stood. Not a crack in the earth: a very large, square-shaped hole. And according to the whispers, that hole had contained something . . . something that had been buried in the earth and was exposed during the storm."

"Anything else?"

"No, nothing else. That's all I could get."

Leon leaned back in his chair, feeling dazed and confused, hardly able to comprehend what he had heard, let alone piece it together. He shook his head from side to side, puffed his cheeks, emptied his lungs, then took a deep breath and leaned forward, getting ready to rise.

"Why are you telling me all this?" he asked.

"Because I want to know what happened. Since I've obviously been excluded, they won't let me hear much; but you, with your contacts of a less inhibited nature, might be able to find out more than me. I have to know what they're hiding."

"Why?"

"You know why. You know my position. This government is weak and frightened of further conflict, so sooner or later it will weaken further and try to surrender the West Bank. We, my own kind, those who cling to the dream of Zion, simply can't sit back and let that happen."

"And you think that what occurred on the Mount of Olives could help to prevent that?"

"I can't answer that yet. I have to know what happened first. At the moment I only know that what they found on the Mount was obviously of considerable importance. They're trying to hide it

completely—from Jew, Muslim, and Christian—and that means it'
very big, very sensitive, almost certainly threatening."

"So, if it's threatening, you can use it."

"Yes, I can use it."

Leon stood up slowly, still dazed and a little fearful, unable to
shake off the feeling that this might be a dream. Yet it certainly wasn'
a dream: Paul's brown eyes were intense; remaining in his seat
having to stare up at Leon, he seemed terribly youthful and desolat
—and undoubtedly dangerous. Leon studied him for some time, hi
gaze steady, before offering a tight smile.

"Tell me," he said, "I have to know . . . How does a pious Jev
with such ambitions manage to sleep at night?"

"By praising our Lord the One," Paul replied.

Leon nodded and walked out, breathing gratefully of the orange
blossom, brushing the purple bougainvillaea aside and walking unde
the palm trees. There were children near his car, Arab children, dar
and beautiful, and he gave them some coins, watched them rushin
away excitedly, then opened the door of the car and climbed in an
drove off down the street. It was a long street, very busy, filled wit
restaurants and gardens, and he passed the tourist buses, a profusio
of palms and citrus groves, and then put his foot down and accelerat
almost viciously, letting the air whip his face as the town of Jerich
disappeared and the Jordan Valley, with its magnificent, desolat
grandeur, spread out all around him.

The sky was a white haze, hammering down its fierce heat
burnishing the hills and plains in golden light and enclosing th
silence. Leon wanted that silence, wanted time to speculate, conten
to be a prisoner in his car while the earth slid past eerily. To her
Moses had led his people; here Joshua had fought his battles; here
also, John and Jesus had wandered, sanctifying the Promised Land
But Leon felt removed from this—like his belief, it was mere histor
—and as the land moved around him, as the wind whipped his face
he thought only of what Paul had said, of what Kate might hav
witnessed, and tried to fit the pieces together in his head and view th
parts as a whole.

The recent events were a mystery, unexplained, the lock unbroken
yet to Leon they now seemed like a curtain rising up on his burie
past. Kate had spoken that same night—before the storm defied natur
—had exposed him as a man in retreat from his own frailty, afraid t
reveal his fear of life and its brutal reprisals. Paul had merely echoe

her words, perhaps unwittingly, striking back; but now, as he pressed
his foot down, as the car raced ahead, as the parched plains rushed
past and the Judean Hills loomed before him, Leon remembered the
ghost that had passed over his shoulder when, facing Paul, he had
thought of Kate's words and realized that his denial of the need for
love was really fear of accepting it.

The ghost had told him that, but what ghost had it been? Not one
ghost, but all the ghosts, that parade of the damned, the faces that had
floated past him in Londonderry and Con Thien, in other nameless
villages lost in flames in nameless countries, the dark, stricken faces
of the women and children, the faces of all the boys who had grown
old and died on their feet. He had retreated from that dying,
embracing the horror as solace, casting off the pain of emotional
commitment and taking comfort in nihilism. Now he saw it and was
lost, wanting something new to cling to—not something, someone
. . . wanting Kate, who alone had recognized him, to give shape to
his life.

14

"Come in," Kate said, and the rabbi opened the room door, breathing heavily, feeling the weight of his abundant flesh, silently suffering his old age. He saw Kate on the bed, lying flat on her back, her hands on her forehead, her long dark hair flowing over her brown arms. She opened her eyes when he entered, the closing door drawing her attention, and he noticed that she looked ill and sleepless, smiling wearily, without humor.

"Jozsef Latinavots," she said. "My good friend, the acting chief rabbi, come to offer me solace."

"Do you need it?"

"Not religion," she said. "I could do with a stiff drink."

Jozsef sighed in despair, long familiar with Kate's intransigence, but wondering, as usual, why this strong and willful woman refused to embrace the peace of belief. He glanced at the chair beside her, and she nodded and he sat down, automatically touching the skullcap on his head and rubbing his beard with his hand. Kate was still lying down, obviously too weary to move, wearing only a white hospital smock, her legs crossed, her feet bare, no longer young but still exceptionally attractive, staring at him with her dark eyes strangely haunted.

"Who sent you?" she asked.

"Major General Eitan."

"Why?"

"He seemed to know we were old friends—he had met your father once or twice—and I assume he thought I might be able to comfort you."

Kate smiled sardonically and closed her eyes, her hands still on her forehead. "Major General Eitan is a considerate man," she said. "Particularly when he keeps you a prisoner."

"Hardly that, Kate."

"No, perhaps not." She opened her eyes and turned her head on the pillow, no longer smiling. "Did he say I was disturbed?"

"No. He merely said that you were under observation and might like to see someone. He felt that I, being a rabbi and an old friend of the family, should be that person."

"Obviously he doesn't know me all that well."

"No, obviously not. On the other hand, regardless of our differences of opinion, I still have great regard for you, Kate."

"Admit it: you love me."

"That, also, I agree. Perhaps I think of you as my daughter. I have known you since you came to Israel, a young woman, but resentful; and watched you mature and draw away from your father, embittered and mocking his faith, cheapening yourself to outrage him. Yes, I love you, Kate—I loved you then and I love you now—but my love springs from sadness and despair that you should so waste your life."

"I don't cheapen myself, Jozsef."

"You are blasphemous and promiscuous. You flaunt your reputation as a woman of easy virtue, advertising your contempt for the Torah and those who obey it."

"I didn't believe, Jozsef; and wasn't capable of hypocrisy. As for virtue, each culture has its own, and I come from America. I'm a mature woman with physical needs—and I cannot repress them."

Jozsef felt himself blushing, embarrassed by her bluntness, and he turned his head aside to fix his gaze on the white-painted wall. "Your lack of faith has always disturbed me, Kate, particularly in view of your parents. When I think of them—their belief, their contributions —I must confess, it bewilders me. . . . You are lost, Kate—and suffering."

Now Kate turned away, rolling her body toward the wall, her hands spreading out to cover her whole face, like a child with a bad dream. Jozsef watched her, disturbed, sensing some change in her, and reminding himself of the recent extraordinary event and how it might have affected her. He felt strangely moved, waiting for something, not knowing what, but sensing that Kate was in turmoil, thrashing about in the dark.

"Why do you deny your faith?"

"I didn't just deny my faith—I despised it—and all other faiths with it." Kate's voice was now shakier, filled with bitterness and resentment, and Jozsef leaned forward a little in the chair, wanting to reach down and touch her. "I saw religious faith as selfishness, as a separating wall, as something dividing men against men and closing their minds to the faithless. My father was such a man—the wors kind: a convert. He spent his life amassing wealth, legally taking from the poor, making very mortal deals and breaking very mortal people and living, as those in banking do, for material success. And yet he was still a Jew—a closet Jew, growing older—and so, when he was wealthy, when the boredom set in, he looked for something to reviv him, didn't find it in his family, and then turned to the religion he had ignored, drowning his conscience in piety."

"You poor child," Jozsef said. "I never realized you felt so strongly. . . . But surely you can see that your father's past way of life had no bearing on what he later contributed to Israel. All th charities . . . all that work . . . that selfless devotion to Zionism . . . Surely, Kate, he was a better man for it, giving all he had earned."

"He gave *part* of what he earned. He used the rest for furthe investments. Money makes money—and what his money made i interest was considerably more than he so ostentatiously donated t Israel. He *bought* respectability, Jozsef. He salved his conscienc without sacrifice. Oh, yes, he had his virtue—his religion absolve him from all sin—but his contribution to Israel, that great abstractio you all pursue, was paid for by his indifference to his wife an daughter, those less worthy beings."

Jozsef sat up straight again, instinctively drawing away from her startled by her venom, deeply wounded by her words, ashame because he wanted to close his ears and respect his old friend. "I d realize," he said, "that you did not want to come to Israel, bu surely—"

Kate rolled onto her back, pulling her hands from her face, then la there, very straight, breathing harshly, staring up at the ceiling.

"No, I didn't want to come. Nor did my mother. Jewish we ma have been, but Israeli we were not. We were *American* Jews, Jozsef and very typical of that breed: Hardly aware of what we were, rarel thinking about it, only reminded of it at weddings or the Bar Mitzva of friends' children, perfectly happy with our simple *goyish* pleasure and American freedoms. No, my mother didn't want it, Jozsef—an God knows, neither did I—but my father, in the selfishness of his ne religion, never asked our opinions."

She stopped talking and turned her head, stared at him and looke away, raising her eyes once more to the ceiling, the dark depths out o focus. Jozsef, feeling the need to defend his old friend, leaned forward again.

"I understand your resentment, Kate, but let me just say this: Your father, if not a perfect man, since few of us are, was always very concerned for your welfare."

"You *really* think he cared, Jozsef?"

"Yes, Kate, I do."

"He didn't give a damn, Jozsef. He hacked our roots out with an ax, determined to cut us off from our past and make us walk in his shadow. First the holidays in the Catskill Mountains, that revered center of Jewish resorts; then active involvement with the United Israel Appeal; then our *goyish* pleasures were curtailed, our gentile friends were pushed out, and then my mother and I had to keep our mouths shut and listen as he unveiled his plans. You understand, Jozsef? His religion had made him whole. And so no longer happy to give mere financial support, he now wanted to become the real thing: an important Zionist in Israel. Well, he got what he wanted—with no arguments accepted: He ended up in King George Boulevard, raising funds for the WZO, right here in the heart of *Yerushalayim,* next door to your Rabbinate. As for myself and my mother, he gave us no choice. Then my mother died—and believe me, she died of loneliness —and after that I despised him and despised his damned religion, and finally despised *all* religions."

"That is blasphemy!" Jozsef snapped. "You will not use such words with me!"

"Blasphemy?" she replied, finally turning around toward him, propping herself up on one elbow and looking straight at him. "Blasphemy against God or my father? And which is worse, Jozsef?"

"Enough, Kate! I understand your rage, but I won't take much more of this!" His own rage pulled him upright, pushing his chair back, turning away from her, then he walked to the door and just stood there, his whole body quivering. "I can't stay if you talk like that. You *know* I can't listen. I came here to help you, to listen. I fear for your health. This strange event has sickened your mind. Moshe Eitan explained that you were obsessed by that man in the next room —just lying here, restless, wanting to see him—and he thought I could help you. That's what I'm here for. I would ask you to be calm. I would like to know why you're waiting for that man to miraculously open his eyes."

There was no immediate reply, so he turned back to face her and saw her sitting upright on the bed, her eyes wide, her lips parted.

"So," she said, "you know."

"Of course," he said. "I was informed. I am still the chief rabbi. When a sacred site, any site of such importance, is destroyed, I am personally responsible for communicating the proper facts to the relevant authority."

"And you were told how we found that man next door?"

"Yes, Kate, I was told."

"And?"

"And *what*?" Jozsef looked at her dark eyes, very large, now too intense, then looked away, feeling oddly confused, his soul filled with intimations of chaos and dark, nameless fears. "If you mean, what do I think about that man, I can't answer that yet. A mystery, certainly. Perhaps even miraculous. I prefer to think of rational explanations, but the mystery remains."

"Who *is* he, Jozsef?"

Jozsef stared at her, suddenly feeling his age, some part of him dissolving and pouring back down through his past: his childhood in Poland, the years of study in various *yeshivot*, then arrival in *Eretz Yisroel*, burying the dead of the IDF, then the National Religious Party, studying the Talmud, learning diplomacy, pushed forward as Ashkenazic chief rabbi of Tel Aviv, righting wrongs, making mistakes, learning humility with the Batei Din, until now, an old man, shaped by sixty years of theology, he stood, the Ashkenazic chief rabbi of all Israel, like a child in an orphanage. His past flew by in a second, without warning, almost mocking, vaporizing as if to confirm that all his learning was useless. He was naked, defenseless, unprepared for Kate's question, finding nothing in the well of his experience with which to answer it properly.

"I don't know," he said.

"No," Kate said, "you don't know. He came out of the ground and he's alive, and no religion can answer that."

"Nor science," Jozsef said.

"I agree," Kate replied. "Neither science nor religion can understand how that man can exist."

Jozsef truly felt his age, at that moment more than ever, thinking of Israel, of his years spent in studying it, of how it was divided now as it had been at its beginning, as divided as it was when Joshua brought down the walls of Jericho, when the Philistines slew King Saul, when

King David conquered Jerusalem, when Jeroboam and Rehoboam split the kingdom in two and the ten lost tribes of Israel were scattered to the four corners of the Earth. The land's history was its curse—it was the focus of disparate yearnings—and now Jozsef, in his age and sorry wisdom, saw it threatened once more.

He looked at Kate and felt the pain, the gentle torture of irony, realizing that she believed in logic and was seeing that logic shattered while he, accepting the Torah and thus believing in miracles, was now faced with the possibility of a miracle that could well destroy Israel. This thought also came and departed, vaporizing like his past; or, perhaps, rather than vaporizing, being crushed by his fear.

"It is pointless to conjecture at this moment. Much worse to imagine things."

"Not imagine . . . *believe*."

He glanced up, startled, wondering if he had heard correctly, his heart beating to the rhythm of inchoate panic and making his flesh burn. Then he saw her dark eyes, somehow changed, illuminated, her lips trembling like those of a mute attempting to talk, vainly fighting to express all the words that had never been uttered. His burning flesh turned to ice, swamped in waves of chilling shock as he recalled what she had said about her lack of religious faith and realized that she had used the past tense. *I didn't believe . . . I didn't just deny my faith . . .* She had spoken as if it was behind her and no longer of consequence. Jozsef suddenly understood, the truth hammering home brutally, and he felt his senses sliding away as he walked toward the bed. He grabbed Kate by the shoulders, felt the bone beneath her skin, started shaking her violently from side to side as if exorcising her.

"Is *that* what you think?" he said, his voice harsh and filled with rage. "Is that your form of conversion? Do you think to find atonement in this madness conceived by the devil? No, child, I won't let you!"

He threw her back against the wall and she tumbled to the bed, rolling over until she lay on her back, breathing harshly, disheveled. She lay thus for a long time, staring up at the ceiling, then slowly turned her head to look straight at him, her eyes cold and defiant.

"He's mine," she said. "I don't know what that means . . . but I know that he's mine."

Jozsef shuddered and turned away, drained by fear and despair, all his learning dissolving to dust and leaving him helpless. He reached out for the door handle, then stopped, flushed with shame, remembering who he was, what he was, and taking faith from this knowledge. He glanced quickly at Kate, saw the drawn face, the white smock, then bowed his head and moved his parched lips, murmuring words that were part of him. He prayed for understanding, for the revelation of truth, for the forgiveness of his own mortal weakness and doubt; and most of all, in the sorrow of his love, he prayed for the salvation of Kate's lost soul.

15

Kate lay on the bed, hardly aware of Jozsef's departure, studying the white sheen of the ceiling, drawn into it, drifting through to the white sky. Half asleep, she searched for peace, swam in darkness and streaming light, her heart beating in rapture and fear, one reflecting the other. Her exhaustion was total, a draining of mind and spirit, yet sleep, in which peace might be found, more frequently eluded her. She was losing herself slowly, the life dripping from her body, and yet, beyond reason or logic, she felt the beating of fresh life.

She opened her eyes, looked around her, saw the window, saw the golden light of late afternoon, a streak of blue sky. Not white: blue; a few thin, drifting clouds; the black, beating wings of a lone bird, drifting on high.

Her body felt hollow, drained of life yet strangely radiant, charged with something other than her blood, the radiance spreading out slowly. She tried to think of what she had been, to apply logic to the past few days, but her thoughts, slipping in and out of shadows, merely teased and confused her. . . . Leon, so intense, his pale body above her, making love with a violent desperation that refused to be stated . . . Then the eye of the storm, a bright star, a brilliant light, something drawing her forward against her will, filling her up with its presence . . . No rational explanations, just the urge for revelation; in Leon's confession, unstated but displayed, was the love she could not feel for him in return, the reflection of her fear of commitment because of what she had lost. . . . The dream, that first evening, the bloody fetus in the Pool of Siloam: someone's child—her child—the life that was aborted so brutally before it saw light . . . And then the brilliant star, that great eye shining down on her; her conviction that her past was being measured and held to account.

She closed her eyes again, searching for logic and failing, having to accept that what had happened on the Mount of Olives had changed her completely. She bled for the rabbi, that loving man, her caring friend; but his words, now that faith had enslaved her, could have no effect on her. No logic could restrain it, no stern advice deflect it; her faith was in the awakening of her flesh and its response to the other. He lay parallel to her, the wall between them soon to fall, and as she weakened, so she felt him faintly stirring and returning to life. . . .

It was darkness beyond measure, black painted on black: above and below and all around, without end, filled with silence. It was Nothing, a void, but He was it, and it Him: an impulse, a pulsation that existed where Nothing could be. He was forming out of time, out of the infinite frozen moment, a consciousness flickering on and off and then dividing the darkness. He saw light and was the light, illuminating His own birth, Himself originating existence and then, being it, swelling out to give form to His own coming.

Existing, He was the light, illuminating Himself, expanding and pushing back the darkness and arousing its forces. He reached out and touched, and withdrew and considered; then sensed the manifestation of thought, which evolved from His being. In thought was dimension: time and space; the conceivable. He conceived and saw the web of time and space around which was the darkness. Beyond the darkness could be nothing; all that would be, must be within it. He therefore stretched Himself forth, expanding time and space, pushing the darkness back and thus creating from Himself all that had been or ever would be.

He existed and was All, blossoming out of the Nothing; and the darkness, now aroused from eternal slumber, saw the light that divided it. Divided, it was wounded, incomplete, without Oneness, and it closed in to make itself whole and heal the scar on the Nothing —that, which being nothing, had been perfection.

Blessed with thought, He was being—time and space; that which is —and in consciousness, which ordained time and space, He was bound to exist. Having originated that which is, being Himself the light of being, He accepted the imperfection of His creation and resisted extinction. The forces of darkness were His womb, offering existence or denying it, and thus conflict, the war between light and darkness, was the pulse that sustained Him.

The Whole was a white hole, a burning light expanding, the light spreading out all around Him and dissolving the darkness. To be whole, He became, stretching defiantly through the Nothing, creating positive and negative, past and future, eternal present; reaching out from the womb of darkness to touch the flesh of the Beyond, giving impulse to the impulse of life and ordaining her future.

"He's awakening," Kate said.

She opened her eyes and jerked upright, her heart pounding, her body wracked, shook her head and saw Moshe by the door, his hand still on the handle. He stared at her, obviously startled, possibly hiding his embarrassment, then he walked in and closed the door behind him, and then stood there, his eyes veiled. She looked at him, feeling frightened, wondering what was happening to her, then leaned sideways and pressed her shoulder against the wall, trying to calm her emotions.

"A nightmare?" Moshe said.

"Yes," she said. "Something like that. I've been having an awful lot of them lately. You should know; you've been watching me."

He nodded, not offended, his gray eyes revealing nothing, and she felt like getting up and slapping his face, just to see his reaction. This urge faintly amused her, almost bringing back her old self, but looking up at his face, at that strong, granite mask, she understood that it might be a mistake, inviting nothing but scorn.

"He's awakening, did you say?"

"No," she lied, "I didn't say that. I don't know. What difference does it make? I was having a bad dream."

His lips moved without humor, the smile never reaching his eyes, and she noticed that his body barely moved, his hands steady on broad hips. He was obviously suppressing something, keeping himself in firm control, and she studied him, wondering what he thought of her, finding nothing to help her.

"I thought you said that."

"Think what you like," she said. "If what you think is as inaccurate as what you say, there won't be any problem."

"I don't understand."

"Neither do I, Major General. You informed the rabbi that that man next door obsessed me—which is true—but you omitted to tell him who asked me to stay here."

"You admit that you're obsessed?"

"I don't think that's the point. The point, Moshe Eitan, is that you *asked* me to stay, whereas the rabbi thinks you're keeping me locked up because I'm out of my mind."

"I simply thought you might like a visitor."

"And simply suggested that I needed help."

"There was a reason," he said. "I had a reason that I can't quite explain." She noticed his dropping eyes, the slight pursing of his lips, the way his hands moved, fingers parting, spreading out on his hips. "Let me try to explain," he said. "It's something to do with you and that man in the next room; with how you seemed to have an instinct about that object and with what was inside it. You were drawn to that object; your body kept straining toward it. You actually said it was a tomb—an accurate description—before you went anywhere near it. That, plus the star. The star was obviously the light we saw. But what made you follow the star and end up at the chapel? So, I was intrigued. Your behavior here has intrigued me more. Superficially you were logical—remarkably so, considering your experience—but beneath it, in some way I can't explain, you seemed to be drifting away from us, becoming more agitated, more restless and sleepless, your talk, whether awake or asleep, dominated by one subject: that man from the Mount."

"I found him. I almost sensed that he was there. I want to know who he is."

"No, it's more than that. His presence seems to have taken you over. I'm not too sure what I mean by that; only you can confirm it. I wanted to ask you, but it didn't seem appropriate—your behavior was too oblique; you seemed frightened and secretive—and so I tried the rabbi, who had been wanting to see you anyway. I said you were obsessed because I thought that might encourage him to ask you the sort of questions I couldn't ask—and because I thought that his being a rabbi, you might tell him the truth."

"I'm not intimidated by any rabbi."

"I'm beginning to find that out."

"There's nothing I can tell you. I just feel things. . . . I feel that I'm tied to that man."

Her own words pushed the door back, revealing his graven image, that face that had materialized from the darkness in a pillar of light. The light, which had divided the darkness, had given life to her emptiness. Still leaning against the wall, her ear close to that white sheen, she tried to hear the sound of his stirring and heard nothing but silence. Perhaps she was mad; she could not ignore the possibility: more than once she had thought that this was so and had longed to be cured. Yet now, even as she thought this, she rejected it with fervor, some part of her, once hidden but gradually taking her over, insisting that what she was feeling was a reality that could not be ignored; that in some way beyond comprehension she was tied to the other.

"His robe," she said, the thought springing from nowhere. "Did you touch it?"

"We removed it."

"Why?"

"We had to remove the robe in order to examine him. Also, we wanted to analyze the robe itself."

"What sort of analysis?"

"Ultramicroscopic and radiological testing; they might tell us what the robe is made of, where it was made, and how old it is."

"You shouldn't have touched it," Kate said.

She regretted the words immediately, not really knowing what she had meant, wondering if His voice had reached out through the silence of sleep. He lay there, awakening, a light growing in the darkness, drawing from her body and mind the strength He required. This concept was extraordinary, defying logic and common sense, yet it gripped her and refused to let her go, both exalting and frightening her. His presence was within her, taking from her and giving to her, and she wondered, with increasing joy and dread, what His nature might be.

"*Why* should we not have touched it?" Moshe was staring straight at her, his face thoughtful, somehow gentle, his gray eyes concealing an emotion that she could not define. A solid man, she thought. Withdrawn but strong-willed. She took comfort from this knowledge, but was still uneasy with him, sensing something other than mere curiosity in the way he talked to her.

"I just said it," she replied. "I don't know why. It just doesn't seem right."

"It's only a robe, Kate."

"I know that."

"You're not religious."

"No, I'm not religious; not that way. . . . I don't know why I said that."

She curled her legs beneath her, feeling weak and a little dizzy, as she usually felt when her menstrual blood was flowing and her body disgusted her. A woman's body could be her prison, administering punishment at regular intervals, inflicting pain and secret humiliation, turning flesh into stone. Sexual desire was little better: a grossly physical appetite; a hunger that obliterated consideration and destroyed common sense. She had always distrusted her body, quietly abhorred the demands it made on her; yet now, as it weakened, so it conversely seemed to be filling with a warmth that both moved and bewildered her. Thinking this, she looked at Moshe and remembered how they had both found Him; and then wanted Moshe to reach out and embrace her as he had that first day. But he made no such move, merely stood there, staring at her, his gray eyes strangely tentative and veiled, as if sheltering a private dream.

"You think there's a bond between you?"

"Yes," Kate said, "I do. I can't help it; that's what I feel . . . and the feeling grows stronger."

"And the dreams . . . ?"

"About him."

"What sort of dreams?"

"It was always the same dream." The words now came easier. "I was dreaming about what had actually happened: the total darkness inside that object, the awful blackness of it, the sense that the emptiness was boundless, beyond time and space. . . . Then that pillar of light, his face radiant in the light, that bearded and remarkably composed face with its terrible beauty . . . Why do I use those words? Because he's not like you or I; because apart from how we found him, apart from the knowledge that he was buried there, apart from the fact that he's still alive, he is someone quite different. . . . I *know* he's normal flesh and blood—the examinations have proven that—but his face, though superficially like that of a normal human being, is also somehow inhuman in its purity; its lack of human contrasts. Beautiful, yes: a terrible beauty. . . . Its perfection is frightening."

"I'm not sure what you mean."

"It's a void . . . a void waiting to be filled."

She glanced at him nervously, wondering what she was suggesting, then dropped her eyes and studied her hands, the fingers tugging the white smock.

"You said it *was* always the same dream. Why use the past tense?"

"Because the dream changed last night, and I relive it when I close my eyes—wide awake, but experiencing the dream as if I were sleeping. I think it's about him, about what's inside his mind: I dream about a light growing out of a perfect darkness, and the light seems to represent him and the birth of his consciousness. That light, which I see in the dream, I also feel in my body. . . . There's something tying us together, a sort of umbilical cord. . . . He's reviving, awakening, and I know that as sure as I sit here. That man, that being next door, will soon be awake."

Moshe went down on one knee and took hold of her wrists, very gently pulling her clasped hands apart and then tugging her toward him. His gray eyes, close to her face, were protective and calming, and he stared at her thoughtfully, as if coming to a decision, and then, for the very first time, offered a tentative smile.

"Yes," he said, "you're right. We think he's reviving. His temperature is rising, his slow heartbeat is quickening, and the EEG is starting to flicker. Not much in either case, but enough. . . . He's returning to normal."

The dream folded in upon her, enclosing her in silence, filling her with fear and exaltation and stripping her senses. She closed her eyes and saw the darkness, the void of the unknown, then a light, blossoming up from her depths, illuminated her being. She started to shake, felt Moshe holding her wrists, and then, licking her lips and opening her eyes, was reassured by his presence.

"I have to see him," she said.

He lay naked on the bed, sensors attached to his chest and wrists, his head wired to the EEG machine which was flickering feebly. Sunlight poured through the window, a rich gold turning gray, illuminating the marble of pure white skin and his startling face. His body was long and lean, the stomach flat, the muscles hard, the skin smooth and absolutely unblemished, almost translucent. His hands were by his sides, palms turned upward, webbed with fine lines, the fingers long and thin, without calluses, extraordinarily delicate.

Kate looked and was captured, her eyes drawn to his face, that mask of inhuman composure and impossible serenity. That face was the light, drawing it in and reflecting it, turning it back upon her and making her burn. The face was a cipher, offering nothing, revealing all, at once innocent and wise, very young and very old, too blank to be real, too vivid to be forgotten, defying, in its terrible beauty and repose, definition and logic.

Kate was captured and held, her heart breaking with grief and love, seeing the child in the man, the man in the child, ascetic lips, hollow cheeks, the dark beard flecked with gray, the nose aquiline, the closed eyes with long lashes, forehead smooth, dark hair matted. A mature man. A child. One dissolved into the other. The face was a contradiction: a blank page, the map of history, a void waiting to receive and be received and thus fill itself up.

Kate sobbed and stepped forward, spread her fingers and reached down, touched his forehead, his eyes, his nose and lips, felt the shock of his living skin. Then she froze and remained there, her fingers at his lips, the unknown opening out and slowly drawing her in past that point where she could ever hope to return as what she had been.

She removed her hand and stepped back, shaking her head from side to side, and then, in her expectation and exaltation and dread, turned around and saw Moshe in the doorway, his gray eyes fixed upon her.

"Oh, please God," she said, "hold me!"

16

"So, gentlemen," Ben Eliezer said, spreading his hands in an oratorical gesture, "the man from the Mount is awakening and decisions are called for."

"Not *quite* awakening," Leonard Rosenberg corrected, scratching his chin with a pencil, his head down and his eyes focused upward, looking over his spectacles. "Physiologically speaking, he is almost certainly returning to normal; but that process could reverse or possibly cease at any point—and either way there is no guarantee that the patient will actually regain full consciousness."

"My point, dear Doctor, is that either way we look at it, we still have a living creature on our hands."

"Quite so; I'll support that."

Ben Eliezer sighed and smiled slightly, sardonically, then glanced across the table, first at Moshe, then at Rabbi Latinavots, before returning his gaze to the table, as if examining his knuckles. "And the man is perfectly normal," he said. "We can take that as read?"

"Yes, Shlomo," the doctor said. "Perfectly normal. Very much a flesh and blood human being—and in excellent condition."

"So," Ben Eliezer said, still studying his knuckles, "where did he come from?"

They all glanced at one another, each foiled by the incomprehensible, each wrestling with his private, conflicting views of what the answer might be.

"We've discussed this before," Moshe said. "We still can't answer the question. We might learn something if that man regains his senses or if analysis of his robe reveals something. Meanwhile, there's no rational explanation."

The rabbi gave a sigh, obviously relieved at Moshe's response, well aware of what all of them were thinking and not wanting to face it.

"Fine," Ben Eliezer persisted. "We don't know anything about him. We only know that there was an object, that that object defied known science, that it had to have been buried there for centuries, and that that man was inside it. . . . Now what does that *mean*?"

"I pass," said Leonard Rosenberg. "I can only repeat that he's a human being. How he managed to stay alive, I don't know—it just doesn't make sense."

"Some cryogenic process?"

"No," Leonard replied. "His blood is absolutely pure. He hadn't been tampered with, he was wearing a simple robe, and there wasn't another thing in that room except for the stone bed."

"So he's been sleeping there for years."

"That's impossible," the doctor said. "I simply cannot accept that. He could not have survived very long in his condition, so the object must have been planted in the ground just before it was found."

"Fine," Ben Eliezer said, "that makes sense. . . . But what planted the object?"

"It *had* to be the unidentified."

"That's equally impossible," Moshe intervened. "That unidentified reached ground level and then simply disappeared; it was therefore some form of energy; nothing mechanical or physical . . . and believe me, nothing *crashed* on the Mount of Olives."

"Thus," Ben Eliezer said, "it must have been buried there—before the Chapel of the Ascension was constructed . . . a small matter of centuries."

Moshe looked at each man in turn, first Ben Eliezer; then the rabbi; then the doctor, Leonard Rosenberg; and finally, General Yaakov Meshel, the current head of the Intelligence Committee, which coordinated the activities of the three Israeli intelligence services. Now the general was leaning forward, his elbows resting on the table, a cigar between the fingers of his right hand, his face hard and aggressive.

"Moshe is right," he said. "We've discussed all this before. It's pointless to continue the conversation without adequate knowledge. At this moment we have to discuss that unidentified and how to explain it."

"We *don't* explain it," Ben Eliezer replied. "We simply continue our denials, sticking to our story of unidentified atmospheric phenomena."

"A temporary measure," the general said. "It won't hold water for long. That unidentified was also picked up by reconnaissance satellites and foreign radar as it traveled from west to east and winked out here. We could use atmospheric phenomena if it wasn't for the storm; but the destruction of the chapel and mosque—and the widespread destruction around Jerusalem—have encouraged speculation about a crash. We can't dampen that speculation and it makes for embarrassment: both the Soviets and the Americans are convinced that we're hiding some hardware."

"Naturally," Ben Eliezer said. "They both think something crashed here—and each side thinks it belongs to the other and wants to know what it is."

"Right," the general said. "They're worried about what we might have here. They're asking a lot of questions and applying considerable pressure; and now the journalists, including Leon Halcomb, are starting to bang on some doors."

"What's so special about Leon Halcomb?"

"He seems to know more than the others. He knows it wasn't a normal accident, he suspects that something was found up there; and, worst of all, he seems aware that we brought someone down from there and are keeping him under guard in the hospital."

Ben Eliezer looked at Moshe, his gaze oblique, his eyebrows raised, and Moshe, understanding the unstated question, shook his head slowly from side to side.

"No," he said, "not Kate Hirschfield. She hasn't spoken to anyone. She didn't leave that room until today—and she was watched all the time."

"Today?" the general said. "Why today?"

"Because I took her next door to let her see that man from the Mount."

The general stared at Moshe, at Ben Eliezer, then back at Moshe, not trying to conceal his amazement at what he had heard.

"She found him," Moshe explained, "and the circumstances were very strange; and now she seems to be affected by his presence in a very odd way."

"Of course, Moshe: she *found* him."

"No, Yaakov, it's more than that. There's an almost psychic connection between them. Kate seemed to know that the object was hollow, she seemed to sense that someone was in there, and since we've kept her in confinement she's developed an instinct for that man—and even knew, without us telling her, that he was reviving."

"I don't believe in psychic connections," the general said. "You should address that to the rabbi."

Moshe glanced at Jozsef and saw his clear discomfort, his hand reaching up to touch his skullcap as if consoling himself.

"Well, Jozsef?"

"I don't think so. I'm afraid I cannot accept that. The woman has not been happy, this event has badly shaken her, and now she has succumbed to this obsession that that man is a savior."

"A *savior*?" the doctor said.

Jozsef shrugged, his face forlorn. "This is a very delicate matter. I'm not at all sure of her motives, so permit me to speculate. . . . The Chapel of the Ascension is one of the most sacred of all Christian sites. It was built over the rock upon which, according to the Christians, Jesus last stood before ascending to Heaven."

"Kate Hirschfield is *Jewish*," Ben Eliezer said.

"Correct," the rabbi said, "but she is also without faith—or, more accurately, in revolt against her faith. Nonetheless, still Jewish to her soul, that faith has to be replaced with another. So we have the earthquake, an extraordinary storm, and Kate is right there when that object comes out of the ground beneath a chapel that has been standing for centuries."

"A *Christian* chapel, Jozsef."

"Of course, Shlomo, but it doesn't matter: the object is a miracle, beyond rational explanation—and the man inside, an even greater miracle, possibly buried for centuries. So, she is seduced, overwhelmed by the inexplicable, and faced with what appears to be supernatural, surrenders her reasoning. The man becomes a miraculous being, possibly a messianic figure, someone who is above normal men and has made her his chosen one."

Something cold slid through Moshe, a chilling portent of the future, the feeling that the rabbi's words, dropped reluctantly from his lips, might mean more than even the rabbi could at present consider. He thought of Kate in the stranger's room, her body quivering like a reed, her eyes filled with dread and exaltation as she fell into his arms. Holding her, stroking her hair, Moshe had felt more than longing; he had felt, just like Kate, a mixture of childish awe and fear, swept away from his old self on the tide of the future which was, since the arrival of the man from the Mount, a path leading to infinite possibilities, all of which stunned the imagination and opened the door to the unknown. He glanced again at the rabbi, sympathizing with his plight, understanding that he, too, was grappling with nameless fears, now faced with implications more threatening than he dared to admit.

"A messiah," Ben Eliezer said.

"I merely speculate," the rabbi replied.

"Your speculations, Jozsef, lead us into more disturbing possibilities. . . . The destruction of the chapel has already shocked the Christian world, but what will be said if they find out about the man we brought down from there?"

Ben Eliezer had raisèd the issue that they had all avoided so far and now Moshe felt the tension in the room, an almost palpable reluctance to face the issue and try to resolve it. He shared that reluctance and could not be proud of it, but the reasons were complex and not related only to politics; rather they sprang out of the soil of faith itself—a faith not only fundamental to the spirit of Israel, but also to the ineradicable beliefs of each individual. Those beliefs were now endangered—or at the least, exposed to doubt—and the questions that would ultimately be raised could only lead to more questions: a confusion that could break the mind and spirit and render faith obsolete. This was what they were avoiding, but Ben Eliezer, a supreme realist, had thrown down the glove that Moshe now felt compelled to pick up.

"It's not only the Christians," he said. "It's also the Jews and the Muslims. We can no longer pretend that the destruction of a Christian chapel was the only thing that happened that night. The Chapel of the Ascension was destroyed, the Golden Gate was smashed open, and many of the graves in the Muslim graveyard on the slopes of the Mount of Olives were exposed by the cracks caused by the earthquake. These are the salient facts of this matter, and they can't be ignored."

"I don't know what you mean," Leonard Rosenberg said. "I'm a doctor and know little about theology, which is what you're suggesting."

"So, Moshe," the general said, stubbing out his cigar, his face hard but no longer aggressive, now carefully composed, "just what are you driving at?"

"An unholy trinity," the rabbi said. "Moshe is right: we have to face it. What has happened embraces the three great monotheistic religions and could lead to the most extraordinary reactions."

"I am listening," Ben Eliezer said. "I am wide awake. Please clarify this matter."

The rabbi was reluctant, perhaps unable to utter the words, so Moshe, less committed to Judaism, broke into his silence.

"Christianity views itself as the fulfillment of Judaism, as the messianic prophecy come to life in the person of Jesus Christ; ergo, only Christ can be the true Messiah. To put it another way, whatever we Jews preach, teach, believe in, and accept was actually fulfilled in Jesus; and the Second Coming of Christ, in which the Christians believe, will not only inaugurate the conversion of the Jews, but ordain the Christian world as the New Israel."

"That is blasphemous," the rabbi said.

"It's what they believe," Moshe replied. "And what matters at the moment is not just what *we* believe, but what the Christians and Muslims also believe."

"What you are suggesting," Ben Eliezer said, "is that the Chapel of the Ascension was built over the rock upon which Jesus, according to the Christians, ascended to Heaven—and that that man from the Mount, whose materialization seems supernatural, might be taken up by the Christians either as the resurrected Christ or as a sign of His Second Coming."

"Yes," Moshe said. "The Son of—"

"That belief is anathema to both Jews and Muslims," the rabbi said, preventing Moshe from uttering the forbidden word. "For both there is no such thing as the Trinity—only the One."

"But certain Muslims," Moshe replied, "particularly many of the Sufis, also believe in the Second Coming of Christ."

"A belief condemned by the Orthodox," the rabbi said.

"True, Jozsef. . . . But the Muslims also believe in a Day of Salvation. Remember that the two main forces in Islam are the Sunnis and Shi'ites. The Shi'ites follow Ali, Muhammad's son-in-law, and believe that he and his eleven successors, all Imams, or leaders, had the correct hereditary succession from Muhammad and were therefore infallible and free from sin. They also believe that the twelfth and last Imam disappeared and went into hiding, waiting to return on the Day of Judgment. The Mahdi is the hidden Imam: a spiritual being who will appear at the end of time to restore peace and justice to mankind and establish the full power of Islam over the nonbelievers—namely, in the case of Israel, the Jews."

"This is beginning to sound worse every second."

"Yes, Shlomo. And it would be best not to ignore the fact that the Muslims also accept Jesus: not as a divine being or the Son of the One, but as one of the righteous individuals—or one of the prophets —selected by the One to be a channel between Himself and His people. They might therefore view this man as the resurrected prophet . . . or as a sign of something even more dangerous."

"You're obviously referring to the Muslim graveyard."

"Yes. The Muslims believe that the resurrection of souls will begin at the Muslim graveyard on the slopes of the Mount of Olives—and since the earthquake devastated the graveyard, opening up many of the graves, there are whispers in certain quarters, by which I mean Arab sectors, that the Day of Judgment is at hand. It therefore stands to reason that if they learn about that man, they might well convince themselves that he's the hidden Imam, the Mahdi, returned to Earth to inaugurate the Day of Judgment."

"And if they did, it would encourage them to try and establish Islam over the Christians and Jews of the Holy Land."

"Exactly," Moshe replied. "And this danger from the Arabs is unfortunately compounded by the destruction—or opening up—of the Golden Gate."

"I don't understand," Leonard Rosenberg said.

"You should," the rabbi said, at last feeling free to talk. "American or not, you are a Jew and your ignorance is shameful." He sighed, shaking his head from side to side, too distraught to be angry. " *'I believe with perfect faith in the coming of the Messiah,'* " he said, quoting the great medieval Jewish thinker, Maimonides, " *'and though he tarry, I will wait daily for his coming.'* "

"No Jew would accept the destruction of a Christian chapel or Muslim graveyard as a sign that that man is the Messiah. That, Jozsef, would *surely* be blasphemous."

"Not Christian or Arab, Leonard. Naturally, what I refer to is the Golden Gate. . . . According to Jewish tradition it is through the Golden Gate that the Messiah will enter Jerusalem when He ushers in the Redemption. The Golden Gate has therefore been walled in for centuries, but that extraordinary storm destroyed the wall and thus re-opened the gate. This could, by itself, be explained as a freak of nature, but knowledge of that man from the Mount could complicate matters. Please remember your learning, Leonard. For we Jews the Messiah is the personality who will, through the power of the Most High, redeem Israel and inaugurate the sovereignty of Judaism. A descendant of the House of David, he will *not* be a supernatural being, nor will he be divine; rather, he will be a person of normal flesh and blood, but one with divine gifts or supernatural abilities. I risk blasphemy as I speak, but now the words must be spoken: that man from the Mount is very much flesh and blood, but his survival, at least so far, would appear to be supernatural—and we cannot ignore what might happen should this news be released."

He lowered his eyes and said no more, perhaps regretting what he had already said, and Moshe, looking around at each of the others in turn, felt the waves of disbelief washing over them and turning to fear. The fear was secular and religious, based on politics and faith, both of which were now being threatened by what remained unexplained. The unexplained was the event itself, what it had produced and might yet produce: that man of unknown origin and the inexpressible possibilities inherent in his return to the world of the living . . . his abrupt welding of the past to the present, perhaps to reshape the future. Moshe stared through the window, saw the sky above the Knesset, bright, flecked with white clouds, very real, defying what he was feeling. Weary, confused, longing to be out there in the real world, he returned his gaze to the room, looked at each of the men in turn, and saw General Meshel shrugging his broad shoulders and pursing his lips.

"Speculation," the general said.

"But relevant," Moshe replied. "If word of that man from the Mount gets out, it could lead to bad trouble."

"True," Ben Eliezer said. "So we have to keep him secret. We stick to our story of atmospheric phenomena, and ensure that Kate Hirschfield keeps her mouth shut."

"Kate Hirschfield is no problem," Moshe replied quickly, her image suddenly floating before him, resurrecting old griefs, returning him to that which had been lost and encouraging helpless need. "We're keeping her in the hospital for another week or so in the hopes that that man will revive. If he does, she'll be useful."

"How?"

"She's a psychiatrist. The man may be in a state of shock. His mental condition could in many ways be delicate; and if so, we'll need her."

"And she's agreeable?"

"She's obsessed," the rabbi said.

"That's why she'll stay silent."

Moshe stared directly at the rabbi, noticing the flush on his kindly face, understanding his grief and anger over Kate, and feeling sympathy for him.

"And Leon Halcomb?" the general asked.

"An anti-Semite," Leonard Rosenberg replied. "If he finds anything out, we'll be in trouble and he'll be a happy man."

"He's convinced we brought someone down—someone other than Kate Hirschfield—and I'd like to know who gave him the news."

"It's not news," Moshe said quietly. "It's probably more like a whisper. Someone probably told Leon about the second ambulance, but that doesn't mean much. Unfortunately the whisper had to come from inside—so we have to face the fact that his source was Jewish."

That silenced the conversation, made them glance at one another, each looking both guilty and outraged, wondering who had betrayed them.

"There are other matters," the rabbi said, his abundant flesh making him sweat, one brown hand reaching up to touch his skullcap before slipping back down to stroke his gray beard. "The Christian world, already shocked by the destruction of the chapel, is now incensed by our refusal to let their Jerusalem representatives—the formal caretakers of the chapel—examine the ruins and decide what to do about them. I have, as you know, received from the Papal See's apostolic delegate in Jerusalem, Monsignor Pio Lazzari, a formal complaint about this matter, and it places me in a delicate position. Since morally I cannot and will not lie about the situation, I have hesitated about replying to the complaint. Now I must either give him permission to take back control over that site or pass the matter into the hands of our security—which, of course, would be embarrassing."

"There is no problem," Ben Eliezer said. "That hole has been filled in. We bulldozed the rubble back to where it belongs, so the site can now be opened to official visitors, including the press. The Vatican is only interested in the chapel and cannot ask about unidentifieds; you can therefore reply, passing the site back to its Christian caretakers, and you will not be asked questions on matters that do not relate to the Rabbinate."

"In other words, I don't lie," the rabbi said. "I simply erase the full facts from my mind."

"That's right," Ben Eliezer said.

Moshe felt the rabbi's discomfort, the ambiguity of his position, perched, as he now was, on the painfully cutting edge that divided the whole truth from a form of deceit. Not the plain dishonesty of a deliberate lie, it was nonetheless a deception based on omission, morally questionable under any circumstances, more so for the rabbi. He knew what the rabbi was thinking and did not envy him his dilemma; already the presence of that man from the Mount was forcing them to alter their own judgments and accept compromise.

"That only leaves the Soviets and Americans," the general said.

"We simply stick to our original story," Ben Eliezer said. "The site is now open and they're welcome to inspect it; and when they do, since there is nothing to find, they might even believe us. Let them come and go home again; they'll find nothing but rubble—no scorching, no radioactivity—just the rubble left behind by an unusual earthquake that also affected other areas around Jerusalem. That's not a major problem and the opening of the site will simply help it. Our major problem lies with the Christians and the Arabs and our own Jews, and how they might react if they find out about that man from the Mount."

He looked at Moshe for confirmation, and Moshe felt sick to his soul, thinking of Kate in the hospital, of her dark, haunted eyes, of the rapture and dread that had made her turn away from that man and throw herself into his own arms. Moshe felt frightened and posses- sive, at once jealous and resentful, more resentful of that man than he had been of Leon Halcomb, more ashamed than he had ever felt before: humiliated by his own brimming selfishness. He looked at Ben Eliezer, at the rabbi, then through the window, his gaze drawn to the clean sweep of the sky where the sun had dominion. Then, putting his head down, keeping his hands flat on the table, he heard his own voice as if coming from far away, distanced by expanding webs of guilt and the shame of betrayal.

"I agree," he said. "We don't have a choice. We must keep that man buried."

17

The sun was sinking when Leon showed his press card to the guard at the wooden barrier that ran across the road, preventing entrance to the devastated area. The guard nodded at him, unsmiling but polite, then raised the barrier and let him walk through. Leon knew the area well, normally living in the hotel above it, but now, as he walked forward, the sky darkening over Jerusalem, he felt totally disoriented and unreal, as if in a dream.

The ruins were quiet and ominous, the dust drifting above the piled rubble, the breeze making an eerie hissing sound that complemented the barren scene. The tower of the Arab mosque, the Chapel of the Ascension, and the tomb of the prophetess Hulda which adjoined the chapel courtyard had originally filled the space between the Mount of Olives Hotel and the road that passed the Church of the Pater Noster; now that area seemed empty, strangely desolate and haunting, the piles of rubble blending in with the strip of waste ground at the opposite side of the road, beyond which, partly obscured behind a stone wall and trees, were the equally desolate evacuated Arab houses.

Moving to the left side of the road, his feet kicking up stones, Leon stepped carefully over the rubble of the fallen wall of the chapel courtyard and stopped near the remains of Hulda's tomb. A steel door lay in the rubble, painted light blue, covered in dust: the door that had led into the grounds of the Arab mosque, at the center of which had stood the Christian chapel. *Ridiculous*, Leon thought. *There's no sense to this country*. He stepped forward and saw shards of glass, pulverized mortar and drifting dust, parts of the Arabic inscription on the broken stone of Hulda's tomb, the television aerials that had been swept across the road from the small collection of modest Arab homes beyond the waste ground.

Leon stopped and looked around him, knowing that Kate had been found here, trying to remember the courtyard walls, the small, dome-shaped chapel, trying to visualize the storm sweeping over it with extraordinary ferocity. His imagination failed him, quietly defeated by the desolation, but the breeze, hissing eerily around his feet, made him shiver unnaturally.

What was he looking for? The earth scorched by an unknown force? The tracks of a bulldozer that had possibly pushed the rubble back over a hole of mysterious origin? Yes, he looked for signs, but his heart wasn't really in it: he had known from the moment that permission had been granted to come here that such permission would not have been granted if there were something to see. Moshe Eitan was not that stupid, and his men had been here for a week: scientists and engineers and security officers, then finally the bulldozers. *Not guards,* Leon thought. *Not your ordinary foot soldiers. They were not protecting people from the dangers of the ruins, but keeping them out while they thoroughly examined this site and then used the bulldozers to put the rubble back where it belonged. . . .* He glanced back at the road and saw the evidence of the earthquake: The cracks formed a jigsaw that covered the whole area and had possibly undermined the Arab houses. . . . *Fair enough,* he thought, *a good excuse for removing civilians . . . but those cracks are only wide enough to break a careless ankle and would certainly not account for the week-long banning of the press and the representatives of the Christian Church from the site. . . .* So there was a mystery —something covered up or removed—and now Leon, watching the shadows growing darker on the rubble, thought of Kate in the hospital near Ein Kerem and wondered why she was part of it.

To think about her made him hurt, the pain emanating from a sense of loss, the conviction that he had to enslave her soul in order to regain his own. Perhaps that's why he had come here, even knowing that he would find nothing: not just to see the ruins and try to imagine what might have happened, but in the hope that up here, where the mystery had begun, he might feel her presence all around him and take small comfort from it. He smiled even as he thought this, shaking his head in self-admonishment, realizing that the intensity of his feelings for Kate had reached a pitch that was almost religious. *Yes,* he thought bleakly, *my soul has become religious: from nihilism to commitment is the leap of a religious impulse; and now, in my inanity and weakness, even this sacred site, which before meant little to me, is wrapping its history around me and drawing me into it.*

The darkness was descending, casting its shadow on stone, and he looked at the rubble piled before him at eye level and realized that it was the Chapel of the Ascension. Could it be possible? Was the sacred rock buried down there? Had a man called Jesus, in the process of changing history, stood on this spot (his countenance like lightning, his raiment white as snow) before ascending to sit by God's right hand? Leon very seriously doubted it, but the imagery clung to him, surrounding him and drawing him in and revealing itself as Kate's dark eyes. He thought about her and tried to be her, trying to imagine her experience, stepping forward, stepping back, gazing around him at the gathering darkness, looking beyond the chilling ruins to the nearby Church of the Pater Noster where, it was believed, Jesus Christ had taught his disciples the Lord's Prayer. . . . *"Thy will be done in earth, as it is in heaven . . . For thine is the kingdom, and the power, and the glory . . ."* and, Leon thought, *the vain dreams of all men who could not accept their fleeting mortality.* He shivered and turned away, looking back from whence he had come, seeing the Mount of Olives Hotel, a glass-windowed cube of limestone, the guard standing at the barrier across the road, his Uzi gun pointing skyward.

"The real world," Leon said, speaking aloud to hear his own voice, hoping to jolt himself back to the objectivity he had lost when he drove toward the hills of Judea and saw Kate's face before him. "Liberty and democracy become unholy," he added, "when their hands are dyed red with innocent blood."

Such was Israel's dilemma, the source of its shame and glory, holding the Torah in one hand, a gun in the other, shedding the blood of the innocent, its enemy's and its own, in an unholy bid to preserve the Holy Land and ensure the dominion of Zion. Such a war might never end, and even now was continuing; and the mystery of the Mount, shrouded in secrecy and deception, almost certainly had to be tied not only to religious matters, but to very delicate political concerns.

Leon tried to work it out, but his reasoning failed him, confused by the return of his restless emotions and the conviction that the mystery that revolved around politics contained within its secular intrigues a much more personal dimension: that it had, at the very least, ripped the veils from his own shame and was now, in some inexplicable manner, binding him tighter to Kate.

He passed through the barrier, murmuring his thanks to the guard, and turned around in front of the hotel and looked back at the ruins. They were now surrendering to dusk, sinking back into darkness, and he wondered what it was he had hoped to find when he climbed up the steep hill. He had come to discover the truth that was being hidden by Moshe Eitan, but as he studied the ruins, glanced at the armed guard, thought of Kate, he was overwhelmed by the conviction that the mystery of the Mount was, apart from politics and the schemes of mortal men, a riddle that was drawing him closer to his own fractured image.

He removed his gaze from the ruins and walked away from the hotel, turning down toward the Garden of Gethsemane and its dark, silent slopes. The sky was now black, the stars bright and multitudinous, and he hastened down the crude, narrow road, between walls of rough stones. Here, in Gethsemane, Jesus had wept over Jerusalem; here the sweat of His agony had fallen to the ground as blood; and here, also, He had been betrayed and given birth to the Christian world. To remember this surprised Leon, casting him back to his Christian childhood, the days when he had believed all he read and held it close to his heart. Those days were long gone, their religious teachings undone, but now he marveled at how deep his roots went and at their will to survive. He had tried to uproot them, to cast them over the wall, but as he hurried down the road, the dark slopes still and quiet, he felt the tide of his history at his unprotected back, pressing down on his shoulders like the mystery he was still trying to solve.

He blinked and looked across the darkened slopes and heard a voice from below. At first he thought he was imagining things and shook his head, almost amused, but then he heard the voice again, very masculine and harsh, obviously coming from farther down the path, on the lower slopes of the Mount. The man was obviously shouting, his voice passionate and angry, sounding barbaric and unearthly in the night, echoing over the dark slopes. Leon listened, strangely moved, unable to understand the words, and then, slightly surprised at his own expectancy, he hurried on down the narrow road.

It did not take very long and he soon saw who was shouting: a man in his late fifties, very tall and emaciated, Caucasian, his skin burnt dark by the sun, beardless but with unwashed white hair that blew around his wild features. He was facing the Basilica of the Agony, standing up on the low stone wall, looking down on a crowd of people, both Arab and Jew, his arms raised and his black coat flapping loosely as he shouted his message. He was obviously some kind of preacher, certainly Christian and possibly mad, and as Leon, intrigued, stood behind the crowd and watched him, he stared fiercely up the slopes that led to the summit of the Mount, jabbing at the summit with one finger, his voice hoarse and outraged.

"They will not let us go up there!" he shouted at the crowd below him. "They will not let us go up there to see because they have denied Him! For He said, Let there be lights in the firmament of the heaven, to divide the day from the night! And let there be lights in the firmament of the heaven to give light upon the earth—*and it was so!* And He made two great lights—the greater light to rule the day and the lesser light to rule the night—but they will not let us go up there to see, *for up there was the light!*"

His right hand cut through the air, slashing down through the darkness, balling into a fist at his stomach as his body shook violently. Leon recognized the words, now distorted but still eloquent, and he felt the chill of dread, some cold and fathomless presentiment, as the old man threw his hands up in the air and started shouting again.

"They will not let us go up there to see because His light filled the dark void! Because He said, Let there be light—and there *was* light! And He saw the light and it was good; and He divided the light from the darkness. And He called the light Day, and the darkness He called Night; and up there, above the rock where He last touched the earth, *He made the light and darkness one and announced His returning!*"

He threw his hands out to the sky, his body curved, his black coat flapping, and the breeze, shivering through his long white hair, made it dance on his head. Leon watched, disbelieving, feeling the urge to walk away, but then the old man turned sideways, facing the slopes of the Mount of Olives, his finger jabbing up at the summit and his voice raging defiantly, and Leon almost lost his senses, the familiar words shattering reason, ricocheting in his brain with intimations of revelations, vaporizing even as he sensed them and leaving him drained.

Leon turned away from him, hurrying on down the hill, torn between revulsion and excitement, feeling touched by some madness. The stones rolled before his feet, tumbling down the dark slope, and then he stopped, hardly knowing what he was doing, and looked back up the ancient path. The old man was still preaching, his voice harsh and obsessed, towering over the silent people, the wind whipping his white hair, his arms raised above his head, fingers outstretched to the sky, while the stars, illuminating the darkness, swam around him in glory.

18

Kate felt weaker every minute, more light-headed, her body emptying, her thoughts drifting like smoke in the night, slowly turning, then vaporizing. She stared down at his face, at his closed eyes, his gray beard, at that mask of inhuman composure and impossible serenity. Her body glowed when she saw him, lighting up from within, the warmth reaching out to touch her cold skin and make amends for her failing strength. He was taking that strength from her, draining her to fill himself, and as his white chest rose and fell, his hands motionless by his sides, she was torn between rapture and fear, wondering what would become of him.

She studied him a long time, almost dreaming, twice removed, only aware that he was coming to life as her strength drained away. She reached down and felt his pulse, placed her hand over his heart, put her fingers to his lips to feel his breath, stroked his forehead, stepped back again. The past had been and gone and now returned to meet the future; between the past and the future was the present, out of which he had called her.

Suddenly frightened, she turned away and lay down on her own bed which was situated, parallel to his bed, at the opposite side of the room. She closed her eyes and breathed deeply, trying to still her beating heart, staring up at the white ceiling, feeling light, almost floating, her thoughts drifting to and fro and then dissolving into blankness and silence.

She slept and awakened, hearing murmuring and movement, turned her head and saw the doctors in white jackets leaning over his pale form. They were checking his heartbeat, his pulse and his breathing, leaning forward to study the EEG screen where a white line was flickering. Kate watched them, feeling nothing, her thoughts circling and returning, her body floating somewhere beneath her as if made of thin air. The men in the white coats seemed unreal, far away, their

voices muted, their hands rising and falling through striations of
sunlight in which, like the basic matter of life, motes of dust were at
play.

She turned away and closed her eyes, letting her body drift freely,
ignoring the doctors as they left him alone and surrounded her bed.
Her wrist was picked up and checked; the cold stethoscope touched
her breast; there were whispers about her weakening condition and its
mysterious cause. She felt amused but didn't smile, the amusement
fleeting and remote, dying away like a light being withdrawn and
fading out in the distant night. Then they moved away, still
whispering, and the door opened and closed, after which, feeling
grateful and at peace, she heard the hymn of his breathing.

She could still hear his breathing, felt his presence all around her,
and she wondered what would happen when he awakened and her
strength was all gone. This thought came and departed, a mere
whisper in her mind, and she raised her hand and spread her long
fingers, watching them shaking and falling. She was too weak even
for that, her body hollow, without feeling, as it had been after the
bloody abortion all those long years ago. Lost, but not forgotten, the
relentless specter of her dreams: the fetus turning in the Pool of
Siloam at His feet, His arms raised in forgiveness. Now she sighed,
her strength gone, the light shrinking in the darkness, heard the door
opening and closing and opened her eyes and saw Moshe looking
down at her.

"*Shalom*," he said quietly.

She could not immediately answer, feeling dizzy and unreal, her
thoughts circling like birds in a mist, resplendent in silence. Moshe
loomed very large above her, his shirt tight on broad shoulders, his
gray eyes, which were usually unrevealing, now strangely gentle. She
kept looking at him, taking comfort from his rugged face, noting the
scar on his left cheek, the broken nose and webbed lines, understanding that in some way she was drawn to his remote, private nature.

"How are you feeling?" he asked.

"Very weak," she replied. "My body feels totally drained and I
can't think too clearly."

"Any pain?"

"No pain."

"The doctors are baffled by your condition. As far as they can tell,
there's nothing wrong, yet you're fading away."

Kate smiled. "It doesn't matter. He's recovering . . . that's what matters. You shouldn't worry about what happens to me; he's the one you should think about."

"I worry," Moshe said.

"I thought you didn't approve of me."

"I'm not talking about approval," Moshe said. "It's the caring that matters."

"And you care for me?"

"Yes, Kate, I care."

"I'm surprised to hear that."

She smiled again and raised her hand, reached out toward him and let the hand drop, not really knowing what she was doing or what she was feeling, too tired to define it. Looking at Moshe, she saw the other, a different face, the same face, first Moshe and then the man from the Mount and then Moshe once more. He was looking down at her, not smiling, his gray eyes gentle, trying to suggest the words his tongue refused to speak, his meaning felt if not stated. She studied him calmly, drawn toward him, drifting into him and becoming him; and then, being of him and within him, gazed out of his gray, wounded eyes. She saw herself on the bed, her wasted body in the white smock, her cheeks hollow and her shivering lips dry, her long dark hair disheveled.

"I'm fading away," she said.

"Yes," Moshe said, "you are."

"Am I dying?"

"No, I don't think so. I think you're feeding that man."

"He's reviving?"

"Yes."

"That's important."

"I know it is."

"Moshe Eitan, that famous warrior and Zionist and private person, is not as harsh as his reputation would suggest."

She saw him smiling reluctantly, the humor finally reaching his eyes, and then she drifted up again, leaving her exhausted body behind, and dissolved into the mystery of his flesh and examined his grief. She saw dead eyes staring sunward, a skein of dark hair covered in sand, a woman and two children spread-eagled, the desert sky as white heat. As it was everywhere, so here, too, there was blood; now dry and matting the skein of dark hair and smearing the limbs of the children. His grief was lacerating, tearing the skin from her own wounds, and she shrank and retreated to herself, staring up from the small bed.

"Don't grieve so much," she said.

"I'm not grieving," he replied. "I'm concerned that you should be in this condition and I'm wondering what caused it."

"You know what," she said.

"I know it's him; I don't know how."

"It's not me you're concerned with—it's him: you're wondering where he came from."

"Not only that, Kate."

"You're also wondering *who* he is."

"Yes," he agreed, "both those questions bother me. But you bother me, also."

"Why?"

"That should be obvious."

"Nothing is ever obvious."

"It's the concern of one human being for another. It's not all that uncommon."

He was no longer smiling and his gravity touched her heart, as did his hesitation to express his true meaning: his need to couch it in clichéd generalities. She thought of the dead eyes staring sunward, the woman and children spread-eagled, and wondered why that vision, with its connotations of Moshe's past, should have come to her at this particular moment. His great tragedy had been well publicized, but she had never known the precise details; and now, growing weaker, her thoughts increasingly fractured, she was convinced that the dead eyes staring sunward were the eyes of his family. Yet how could she know that? As she weakened, so her mind seemed to expand to take in past and future. The other lay in the bed opposite, breathing evenly, reviving, and as He came back to life, taking her physical strength, so He seemed to be compensating her with unusual powers.

"There's no need for concern," she said.

"Concern is natural, Kate."

"I feel frightened for him; not for myself. I even feel strangely happy."

"Happy?"

"All warm."

"Your temperature's dropping."

"I feel warm."

"You're not warm, you're cold. Your skin is cold to touch. Your heartbeat is slow, your circulation is all wrong, and you haven't been able to eat for two days. There's no reason. We're worried."

"Don't."

"You should sleep."

"I'm *always* sleeping."

"Then sleep a bit more."

She smiled and closed her eyes, oddly comforted by his presence, and let herself drift toward the light that rose out of the darkness. The light grew like a white flower, its petals unfolding, stretching out in every direction to divide the darkness and reduce its domain. Then the light warmed her, surrounded and enveloped her, and she felt her spirit expanding across the void to explore the unknown. Past and future were as one, the frozen moment of His existence, and His growing, which flowered around her in majesty and silence, was the sign that she would soon be renewed.

"All right," she said, "I'll sleep."

"Good," Moshe replied.

"Don't stay away for too long. I think he'll soon wake up."

"No, I don't think so. I think it's too early. His pulse and heartbeat are improving but they're still much too slow; and his temperature, though rising steadily, is even lower than yours."

"Have you made an estimation?"

"A few more days."

"No," Kate said. "You're wrong."

She opened her eyes when she heard his sigh, saw him shrugging his broad shoulders, reaching up to stroke the small scar on his cheek, as if reminded of old pain. He was looking steadily at her, his gray eyes very grave, studying her with a muted intensity that said more than words could. She realized this dimly, in some distant recess of her mind, but her feelings at that moment all belonged to the other who, breathing evenly in the adjacent bed, was dominating her senses.

"So," Moshe said, "I'll go."

"Yes," she replied. "I'm fine."

"Don't forget to ring the bell if you need anything."

"Don't worry, I won't."

He leaned forward and then stopped himself, straightened up and pursed his lips, then nodded, gave a hesitant smile, and turned around and walked out. Kate watched the door closing, feeling mildly desolated, then she turned her head and looked across the room at the one in the other bed.

He was lying flat on his back, a sheet covering his lower body, his hands by his sides, the sensors attached to his wrists and chest, dark wires running from his head to the EEG machine, his profile silhouetted in the striations of sunlight pouring obliquely through the window just above him. He looked like a dead man, horizontal, very straight, but his chest rose and fell as he breathed in and out, and Kate, hearing the sound of that breathing, felt herself straining toward him.

She closed her eyes and put her head back, trying to slip into his mind, saw the darkness, then light, a spot of light growing larger, a pulsating light that soon became a sun obliterating the Nothing. The Nothing was her own body, the void created by His need, but now the light, which was He, giving birth to His being, flared out to touch the darkness with glory and return her to wholeness.

The darkness rolled back, the seas parted, the land appeared, the herb yielded seed and the tree yielded fruit, and the moon and the sun shared the heavens and let the stars shine in glory. Out of the whirlwind came His voice, giving substance to the silence, and the seed, which was scattered on His breath, brought the years and their seasons. He wept over His creation, moved by pity and love, and His tears formed the clouds and shed rain upon the stones of the Earth. The waters were abundant and the skies received the living, and the dry land grew green and fed the beasts both in darkness and light. To be whole, He became, and cast Himself around the firmament, and saw that His creation, which was good, was devoid of His image. And He breathed and raised the dust, and into the dust He breathed His life, and His image rose up and was touched with the wonder of innocence. In this innocence was dread, the isolation of singularity, and He, observing the reflection of His own anguish, split His image in two. She sprang forth from the other, to the fierce and blinding light, the female to his male, the plurality of his Oneness, and then He came out of the whirlwind and touched her to give life to the living.

Kate experienced great joy, a transcendental exultation, and felt the life pouring back into her flesh as He awakened to sunlight. She turned her head and saw him moving, raising his right hand and clenching his fist, flexing his fingers to feel his coursing blood and confirm his existence. The hand dropped back to his side, and he breathed deeply, his head unmoving, still silhouetted in the sunlight pouring obliquely from the window above him.

Renewed, Kate sat up, her heart pounding, her blood warm, released from the languor of exhaustion, her skin alive and receptive. She felt fearful and triumphant, filled with love and trepidation, and as she swung her long legs off the bed, her thoughts collided and scattered. The room expanded and contracted, the light flared up and died, and she blinked and licked her lips and walked forward toward the inpouring sun. The sun was the light, a stream of gold above his head, illuminating the naked contours of his face as she reached out to touch him.

He stared at her, not startled, his eyes silvery-gray and neutral, reflecting light and her miniaturized image in some space beyond knowing. His serenity was absolute, a beginning and ending, couched in the acceptance of being and brooking no doubts. Kate looked and was enslaved, transported out of her self, surrendering to the imperative of his presence and embracing his will. She gazed down and was frozen, no longer able to act, simply waiting, with the patience of the lost, for his words to reveal her.

"*Be*," he said, and thus became, his voice the signature of his birth, a whisper resonant with innocence and wisdom, at once a statement and order. "*Fore*," he said after a pause, his lips shivering with the effort, as if the word were an indecipherable hieroglyphic, barbaric and strange. "*Abra*," he added, staring at Kate, destroying the myth of her maturity, the word conjuring up the mysteries of her childhood with its promise of magic. "*Ham*," he said, raising his right hand, studying his fingers, looking puzzled, as if the word, ricocheting in his head, had led him into confusion. "*Was*," he said, dropping his hand, his silvery-gray eyes focused inward, gazing back along the years to some beginning in the mists of lost time. "*Was I*," he continued, speaking slowly, savoring the words, tentatively knitting them together in search of sense, being foiled, almost sighing. "*I*," he said, isolating it, inching along the blade of meaning, letting the word drop like a pebble on ice, ringing lightly in Kate's ears.

"Before *Abraham* . . . was I," he said, trying to place the emphasis, raising his head and then letting it fall again, as if too weak to move. "Before Abraham *was* . . . I," and then he seemed to sigh again, the ages whispering as they glided through the silence of his interminable pause.

He closed his eyes and licked his lips, breathing evenly, his hands at rest, confused and yet perfectly calm, accepting one for the other. He lay thus for a long time, relaxed, very human, his body colored by rays of golden sunlight, his bearded face strangely ageless. Then he looked up at Kate, his silvery-gray eyes hypnotizing, drawing her in to distant moons and wheeling stars and unsung planets, then reached up and touched her shoulder, his fingers exploring flesh and bone, and then took a deep breath, experimenting with his lips, and eventually, triumphantly, yet perhaps with a hint of sadness, gasped the words of revelation and faith and ineradicable commitment.

"*I am,*" he said.

PART THREE:

Ministry

"Think not that I am come to destroy the law, or the prophets: I am not come to destroy, but to fulfil."

—Matthew, 5:17

". . . and upon this rock I will build my church; and the gates of hell shall not prevail against it. And I will give unto thee the keys of the kingdom of heaven: and whatsoever thou shalt bind on earth shall be bound in heaven; and whatsoever thou shalt loose on earth shall be loosed in heaven."

—Matthew, 16:18–19

MURDER?

Think not that I am come to destroy the law, or
the prophets: I am not come to destroy, but to
fulfill.

—Matthew, 5:17

. . . and upon this rock I will build my
church; and the gates of hell shall not prevail
against it. And I will give unto thee the keys of
the kingdom of heaven: and whatsoever thou
shalt bind on earth shall be bound in heaven: and
whatsoever thou shalt loose on earth shall be
loosed in heaven.

—Matthew, 16:18, 19

19

Having spoken, he fell silent, his brow furrowed in thought, as if his words, springing out of the vast silence of his gestation, had unlocked the door to human doubt. His confusion was obvious, rippling across his prismatic blankness, shadowing his impossible serenity and etching fine lines in his face. He blinked and gazed at Kate, his silvery-gray eyes growing dimmer, still magnetic but less alien than before, the pupils shrinking to normal size. Then he stared around the room, pursed his lips experimentally, raised his right hand, then his left, turned them slowly, flexed his fingers, taking in the geometry of flesh and bone before letting them fall again.

Kate stared at him, speechless, both exultant and disbelieving, his words echoing in her mind and fading away to leave a threatening silence. Why threatening? She wasn't sure. It was something in his silence; something forcing her to concentrate on his face and its subtle metamorphosis. The same face, yet different, altered almost imperceptibly: his skin neither white nor dark, his features faintly Semitic, the dark beard flecked with gray, the eyes now also gray, his serenity finally shattered by awareness and unspoken questions.

Staring at him, Kate felt dazed, her emotions in turmoil, trying to reconcile her excitement and fear and take a grip on her senses. She shook her head from side to side, her thoughts spinning and colliding, only aware, as she reached out for the bell above the bed, that her heart was beating dangerously fast. His eyes followed her shaking hand, saw the bell, returned to Kate, and her hand, which was dangling in the air, seemed to freeze of its own accord.

"No," he said, speaking quietly, his voice gently commanding, slipping through the silence like the blade that hypnotizes its victim. She heard the voice, or felt it, and her hand dropped away, still shaking as it hung by her side, the fingers opening and closing. She stared at him, confused, wanting to protect him and frightened of him, feeling even in the warmth of her concern that his presence was dangerous.

"Who are you?" she asked, and her fear disappeared immediately, giving way to concern and a strange kind of love as he blinked, glanced around him, and again looked confused, shaking his head gently from side to side and stroking his beard.

"I don't know," he said, his voice soft and oddly resonant, speaking English with an untraceable accent, his words clear and precise.

"Do you know where you are?"

"Where I belong," he replied. "I only know that I am where I belong and that time will reveal me." He looked directly at her, his gray eyes compelling, while the early-evening light, growing dimmer, sketched dark lines on his face. "You have been with me for a long time," he said. "What is willed, will be done."

"What is . . . *willed*?"

"It was willed."

He looked away, almost startled, as if someone else had spoken, his eyes widening and studying the sunlight fading over his face. . . . A gray light, on gray eyes, the eyes merging with the light, disappearing until his head turned slightly and the pupils contracted. He was still lying down, his upper body pale and lean, his lower body covered in the white sheet, his hands clasped on his stomach. When he looked along his own body, saw the sensors on his chest and wrists, his brow furrowed in puzzlement. He sighed, almost smiled, then used his right hand to tug the sensor off his left wrist, reversed the procedure to remove the sensor from his right wrist, then tugged the sensors off his chest, and raised his hands to his head as if about to remove the EEG wiring. His hands stopped in midair, hovering just above his forehead, then his brow creased in thought and his hands started shaking, moving away and then coming back again, the fingers outstretched and searching. He sighed, took a deep breath, then removed the metal cap, stared at it and shuddered a little, and then threw it away. It hit the far wall and then bounced on the floor, ringing out like a bell, and Kate felt her body twitching with shock before his gray eyes returned to her. He studied her for a very long time, breathing evenly, calmly.

"No fear," he said eventually, his voice hollow, almost echoing, an ethereal sound that writhed through the silence to reach out and touch her. "In my dreams, which were many, was this one recurring lesson: The darkness will roll back to reveal the light and there is no need to fear. Now, I am confused, and my words are not my own, and in my ignorance I only know one thing: that I do not know what fear is."

Kate opened her mouth to speak but no sound came out immediately, and she licked her dry lips and rubbed her eyes, feeling renewed but unreal.

"You remember nothing?" she managed to say.

"The long darkness," he replied. "The light grew out of darkness and the dreams were mere fragments that comforted."

Kate thought of her own dreams, which had blossomed as her body weakened, filling her with the love and fear that now bound her to the man on the bed. He was breathing deeply and evenly, his gray eyes fixed on the ceiling, his fine-boned hands resting by his sides, not moving at all.

"I feel weary," he said. "I have slept a long time. My body is weak and my mind is no more than an empty well. Who speaks? My voice is strange. The fragments float in a darkness. The Teacher of Righteousness is with me, and once showed me the way."

"The Teacher of Righteousness?"

He glanced at her in confusion, his face creased and more human, his lips shivering with the effort of speaking the very words that confused him.

"Yes," he said, "the Teacher of Righteousness. He came before me and showed the way. In the darkness of the caves, which in darkness I could see, were the scrolls revealing the lineaments of the life that gave shape to my own." He slowly raised his pale hands, spread his fingers and placed them around his head to gently rock it from side to side. "My head is empty," he continued. "Filled with light, containing nothing. I cannot plan my words and my speech belongs elsewhere; it comes forth from the emptiness inside and must be a foundation. The Tower of Babel, reaching Heaven, scattered words across the Earth; and those words, of which I drank, remain with me as light to the darkness. The foundation is language, that which webs the incompati-

ble, and my words, which I do not understand, will in time weave my
meaning."

Kate listened and then leaned upon the mystery of his speech,
drawn in on the ambiguity of his words and their haunting, faintly
familiar resonance. . . . Familiar? Yes. It was the resonance of her
childhood memories: the words, often strange and obtuse, that had
been preached in the synagogue. She was startled, a little frightened,
unable to accept what she was hearing; but he drew her eyes toward
him, his own gray gaze luminous, and she felt herself surrendering to
his will as the fear fell away again.

"Where am I?" he asked.

"In Israel," Kate replied.

"What is Israel?"

"A country . . . a place . . . You don't know this at all?"

"This is part of the Earth," he said. "I know the Earth is but part of
the whole. I also know that the Earth, which abides and will endure, is
where I have walked and will walk until the darkness descends
again."

"You've been here before?"

"Yes."

"You remember?"

"I *know*. I stand upon the rock of my faith and have no cause to
question it."

He moved his head a little, surveyed the room, closed his eyes,
murmured something, and then opened his eyes again, staring up at
the ceiling.

"How do you feel?" Kate asked.

"Feel?"

"I mean your body."

"My body is whole," he replied, "but of little importance." He
spread the fingers of both hands, pressed them down on the bed, and
then, with what seemed to be a great effort, slowly pushed himself
upright. He shook his head from side to side, shrugged his shoulders,
stretched his spine, then sat there, his arms angled behind him, his
body pale in the darkening light. "Blood and flesh," he said.
"Feeling . . ."

Kate took a step forward, wanting to reach down and touch him,
but then, having made that one step, remained where she was. She felt

remote from herself, both fearful and excited, all her senses concentrated on the face of the man on the bed. A contradictory face, at once gentle and imperious, the face of an ancient prophet or warrior, beautiful and fierce. The afternoon light was gray, the room darkening, growing colder, and Kate shivered, feeling lost and ineffectual, wondering what she could say to him. This problem, unexpected but real, was soon solved when he looked at her.

"Where did you find me?"

"You remember nothing?"

"No."

"You were in some sort of tomb on the summit of the Mount of Olives. That tomb—or whatever it was—appeared to have been buried there, but we don't understand how it got there."

"I must see it," he said.

"You can't see it," Kate replied. "It disintegrated, leaving nothing but dust. Now there's nothing to see."

He did not seem perturbed. "Dust to dust," he murmured. "Life rose from the dust and returns to it when we pass over to the other side."

"The other side?"

"The real world."

He swung his legs off the bed and placed his feet on the floor, his toes, very white, the nails long, curling down to the tiles. "Cold," he murmured and leaned forward, rocking slightly to check his balance, letting his feet take the weight of his body, his toes rising and falling. The room was growing darker, shadows gathering in the four corners, but the light from the window, now a gray haze, slanted down on his shoulders. He stood up very slowly, as if checking that he could do so, and the white sheet fell to the floor with a rustling sound. Kate saw only his eyes, now closing, now opening, silvery-gray and wandering restlessly around the room, very bright and intense. He stared at her as if trying to recognize her, then ran his hands lightly down his face and gazed up at the ceiling.

"I remember little," he said, "but the fragments are enough, increasing with each passing moment and giving shape to my thoughts. I am calm and unafraid. I speak these words before I know them. My coming was ordained in the scrolls in the dark caves, the rituals of my drama rehearsed by the Teacher of Righteousness. I know the name, but not the man. His face is blank, his source a mystery. He was there before I came into being, long ago, in a strange land."

"What land?"

"That is unknown. The sun shines on parched earth. A land of great beauty and desolation, where man's spirit abides."

"How long ago?"

"I do not know where or when. I know of a time before my own, but in my mind they are one. My memories are like clouds, now obscuring, now revealing, offering isolated glimpses of things that do not make sense to me: a people called the Essenes, the curled edges of ancient scrolls, a drachma, a denarius, a pinnacle of stone, the presentation of a child in the Court of Gentiles when his keepers, male and female, offered the winged creatures as sacrifice."

Kate shivered, feeling cold, frightened by what she was hearing, but hypnotized by the glittering brilliance of his gray eyes and his extraordinary bearing.

"You mentioned the Court of Gentiles," she said. "Do you know what that was?"

"No. I can only see it. The recollection is very clear. The sun shines on the sloping stone and colonnades and makes everything bright. There is a barrier. The Court of Women. I do not know what such names mean. The Court of Women or the Court of the Israelites . . . perhaps one and the same." He closed his eyes and shook his head, pressed his right hand to his brow, removed the hand and let it fall to his side, and then looked straight at her. "The Court of the Israelites," he said. "And you say I am in Israel. . . . The child of which I speak was myself, the presentation near here."

Kate's feeling of unreality deepened, increasing her fear and awe, unraveling all the teachings of her past and leaving her naked. She stared at the wall above his bed, wanting to press the alarm bell, but his gaze, at once calm and commanding, seemed to paralyze her muscles. She felt her senses sliding away, releasing her buried primal self, and she stifled the scream rising from her center and cloaked it with faltering words.

"A . . . presentation?"

"A sacrifice."

"What kind of sacrifice?"

"The child, being myself, was of age and was confirmed in His presence. The sacrifice . . . relates to this."

Again he stopped talking, the doubt rippling across his face, while the light, growing darker each minute, turned his body to stone.

"I think my keepers were my parents. I was wrapped in swaddling clothes. They carried me up some steps to the just and devout one who confirmed the uniqueness of my birth. And the prophetess, also, serving then in the temple, looked upon me as the light of redemption and offered thanks to the Lord. And the priest took one of the birds to the lower corner of the altar, wrung its neck and sprinkled its blood on the altar and then put it aside. The other bird was then killed, but also gutted and salted, its blood offered to the top of the altar, its carcass thrown to the flames."

Kate thought of distant times, of strange temples under the sun, of men in robes sacrificing birds upon an altar of flames. This vision filled her mind, briefly obliterating his features, pushing back the walls of the room and letting the past live again. The sky was a white haze, the land harsh and awesome, and the great walls of stone materialized like a mirage in the wilderness. Surveying it, she was part of it, her shadow etched on the temple floor, and she held the precious child to her breast while the altar flames flickered. The child was father to the man, the man destined to change history, and she closed her eyes and opened them again to see the one who was full grown.

He was standing in the same place, his gray eyes slipping away, and the walls of the room moved back in to reinstate some reality. Kate stared at him, speechless, unnerved by what he had made her witness, then was calmed by the sound of his voice, strangely distant yet resonant.

"I do not know what that means, but I remember my own infancy. Between the events of that day and my thirteenth year there is nothing at all. My thirteenth year was my true beginning. I know this because I utter it. I see the priests in the shadows of the colonnades of the temple, and know that in their presence I waxed strong in spirit and wisdom. I forsook my father and mother, learned detachment and concentration, and assumed my responsibilities as a student of the affairs of the Most High."

He turned away from her, examined the door of the room, then took a step forward, very slowly, as if learning to walk. His second step was also hesitant, his third taken with greater confidence, then he walked up to the door and turned around and walked back to her. He stopped in front of her and took a deep breath, looking down at his own feet, raised and lowered his arms and walked away and stopped once more in front of her. His gray eyes, gleaming unnaturally in the deepening gloom, drew her into their depths; in those depths there was flame and smoldering flesh and the bleached bones of history.

"At first you knew nothing," Kate murmured dreamily, "but now you're remembering things . . ."

"Mere fragments," he replied. "They pass through my thoughts like clouds. My infancy, my thirteenth year in the temple, then my first great temptation. Between these, there is nothing but the darkness and the silence of passing time."

"Your parents?"

"I don't know."

"And the Teacher of Righteousness?"

"I don't know. . . . Someone who lived before my time and recorded my coming."

"This awakening?"

"No," he said. "My former awakening . . . in that time I now speak about."

Kate shivered and lost herself, retreating back into her mind, gazing out of the long tunnels of her eyes at the creature before her. His face was now more human, etched with lines of experience, gaunt, almost primitive, yet inexplicably civilized and noble, touched with strange beauty. He was a normal human being, a creature of flesh and blood, but his genesis and the speed of his recovery had contradicted such facts. Staring at him, Kate felt childish, returned to innocence, filled with wonder, overwhelmed and frightened and excited, cast adrift from the rational world. The mystery of his presence teased her, threw her from one shore to the other; then, drowning in quiet desperation, she sank down through her deepest fears.

"What else do you remember?" she asked him, hardly hearing her own voice.

"I see a ribbon of water. A line of people stretches to it. I wade in the water and am dazzled by the sun, and the man with the face of a prophet takes hold of my shoulders. He immerses me in the water, crying words I cannot hear, and I rise up as the heavens open out and a white dove appears." He stopped talking and closed his eyes, looking back into his past, obviously trying to weave some meaning from his words, bowing his head in defeat. "I do not know what this means, but I know that it was willed; and after it—how long I cannot say—I was tempted and tested."

Kate started to speak but immediately forgot what she wanted to ask, the sound of his voice emptying her mind and letting him pour himself into it.

"I see myself in the wilderness, refusing to turn stone to bread; on a mountain with the desert at my feet and the Evil One whispering. He, who is my opposite, wishes to tempt me but fails; he then guides me to a pinnacle of the temple beneath the sun, where, to challenge my powers, he commands me to throw myself down and let the angels protect me. I refuse to tempt the Lord as the Evil One tempts me; and after this, turning away from his seductions, I embark on my calling."

Fascinated, Kate stared at him, hardly aware of his nakedness, her gaze drawn to the glittering gray of his eyes and their invincible calmness. He was not returning her gaze, but instead was looking inward, his brow wrinkled as he tried to survey the voids between his sparse recollections. Then he raised his eyes again, looking at her and into her, his power flowing out all around her to render her helpless. She held her breath and clenched her fists, experiencing fear and love at once, wanting desperately to press the bell on the wall but unable to do so.

"You still don't know who you are?"

"No," he replied. "The words offered tell all there is to know for the present; perhaps time, if not obstructed, will reveal more. . . . I have patience. You must practice it."

He looked directly at her, his gray eyes unblinking, growing brighter in the deepening darkness and resembling cats' eyes. Kate shivered, more confused, no longer sure of his nature, thinking of good and evil, of purity and amorality, and wondering what the voids in his recollections might eventually reveal.

"The words uttered," he continued, "were uttered before I knew them, but already I am learning to express my thoughts and color the voids. Soon I will be full grown, my body and spirit one; and then, by the grace of the Most High, I will learn of my purpose. In the meantime, until time itself reveals me, you will stand by my right hand."

An imperious request, offered quietly and implacably, it cut through Kate's confusion and doubt to leave only the fear. She tore her eyes from his face and stared wildly at the wall, thought of Moshe, and then raised her right hand to press the alarm bell. Yet even as she made this move, her fingers wavering in the gloom, she was bathed in a wave of heat, her raised arm became numb, and she thought she heard his voice inside her head, a sound stripping her senses. She stepped back, her heart pounding, wanting to scream but simply gasping, the breath drawn from her lungs by the wave of heat that seemed to pour from his body. Then the light flared up around him, a shimmering haze distorting his features, and Kate blinked and it faded away, taking with it the burning heat. Kate gasped and licked her lips, trying to control her pounding heart, then fearfully, helplessly, as if no longer in charge of herself, she dropped her hand and looked directly at his eyes, hypnotized by their brilliance.

"What is that?" he asked.

"It's a bell . . . to call those listening."

"Those listening?"

"We're being taped. They can hear us in another part of the hospital. But they won't come until I ring the bell. They want to talk to you, also."

"They are men of authority?"

"Yes."

"That is good," he said. "With such men I can give and receive and eventually find revelation. What is willed, will be done."

The brilliance faded from his eyes and the room returned to normal as he stepped back, gave an audible sigh, and then nodded at her. The fear fell away from her and was replaced with a protective love as inexplicable as the paralysis that had preceded it. She was transported out of herself, her will now his will, and she stepped forward and saw in his gaunt face a terrible weariness. He covered that weariness with his hands, bowed his head and murmured something, then moved away and sat down on the bed, leaning forward, breathing deeply. Kate was overcome with emotion, with a desperate, overwhelming yearning, and she turned aside, too shaken to say anything, and pressed the bell with one finger.

She stood there for some time, keeping her finger on the bell, thinking of the bright star, of the storm advancing toward her, of the black monolith rising out of the rubble, of Moshe holding her in that ultimate darkness as their hearts beat together. She also thought of the stranger's recovery, of her own weakening as he grew stronger, of her dreams about his life growing out of the void and her belief that a bond existed between them and might never be broken. And then she thought of his mesmeric powers, of the light and heat that had emanated from him; and she shook, feeling fear and love at once, and wondered what was to come.

Footsteps raced along the corridor and then stopped outside the door; Kate looked up as the door opened and Moshe walked into the room, his eyes, also gray, very bright and intense as he stared at her, nodded, then studied the man on the bed, obviously shaken by the revelation of his recovery. The man raised his head, spread his hands out in the air; then, his face still gaunt with that terrible weariness, and yet, in contradiction, almost radiant with inner calm, quietly offered the words that gave substance to his being and separated him from all other men.

"My name is Joshua," he said.

20

Leaving the hospital in the early hours of the morning, walking away from the room in which the miraculous had occurred and his own world, once orderly, had exploded, Moshe felt his heart beating and electrifying his blood, while his thoughts, uncontrollable, swirled around the image of Kate, her dark eyes reflecting rapture and fear before the man from the Mount. He stopped once and took a deep breath, blinked his eyes, and glanced around him, seeing the long reception area, very quiet, almost empty, trying to will himself to accept that it was real and not part of a strange dream. A medical orderly walked past, his white smock rustling in the silence, and Moshe bit his upper lip and then walked on, heading straight for the exit.

Kate's face floated before him, making his heart pound all the more, drawing his buried self out of its tomb and resurrecting his lost hopes. He thought of his wife and children, of how their deaths had affected him, and understood that the appearance of the man from the Mount was, with its mystery and terrifying implications, tearing him from the rock of his former self-control and leaving his emotions, long hidden from further wounding, exposed and responsive to Kate's presence.

He walked through the swinging doors and stopped again on the top step, breathing deeply of the chill morning air and gazing up at the cloudy sky. There were no stars up there and the silence was complete, but he felt, as he had never felt before, that the void was alive. What manner of man was he? What had kept him alive? Moshe remembered the ringing bell, his urgent race along the corridor, the door opening to reveal Kate's haunted eyes, the naked man just behind her. After that it became unreal, a mere confusion of noise and motion, people coming and going as in a dream because no one could grasp it. Moshe recalled it unclearly, still too dazed to take it in: the startling words on the tape recording, the interrogations leading nowhere, the man's ambiguous recollections and invincible calm as Kate, like someone caught in a trap, retreated into herself. Once Moshe reached out to touch her, ignoring the doctors and security officers, and this memory—of his fingertips at her pale cheek—had a pure, brilliant clarity. All else was but a dream that would surely soon dissolve: the security officers taking over, the man facing them with frightening ease, the door finally shutting him in as Kate was led along the corridor and laid down on a bed in another room. Moshe had stood by her bedside, looking down at her closing eyes, wanting to drown in her lips, on her body, and walking out with reluctance. Was it logical? No. But it had exploded his last defenses. Confusion and fear, love and yearning and pain, had rolled over him and swept him away from the chains of his past.

Moshe knew what was happening to him, but he didn't quite know why; it had started on the Mount of Olives when he first laid eyes on Kate and saw, in the stricken darkness of her face, his wife and children in death. A nightmare and dream, a beginning and ending: the ending of his self-willed emotional isolation, and the beginning of his obsession with Kate and her strange, secret pain. So it was happening and he had to accept it; but now, as he stood and watched the dark clouds in the black sky, he could no longer ignore the nagging possibility that Kate's helpless involvement with the man from the Mount was, like his own helpless involvement with Kate, preordained and impossible to break.

Moshe lit a cigarette, inhaled deeply and blew the smoke out, then walked down the steps and turned left toward the small, modern synagogue. Still shaken by what had happened, his every thought including Kate, he was startled out of his reverie when a dark figure emerged from beneath the Marc Chagall windows of the synagogue. Moshe froze where he stood, his body tensing for action, but then, as the shadowy figure walked forward, he recognized Leon Halcomb.

"Not you again," he said.

Leon stopped just in front of him, swaying slightly and steadying himself, removing a silver hip flask from his lips and grinning laconically. He had obviously been up all night and was clearly very drunk, his tie loose, his face sagging with exhaustion, his eyes blinking repeatedly.

"An early morning call," he said, grinning, "but I've been waiting for hours."

"What for?"

"A few answers."

"You're drunk."

"That's very true."

"I'm not accustomed to talking to drunkards, particularly at this time of the morning. Go to bed, Leon. Sleep it off."

Leon winked and cocked his head, waving one hand in refusal, leaning forward and then straightening up again, trying to keep his eyes open.

"Unpleasant, Major General. Not sociable. I'm only doing my duty."

"What duty?"

"The journalist *par excellence* never sleeps. You should know that by now."

"This is ridiculous. Get out of my way, Leon."

"No."

"If you don't move, I'll have you arrested."

"Kindly have me arrested."

Moshe sighed and shook his head, feeling contempt rather than anger, then, remembering the relationship between Kate and Leon, let the anger and bitterness swell through him. He tried not to think about it, to retain his objectivity, but a vision of Leon and Kate coiled together simply filled up his head. He looked at Leon and dropped his eyes, trying to obliterate the image, then shook his head slowly from side to side, shame and guilt whipping through him.

"All right," he said, wearily raising his head. "What is it this time?"

"The same as always," Leon said.

"You know that's not possible."

"Why?"

"We have our reasons."

"Either let me see Kate or give me a reasonable explanation. Damn it, Moshe, you know you've no right to hold her, and I'll soon have to use that fact."

"Any mention of Kate in your column and you'll be out of this country."

Leon visibly stiffened, his shoulders straightening, his hip flask motionless, the hand holding the flask near his lips, his eyes staring across it. Moshe saw his eyes clearly, even through the starless night, and realized that Leon, if drunk, had not lost his sharp wits. For a moment he almost admired him—or at least respected his tenacity

—but then when Leon grinned, offering the blade of his mockery, Moshe felt his detestation returning like phlegm in the throat.

"Are you threatening to deport me?" Leon said dryly.

"Something like that," Moshe replied.

"Then you must be holding Kate against her will."

"No, Leon, we're not."

"She can't still be in shock."

"I'm not at liberty to discuss her condition."

"Nor, may I assume, are you willing to expand on your rather curt answers."

"You assume quite correctly."

Leon grinned and dropped his eyes, studying the darkness around his feet, nodding his head as if talking to himself and then raising his eyes again.

"This is a very strange business," he said softly. "I just can't work it out."

"I'm not sure what you're getting at, Leon. We've discussed all this before. There's nothing more to add. The destruction was caused by some unknown phenomenon and those people, including Kate, are being kept under observation for that reason."

"What about the Soviet and American belief that something actually crashed on the Mount of Olives?"

"Nothing crashed and you know it. If anything had crashed on the Mount of Olives, Kate would not be alive right now."

"It could have been something small," Leon insisted. "Perhaps a satellite exploded and part of it—a very valuable part—destroyed that church on the Mount."

"You've been reading the wrong newspapers," Moshe replied.

"Well," Leon said, "we can only hope that you come up with a rational explanation pretty soon, because apart from my personal interest in getting Kate out of there, the lack of an explanation is already starting to cause you embarrassment."

"You've lost me again, Leon. Absolutely."

Leon nodded and grinned, obviously amused at Moshe's denial, then he put the hip flask to his lips, had a drink, lowered the flask, then wiped his lips with the back of his right hand and kept his clear eyes quite steady.

"You know exactly what I mean, Moshe Eitan. You know exactly what the Chapel of the Ascension, the Golden Gate, and the Muslim graveyard mean to certain Christians, Jews, and Muslims respectively. It's no secret at all that the Christians are extremely disturbed by the destruction of the Chapel of the Ascension and are demanding a coherent explanation. Nor is it a secret that the opened graves in the Muslim graveyard have encouraged a lot of Arabs to believe that the Day of Judgment is at hand—and that last week there were moderately violent demonstrations by some of those Arabs. Finally, word of mouth has it that the recent embarrassing clash between Neturei Karta zealots and your own conscript troops started because the zealots wished to worship at the Golden Gate and were incensed that that area, like the Muslim graveyard, had been cordoned off. Word of mouth, frequently reliable, also insists that those zealots are convinced that the opening of the sealed Golden Gate is a sign that the Messiah will soon be coming to usher in the Redemption."

Moshe felt his heart beating fast, but he kept his gaze steady, trying to look more assured than he felt, a distant fear creeping toward him.

"I'm tired of this," he said. "It's four o'clock in the morning. I think I'd like to go home to bed and forget this whole thing."

"You sleep alone?" Leon asked.

"What was that?" Moshe said, startled.

Leon took a step forward, tilted his head, and grinned mockingly, his eyes glinting in the now moonlit darkness, his gaze steady and sharp.

"I just wondered," he said. "You've been a bachelor a long time. Not a thing has been revealed about your personal life since the death of your family. Interesting, yes? Moshe Eitan, the Jewish hero. Idolized by half the women in the country, but has no private life. No woman has told her tale, no pleasant vice has been reported, and Moshe Eitan, the macho warrior and *folks-mensh*, seems as pure as the driven snow. Give me a story, Major General. A real exclusive for the masses. The real man behind the public image, naked and unafraid."

The rage took hold of Moshe with sudden, shocking force, blinding him to all but Leon's face as it wavered in moonlight. He balled his fists by his sides, clenched them tight but kept them there, trying to fight the enormous tension in his body and his urge to do violence. He saw Leon staring at him, his grin mocking, his eyes observant, and he wrenched himself back to common sense and slowly unclenched his fists.

"My private life is my own," he said.

"Do you actually have one?" Leon replied.

"Your anti-Semitism is becoming obscene, Leon, but you've no right to ask that."

"I'm not anti-Semitic, Moshe. I'm against Zionism; there's a difference. If I were anti-Semitic, I wouldn't be concerned for Kate Hirschfield."

"You're concerned only for yourself. She's your mistress, as is well known. Your concern is for your own empty bed, so let's leave it at that."

Moshe regretted the words immediately and recoiled from his own vehemence, stepping back and then a little to the side as if about to move off. Then he stopped, suddenly numb, feeling Leon's eyes upon him, and turned his head to look directly at him and see what he was thinking. Leon was leaning slightly forward, the mocking smile no longer on his face, his ascetic lips tight. Moshe watched him, feeling cold, a touch of fear creeping over him, and then Leon, as if realizing something, straightened up and sighed loudly.

"Is that it?" he said. "Two motives disguised as one? One motive is the mystery of what happened on the Mount; and the other, more touching, is that the great Moshe Eitan has romantic designs on Kate Hirschfield. Don't tell me it's true, Moshe!"

Moshe started to walk away, feeling torn by rage and guilt, but Leon, moving forward very fast, grabbed hold of his elbow. Moshe tugged his arm loose and looked around to see Leon's flushed face.

"It's true, isn't it?" Leon said.

"Don't be ridiculous," Moshe replied.

"Damn it, Moshe, it's written in your face: her very name gets you jumping."

"You're drunk, Leon. You're talking nonsense."

"Damn you, Moshe, tell the truth! You can't bear to hear her name mentioned—particularly from my lips."

"That's enough; I'm going home."

"I want to see her."

"You can't."

"Two motives instead of one, Moshe. I know it! *That's what you're hiding!*"

Moshe turned and hurried away, whipped forward by Leon's voice, something breaking and crashing down inside him, leaving him wounded. His rage gave way to guilt, a shameful acceptance of the truth, and he marched across the garden toward the parked cars with his heart pounding furiously. Then he heard Leon's voice, ringing out of the night behind him, loud and precise and filled with rage, almost out of control.

"You won't get her, Major General! You hear me? *You won't get her!* And don't pretend you're just doing your duty! *You won't keep her that way!*"

Too ashamed to face Leon, Moshe didn't look back, but instead kept walking toward the cars parked above the valley's vast darkness. He climbed into his own car, slammed the door, and drove off quickly, relieved when the hospital fell far behind him and the darkness surrounded him. The clouds above were thinning, letting moonlight filter down, illuminating the desolate, silent land on both sides of the car. He drove slowly and carefully, too disturbed to go faster, still shaken by what Leon had said and by his own urge to deny it.

He glanced down at Jerusalem, now sleeping, couched in darkness, and shivered, thinking of what the storm had brought and what it meant to the future. The public or private future? In his mind they were the same. He could no longer separate his love for Kate from his personal history; nor could he divorce it from the events on the Mount of Olives and his own emotional involvement in those events. And this confusion, aroused by his extraordinary experiences with Kate, was what Leon had sensed and laid bare.

Moshe pulled into his driveway, climbed out of the car and locked the door, stared down at the darkened domes of Jerusalem, and then looked at his house. A light shone from the back lounge, beaming out over the patio, and Moshe, knowing who was inside, thought of Leon and shivered. *My private life,* he thought. Whatever made him think of that? He remembered Leon's words, his invidious suggestiveness, and was lacerated with shame and trepidation as he walked toward the house. *Does Leon know?* he wondered. Or was it just jealous spite? The questions coiled like thorns around his heart as he opened the front door.

He locked the door behind him and walked straight through to the lounge, feeling burdened with the weight of Leon's words and his own guilt and shame. Leah was sitting in an armchair, drinking a Sabra, her long legs crossed, her dark hair flowing onto her dark dress and the curve of her breasts. She glanced up when he walked in, smiled sleepily, waved one hand, her fingers long and thin, devoid of rings, her long nails bright with polish. Dark eyes, like his wife's eyes, like Kate's eyes, dark as death, each face blending into the other and stripping his senses. He stopped just in front of her, tried to smile, and failed dismally; instead he reached out and stroked her hair, then let his hand fall away.

"You're very late," she said.

"I was held up at the hospital."

"I'll have to charge you extra for that."

"You always do," he replied.

My private life is my secret shame, he thought, *and Leon somehow knew it; and now, on top of my jealousy and rage, I will have to live with his knowing. Yet why do I do it? Why not someone who cares? Why must it always be someone who sees it as trade?* He glanced around the room, surveying the photographs of his family, concentrating on his wife with her dark hair and dark eyes, wounding himself by looking back down at the whore and facing what he was doing. No involvement, he thought. The denial of emotion. A pathetic charade involving dark hair and dark eyes but no involvement other than that: their flesh bought but not yielding. Now he knew what he was doing, had been doing all those years, and as he dropped his jacket onto the floor, he saw Kate entering the picture.

"What do you want, Moshe?"

"The same as always," he replied.

"You won't solve the problem that way," Leah said. "My hands won't make her go away."

"It's all I can do, Leah."

"I doubt that, Major General. You won't betray your wife by coming inside me; you'll just put her to rest at last."

He glanced down at her and smiled, shaking his head from side to side, saying nothing but feeling the anguish swelling out deep inside him. She was wrong: he couldn't do it. He hadn't been able to do it for years. He had loved, and his love had been so true that his wife's death had numbed him. An emotional and physical paralysis, a retreat from further wounding; he had wrapped himself in ice and drifted away past all hope of returning. Now he looked down at Leah, his secret whore, almost an old friend, saw his wife and then Kate, one face superimposed on the other, and realized that what he was seeking in Kate was his own resurrection.

His emotions swelled up and threatened to burst his beating heart, grief and love and inextricable guilt bringing tears to his eyes. He undressed very quickly, dropping his clothes to the floor, then sat down in the chair and started shaking as if with some fever. Leah stared at him, startled, opening and closing her lips, then she undressed and knelt on the floor and placed her hands on his thighs. He tried to smile but couldn't make it, so closed his eyes and put his head back, concentrating on the softness of her lips and the artful play of her fingers. Then Kate entered his mind, her dark eyes revealing death, the dark eyes of his wife staring sunward, gazing into eternity. He opened his eyes and looked down, seeing himself in Leah's fingers, knowing he was asking her to give him a substitute for the more basic human need to lose his guilt and pain in Kate's body.

Understanding this, Moshe broke, groaning aloud and then sobbing, letting the waves of pain pour out and leave him spent in the peace of acceptance. He sobbed a long time, very quietly, without shame, and then stood up, waved one hand in rejection, and walked into his bedroom.

He lay down and closed his eyes, drifting gently in the darkness, then sat up when he heard Leah's footsteps, the door opening and closing. He then reached for a cigarette, lit it and inhaled, blew the smoke out as he climbed off the bed and walked back to the lounge. The room was empty and silent, chilled with memories of grief, and eventually he looked around him, studying the photographs of his family, and accepted that he had made the room into a mausoleum for the shards of his broken past.

My wife and children were killed, he thought, *and the pain was too great: my emotions, stripped bare in that moment, turned cold as the dead*. He shuddered again as he remembered (*the dead eyes staring sunward*), then inhaled far too deeply on his cigarette, still aware of his beating heart. *I had to live with it*, he thought, *and the pain was unforgettable; and fearful of ever suffering like that again I turned away from involvement*. He blew smoke to the cold air, watched it drifting away, dissolving in the air like his will, disappearing forever.

What he faced was the truth, the revelation of his self-defeat, the knowledge that he had suppressed the very emotions that gave men dignity and instead had filled the wastelands of his scorched soul with patriotism and duty. No love had been admitted, no possible pain invited, and his physical needs, divorced from his emotions, had been coldly appeased. The occasional whores had been necessary, preventing the humiliation of self-abuse, but their hands, while drawing the semen from his agitated loins, could not obliterate the shame of a transaction that ignored deeper feelings. Now those feelings had returned, exploding out of his hidden depths, ignited by the miracle of

the man from the Mount, then given new life and absolute commitment in the mirror of Kate's eyes.

The miracle of the Mount had indeed introduced him to Kate, but
his feelings for Kate were not miraculous. He loved her and wanted
her with him in the most earthly way.

Moshe took a deep breath, stubbed his cigarette out, straightened
up, and glanced around the room in which his hopes had been buried.
He shook his head from side to side, silently admonishing his own
stupidity, then walked around the room, took his family photographs
down, and then, feeling sadness and joy at once, locked them up in a
cupboard. Finally, still naked, hardly aware of the cold, his thoughts
filled with Kate and the possibility of redemption, he stood on the
patio and looked down on Jerusalem which, like the dream of his lost
years, was emerging from darkness.

Jerusalem the Golden. His home. What would become of it?

He wept again before dawn broke.

21

The Range-Rover braked to a halt in front of an old villa high in the hills above Tyre, near the southern border of Lebanon. The villa was the headquarters of the local Fatah command; and Leon, examining it, was struck by its modesty, not failing to note its peeling yellow walls and loose, broken tiles. Below the mountain clearing were the sun-scorched valleys of citrus trees, above it loomed the encircling, snow-capped mountains. The clearing itself was surrounded by cyprus trees and filled with trestle tables and long wooden benches. The tables were covered with unused plates, mugs of coffee, and bottles of beer; and the people who should have been sitting there, Lebanese and Palestinian, were gathered together at the far end of the clearing, listening to their leader, the famed Rashid Idriss.

Climbing out of the Range-Rover, the dust drifting lazily around him, Leon felt the fierce heat, experienced a fleeting spasm of nausea, and quietly cursed himself for having drunk too much the previous night in Beirut. The drinking, excessive even by his normal standards, had followed a restless sleep during which he had dreamt of Kate in the storm over the Mount of Olives, her dark hair streaming out in the wind as she drifted away from him. Now, as he placed his feet gingerly on the ground and heard Rashid Idriss propagating the Palestinian cause, he understood that the dream, which refused to leave his head, was the product of his increasing frustration at not seeing Kate for so long. She was still locked up in the hospital, well protected by Moshe Eitan; and Leon, standing between his two Fatah commando guards, realized that his negative feelings about Moshe Eitan were not based solely on political differences.

Moshe's most immediate enemy, Rashid Idriss, was still giving his speech to the people gathered in front of him under the cyprus trees at the far end of the clearing. His audience consisted of Palestinian refugees, the more committed aristocrats of Beirut, uniformed Fatah commandos, and dark-eyed Arab children, some ragged, some beautifully dressed. All of them were listening with the attention of the devoted as Rashid, exceptionally youthful for a man in his early forties, eloquently harangued Zionist Israel, praised the tenacity and courage of his own fighters, and implored those in a position of strength—the sophisticated and wealthy Lebanese—to support the Palestinian cause. His voice, which in normal speech Leon had found to be strikingly quiet, was now surprisingly loud and impassioned, almost messianic.

"We must not give in!" he finished. "Without a homeland we are nothing! Our people are of the desert and the mountain and the river; and, by the will of Allah, will remain so when the Zionists are dust. To this end, and for the sake of our children, we must continue to fight. Those who carry the guns must fire them, those with wealth must lend their support. We must not be divided, one Arab against the other, while the Jews increase their expansionist activities. Palestine belongs to the Palestinians! *Revolution until victory!*"

Rashid raised his balled right fist in a dramatic gesture, and the people around him cheered and applauded. The Fatah commandos, including those at each side of Leon, then started to chant "Revolution until victory!", raising and lowering their weapons in unison. Stepping down from the bench upon which he had been standing, Rashid disappeared into the jostling mass of excited men and women, many of whom were obviously attempting to embrace him or kiss the back of his hand.

Familiar with such scenes of politically based adulation, but in no way moved by them, Leon lit a cigarette, inhaled deeply, and then cast his eyes around the clearing. The smell of chicken stew and boiling rice led his wandering gaze to the aproned Arab women who were stirring the contents of some large, steaming cauldrons near the encircling trestle tables; beyond the tables, beneath more trees, were the Range-Rover, Mercedes, and BMW cars that had brought most of the people up from Beirut or the nearby refugee camps. Looking back at the tables, Leon saw the aproned women setting down jugs of coffee and tea, bottles of beer and plates for the food, while those around Rashid Idriss, hugging one another and talking excitedly, moved away to take their places on the long wooden benches.

Emerging from the tight circle of his most trusted men, Rashid, wearing his uniform, his eyes shaded beneath a peaked cap, walked up to Leon and stopped just in front of him with one hand outstretched. They shook hands, and then Rashid stepped back a little, tilting his head and offering Leon a modest smile, his brown eyes slightly mocking.

"So, Mr. Halcomb, you made it to our little gathering. I hope you enjoyed your stay in Beirut and were not led astray."

"And why should I be led astray?" Leon asked, sensing the seriousness behind Rashid's gentle mockery.

"I am told you are a man not averse to pleasure—and Beirut, for such a man, could be a temptation."

"I was tempted only with thirst . . . and that was well satisfied."

"Good," Rashid said, his eyes directly on Leon's face. "I had hoped to meet you sooner than this, but"—he raised his hands in apology—"I was unfortunately delayed."

"That was a nice speech you made."

"A bit theatrical, but necessary."

"One of the benefits of formal education."

"Quite so, Mr. Halcomb." Rashid turned slightly sideways and indicated the only empty table. "Come. You will sit with me. We will eat and then talk. I am very glad you accepted my invitation and there is much to discuss. But first, a little Arab hospitality—if your stomach can stand it."

Taking note of the last remark, Leon flushed and inhaled on his cigarette, his stomach less unsettled than before but not yet in good shape. Saying nothing, he followed Rashid across the clearing and sat beside him behind the trestle table. It soon became clear to him—after the Arab women had served the chicken stew and rice—that no one else would be joining them at the table. Rashid, as if confirming this fact, indicated that Leon should eat.

"You live humbly," Leon said, gazing down at his steaming stew.

"To lead the people you must be *of* the people," Rashid replied. "My formal education has not made me forget that I'm an Arab. I eat as my people eat, and drink as they drink. A man only needs food for sustenance; all else is pretension."

Leon nodded and smiled, and they both started eating, washing the chicken stew down with beer and talking only of small things. The stew was simple but delicious, settling Leon's upset stomach, clearing his head, and making him feel more alert, his curiosity aroused. Well aware that Rashid would not invite a journalist to this place for a routine interview, he wondered just what was forthcoming; and also why he had been singled out in particular. Rashid studiously avoided the issue until the meal was finished when, with a gentle sigh, he turned around to face Leon, his liquid brown eyes very steady, his lips forming a slight smile.

"You enjoyed the meal, Mr. Halcomb?"

"Yes. May I smoke?"

"Of course. Your pleasure is my pleasure.",

Leon lit a cigarette and inhaled gratefully, leaning back against the hard wooden bench. The other tables were completely full, the people leaning toward one another, drinking and waving their hands excitedly, their voices rising and falling. Around the clearing, at various points beneath the trees, the armed commandos kept watch.

"I am told that you've been trying to arrange an interview with me for some time," Rashid said. "This is true?"

"Yes," Leon said.

"Why? I can't tell you anything that I haven't already told the press. My views, as you well know, have been widely publicized."

"If you know that I've been trying to arrange a meeting," Leon said, "then you'll also know that I wanted something other than a redundant interview."

Rashid smiled in acknowledgment of that truth. "Correct," he said. "I was told it was something else. I was also told that you refused to discuss it with anyone but me personally."

"Correct again," Leon said.

Rashid's smile revealed real amusement combined with sly mockery. "So," he said, "you're after something else. What might that be?"

"What I want is something that could give me an exclusive and be of considerable value to your cause."

"Your concern for the Palestinian cause is very touching. Now what do you *want*?"

The sudden change of tone was enough to convince Leon that Rashid, with his dark poet's eyes, could be steel at the bargaining table.

"What I want," Leon said carefully, "instead of a redundant interview, is the opportunity of presenting an intimate portrait of your men by traveling with them, let's say for a month, as they move around the country. More precisely, I want to travel with you, wherever you go."

He kept his gaze steady as Rashid leaned back a little, removed the smile from his face, and studied him with those dark, thoughtful eyes for a considerable time. Eventually, when the silence became too much, he offered another slight smile.

"And why should I let you, Mr. Halcomb, enjoy such a privilege when I've denied it to every other Western journalist?"

"You read all the Western newspapers, Rashid. You must know what I've written."

"I assume you're referring to your anti-Zionist tirades."

"Quite."

"You are not the first Western newspaperman to take a stand against Zionism. Indeed, such a stand has become increasingly popular, and may well be a profitable stand for a journalist to take."

"I was attacking Zionism when the Western press was spitting on the Arab world. You know that, Rashid, as you also know that I gave a great deal of space to Arab grievances when no one else would."

Rashid smiled and raised his two hands in the air as if begging forgiveness; nonetheless a hint of mockery was still present.

"Yes," he said, "that is true, and your efforts have been appreciated; but I still must say no to your request."

"Why?"

"Let me answer your question with another question. Do you really think you can explain the Arabs by traveling with them?"

"Yes."

"But you've already expressed our grievances in your columns."

"That's right," Leon said. "But the West isn't interested in those grievances because they don't trust the Arabs."

"They don't trust the Arabs because they don't understand the Arab mentality."

"Correct."

"And you do?"

"Also correct."

"Wrong," Rashid said. "You assume too much, my friend. You may sympathize with us Arabs, but you do not understand us; for this reason when you try to explain us, you simply cause more distrust. How can you understand us? Even our poetry defies you. We come from the endless deserts, from bitter, harsh lands, from the places where no white man can endure let alone comprehend. You do not understand us. You analyze us by Western standards. And such standards, created out of your own needs, have no relevance to us. Custom alone does not separate us; nor does language or politics; God's anvil, the desert, serenely beautiful and merciless, has shaped us in a manner that defies your relentless Western scrutiny. To you we are cruel—to ourselves and to others—but our cruelty, which you view as barbarism, is the desert's quick justice. There are no laws in the desert—the rule of law is the white man's sword; in the desert, which respects no human need, there is only the burning sun. Life or death is all that matters: survival is all; we spring from the wandering nomads whose one enemy was nature and who found, to their cost, that there was only safety in numbers with the individual subordinated to the whole. How can the white man judge us? He believes in freedom and mercy. But for us—who live where human life is scarce —freedom and mercy are dangerous. Such concepts are a Western luxury, the very foundation of your civilization; but such concepts, if practiced by the Arabs, would bring about our destruction. No, Mr. Halcomb, you do not know us at all. You may sympathize with us —and even try to accept us—but as long as the wind blows on the desert, you will not understand us."

There was a sudden cacophony, blaring from loudspeakers in the trees, and from under the trees came a detachment of armed commandos, all marching in time to the music. Rashid turned away to watch them, nodding his head in approval, and the soldiers marched around the clearing, passing the diners at the tables, and eventually stopped in front of Rashid, presented arms and then stood at ease. The diners all applauded, standing up, their hands raised; and then, at a nod from Rashid, the commandos broke ranks and went to join their families at some tables still laden with food and drink. The music was still playing, very loud and discordant, when Rashid turned back to face Leon, who saw the steel in his brown eyes.

"Did you examine them?" Rashid said. "Did you notice how young they were? All Arabs, Mr. Halcomb, not one of them over twenty, and yet all of them have killed and will kill again without what you call conscience. That also is a Western luxury, a romantic notion of protected children; but *my* children know only one thing: that the homeless are lost. To dispossess the Arabs is to rob them of their pride; and an Arab without pride values nothing except getting it back. Homeless, they are lost and thus have nothing to lose; stripped of pride, their whole life becomes meaningless—and other lives, equally so. Thus they will fight and die, and then their sons will replace them, one generation after the other until the Jews yield. How can you understand? Nothing matters to you that much. You, with your ephemeral Western values, are divorced from such passion."

Leon picked up his glass and had a long drink of beer, a nervous pulse beating in his stomach as he put the glass down again. When he picked up his eyes, he saw Rashid leaning forward, his brown eyes very large and intense, beads of sweat on his forehead.

"Let's talk about Western values. What are your values, Mr. Halcomb? In one sentence you say that you want an exclusive and that it could be of value to our cause. In other words, my journalist friend, you are trying to convince us of your sincerity whilst helplessly admitting to your own selfish interests. Our cause means nothing to you. It's your exclusive that matters. It is true that you defended us while your fellow journalists reviled us; equally true is that by doing so, you became a controversial figure who was able to command a much bigger fee. Where were you before you defended us? On the fifth column of some back page. In defending us you got what you needed: a great deal of attention. And yet now you need an exclusive. Why is that, my good friend? It's because the Arabs are no longer being reviled by your fellow journalists and your lone stand is no longer quite so bankable. In short, Mr. Halcomb, you need something that will set you back on your feet."

Leon felt his cheeks burning and he lit a cigarette, his hand shaking when he put it to his lips and inhaled very deeply. He blew the smoke out slowly, squinting through it at Rashid, trying to control his face while his emotions collided in some dark pit where fear had dominion. He tried to speak but felt choked, his denial drowning in bile, rising up to his throat from the nausea in his stomach and emerging through his lips as a whisper devoid of conviction:

"That's not true," he said feebly.

"Yes, it is, Mr. Halcomb. Did you think I would let you come here without having you checked? I know all about you, and you are a man with some problems: Your column is no longer popular, your income is falling dramatically, you drink far too much for your own good, and your reputation is crumbling. Also you are a romantic, an idealist with no beliefs; and your cynicism, once directed at others, is now aimed at yourself. Idealists are pathetic: in the end they can't face life; your contempt for yourself is now evident in your work and represents your increasing sense of shame at your lack of commitment. No, Mr. Halcomb, it's not the Arabs you care for: what you care for is an exclusive that will pull you out of debt and disguise your feelings of failure in material success. You are, in short, a very desperate man who thinks the Arabs can help him. All right, Mr. Halcomb, we will help you—but the price will be high."

Leon, holding the cigarette near his lips, started shaking again. He lowered his hand to the table, nicked the cigarette and glanced around him, feeling sweaty and ill and bewildered, the truth making his ears ring. Failure based on disillusionment, desperation based on fear: the truth in Rashid's words hammered home and shattered all his defenses. Kate had seen it as well, had plucked the defeat from his cynicism; and now, remembering the intensity with which he had made love to her, he understood that her revelations had stripped him down to the bones of his terror. It was the terror of lost faith and its consequent loss of will; and finally he would have to face the cost, no matter how high.

"All right," Leon said. "What do you want from me?"

Rashid's face moved away a little, a slight smile on his lips, his brown eyes still direct but much softer, almost benign.

"I want to know what happened on the Mount of Olives," he said, "and I want to know what was brought down from there."

Leon suddenly felt claustrophobic, sensing the trap closing in on him, as if his life, with its succession of failed hopes, was narrowing down to oblivion. He had reached middle age and had little impetus left; his only motivation was the fear of insecurity, and now Rashid, understanding the full extent of that fear, was about to push him close to the edge where decisions are made.

"Unknown atmospheric phenomenon," he said. "That's the official explanation—and very possibly it's all that they know."

"I'm sorry," Rashid said, "I cannot accept that."

"Why?"

"There is too much talk about something discovered on the Mount of Olives, and such talk is normally based on some kind of truth. It is said that the Jews cordoned off that area and worked throughout the night with bulldozers, obviously trying to cover up *something*. Also it is known that the Arabs who lived in that area were evacuated from their homes and are still being held by the authorities without explanation. Finally my sources tell me that you, Leon Halcomb, have been spending a lot of time at the Hadassah Medical Center, trying to find out why Kate Hirschfield has been held there under guard since the night she was brought down from the Mount. It is clear from all this that something strange is going on—and like you, I want to find out what it is."

"And you want me to get you that information."

"Correct. That's our deal."

Leon thought about Kate and felt sick to his soul, aware that if he did what Rashid wanted, he would never forgive himself. He glanced up at the bright sky, blinked and stared around him, saw the commandos beyond the crowded trestle tables, heard singing and laughter. Lighting another cigarette, he noticed that his hand was shaking, and understood, as he looked back at Rashid, that this was caused by his shame.

"They won't let me in to see her," he said, trying to delay the issue, but realizing, even as he spoke, how lame his words sounded.

"So," Rashid replied, "they will not let you in to see her. But sooner or later they will have to release her, and then you can talk to her."

"That doesn't mean she'll tell me what happened," Leon said, still trying to wriggle out of his bed of thorns. "If, as you seem to think, the Israelis are trying to keep the facts hidden, they won't release her without swearing her to secrecy."

"You weary me, Mr. Halcomb. Why do you make excuses? The woman is your mistress, she obviously trusts you, so if you promise to keep your mouth shut, she will almost certainly tell you."

"I get her to tell me, and then I betray her."

"It's your choice, my friend."

Leon looked at Rashid's brown eyes, into their calm, liquid depths, and felt his will slipping away with the remains of his pride. He inhaled on his cigarette, felt nauseated, and almost choked, coughed and then stubbed the cigarette out and wished his heart would stop beating. The people around him had grown silent while an Arab sang a mournful song, his guitar weaving intricate refrains around his high, tragic voice. Leon listened and was captured, thinking of when he had last seen Kate, then was suddenly torn between his desperate need of her and the thought of betraying her. The pain swelled up inside him, almost bursting his heart, and then he tried, even knowing that he was lying, to deny the inevitable.

"I won't do it," he said.

Rashid studied him a long time, his brown eyes calm but thoughtful, then he shrugged and opened the fingers of his right hand as if releasing trapped air.

"Fine," he said. "It's your choice. Only you can decide. I leave the offer open should you happen to change your mind later on."

"I won't," Leon said.

"Perhaps not," Rashid replied. "But then we never really know what we will do until we have to decide. Only you can decide what is most important to you: the respect of Miss Hirschfield or your whole future. No information, no exclusive. No exclusive, no future. The choice is all yours, Mr. Halcomb, and soon you must make it."

Leon put his head down and closed his eyes and surveyed the darkness, trying to lose himself somewhere in the void at the back of his head. The sound came out of the darkness, first a sibilance, then a screech, then a roaring that erupted all around him and tore through his mind. The air was sucked from his lungs in a terrible, soundless shriek, and he opened his eyes to see the earth spinning over and slamming down on his face. Pain exploded from his head and hammered right through his body as he choked on dirt and stones and felt the ground shaking under his belly. There was screeching, more roaring, waves of heat and raining soil, and something slammed into his spine and stopped his movement as he opened his eyes again. He saw mushrooming earth, sheets of flame in boiling smoke, a screaming woman racing after a burning child, bodies spinning and breaking. Above the smoke something glinted, a Phantom jet climbing high, looping over, and swooping back toward the clearing at high speed.

The ground erupted again, spewing earth and vegetation, human screams daggering out of the explosions as the flame and smoke blended. Leon grabbed hold of the tree trunk, tried to stand and collapsed, looked around him, and saw the Arabs running back and forth through the murk. A man jackknifed to the ground, a shredded woman shrieked and writhed, a bloody child stood with his thumb in his mouth, the smoke swirling around him.

Leon tried to stand up again, heard a roaring, felt the blast, was jerked away from the tree and pulled around, and found himself facing Rashid, his brown eyes, very bright, filled with anguish and rage, almost unreal as they floated in the smoke that grew darker each second. Rashid was shouting at him, jabbing his finger toward the trees, and then he grabbed him by the shoulder and pulled him forward through the bedlam and chaos. Leon followed, or tried to follow, his spirit willing, his flesh weak, but he was picked up in a maelstrom of light and noise and hurled back to the earth. There was no fear at all, just the familiar disbelief, and he rolled across the ground automatically, his hands over his ears. The ground shuddered and growled, then the growling became a roaring filled with shrieking and hissing and spitting and dull, thudding sounds. Leon lay on his belly, opened his eyes and looked ahead, saw a man rising out of the swirling smoke, his arms outstretched and pleading. Ringed with fire, he became a torch, a flaming figure staggering forward, some sound that was not remotely human coming out of his melting lips. The smoke swirled and devoured him, passed on across the clearing, left behind it a smoldering black rag that sank down to the ground. The bloody child still stood alone, sucking his thumb and staring blankly, then a white-robed figure swept him away as flames licked at the empty space. Leon lay there, stretched out on his belly, staring into the chaos.

Death. Devastation. The Israeli jets shrieking. People screaming and bawling and falling down and waving fists at the sky. It took only a few minutes, but seemed to go on forever, the jets shrieking overhead, the ground erupting and roaring, the smoke swirling around the Arabs as they raced to and fro, tripping over the fallen bodies, grabbing hold of one another, weeping and screaming and cursing, the villa blazing behind them.

Leon lay there and watched, the smoke stinging his eyes, feeling bruised and exhausted and filthy, only saved by his outrage. The anger defeated fear, gave him someone to hate, and eventually, as he watched the Israeli jets flying away, also gave him the justification he needed for what was to come. The jets disappeared, leaving drifting smoke and silence, and Leon climbed to his feet, shaking his head, clearing his ears, then heard broken sobs, children crying, people groaning, and turned his head, when a hand touched his shoulder, to see Rashid's brown eyes.

"We are cruel?" Rashid said. "The Arabs are cruel? Take a good look around you, Mr. Halcomb, and tell me of justice!"

Leon stared and saw the smoke thinning out above the clearing, drifting away from the smoldering trees and blazing villa, and making the blue sky look gray. The clearing itself was a shambles of broken tables and chairs, countless shards of glass glinting from the charred, blackened earth of the shellholes. Here a dismembered head, there the bright splash of intestines, all around the blistered flesh and shivering limbs of the mortally wounded. A woman wailed and rocked her child, a bloody bundle in her arms; a man sat up and looked at his mangled leg and then screamed and fell back again. Blood flowed and congealed, soaked the earth, dried on hot stones, and the boy with the thumb in his mouth gazed around him with blank eyes. Leon stared and saw it all, the pure horror, his excuse, then he turned back to Rashid, his stomach heaving, and heard the shame in his own voice.

"I'll do it," he said.

22

He was not a supernatural being but a man of flesh and blood, yet unmistakably one with divine gifts or supernatural abilities. Kate, in her fear and love, had understood this from his awakening, but as the days passed, and his empty mind was filled, she had the proof to contend with.

He learned remarkably quickly, never forgetting what he heard or read, sublimely calm as he sat like a prisoner in his room—asking and answering questions, reading books by the dozen, letting the facts of contemporary life color the darkness of his mind—or lay on a table in the laboratory, being examined by physicians and psychologists, his silvery-gray eyes bright and undisturbed, his bearded face in repose.

He still called himself Joshua and remembered the Teacher of Righteousness; but other than what he had told to Kate, his past was an empty page. He had told Kate all he knew and could not fill in the blanks; knew nothing about his own resurrection and appeared to care little. He existed; it was enough. "I am that I am," he said. The statement was startling for many reasons, not least for its arrogance, and it led to a further flurry of examinations by very concerned men.

The hypnotists tried and failed, unable to capture his mind, but then, almost amused by their perplexity, he put himself into a deep sleep. No fresh memories were unveiled, no hidden secrets revealed; in his trance he merely repeated, word for word, the fragments passed on to Kate. He then awakened of his own accord, obviously refreshed, smiling slightly, and hypnotized the hypnotist sitting above him by simply waving one hand.

"What do you see?" he asked.

"What you described," the hypnotist replied. "I see the scrolls in the dark caves, the Teacher of Righteousness, yourself as a child being presented in the temple; and now . . . yes, I see you . . . you look like a mature child, perhaps thirteen or fourteen years of age, sitting in the shadows of the colonnades, having words with the priests."

"You are seeing what's in my mind?"

"I am seeing what you remember. . . . Baptism in the water, a white dove, meditation in the wilderness, your temptation . . . You are now a grown man."

"You may wake up now."

The hypnotist awakened and retreated in confusion, taking with him his very frightened colleague and saying nothing to Kate. Joshua sat up on the bed and stared at her, smiling slightly, making her feel love and fear as a single emotion that defied human reason. She wanted to walk out of the room, to be alone with her thoughts, but his eyes, with their silvery-gray neutrality, seemed to drain her of will.

"Love and fear are the same," he said, as if reading her mind, "for love is the surrender of that self which we need to protect us. If you cannot forget the fear, you must accept it and learn to feed off it."

The linguists were also foiled, pacing back and forth, muttering, making tape recordings of his voice, analyzing his speech patterns, trying to trace his accent back to its time and source, but getting hopelessly lost. The Tower of Babel was in his speech, a veritable multitude of voices; he spoke every known language with a casual, startling fluency, his accents fitting the region requested with unbreakable accuracy. The linguists were stunned, unable to believe their own findings, knowing no more at the end than they had at the beginning, having to confess that his origins were a mystery, his time indefinable.

"What do you hope to find?" he asked them. "There is only one voice. It is the voice of each and every individual and belongs to the whole. I do not select my speech. I speak in the tongue of the one addressing me. I speak without thought or calculation and let the words build their own shape."

"You speak every known language."

"There is only one language."

"You have every possible accent at your command."

"There is only one accent."

He stared at Kate as they left, offering nothing, demanding nothing, quietly forcing her to travel down through her Self to some point beyond nakedness.

"You are everything," he said. "And without you, there is nothing. Through ourselves we make the universe manifest, and without us, it cannot be. You must not be frightened of this. You must accept your fleeting grace. You are here, we are here, in this room and outside it, as we were in the past and are now and will be in the future. This concept must not destroy you; it must give you strength and faith. In me, and in yourself, you must believe and thus find your true nature."

The psychologists crowded around him, wearing white coats and bland smiles, speaking softly as they tried to find the key to the hieroglyphics in which his nature was couched. They examined his learning and thinking, his intelligence and personality, his motivation and emotion and behavior, his group dynamics and sensation-perception and possible psychoneuroses. He understood them and responded, teasing their lust for the unusual, playing tricks with their mazes and one-way mirrors and sound-wave generators, producing images on their spectroscopes and distortions on their colorimeters, spending days in the black silence of the anechoic room and emerging without the slightest sign of change, his silvery-gray eyes unblinking. The psychologists stopped smiling, but started rubbing their furrowed brows, utterly baffled by this apparently human creature who defied normal laws.

"We have a ghost on the spectroscope. An image that shouldn't be there. You were photographed in that chair and we saw that you didn't move; yet here, in the photograph, standing right beside the chair, is a figure that shouldn't exist."

"I briefly left my mortal shell. It seemed natural to do so. It is good to be released from the flesh, though it cannot last long."

"The electroencephalograph went crazy: it contradicted itself. It gave a normal alpha reading of approximately eleven cycles, yet it also showed extraordinary, almost violent, activity in the deeper levels of the recticular formation. That just doesn't make sense."

"I felt peace and excitement. I meditated and felt joy. I was calm, yet my spirit soared aloft to embrace sun and sky."

"You spent five days in the black room. You made no sound or movement. You hadn't changed a bit when you emerged. What happened in there?"

"Nothing."

"You weren't affected?"

"I didn't know that was expected. I was conceived out of darkness and silence and returned to it willingly."

"You're not human."

"I am."

"Perhaps physically; not otherwise."

"I only know that I am as you were—before your weakness stole from you."

"*My* weakness?"

"The weakness of Man . . . his flight from the Whole."

The last psychologist departed, the light of terror in his eyes, and then Joshua turned his gaze upon Kate where she stood by the window. She stared back, her thoughts colliding, feeling divorced from her body, torn by love and the fear of an awareness beyond what she had known before. She kept staring, trying to think, concentrating on his appearance, wondering why he had insisted on the white robe that now draped his lean body. He was a tall man, starkly handsome, at once gentle and imperious. The child in her saw a father, the woman in her saw a son, and somewhere between the two, lost in time, was the ghost of her former self. He had insisted that she stay with him, offering no explanation, and yet now, in her resentment, desperately yearning to be free, she understood that without his consent she lacked the will to walk out.

"I have patience," he said. "You must practice the same. I do not know why I want you here with me, but I know it was willed. You were called and came to me, giving energy and light, and now, as I evolve out of ignorance, you will act as my beacon. What I bring, you have been seeking; what you offer is my reward; you and I, we are one and the same and but part of the Whole."

The parapsychologists soon took over, using the notes of the failed psychologists, experimenting to check the extent of his powers and understand how they worked. They strapped him into an electroencephalograph and cardiograph harness, checked his resting physiology, and discovered that he had a magnetic field surrounding his body that was only eight times less powerful than that of the Earth; and that his brain-wave patterns could, at his conscious bidding, generate fifty times more voltage than normal. When this happened, windows cracked, tables shook, test tubes broke, while those standing close to him developed headaches or nausea and dizziness.

"How did you get such power?"

"All men have such power. All men are of the earth and the sky, but refuse to have faith. What is willed, will be done; transcendence lies in faith. Rejecting faith, man rejects his hidden strengths and squanders his riches."

"Your powers are very unusual."

"They are commonplace, but ignored."

"You're suggesting that you're just a normal man?"

"There are no normal men."

He proved his point by displaying his aura without using colored-glass screens, standing radiantly before them like a thermographic photograph, his figure suddenly shimmering in a luminous orange and red surround, his hair and beard black, his nose yellow, his ears green, striations of light spreading out from his fingers and disappearing some distance away.

"I am normal," he said. "You have seen all this before. I merely show you what you see with your cameras and once saw with your eyes. You are blind and I give you sight. You lost your vision when you lost your faith. What I radiate, you radiate also, but your eyes now reject it. I am flesh and blood. Normal."

They refused to believe him and continued to experiment, testing his psychokinetic energy, his eyeless sight and thoughtography, first placing him in a restraining jacket, then in a Faraday cage, then inside the thick steel walls of a radiation counting chamber from where, with stunning ease, he reproduced his thought images on the photographic plates in another room. He stared at objects and made them move, described objects when blindfolded, removed the blindfold and stared at some papers and set them on fire. All of this he did calmly, with quiet, weary patience, until finally, both excited and fearful, the parapsychologists surrendered.

"You're unbelievable," someone said.

"Believe and you will see."

"Your physiology is normal, but that's all: otherwise, you're a miracle."

"Such a word has no meaning."

Alone again, Kate stared at him, finally feeling fear for him, realizing the full extent of his innocence and what it might lead to. He knew not where he had come from, nor why he was here, and his ignorance about the world, particularly combined with his strange powers, could lead to a multitude of dangers. Kate thought of this with grief, with a stabbing, maternal love, her fear of the unknown giving way to a fear for his future. Then she thought of herself, of the horror expelled from her bleeding womb, and the guilt that had haunted her for years rose like smoke in her mind. Choked with shame and remorse, wanting to cleanse herself of sin, wanting, even more, to nurture this full-grown child to manhood, she walked across the sunlit room and raised her hand and touched his chest with her fingers.

"I'm real," he said. "You know that."

"I just wanted to confirm it."

"You worry for me and resent me at the same time, wondering when I will free you."

"I can leave anytime."

"You may desire it, but you won't. You see your life in the mirror of my eyes and are starting to question it."

"You frighten me."

"No. You are reflected in my eyes. You look into me in order to see yourself, and that brings on the fear."

"What fear?"

"Your past shame."

"I did nothing to be ashamed of."

"You lie to yourself in order to kill the pain, but it won't go away. Admit what you now deny, for in shame there is repentance. Stop dreaming of the child in the pool of blood and let the healing bring new life."

Kate gasped and stepped away, covering her face with her hands, terrified by his knowledge of her thoughts and their haunting persistence. She felt his hand on her head, his fingers outspread through her hair, his palm pressing down on her skull with a gentle insistence. Her knees bent and touched the floor, the stone cold against her skin, and, obeying his command, she bowed her head and then opened her eyes. She saw the curve of her own breasts, the white blouse stretched across them, her legs, pressed together, in blue denim, her hands on her thighs. Then her clothing seemed to melt, turning to liquid and vaporizing, and she saw her naked skin as a jigsaw of shadow and light. She tried to scream but heard nothing, tried to move but was helpless, and then, as her body became translucent, she surrendered to wonder. Her flesh was shifting sand, the sand alive with sound and color, eddying and swirling and parting to reveal further wonders. Her enzymes were the stars, her blood cells the great moons, her hemoglobin streaming out like crimson mist across the cosmos within her. Her beating heart was the pulsating sun, her blood was oxygen and fire, and her consciousness, the manifestation of all that was, traversed time to the infinite. In that void there was nothing, and being nothing, nothing to fear, and she saw it and touched it and embraced it and returned to her mortal shell. She blinked and shook her head, no longer shivering with panic, then she raised her eyes, studying his strange, ascetic face, feeling his hand slipping away from her head and seeing it fall to his side. She stood up, very slowly, not too sure if she would make it, made it and stepped back again, opening her mouth, saying nothing.

"I am that I am," he said. "That which is, has its purpose. The questions on your lips will not be asked because there cannot be answers. I have patience. You must practice it. Time alone will reveal our meaning. I am, as you are, a stranger in a world filled with strangeness. Nothing is without its reason. Your own shame has shaped your life. Your shame is what leads you to repentance and the need to affirm. To affirm is to live. Not exist, but embrace. We embrace the pain and doubt to find faith and once more stand in grace. Your pain and doubt are your unanswered questions and I cannot assist you. I am that I am—that is all. There is no other answer."

The security officers returned, having despaired of the academics, and sat in chairs facing the bed upon which Joshua was sitting. He gazed at them with interest, neither amused nor resentful, simply waiting with the patience of the innocent for their words to reveal him. The security officers were nervous, both embarrassed by the inexplicable, their eyes wandering from Joshua to Kate and then back again. Kate watched them from the other bed, saying nothing, feeling frightened, wondering what they would do when they had to accept the unacceptable.

"Tell us who you are."

"I cannot answer that question."

"You can't or you won't?"

"I can't. I don't know."

"And you don't know where you came from?"

"You already know all I know."

"According to what you told us—and if we accept that it's true —we would have to assume that you're two thousand years old."

"You assume. I do not."

"You deny it?"

"I do not assume it."

"We want to know how you were buried on the Mount of Olives and you refuse to cooperate."

"I do not refuse to cooperate. All your questions teach me something. Like you, I would like to know the answer, but my mind is a blank."

"We refuse to believe that."

"You must believe what you believe. You must accept or reject as you feel, but I cannot assist you."

"Who sent you?"

"I don't know."

"What's your mission?"

"I don't know."

"We just can't believe that. We think you're trying to bluff us. You have a remarkable brain, you speak every known language, your rate of learning is too fast to be natural, and you are, given the circumstances in which you were found, too calm and collected to be innocent. Who taught you all you know? Who trained you in parapsychology? And why, if you honestly don't know who you are or where you came from, are you not even remotely disturbed?"

"Why should I be disturbed? What is willed, will be done. You will show me who I am in due course, so there is nothing to fear."

"*We* will show you who you are?"

"It is you who seeks to know."

"And you?"

"I am merely a witness. Let events take their course."

"We could keep you here forever."

"If you do, it was intended."

"We could probably have you shot as a spy."

"Every death has its meaning."

The security officers departed, shaking their heads in disbelief, but Kate stayed where she was on the bed, trying to order her thoughts. She no longer feared him; now she was frightened for him, aware that his innocence was being misconstrued as some dangerous ploy. The security men were suspicious, the chief rabbis were nervous, and the full facts about him, if disclosed to the general public, could be misconstrued in even more dangerous ways, perhaps leading to havoc. Yes, she was concerned, and now she studied him, thinking of how his ignorance about himself could be used and abused. The Jews could claim him as their Messiah, the Muslims as their Mahdi, the Christians as their Christ in His Second Coming. She found his eyes fixed upon her in merciless scrutiny, and then she thought about his strange powers, his ability to work miracles, and wondered what would happen if his serenity was turned into anger.

"You show nothing," she said.

"There is nothing to show."

"You don't show what you're feeling inside, and I find that disturbing."

"I show what I feel. What you see is what I feel. If what I show is less than you expect, you must examine yourself."

"I don't understand that."

"You have feelings I lack. You have anger and fear and grave doubt, and in me they are missing."

"Why?"

"I don't know. Perhaps because I am unformed. With time we gather experience and feeling, but my time is still short."

"You don't relate to people."

"I am watching and listening. I am taking in what they say and do and will soon learn their meaning."

"Meaning is not feeling."

"Without meaning there is no feeling. Men rarely mean what they say; how they say it means more. They speak with their bodies, not only their tongues, and the manner in which they gesture when they speak reveals more than their words do. I watch and I listen, and take in what is revealed, and in this way I learn what feelings are and what they resolve."

"You're talking about logic."

"Without feeling there is no logic. Logic is the purest expression of controlled emotion; lack of feeling is madness."

"I cannot accept that."

"That's why you are torn. You have tried to separate your reason from your feelings, and now are paying the price. You are divided within yourself, emotionally crippled and confused, afraid that by surrendering to feeling you will lose your integrity."

"What integrity?"

"I think you know: the integrity of your mind. You view logic —separated from feeling—as the ultimate virtue."

"And that isn't so?"

"No, it is not. The mind and emotions are one—and divided, they fall."

"And yet you feel nothing."

"I feel what you feel. Through you I am learning to respond to conflicting emotions."

"You have not displayed emotions."

"I only know them through you."

"Knowing is not the same as feeling."

"That will come if required."

The door opened and Moshe walked in, followed closely by two guards, both of them carrying Uzi guns and looking uncomfortable. Moshe stood in the middle of the room, his large hands on his hips, staring first at Joshua and then at Kate, as if searching for words. Kate returned his stare, feeling a sudden rush of emotion, seeing something in his eyes, a quiet despair, that made her want to console him. He kept his eyes on her, as if signaling a message, a pained plea for forgiveness or understanding for what was to happen. Then she realized that she was standing, had stood up without knowing it, her heart beating in the conviction of trouble, her throat dry, her legs shaky. She just stood there, staring at him, then at Joshua and back again, until she saw him dropping his eyes to the floor and slowly looking back up, his face pale in the sunlight.

"I have to take him away," he said. "We're handing him over to Shin Beth. They're not satisfied with what he's told us, so they want to personally deal with the matter. I'm sorry, Kate. I can't do a thing about it. I simply have to deliver him."

"Shin Beth?" Joshua said. "What is this?"

"Internal security and counterintelligence," Kate said. "They're not as patient as doctors."

She stared at Moshe and saw him grimace, his pale cheeks turning red, and her anger, which had rashly boiled up, quickly turned into sympathy. Torn, she turned away and covered her mouth with her hand, took a deep breath and turned back again, her eyes fixed on them both.

"You will take us?" Joshua said.

"Not both of you. Only you."

"I will go, but she must be by my side. What is willed, will be done."

"I'm sorry," Moshe said, "but you have to come alone. Your insistence on having Kate with you has made them suspicious."

"Suspicious?"

"They think you're using her, that you've got some hold over her, that somehow or other you're tied together and have to be separated."

"We will both go together."

"I'm sorry, you won't."

"I am merely a witness. Let events take their course. But I tell you, we will both go together. She must stay by my side."

Moshe shrugged and stepped back, and then the two guards

marched forward, both lowering the barrels of their Uzi guns and pointing them directly at Joshua. Alarmed, Kate stepped forward, something cold slithering through her, the cold scorching her and making her burn as she looked right at Joshua.

He was still sitting on his bed, staring up at the gun barrels, but his face, which before had been serene, now looked almost anguished. He shook his head from side to side, closed his eyes and leaned forward, then his whole body started to tremble as if with some fever. Kate opened her mouth to scream, smothered the scream with her hand, saw the egg-shaped, silvery haze around his body, his head emitting striations of light. One of the soldiers stepped back, his weapon clattering to the floor, while the other, falling down to his knees, was diffused in the shimmering haze. Kate screamed when Moshe walked forward, trying to warn him to get out, but a roaring drowned her voice as the room began to shake and the walls, suddenly webbed with enormous cracks, spat plaster and dust. Moshe stumbled and fell, his hands slapping on the floor, pushed himself back to his knees and lowered his head and covered his ears with his hands. Kate sobbed and started forward, her head filled with the roaring, then was blinded by the light and thrown back by some invisible force. She felt the wall against her shoulders, a sharp pain in her back, then fell onto the bed and looked up and saw a whirlpool of light. Moshe was still on his knees, a dark form angled backward, his body jerking as if being whipped, the light swirling around him. The light seemed to come from Joshua, spinning out of some source around him, roaring and screeching around the room and tearing plaster from brick. She could hardly see Joshua, only a shadow shaking violently, a dark form in a maelstrom of light and sound, an explosion of energy.

Another figure materialized, rising up from the floor, raising his arms in the eloquence of entreaty and then jerking backward. He hit the floor and rolled over, smacked forward by the light, reached up and grabbed Moshe by the shoulder, and dragged him down with him. They were swept away together, plaster raining down upon them, then stopped in a tangle of arms and legs at the wall by the door. The light raced through the door, carrying lampshades and bedsheets, then the door screeched and broke loose from its hinges and vanished into the corridor.

Kate clung to the bed, her eyes dazzled by the light, almost deafened by the terrible roaring, a fierce wind tugging at her. She saw Joshua on the bed, a diffused form in white fire, the light streaming around his body and then roaring out through the door. He was burning, disintegrating, melting into the maelstrom, while the third soldier, screaming dementedly, was swept out of the room. Moshe was still by the wall, wrapped around the other soldier, both of them being pummeled by the light as if by a hurricane.

Kate sobbed and closed her eyes, felt the bed shaking beneath her, gripped the mattress and hauled herself forward and huddled into the wall. She tried to blot out the roaring, tried to resist the clawing force, but her head started splitting in two as her body was hauled back. Her fingernails tore at the mattress, fingers bending and digging in, but her body, stretching out to its limit, eventually made her let go. She felt as if she were being devoured, sucked into an enormous throat, and then, when the roaring seemed to be all around her, she screamed and fell down.

She hit the floor and rolled over, coming to rest on her back, and then lay there, not moving any farther, as the roaring receded. Still motionless, she looked up, saw the havoc settling down, the light retreating from the walls and then shrinking to a globe around Joshua. There was a distant, rushing sound, like water pouring down a faucet, then the light around Joshua flared up and shimmered briefly and then disappeared into his body.

Kate stared at him, mesmerized, then managed to look the other way; she saw Moshe and the soldier rolling apart and lying flat on their backs, both gasping for breath. Her heart went out to Moshe, a love she scarcely recognized, then she turned her head back the other way and again looked at Joshua. He was in the same position, bent forward, not moving; then he put one hand down, tugged aimlessly at his white robe, then raised his head and stared directly at her, his face human and anguished.

"It was rage," he said quietly.

23

Hardly feeling like a human being, let alone the Ashkenazic chief rabbi, Jozsef lowered himself into his chair at the crowded committee table just as Moshe was finishing his curt, precise summary of the recent events. Making himself comfortable, though still sweating too much, Jozsef nodded at Ben Eliezer, silently apologizing for being late, then looked at the people sitting around the table, none of whom seemed too happy. Moshe and Kate were side by side, the former addressing the table, the latter rubbing her closed eyes with her fingers; both seemed almost haunted. Leonard Rosenberg, the medical director, and General Yaakov Meshel, the head of the Intelligence Committee, were sitting together at the opposite side, Leonard doodling abstractedly on a sheet of paper, the general staring at Moshe. To Jozsef's surprise Paul Frankel was also present, his dark, handsome face expressing shock at what he was hearing.

"So," Moshe said eventually, glancing at everyone in turn, "those are the up-to-date facts of the matter. It's now open for discussion."

"This is extraordinary," Paul Frankel said.

"A constructive start," Ben Eliezer replied. "We appreciate your shock, Lieutenant Frankel, but please try to control it."

Paul glared at the prime minister, then blushed and lowered his eyes, a slight tremor running through his body as he picked up a pencil.

"For a start," Ben Eliezer added, "perhaps someone can tell me why Lieutenant Frankel, a relatively inexperienced officer, should have been invited to sit in on this meeting."

"I felt that Shin Beth should be involved," General Meshel replied.

"I asked for Military, not Internal Security to handle the matter."

"I wasn't satisfied with their results," Yaakov replied, glancing at Moshe, "so I felt that Shin Beth should be given a chance."

"And Lieutenant Frankel?"

"Although he is, as you say, a relatively inexperienced officer, he is also, unquestionably, one of our most successful interrogators."

Jozsef glanced across at Paul and saw his flickering smile, a helpless demonstration of pride as he lowered his eyes again. Ben Eliezer, clasping his hands beneath his chin, kept his eyes straight ahead.

"Shin Beth wants that man," he said, "but Shin Beth has already failed. In insisting that he be separated from Kate, his first contact, they encouraged him to practically demolish his room."

"No one could have anticipated that, Shlomo."

"And are you still going to try to separate them?"

"I don't think we should try that for the moment," Moshe said. "We have no way of dealing with such abilities; we don't know what he's capable of."

"And naturally we still don't know who he is or where he came from."

"No, I'm afraid not. At least nothing other than tentative speculation based on what he remembers."

The prime minister sighed and rubbed his face with his hands, removed his hands and looked up again, staring directly at Jozsef.

"So, Jozsef," he said, "you have heard the tape recordings. What is your assessment of this man?"

Jozsef felt himself blushing and lowered his eyes to the table, unable to utter words that might verge on the blasphemous. He felt sweaty and ill, infinitely wearied by age, all his teaching reduced to dust in his mind, blowing through it and blinding him. Raising his eyes, he glanced at Kate, his heart going out to her, now accepting that what she was enduring was what tortured him also.

"I am lost for words," he said. "The situation is without precedence. I'm a rabbi—a man of faith, not of reason—but the facts overwhelm me."

"Precisely, what *are* the facts?" Ben Eliezer asked.

"It is unlikely," Moshe said quickly, "that Shin Beth will get much further than we have. The man has been examined by physicians, psychologists, parapsychologists, and linguists; and apart from ascertaining that he possesses extraordinary powers, we know no more now than we knew when he first spoke to Kate."

"Those powers are really very unusual, Moshe. One might even describe them as miraculous—if not downright inhuman."

"Not necessarily," Moshe replied. "The man is flesh and blood, physiologically a human being, and his powers, although extraordinarily advanced, could be explicable in human terms."

"I find that hard to accept," Leonard Rosenberg said.

"I'm talking about parapsychology, Leonard. We know that powers such as this man has demonstrated have also been observed, to an admittedly much lesser degree, under laboratory conditions in various institutions. The Soviets and Americans are particularly interested in this field; and subjects like Ted Serios, Nelya Mikhailova, and Rosa Kuleshova are proven cases of advanced psychokinetic personalities."

"Don't suggest that he's a secret agent," Kate said sarcastically. "We both know that's ridiculous."

Moshe glanced at her and then looked away, his face flushed with anger. "I'm not suggesting any such thing," he said.

Leonard Rosenberg leaned across the table and said: "We are talking about a man who can see when blindfolded, who can transfer his thought images onto photographic plates, who can make objects move and shatter glass without touching them, who can hypnotize his hypnotist, and speak every known language and adopt every accent down on record. No need to mention the devastation he caused when he simply got angry."

"I appreciate that, Leonard, but I'm merely pointing out that if this man's abilities have, to a lesser degree, been demonstrated by other human beings then, extraordinary or not, he could still be an ordinary human being."

"Human, yes," Leonard muttered. "Ordinary, definitely not."

"Let's accept that he's basically human," Ben Eliezer intervened. "Have we analyzed his ambiguous statements and, if so, do we now have some idea of what they mean?"

"*I'll* tell you what they mean," Kate said, leaning forward, her face pale and drawn, her eyes shadowed, her whole body tense. "Since your code-breakers are likely to invent something that doesn't exist, I thought I would give you the simple facts and let you make your own minds up." She glanced quickly at Jozsef, then at Moshe, and then stared down at her notes. "The first thing to bear in mind is that although he remembers little, he is convinced that he has been on earth before. He doesn't know where or when, but certainly his recollections are of biblical times; while the land, as he describes it —great beauty and desolation, the sun shining on parched earth—is remarkably similar to Israel."

"It is also remarkably similar to Africa or Spain," General Meshel said, "but we'll ignore that minor point for the moment."

"No," Kate replied, "I'm afraid your sarcasm is out of place. He mentions a people called the Essenes, a drachma, a denarius, the Court of Gentiles, and the Court of the Israelites. . . . Not Africa or Spain, General Meshel, as I think you'll agree."

"Such descriptions could have been learned overnight from a school history book."

"We'll have to accept—at least for the sake of our hypothesis—that his recollections are genuine."

"With reluctance, my dear."

Kate nodded, her pale cheeks flushing with anger, and then looked down at her notes.

"No Christian," she said, "would have trouble in translating these statements. His first memory is of the presentation of a child, himself, in a temple that included the Court of Gentiles, the Court of Women, and the Court of the Israelites—all of which were, of course, part of Solomon's Temple, now the Haram es-Sharif, the noble enclosure, atop Temple Mount in Jerusalem. In discussing this presentation, he first mentions the Court of Gentiles and then talks of the sacrifice of two birds. He was, according to his recollection, wrapped in swaddling clothes and taken to the Temple by his parents. He clearly states that he was carried up some steps to a 'just and devout one' who confirmed the uniqueness of his birth, that a prophetess serving in the Temple offered thanks to the Lord, and that a priest then sacrificed the two birds, sprinkling the blood of one on the lower corner of the Altar, burning the other on top of the Altar. Whether or not this actually happened to Joshua, we *do* know that in the period he recollects, the first born male, after being circumcised, would have been presented in the Temple, that his parents would have had to enter the Temple via the Court of Gentiles, that there they would have bought themselves two pigeons, that they would then have passed through a barrier and climbed up some steps to the Court of Women, through a gate and then as far as the step marking the end of the Court of the Israelites, where the priest would have sacrificed the two birds in the manner described. Indeed, such a ritual has its roots buried deep in the history of Israel and its details are minutely prescribed in the Mishnah. Also, according to St. Luke, this happened to the child Jesus—and according to Joshua, it happened to him."

"This strikes me as blasphemous," Paul said. "We should not have to listen to it."

"Go on," Ben Eliezer said.

"He claims that between his presentation in the Temple and his thirteenth year he has no memory of anything at all. This is particularly interesting in that there are no written records of Jesus' life between *his* presentation and his thirteenth year—and indeed this whole period of Jesus' life is an absolute mystery."

"This is Christian doctrine," Paul said angrily. "We are all Jews in here."

Ignoring him, Kate continued: "According to Joshua's next statement, he is sitting in the shadows of the colonnades of the Temple, learning from the priests, thus assuming the responsibilities of a student in the affairs of the Most High. Here, I need only point out to you that just as we Jews celebrate the Bar Mitzva, when the thirteen-year-old male assumes the responsibilities of adulthood, so, too, in the time of Jesus, did the thirteen-year-old male assume his responsibilities by going to the Temple to be taught by the priests. He would neither communicate with nor return to his family until his teaching had ended—and here, again, in recalling his own teaching, Joshua states that he had forsaken his parents to go to the Temple. Likewise, according to the New Testament, Jesus forsook his father and mother, and went, at the age of thirteen, to be taught in the Temple."

"Your parallels are singularly disgusting," Paul said, "and should be erased from the minutes of this meeting."

"His next statement is this," Kate continued as if in a trance. " 'I see a ribbon of water. A line of people stretches to it. I wade in the water and am dazzled by the sun, and the man with the face of a prophet takes hold of my shoulders. He immerses me in the water, crying words I cannot hear, and I rise up as the heavens open out and a white dove appears.' " She raised her head and stared at everyone in turn, her stance almost defiant. "At the risk of offending you, I must speak like a Christian and point out that that statement has striking parallels in Matthew 3:16, Mark 1:10, Luke 3:22, and John 1:32—all describing John's baptism of Jesus Christ."

"I must protest!" Paul exclaimed.

"Protest denied," Ben Eliezer said. "We are not necessarily accepting what she says, but we must hear her out."

"His next three memories are visions of temptation," Kate continued, "and each one of them is recorded in the New Testament as relating to Jesus. First, in the wilderness, he is tempted to turn stone to bread; next, on a mountain, he is offered the world for his soul; and finally, he is taken to a pinnacle of the Temple where he is tempted to throw himself down and let the angels protect him. For those of you unfamiliar with the New Testament, I will simply point out that all three incidents are recorded in Matthew and Luke, where they describe Christ's temptation by the Devil. Joshua recounts exactly the same temptations, but calls his tempter 'the Evil One.' "

"Luckily our man called himself Joshua," Ben Eliezer said, not without a certain note of relief.

"Unfortunately," Kate said, "Jesus and Joshua represent the same name: 'Jesus Christ' is merely the Greek translation for the Hebrew 'Joshua the anointed.' And Joshua's very first words—'Before Abraham was, I am'—have long been attributed to Jesus."

A sudden, shocked silence descended upon the table as each of them took in what they had heard and tried to grasp its full import. Jozsef studied them all in turn, his heart beating far too quickly, his spirit plunging down to some cavern where fear limned the darkness. Jesus the Jew, he thought, that most remarkable and ambiguous man; who divided the Jewish world into Jews and Gentiles and branded the Jews as the killers of Christ, the Earth's most despised race. Then, of course, there was the irony—the Christians worshiped a Jewish prophet—but beneath that, like the thorns beneath the rose, lay the nightmare of vengeance. Two thousand years of persecution—the endless blood of the Crucifixion—as the Christians, avenging their Jewish Christ, tried to obliterate Judaism. Jozsef thought of it with woe, with a fresh, frightening clarity, and wondered, even as he glanced across at Kate's dark, haunted face, how he could possibly handle this extraordinary event.

"Let me get this straight," General Meshel said slowly, his voice no longer harsh with cynicism, his eyes directly on Kate. "Can I take it that you're suggesting this man is the resurrected Jesus Christ?"

"I'm not willing to suggest anything," Kate replied. "I'm merely pointing out that his fragments of recall are all remarkably similar to the known facts on Jesus Christ, that all our tests have proven that he is not consciously lying to us, that he thinks he is called Joshua, which simply means Jesus, and that like the original Jesus, he is a normal human being, but one with unusual powers of the kind shared by few men."

"Hypnotically induced amnesia and the implantation of his few recollections could conceivably have been arranged in a Soviet or American military laboratory. As for his extraordinary powers, they could be the results of intense parapsychological training in some similar environment."

"No," Leonard Rosenberg said. "No kind of hypnosis could defeat our psychological tests, let alone account for his unprecedented command of every known language. Nor could any kind of parapsychological training account for the manner in which Joshua devastated his room. Human he may be, but natural he is not: he's a very rare kind of human being, beyond rational analysis."

Jozsef clasped his hands together and started cracking his knuckles, a sound that seemed shockingly loud in the room's stricken silence. Embarrassed, he stopped immediately and placed his hands back on the table, lowering his eyes and then raising them again to stare shyly around him. Ben Eliezer returned his stare, automatically, scarcely seeing him, then sighed and looked down at the table as if deep in thought. General Meshel was staring at Kate, his eyes narrowed, no longer cynical, his right hand tapping a pencil up and down, his left holding a cigarette. Leonard Rosenberg was leaning back, his hands clasped behind his head, his head shaking from side to side in disbelief, his eyes fixed on the ceiling. Moshe and Kate both looked haunted, glancing uneasily at one another, their eyes locking and then breaking apart before meeting again.

Then Jozsef looked at Paul Frankel and immediately felt more uneasy, aware that the lieutenant was an extreme Orthodox Jew —perhaps more extreme than he was willing to show—and disturbed by the intensity of his gaze as he leaned toward Kate.

"You claim that you're unwilling to suggest anything," Paul said, "but in fact your every word suggests that you believe this man is the resurrected Christ of the New Testament."

"I don't know *what* I believe," Kate replied. "I'm just very disturbed. The facts are almost beyond comprehension, but they can't be disproven."

"Neither his recollections nor his powers constitute proof that he is the Christian Jesus—and if he were, it should little disturb us, since we are Hebrew, not Christian."

He stared at Jozsef for confirmation, his dark eyes very intense, and Jozsef, even against his every instinct, faced the issue that was normally avoided by Jew and Christian alike. There was the Jesus of the Jews and the Christ of the Christians, and this division, ironic in the extreme, was also destructive. Christianity and Judaism had sprung from the same root, but neither religion was willing to recognize the fact. Nor was either religion, in the duplicity of self-righteousness, willing to accept the Jewish background of the man called Jesus. Yet Jesus was a Jew, immersed in scripture, taught by rabbis—not, in Jewish eyes, the Son of God, but most certainly a prophet. Judaism and Christianity had therefore much in common, but were divided over the interpretation of this one man and his extraordinary impact. Now there was the man called Joshua, another Jesus of mysterious origins, and already, like his remarkable predecessor, he was causing dissension. Whether resurrected or not, whether the same man or another, his very presence on the soil of Israel could lead to terrible consequences. Jozsef thought of this and trembled, looked at Paul and felt despair, suddenly wishing that Jew and Gentile could be one as they had been in the beginning. Then, lowering his eyes, trying to keep his voice steady, silently praying for guidance and understanding, he let his words find their own way.

"I'm afraid we must be disturbed," he said, "since Kate omitted one recollection. This man, Joshua, also made mention of the Teacher of Righteousness, of scrolls in dark caves, of how the Teacher of Righteousness went before him and showed the way and the scrolls revealed the lineaments of the life that gave shape to his own. Presumably, then, the scrolls showed the path he would have to follow, and revealed it through the actions of a predecessor, the Teacher of Righteousness."

"You are talking about the Dead Sea Scrolls," Paul said.

"Correct," Jozsef said. "The Dead Sea Scrolls, discovered by a Bedouin shepherd in the remote caves of Qumran, revealed a prototype for Jesus a century before his birth, this man a leader of the Jewish sect known as the Essenes—which Joshua also mentioned. No matter: the Dead Sea Scrolls revealed that the Essenes had developed a curious hybrid of Judaic creed that diverged from both Saducee and Pharisee Judaism, still managed to resemble both in certain ways, but bore a distinct resemblance to the future Christianity, including a protocol for seating foreshadowing the Last Supper and a ritual foreshadowing the Christian communion. The central figure of this sect was a mysterious figure known as the Teacher of Righteousness. Viewed by his disciples as the suffering servant of God and the instrument of salvation for mankind, often called the *nezer*—the

Nazarene—and believed to be the 'shoot' of the House of David and
the rock upon which the future Church would be built, he was also
destined, like the later Jesus, to be slain at the hand of a 'wicked
priest.' The name of the Teacher of Righteousness is not known, but
after his execution, about 65 to 53 B.C., his disciples, convinced that
he would reappear among them, settled in the area around Qumran
and awaited his return, doubtless also then writing the Dead Sea
Scrolls and preparing themselves for Judgment Day."

Jozsef slowly raised his head, feeling weary and confused, glanced
at Paul, and then looked across at Kate, feeling drawn to her haunted
face. Her eyes, dark and luminous and strangely passionate, made
him feel less self-conscious.

"As you can see," he continued, "the resemblance between the
Teacher of Righteousness and the later Jesus Christ is rather remarkable. More important, however, is that the discovery of this curious
sect and their leader shattered the myth of the originality of
Christianity and confirmed that it had evolved out of Judaism. While
this dismayed the Christians, it also dismayed us Jews; since we now
had to face the fact that many of the Christian rituals reviled by us had
been conceived and practiced by Jews two centuries before Christianity existed. Therefore this man Joshua—whether or not he is the
resurrected Jesus or another man altogether—could be claimed quite
legitimately by Christian and Jew alike—and the resulting conflict
between our two religions would be quite catastrophic. And, it should
be noted, there is no question at all that Joshua believes his future
course was foreshadowed by the Teacher of Righteousness."

"He also states," Kate quickly added, "that his last recollection is
of his last temptation—and that after it, he turned away from further
temptation to embark on his calling. We can take it, then, that he
believes he is on the Earth for some undefined purpose."

Jozsef watched her head turning, her eyes looking at every face,
and he felt his love and sorrow rising up as if to sweep him away. Yet
he also felt exultant and helplessly grateful, sensing that his lost child
had been found and returned to the fold. She, who had lost faith, was
finding it again; and no matter the basis of that faith, it was something
to build upon.

Thinking of this, he was stunned, his exultation draining away,
suddenly turning back into confusion and the cold blade of doubt. For
indeed what was he accepting? That this man was the Chosen One?
That this man, in his mystery and power, was the tool of conversion?

Jozsef looked at Kate and shuddered, again swept by love and sorrow, wanting to reach out and take her in his arms and then pray for salvation—not just hers, but his own.

"So," General Meshel said, "we have circumstantial evidence, but not quite enough to prove our case. No matter what you say, we are still left with a man whose origins simply cannot be ascertained. And I, for one, really cannot accept that he lived in Jerusalem two thousand years ago."

"Which brings us to Joshua's shroud," Moshe replied.

Jozsef looked across the table at Moshe and saw his drawn, weary face. Moshe leaned forward and placed his elbows on the table and then raised his hands, his eyes fixed on the general.

"Shortly after finding Joshua," he said, "we removed his shroud, or robe, and sent it in a sealed container to the Weizmann Institute for analysis. While a proper, scientifically verifiable report will take another year to complete, we feel that the results obtained so far are well worth reading out at this meeting; and since Leonard has been in charge of the program, he will give you the details."

Letting his chair fall forward, Leonard leaned over the table, glanced nervously at Jozsef, then put his head down and started reading, his voice sounding shaky.

"So far, tests on the shroud have included ion microprobe analysis, X-ray fluorescence work, X-ray transmission work, spectroscopic examination, infrared thermography, radiological testing, and incomplete radiocarbon dating. The basic material proved to be linen. To ascertain the precise nature of this linen, selected threads were removed from the robe with microscopy pincers and examined under the microscope, then viewed under polarized lights for the best possible contrast. The fiber showed no signs of disintegration. The style of weave was revealed to be a three-to-one herringbone twill of the kind common to Palestinian, Roman, and Egyptian linens during the first century A.D., albeit in silks rather than linen, this suggesting a fairly costly manufacture. Also found were traces of cotton, the fiber corresponding to the species *Gossypium herbaceum*, which is characteristic of the Middle East. A more precise estimate of the geographic origins of the material was obtained through the analysis of particles of dust removed from it, particularly a one-by-one examination of various pollen grains. Electron microscope examination of such grains revealed typical halophytes: plants common to the desert region of the Jordan Valley and specifically adapted to live in a soil with a high content of sodium chloride, such as that found almost exclusively around the Dead Sea. Tentative dating of the linen was obtained with a carbon-fourteen test—a technique used most successfully on the linen wrappings of the Dead Sea Scrolls—and from these still incomplete tests we have obtained a dating plus or minus two hundred years. This tentative dating places the linen in either late B.C. or early A.D. Our preliminary assessment, therefore, is that the robe originated in the Middle East, was certainly worn in the area of Palestine, and was almost certainly woven at least eighteen centuries ago, possibly earlier."

No one said anything for a considerable time, all too stunned by what they had heard to fully accept it. Jozsef closed his eyes briefly, sinking down through his mind, trying to reason through the chaos caused by panic, and failing quite dismally. He opened his eyes again, looked at every face in turn, saw Moshe's veiled eyes, Kate's haunted expression, then concentrated, with increasing trepidation, on the handsome face of Lieutenant Frankel. Paul was leaning across the table, staring at everyone in turn, his eyes bright but slightly unfocused, as if staring inward.

"It's a miracle," Paul said. "We can no longer doubt that. But that doesn't mean we have to accept that this man is the original Jesus Christ. Jesus Christ was crucified—the Turin Shroud was the proof of that—so this man should have scars on his hands and feet, like those shown on the Turin Shroud."

"No scars," Moshe said wearily. "No scars at all."

"Then he isn't Jesus Christ," Paul replied with some intensity. "Jesus Christ, as we know, was a zealot who was crucified, and clearly this man was not crucified."

"There could be reasons why the scars no longer show. They could, after all, have been erased with passing time."

"If we are to accept that that man is nearly two thousand years old, if we are to accept, as the tests show, that neither he nor his shroud were damaged, then we must also accept that the condition we found him in was the exact same condition he was in when he was buried, in a manner defying our comprehension, in that tomb on the Mount. In other words, if he had been crucified, the scars would still be there."

"Very good," Ben Eliezer said, "but it doesn't solve our problem. I still want to know what we have here."

"Was he circumcised?" Paul asked.

"Yes," Leonard replied.

"A Jewish prophet," Paul said fervently. "Perhaps even the Messiah. He is not a supernatural being but a man of flesh and blood, yet unmistakably one with divine gifts or supernatural abilities. Such will be the Messiah and such is this man—and his presence here, combined with the opening of the Golden Gate and the fact that he was brought down from the Mount of Olives, surely testifies that he is the Messiah and the age of Redemption is at hand."

"No!" Jozsef cried hoarsely. "I will not permit this! You are abusing Jewish folklore and tradition to fortify your delusions!"

"*My* delusions?" Paul replied, his resentment finally breaking loose. "You do not believe in the coming of the Messiah as ordained in the Torah? No, Jozsef, probably not; your blasphemous modernism is well known. Your liberal view of Judaic creed has been noted and has caused much resentment."

"I do not encourage fanaticism or antiquated religious bigotry —neither that of the Neturei Karta zealots nor that of Gush Emunim. That I attempt to interpret the Talmud with an open mind is not blasphemous, but sensible."

"It is—"

"Gentlemen, gentlemen," Ben Eliezer said firmly, "this is no time for theological debate—we must consider the facts."

Jozsef was grateful for the interruption, feeling ashamed of his anger, but understanding, as he settled back into his chair, that the young lieutenant was dangerous. A wave of grief then passed through him, an intimation of tragedy, and he found himself thinking yet again of Jewish conflict and separatism. Lieutenant Frankel, a zealot, far too pious for his own good, was unfortunately a very common kind who could not be ignored. Never before and not now—most assuredly not now—since public knowledge of the man from the Mount could lead to public disorder. And if fanatical Jews and Christians could adopt this man, then so, too, could the Arabs.

"So," Ben Eliezer said, glancing skeptically at Paul, "we have a man who might be approximately two thousand years old and carries in his head recollections that suggest the life of Jesus Christ. He has no scars at all, which at least suggests that he wasn't crucified, but he certainly possesses abnormal powers and thinks he is here for a purpose. What do we do, gentlemen, to make our speculations concrete? Wait for another year in the hope that the completed shroud tests will, given the wonders of science, produce all the answers? I think not: we need something else."

"I want to take him out," Kate said. "I want to show him around Jerusalem. I want to see how he reacts when we take him to some places where Jesus was reported to have walked. That may or may not prove something, but we've little to lose."

"He might run away," Moshe said.

"No," Kate said, "he won't. He doesn't know what he's here for or what he's supposed to do, so he simply does what he is told and lets events take their course. Also, he's convinced that it's through me that he will find what his mission is. So he will go where I take him and return without argument."

"He did not let events take their course," Leonard said, "when Moshe attempted to separate him from you."

"True," Kate replied, "but again, what he did was designed to keep me close by his side."

"We'll need witnesses," Ben Eliezer said.

"I'd like Moshe to come with me."

"I'd like Shin Beth to be represented," General Meshel said, "so you can also take Paul."

"I'm a Jew," Paul replied. "Some of those sites are forbidden to me. My beliefs would not permit me to enter Christian houses of worship."

Jozsef noticed Paul's sharp glance, a blend of contempt and accusation, and he felt his anger rising again at the young man's self-righteousness. He tried to control it, unwilling to let rage blind him, determined to stay as calm as possible and get at the truth. He looked at Kate and then Moshe, saw them staring at one another, suppressed emotion rippling across both their faces and erasing their weariness. Seeing this, he felt better, oddly comforted and energized, and he turned his head again and looked at Paul, keeping his eyes very steady.

"This is an important matter," he said, "for Jew and gentile alike; and may also be of considerable importance to the Muslims. If, as you say, this man might be the Messiah, it is your duty to confirm or deny after seeing the evidence. You may enter the Christian sites if not entering to worship and if, in the witnessing of what transpires, you return with the truth."

He stared at Paul for some time, finally saw him nodding slowly, then turned away and glanced blindly around the table, feeling strangely excited. The silence was uneasy, a mute sigh that filled the room, only broken by the sound of the wind beyond the walls of the

Knesset. Jozsef dwelt on what he felt, trying to analyze his excitement, failed, and then experienced deep shame at his sudden lack of
despair. He was behaving unnaturally, perhaps even immorally;
letting his curiosity threaten the very tenets of his faith, and possibly
yearning, in hypocritical ignorance, that Paul's vision of the Redemption might be true. Feeling hot, he mopped his brow, lowered his eyes
and studied his hands, then raised his eyes again and looked across the
polished wood of the long table. Moshe and Kate had moved slightly,
their bodies turned toward one another, their eyes locked in some
silent communication that involved pain and yearning. Startled,
slightly shocked, feeling almost like a voyeur, Jozsef coughed into his
fist and moved his eyes until he found the prime minister.

"So be it," Ben Eliezer said.

24

He said nothing as they drove along the Hebron Road, passing the Kibbutz Ramat Rachel and the Mar Elias Monastery and then descending into a biblical panorama of orchards and fields where the black-garbed Arabs tended their sheep and goats. Nor did he say anything when they stopped the car and showed him Shepherd's Field, where the angel had announced the birth of Jesus to the shepherds tending their flock. Nor did he say anything when they drove on to Bethlehem, climbed out into the noisy Manger Square, and walked past the taxis and tour buses to the Church of the Nativity. Finally he said nothing when they stood in the Grotto of the Nativity, but merely stared at the star on the floor, glowing golden in the candlelight, then returned the curious stares of the few tourists and their Arab guides and went in to examine the Chapel of the Manger. Seeing nothing recognizable, obviously getting no reaction from it, he shook his head from side to side in a negative gesture and let them lead him back out.

They all remained silent as they drove back around Jerusalem, then headed north across the beautiful plain of Esdraelon, Moshe following the winding road as it ran up through fruitful forests and then fell down to the natural amphitheater in which Nazareth nestled. Joshua maintained his silence as they drove through the modern town, his silvery-gray eyes curious but registering no shock as they passed cars and buses and donkeys and carts, along streets lined with cafés and shops, filled with Christians and Muslims. They stopped and disembarked outside the Roman Catholic Church of St. Joseph, but again, although he gazed at it with interest, he did not seem perturbed.

"It means nothing to you?" Paul said.

"No," Joshua replied.

"Then you cannot have been the son of the carpenter Joseph."

"I never claimed to be," Joshua said.

Leaving the church, they led him to the Basilica of the Annuncia-tion, first taking him through the upper church with its modern mosaic panels, then down to the dark and shadowy grotto in the lower church, lit only by flashes of color from its small windows. There he stood for some time, the surrounding pillars casting shadows upon him, his head leaning into the beams of light and then moving back again, his eyes lost in the darkness. Finally he stepped back, letting the gloom dissolve his features, and spoke, his voice hollow in the cave, very quiet, almost spectral.

"There is nothing of me here. I feel something nearby. I think of the great Via Maris, which linked nation to nation. There were pilgrims and merchants and soldiers near the foot of the hill. That is all I can see."

"The great highway," Kate said, speaking for the first time. "It ran between Egypt and the nations of the North and the East, passing a short distance from Nazareth and then traveling across the plain of Esdraelon. It existed during the time of Jesus Christ."

They left the basilica and took him to the Greek Orthodox church, down the small stairway, then along an ancient, marble-lined passage to the well at which it was believed the archangel first appeared to Mary and the boy Jesus would have come to collect water. He stood for some time, staring down at the well, his noble brow furrowed in concentration, his hands opening and closing. Then his hands closed, became tightly clenched fists, and a tremor ran visibly through his body and then passed away. Kate watched him and went dizzy, closed her eyes and saw two shadows, a woman and a boy bending over, their hands dripping water. She shivered and felt fear, opened her eyes and saw his face, turned toward her and offering a glance that calmed her immediately.

"You saw it," he said.

"Saw what?" Moshe asked.

"A woman and child," Kate replied. "Possibly just in my mind. I closed my eyes and seemed to see them by the pool for a second or two."

"And you?" Moshe said to Joshua.

"It was in my mind," Joshua replied. "She rolls back the stones of my past and releases the shadows."

"Who were they?"

"I don't know."

"You don't think the child was you?"

"I have no idea who the child was; I saw little, felt nothing."

"Let's get out of here," Kate said.

"Why, Kate, are you frightened?"

Kate shivered. "Maybe. I feel strange. I want to leave here righ now."

They left and headed back toward the town center until they arrive at the Greek Catholic church, said to be the site of the synagogu attended by Jesus. Once there he lowered his head, closed his eyes and started shaking, then opened his eyes again and stared at Kat with a hard, bright intensity. Kate immediately felt faint, closed he eyes and saw more shadows, felt anger rising up and coming towar her and pushing her backward. Then she felt Moshe's hands, restin lightly on her shoulders, holding her upright as she opened her eye again and looked straight at Joshua. His eyes, with their silvery-gra luminescence, seemed calm but unnatural.

"I might have been here," he said. "A great anger was directed a me. There was much debate and anger near this place, and I feel I wa part of it."

Kate turned to Moshe and Paul, her lips dry, her heart beating "According to St. Luke," she said, "when Jesus taught in th synagogue, he so angered the townsmen that they dragged him awa and attempted to throw him off the brow of a nearby hill. Th traditional site of that hill is now located at Djebel-el-Qafse, approxi mately a mile from here. The anger that Joshua sensed—and that sensed—could have come from that incident."

"A Christian myth," Paul said, "with no basis in fact. You hav recently studied the New Testament in detail and now remember you reading. You are, in short, trying to convince yourself regarding you own dubious parallels."

"But Joshua felt it as well," Moshe said quietly.

"Perhaps," Paul said. "But how do we interpret it? It seems certai that he lived in the times of which he speaks, but not necessarily a the Son of the One: more likely a prophet."

From Nazareth they drove through a stunning wasteland of rock gorges and parched hills, the sun blazing down mercilessly on an eve bleaker landscape, until they arrived at the verdant green of the palr trees and fruit orchards of Jericho; then they drove on to the Wac Qelt gorge and the towering, spectacular cliffs where Christ was sai to have spent his forty days in meditation. Taking Joshua to the walle enclosure on the summit of the Mount of Temptation, where Jesu was said to have been tempted by the Devil, they all stood there in breathless silence, awed by the stupendous panorama stretched out below them—the barren wilderness shimmering under the sun and rolling away to the sky—then glanced uneasily at one another, neither willing to speak, and eventually turned their eyes upon Joshua, wondering what he would do.

He stood near the edge of the cliff, the wind blowing his white robe out, his long hair whipping wildly around his face as he looked down on the magnificent desolation of the hills and valleys of Jordan. Kate stepped forward to touch him, then stopped, feeling frightened; closed her eyes and felt the presence of evil as a palpable force. She clenched her fists and started trembling, her heart pounding much too fast, then heard a whispering that seemed to surround her and was filled with pure malice. A specter. A presence. An invisible, malignant force. There were visions of torture and pain and the most pitiless hatred. A scream rose up from her center, bubbling into her throat, and she shook her head wildly from side to side, trying to stifle her terror. Then someone's hands grabbed her, Moshe's hands, large and firm, and she opened her eyes to see the sweeping wastelands shimmering under the sun. She blinked and stared at Joshua, saw his silvery-gray eyes, their bright serenity drawing her out of herself and leading her into calm pastures.

"What was it?" she asked.

"You nearly walked off the edge," Moshe said. "You closed your eyes and started to walk forward and nearly fell off."

"It was the Evil One," Joshua said. "As he was, so he is. He stretches around the firmament like a cloud, dividing darkness from light."

"You saw him?" Moshe said.

"No," Joshua said, "I felt him. The Evil One exists by wind and fire and is part of the Nothing."

They left the Mount of Temptation and drove on through the wilderness toward the sleepy Arab village of El-Azariye, or Bethany, where they stopped at the modest tomb of Lazarus, close to the nineteenth-century Franciscan church. Joshua immediately went down the stairs and stood in front of the shrine, his white robe looking spectral in the gloom when Kate walked up behind him. They both stood there for some time, neither saying a word, hardly aware of the few tourists who murmured piously around them, all of them mistaking Joshua for an Arab and averting their shocked eyes accordingly. Joshua shivered again, and Kate closed her eyes and drifted, the darkness rolling back across the curtain of her eyelids to reveal dark-shawled women kneeling low in lamentation, their hands rising and falling in prayer above a man in the shadows. Kate experienced terrible grief, then was filled with exultation; heard the cries of surprise and disbelief and then opened her eyes again. She saw Joshua staring at her, his eyes unnaturally bright, and she shivered and hurried from the tomb and let him find his own way out.

"Well?" Paul said.

"He knows the place," Kate replied.

"That doesn't necessarily mean he was the Christ."

"I never stated such," Joshua said.

They drove him to the Jordan River where it ran east of Jericho and stood on the traditional site of Christ's baptism. "Let it be now," he said, his face radiant in the light, while Kate, her feet cleansed by the flowing water, felt the shock through her body. The water came up to her ankles, but she felt submerged in it, first struggling in darkness and cold and then emerging to light. Something fluttered above her head, a white bird traveling east, and the heavens opened out in her mind and filled her spirit with warmth. She opened her eyes and saw Joshua, felt the tears on her cheeks, raised her right hand and wiped the tears off, and then turned to face Moshe. He was standing close to her with Paul standing just behind him, Moshe concerned and Paul looking bewildered, neither moving at all. Kate smiled, or felt that she was smiling, and dropped her hands to her sides.

"You were crying," Moshe said.

"Yes," Kate replied.

Joshua stepped forward and touched her with his hands, his fingers light on her shoulders. "Tears of joy," he said. "The waters carry the joy with them. It was here that the prophet called my name and ordained my deliverance. What was willed, will be done."

"What *was* willed?" Kate said fearfully.

"It was willed and will be repeated. The seasons come and go and repeat themselves; and just as it is with the seasons, so it is with mankind."

Kate felt a great fear that only deepened in intensity when they arrived at the deserted caves of Qumran by the banks of the Dead Sea. They stood in the Wadi Qumran, the ancient cliffs towering above them, the caves pockmarking the cliffs like dead eyes, a lunar silence surrounding them. Joshua gazed along the cliffs, his eyes scanning the dark caves, then he turned and looked across the Dead Sea as if searching for something. The sun beat upon the smooth sea, cutting through the cloud of haze, the hills of Judah sweeping down to the western shore on the opposite side. Joshua turned back toward the caves, stepped forward and then stopped, bowed his head, and covered his face with his hands as if silently weeping. Kate walked across to him, feeling nothing but his love, seeing nothing but the radiance around his face where the sunlight exploded. In that dazzling light he changed, becoming someone much darker, a man wise and burdened beyond his years, knowing what was to come. Kate reached out to touch him, her fingers spread and shaking slightly, and felt the burning skin of his forehead, a slight shock charging through her. Dazed, her body hollow, she removed her hand and stepped away, then noticed, as a cloud covered the sun, that Joshua looked perfectly normal.

"It was not I," he said. "But here my coming was prophesied. Here the Teacher of Righteousness told the tale of the trial to come. He was here before my time, and before my time he knew me, and his life, a mere prelude to his death, precisely mirrored my own. He was here and is here in my head with the light shining out of him. I must leave this place and never come back because the trials begin again."

"The trials?"

"Those that will come. For myself . . . and for you."

The fear clamped around Kate as she turned toward Moshe, letting him hold her hand and lead her to the car, his silence offering solace. In her fear was a desperate love, the pain of yearning and hapless need, and as she sat down in the back of the car she wondered who had aroused it. Almost certainly Joshua, but not him alone; beyond Joshua, in some realm where the past and present met, she was being tortured by the need to express a more common commitment. Joshua slid into the seat beside her while Paul clambered into the front, then Moshe closed his door and turned the ignition on and drove off very slowly. Kate studied his broad shoulders and the nape of his neck, then turned her head and studied Joshua's profile as the sun passed across it. A remarkable profile, at once noble and strangely primitive, it belonged to every race and every creed and refused to divide them. Kate sat back in her seat, closed her eyes, and drifted away, letting the droning of the car soothe her nerves in an impermanent peace.

They drove back to Jerusalem and up to the summit of the Mount of Olives, disembarking near the Intercontinental Hotel and walking across to the amphitheater with its breathtaking view of Old Jerusalem. Joshua studied the lovely sheen of the golden Dome of the Rock, let his eyes wander across to the silver dome of the Mosque of El Aqsa, then finally fixed his gaze on the majestic, conical roof of the Dormition Abbey.

"Zion," he said. "I know it as Mount Zion. Beyond that, I know nothing at all. That hill is Mount Zion."

Kate glanced at Moshe and saw him looking at Paul, whose brown eyes, like stones in the darkness, reflected pale light. Obviously shaken, he turned away, murmured something, and then walked on, and they followed him down the short, sloping road and back up to the waste ground. The ruins of the Chapel of the Ascension were desolate and strangely ominous, a fine dust drifting languidly across the rubble and settling over their shoes. Joshua studied the ruins at length, walking back and forth in silence, while Kate, remembering the night of his discovery, started visibly trembling. He noticed and walked toward her, stopped in front of her, and put his hand out, touching her cheek lightly with his fingers and offering a gentle smile.

"No fear," he said. "There is no reason to fear. What was done has been done and cannot be undone and has, like you and I and our brothers, a reason for being. I know it was here, and that my coming was preordained, but I still do not know what came before and perhaps never will. You were called and you came and now the fear grips your heart, but beyond the fear is love and redemption which exist by your faith. No fear. You must not have fear. Let your faith fill your heart."

"You remember nothing else?"

"No," he said. "Nothing else."

"Naturally not," Paul said. "The famed ascension is pure myth. You were, and probably still are, a prophet. By my faith I believe this."

They both stared at him silently, as if staring at a stranger, and he turned, his face flushed with confusion, and walked across the sad ruins. They followed him, walking slowly, their feet kicking up the stones, and then entered the Pater Noster Church, blending in with the tourists. Here, set into the tiled walls, were the words of the Lord's Prayer, written out in sixty-two different languages; and he looked left and right, his gaze scanning every language, and then murmured the words to himself. Paul shivered and turned away, his brown eyes displaying fear, and they followed him through the colonnaded courtyard, back out to the sunshine.

They did not return to the car, but instead walked down the narrow road to the Franciscan Church of Dominus Flevit. Joshua changed almost instantly, his silvery-gray eyes turning moist, and then, for the first time, his head turning away from them, he covered his face with his hands, bowed his head, and quietly wept.

"For Jerusalem," he said, his voice hollow as the wind. "For the days shall come upon it that its enemies shall surround it and not leave one stone upon the other nor let the dust settle."

He dried his eyes and walked away, leading them down the stony path, then stopped at the Basilica of the Agony, his eyes widening in shock. There were Arabs with camels, Jewish hawkers with souvenirs, and the tourists were queuing up with their money, their hands reaching for history. He did not respond immediately, barely able to accept the scene, then he stared across at the Old City, looked back at the crowd before him, and eventually uttered an indistinct imprecation and reached out toward a hawker. His hand chopped down through the air, then swept viciously sideways, sending postcards and assorted souvenirs flying off the small stall. The hawker looked up in shock, his customers gasping and jumping back, then Joshua turned, his rage almost demonic, and walked away like a blind man. He ignored the mosaic scene of Christ praying in Gethsemane, but instead walked on into the garden without speaking to anyone. Kate followed him in, Moshe and Paul hurrying after her, saw him standing very quietly, surveying the cacti and bougainvillaea, then dropping to his knees beneath a gnarled olive tree, one hand reaching out to touch the trunk, his tears falling to earth.

Kate suddenly felt incorporeal, as if her blood were draining out of her, but she walked forward, ignoring Moshe and Paul, and laid her hand on his shoulder. He shivered as if with fever, shaking his head from side to side, but probed the tree trunk with the fingernails of his right hand, digging deep for the truth.

"It's an olive tree," he said. "Such trees never die. When an old trunk is decrepit, it sprouts new wood and thus always renews itself. This tree lived when I walked here, when my tears turned to blood, and it lived through the silence of my great sleep and will witness my passing. It is, like the sun and the moon, more lasting than memory. It endures. We pass on."

His body shook as he wept again, his head turned away from Kate, then he stifled a final sob and stood up and dried his eyes with his hands. He stared at Kate as if haunted, then at Moshe and Paul, kept his eyes fixed on Paul for some time, and then shivered and walked away. They all followed him out, Kate's heart pounding dramatically, something inside her reaching out to Moshe as if begging for help. He walked beside her, his head down, shoulders slumped in despair, and her rioting emotions converged in the well of his quiet strength.

They entered the Grotto of Gethsemane, which Joshua viewed without reaction, then went under the Crusader arch and walked slowly down the stairs to the Orthodox Church of the Assumption. At the bottom, in the gloom, surrounded by hundreds of votive lamps, a dull gleaming illuminated the sepulchre and the scent stung their nostrils. Joshua looked at the milling tourists, at the priests in black robes, saw the boxes being extended for coins and turned his eyes back on Kate.

"I came here," he said, "without knowing why I came; and now that I am here, I am lost, feeling nothing within me."

"It's for Mary," Kate said. "The mother of Jesus. It's supposed to be the site of her burial and assumption—though the Dormition Abbey, which you seemed to recognize, claims a similar honor."

"This is a temple for the gathering of coins. I feel nothing but anger here."

They walked up Jericho Road and turned left into the Old City, passing under the great arch of Lion's Gate, at the beginning of the Via Dolorosa. Here the tourists were numerous and the Arab touts highly vocal, many of them no more than children, their large eyes dark and beautiful. Joshua looked at them with kindness, at the Via Dolorosa with suppressed revulsion, then Kate led him into the grotto beneath the Church of St. Anne where Mary, the mother of Jesus, was presumed to have been born. He studied the grotto with detachment, obviously receiving nothing from it, and then was shown the adjoining excavations of the Pool of Bethesda where Jesus was said to have cured the crippled man. Again there was no reaction, so Kate led him away, walking him along the narrow, shabby Via Dolorosa to the El-Omariye School, the first step along the Stations of the Cross.

In the courtyard of the school, opposite the Franciscan monastery, Joshua reached out and held Kate by the shoulder to let his tension pass into her. She closed her eyes and saw a bowl, two hands emerging, dripping water, heard the words of condemnation in her head before they led her away. She opened her eyes and saw Moshe, staring at her with great intensity, the Chapel of the Flagellation behind him, its refurnished walls dark. Joshua looked at her and held her, his fingers digging into her shoulder, and she closed her eyes again and put her head down, staring into herself. There was the humiliation of mockery, the sudden stinging of the whips, then she felt the thorns biting into her head and heard the roaring of vengeful crowds. Held tightly, she was led away, wanting to sob, unable to do so, turned a corner and stumbled to her knees, opened her eyes and glanced up. Moshe and Paul were staring at her, looking down with startled eyes, and between them, on the wall of the Polish chapel, was the relief showing Jesus bearing the cross. Clinging to Joshua, she stood up and saw him gazing at the relief, his face displaying tension and bathed in sweat, his silvery-gray eyes too bright. He turned his head and stared at her, his eyes growing slightly darker, then they all continued on, following the Via Dolorosa until they arrived at the Armenian Catholic church, the fourth Station of the Cross. Here Joshua closed his eyes, the tears shining on his cheeks, while Kate, feeling the anguish of a mother, shuddered helplessly beside him. She reached out and touched Moshe, her fingers outspread on his face, desperately wanting something human to cling to, feeling the warmth of his lips. Then they walked on, and stopped again at the Franciscan oratory, where Kate, as if unburdened of a terrible weight, straightened her spine and breathed deeply. Joshua likewise seemed relieved, but then shuddered and walked on, his right hand, resting lightly on Kate's shoulder, keeping her close by his side. They came to the Church of St. Veronica but did not go inside, satisfied when Kate reached out, automatically and blindly, to gently wipe the sweat from Joshua's face with the palm of her hand. In that moment there was love, an outpouring of grief and warmth, but then they walked to the crossroads of the Via Dolorosa and Khan Ezeit, and there, where the clamor of the bazaar filled their ears, Kate blacked out momentarily and slid down to her knees, her hands clinging to Joshua's white robes, her head shaking from side to side. Joshua looked down with pity, placed his hand on her head, and then, as the passersby looked on with interest, gently pulled her back to her feet and placed his hand on her shoulder. Kate glanced at Moshe and Paul, saw them staring at one another, turned away when she saw Moshe looking at her, his gray eyes filled with fear. Moshe turned away then, leading them farther along the route, and they soon came to the stone relief on the wall that marked the eighth Station. Here Kate began to sob, uncontrollably and visibly, and the passersby—Muslim, Jew, and Christian—gathered around to look on. Joshua moved away from Kate, his hand dropping from her shoulder, and then, his eyes surveying the curious crowd, spoke loudly and forcefully.

"Do not grieve for her," he said. "Instead grieve for yourselves. Grieve also for your children and the days they will surely inherit. For the day is coming to Jerusalem when the barren shall be beholden, when the wombs that never bear and the breasts which never give milk shall be blessed instead of cursed for their sterility. It is then that you will beg for the mountains to fall upon you, for the hills to cover you up, and for the green tree, which refuses to die, to shed its leaves and turn dry. Jerusalem, your Golden City, will fall, and only faith will redeem it."

Paul gasped and stepped away, covering his mouth with his left hand, his dark eyes showing fear and stunned reverence, a spasm lancing his body. He glanced at Kate and then at Moshe, surveyed the people scattering in embarrassment, then turned his gaze back upon Joshua, who was staring straight at him. Paul stood there, transfixed, licking his lips, and then stepped up to Joshua.

"What made you say that?" he asked.

"It seemed fitting," Joshua replied.

"And you still do not know who you are?"

"I only know I was called."

Paul sobbed and turned away, wiping his eyes with one hand, and they followed him up the Via Dolorosa to the Ethiopian Convent, the ninth Station of the Cross. Inside it was gloomy, the monks striding back and forth, and Kate wiped her eyes and bit her lower lip, her eyes following Joshua. She felt nothing in this place, only the heartbreak of her love, and her feelings, pouring out into the gloom, became one with the silence. Joshua watched her, his gaze curious, a gentle smile on his lips, then he touched her cheek lightly with his fingers and led her back out.

The Church of the Holy Sepulchre was on the Hill of Golgotha, and when Joshua entered through the Crusader portal and glanced around the exotic interior, seeing the artifacts and hanging lights of the numerous sects who shared the church—Syrian and Armenian, Coptic and Abyssinian, Roman Catholic and Greek Orthodox—and then saw the workmen's scaffolding, their clutter of ladders and tools, he stopped, briefly foiled by the sight, momentarily frozen. The holiest of holy sites to all Christian denominations, it was filled with chattering tourists and black-frocked priests and their acolytes, long queues forming to view the final Stations of the Cross, coins dropping into strategically placed boxes, cameras clicking incessantly. Joshua stood there for some time, just inside the busy entrance, his gaze scanning the golden chapels and illuminated paintings and religious figures, then turning, saw the nearby Stone of Unction, and started visibly shaking.

Kate walked up to him and held him, her hand resting on his shoulder, and then closed her eyes and dropped down through herself to where his anguish was buried. There was thunder and lightning, the pouring rains of grief and loss; and the pain, more appalling than endless night, was a fuse to redemption. She entered into the pain, traveling through it to freedom, letting the darkness drain the agony away as light flared in the distance. Then she groaned a protestation, then felt shame and affirmed again; and the light, spreading out through the darkness, swept around her and soothed her. The peace of understanding, the glorious warmth of acceptance: her tears flowed between the banks of the River Jordan and made her one with the Holy Land. Kate opened her eyes again, saw the high-domed rotunda, the hanging lamps shedding light on Joshua's eyes and making them luminous.

"We must leave here," he said. "I cannot stay in this place. In here is the anguish and glory of the mystery to come. It is too soon to know, and my way must be in innocence; and this place, in which pain and death reside, is the end of my journey. I feel it; and my body is breaking; and the time is not right yet. We must leave on the instant."

They walked along Rehov Hayehudim, between the Jewish and Armenian quarters, left the Old City by way of the Zion Gate and continued on to Mount Zion. Beneath the gold and polychrome mosaics of the sanctuary of the Dormition Abbey, in the crypt where the Virgin Mary was said to have spent her last days, he stared boldly at the effigy of the mother of Jesus and again showed no visible response.

Retracing their steps, they crossed to the opposite side of the abbey and entered the Coenaculum above the Tomb of King David. A small and humble room with Crusader archwork and Turkish prayer niche, it seemed fitting as the setting for the Last Supper, strangely desolate and sad. Joshua gazed around quietly, his hands motionless by his sides; and yet even as he shook his head in a negative gesture, Kate surrendered to grief.

She closed her eyes and drifted away, then returned in another time, saw the breaking of bread, the cup passing from mouth to mouth, the feet of the twelve apostles being washed by the one on his knees. The grief and sadness overwhelmed her, being torn from love and faith, and she opened her eyes again and looked at Joshua, whose expression was calm.

"No," he said, "it was not here. Yet what you felt was the reality. What you felt was the manifestation of the need of those who have come here for centuries. There was a parting of love and sorrow, a final partaking of bread and wine; what happened did not occur here, but somewhere over the valley."

He walked out of the Coenaculum, moving quickly and decisively, and they followed him back through the Zion Gate and then down the untended slopes of the Kidron Valley. He seemed to know where he was going, and looked neither left nor right, and he eventually led them up the side of the inconspicuous Mount Ophel to the mosque above the Upper Pool of Siloam. Standing on the edge of the slope, a breeze making his white robe shiver, he gazed down at the long, narrow pool with a peculiar intensity. Kate was standing just behind him, between the silent Moshe and Paul; and thinking of her recurrent dream, and of what it represented, she was unable to move to the edge and gaze down at the water.

"He knew it was here," Paul whispered. "He came here quite deliberately. And according to the New Testament, this is where Jesus Christ healed the blind man."

"Also," Moshe replied, "according to the New Testament, Jesus made clay with his spittle and healed the man by rubbing it on his eyes. That was not a ritual prescribed by Jewish tradition."

"That means little," Paul said fervently. "Jesus the prophet was a Jew. The Jews, according to the Mishnah, used this very water for purification both in the ancient ceremonial of the Red Heifer and for the water poured out before the Lord at the Feast of Tabernacles. Jesus was Jewish. So is Joshua."

His passion disturbed Kate and made her turn away from him, again thinking of how dangerous Joshua could be. Her eyes fell on Moshe's face, noting his concern and confusion, and she quickly averted her gaze, feeling torn, not understanding her feelings. Then Joshua looked over his shoulder, waved one hand to beckon her forward, and she did as she was bid, moving tentatively to the edge, aware that Moshe and Paul were close behind her, both breathing too heavily. Joshua looked directly at her, smiling slightly, his silvery-gray eyes consoling.

"Admit what you have denied," he said, slightly amending a previous statement. "Stop dreaming of the child in the pool of blood and let the healing bring new life." He pointed down at the pool with his right hand, his index finger extended. "Look, and will the blood. Do not turn away from it. Let the water turn to blood and accept your shame and then put it behind you. In this way you will mend yourself."

The fear gripped Kate in a vise, almost making her cry out, but she forced herself to lean slightly forward and look down at the pool. It was a long, narrow pool, the water very clear, coming out from an arch beneath the mosque, still fed, as it had been for centuries, by Hezekiah's underground channel. There were a few ancient column drums thrusting out of the water, but otherwise the pool was quite normal, reflecting the masonry above it.

"Will the blood," Joshua said. "Make it flow. Cleanse yourself and be freed."

She looked down and saw the water, her own rippling reflection, a thin line of light dividing her face and emphasizing the shadows. She looked down and was hypnotized, devoured her reflection, and then looked up, saw herself high above, looking down, her eyes widening in disbelief. The water rippled and swirled, formed a gentle, graceful whirlpool, and out of the vortex, as if bubbling up from a faucet, came a flower of rich blood. The blood spread out through the water, was drawn into the coiling current, spread out farther, and moved around the much darker red of its center. Then the darker red changed, growing larger and more irregular, becoming a fetus turning slowly in the eye of the bright, bloody whirlpool.

Kate gagged and almost choked, feeling the terror searing through her, turned her hands into fists and kept staring as her fear turned to shame. Not shame, but something else—perhaps a murderous sense of loss—almost certainly the knowledge that fear itself was the greatest destroyer. She kept looking at the Pool of Siloam, at the bloody fetus in its bed of blood, and she sobbed and out of her blind weeping eyes beheld the truth she had buried. In shame was redemption and from that she gained new life. The swirling ripples contracted, drawn back in to their own vortex, then the blood, first gurgling and then sighing, became a bubbling red flower. The petals of the flower folded inward, became a red bud in the water, then the red bud sank down below the surface and soon disappeared.

Kate looked down, entranced, slowly awakening to rejuvenation, saw the clear, unblemished water, her own rippling reflection, a thin line of light dividing her face and emphasizing the shadows. After a long time she looked up, seeing Joshua, Moshe, and Paul, the three of them forming a semicircle around her, only Paul's eyes averted.

"I saw it," Moshe said. "We all saw it. You didn't imagine it."

An anguished sob broke from Paul and he fell down to his knees, leaning forward across Joshua's sandaled feet, his hands covering his face.

"Not the Christ of the Christians," he sobbed, "but the Jesus of the Jews. Not a supernatural being but a man of flesh and blood, yet unmistakably one with divine gifts or supernatural abilities. Such will be the Messiah and such have you proven yourself. Not the Son of the One, but His messenger. Indeed you *are* the Messiah!"

Kate stared at Moshe and saw his gray eyes, drawn by love, bound with fear. Her heart turned like a leaf in the wind and flew out to be captured.

25

"It's been a long time," Leon said. "Imprecisely, nearly two months. I just want you to know that I've been faithful, doubtless due to senility."

Kate smiled wanly but did not reply, still looking a little uneasy, her body long and angular in the bikini, her gaze fixed on Eilat. Leon navigated out of the lagoon, gradually leaving the marina behind, slipping past the yachts and small boats, the wind surfers and scuba divers, staring across the brilliant blue of the water to the Moab mountains and Aqaba. He only looked at Kate occasionally, feeling as uneasy as she obviously did, well aware that their long separation had, more than expected, made them feel unfamiliar with one another. He wanted to believe that this was so, but felt a little uncertain; in his depths he sensed that Kate had somehow changed and was no longer close to him. This possibility, in his mind but inadmissible, sent a chill rippling through him.

"You were very quiet in the car," he said.

"I'm sorry. I didn't mean to be. It's just that I've been so long in that damned hospital, it feels strange being out."

He believed half of the statement and decided not to question it, his every nerve alive to the tension that almost palpably came off her. He was standing in the open cockpit, at the navigating controls, and Kate was sitting beside him on one of the companion seats, her knees bent, her feet up, her long hair blowing freely in the breeze, her eyes hidden behind a pair of sunglasses that emphasized her high cheekbones.

"You don't look well," he said.

"I don't feel so good either. Two months of air conditioning is enough to make anyone look ill. That's why I suggested coming here, instead of sitting in some bar. I wanted clean air and wide open spaces and the salt of the sea."

"I'm disappointed," Leon replied. "I had assumed it was nostalgia.

We've spent a lot of time together on this boat, which is why I still treasure it."

"You can afford it, Leon."

"Not any longer, my pet. If something doesn't break soon, I'll have to leave here and look for real work."

Feeling guilty and furtive, understanding what he was doing, remembering Rashid and the bargain they had made, he turned his head to look down at her. She was leaning into the hull, her breasts pressed against the railing, her face turned toward the mountains of Moab beyond the languid blue water. Her strange beauty tugged at him, tearing his heart and stirring his loins, and he turned away and looked straight ahead, trying to keep his voice casual.

"I thought they were keeping you a prisoner."

"No, Leon, they weren't."

"Major General Moshe Eitan said you were suffering from shock and were therefore being kept under observation. I refused to believe this of my Kate, but the great man insisted."

"I can't talk about it, Leon."

"Was it shock?"

"Just a little."

"Obviously you don't want to talk about it."

"I'm sorry. I can't."

"Security?"

"Yes, Leon. You know that."

"I'm still a journalist, my pet."

Leaving the lagoon, he entered the Red Sea proper and headed south toward Coral Island, feeling relieved that the bustling port was now behind him, appreciating the cooler air. Glancing down at Kate, he saw her waving hair, her curved spine and broad hips; and the tension, which he felt almost physically, was clear in her posture.

"You haven't recovered yet," he said.

"I recovered a long time ago. I was kept in the hospital because they didn't want the matter discussed."

"You mean what happened on the Mount of Olives?"

"Don't play innocent, Leon. You've been grilling Moshe Eitan since it happened, so you think there was something. Unfortunately you want to know more and I can't help you there."

"The whole world is curious about it."

"What was reported was the truth: the Israelis don't know what it was—and neither do I."

He didn't believe that for a minute and her flushed cheeks showed the lie, before her face, automatically and primly, turned farther away from him.

"Was something brought down from there?"

"You've already asked Moshe that."

"Moshe Eitan has obviously relayed all our conversations straight to you; the pair of you must have talked a great deal."

She turned her face toward him, her eyes hidden behind the glasses, the wind blowing her hair around her lips, which were definitely not smiling. She studied him in silence for some time before looking away again.

"Yes," she said, "we talked a lot. We were forced together a lot. It was a security situation, after all, and Moshe was in charge."

"A dedicated man," Leon said.

"No sarcasm, Leon. Please."

"I'm sorry," Leon replied. "It's just that I got drunk one night, confronted the major general, and ended up getting the very strong impression that he was particularly fond of you."

Kate refused to reply, but continued staring out to sea, and Leon reached down and picked up his glass of gin and had a long, cooling drink. Straight ahead was the Red Sea, a clear, alluvial blue, the barren mountains rising up to the white clouds in an equally blue sky. Over there, at the base of the mountains, was the Jordanian city of Aqaba.

"Well, was he fond of you?"

"I don't want to discuss this, Leon."

"I want to know why he kept you in that hospital if nothing was found up there."

"What's more important to you? What Moshe feels for me or what was found on the summit of the Mount of Olives during the storm?"

It was a clever, mean question, cutting through to the bone, and Leon felt himself flinching with shock. What was more important to him? A future with Kate or his future in general? If he denied Rashid what he wanted, he might still have a future with Kate, but his future in general would be in danger; if on the other hand he decided to betray Kate, he would gain the world but possibly lose his soul. Now, thinking about this, his heart briefly lurched, his indecision placing him on that ledge where fear leaves the nerves bare.

"I don't know what you mean," he lied.

"Yes, you do," Kate replied. "We came on this trip because we haven't seen each other for two months, but already you're starting to ask me questions that you know I can't answer."

"Does that anger you?"

"Yes. You're trying to use me and I won't let you. They let me out on the grounds that I kept my mouth shut, and whether or not what I know is important, I won't break my promise."

Leon had another drink and kept the boat on an even course, glancing across the brilliant water to the southern outskirts of Eilat, seeing the small, glass-bottomed boats above the coral reefs, people swimming and diving.

"Okay," he said. "I take your point and I'm sorry. I'm a journalist and I can't help myself, but I promise to try. The subject, quite obviously *verboten*, will be mentioned no more."

"Fine," Kate replied, turning toward him but lowering her eyes, not smiling as she picked up her glass and had a very long drink. Finished, she put the glass down and bent her neck across the railing, exposing her face to the sun, her dark hair dangling loose. Her body, long and lean, still suntanned, was a magnet to Leon's eyes.

"You're still beautiful," he said.

"My lower half," she replied. "I'm too thin and my breasts are too small, but my legs have some merit."

"Such legs drive men wild."

"Don't get wild, Leon. Please."

"You sound as if you really mean that."

"I don't know . . . I'm not sure anymore."

She didn't smile when she said it, and that made him feel more uneasy, more convinced that she had definitely changed in some as yet unknown manner. He looked at her closed lips, at her almost gaunt cheeks, let his eyes travel down to her breasts, then on down her long legs. No, she wasn't beautiful, at least not obviously so, but her sensuality and attractiveness were of the kind that few men could resist. Understanding this, he studied her, thinking of sex and feeling love, his emotions rampaging over his physical desire and making him feel a deep pain. He looked away, had a drink, put the glass back on the shelf, saw the rock of Coral Island ahead, and tried to keep his voice steady.

"You mean you're not sure of me?"

"I don't know, Leon. I'm tired. I spent an awful lot of time in that hospital, and it wasn't all pleasant."

"All right," he said. "I promise not to ask you about the hospital. I simply want to know why it changed you and how it affects me."

"Why should it affect you?"

"You admit, then, that you've changed?"

"I don't know what you mean when you suggest that I've changed, but since you seem to believe that it's true, how would it affect you?"

"I believe we had a relationship."

"We had sex; that's not a relationship."

"I thought we were friends in *and* out of bed."

"That's still not a relationship."

Leon sighed, exasperated, still not used to her intransigence, but also feeling, as he had not felt before, that she was truly eluding him. He poured himself another drink, filled Kate's glass up, and glanced at her, wishing she would remove the sunglasses and let him study her eyes. As if reading his mind, she put her hand up to the glasses, slid them slightly down her nose, and then changed her mind and slid them back up. Leon gave another sigh and returned to the open cockpit, had a mouthful of gin, and put the glass down, feeling worse every minute. Coral Island was just ahead, the rock supporting a Crusader fortress, the remains blending in with the barren island and looking beautifully desolate. He maneuvered the boat between the island and the crowded beach not far away, then continued his southerly direction toward the fjord, which was where he would drop anchor.

"So," he said lightly, "we didn't have a relationship. We simply had regular sex and were good friends, which is something quite different."

Kate had another drink and raised her head, her eyes obviously fixed on him. "All right, Leon, just don't get upset. You never made claims before."

"You claim something when you go to bed."

"Not necessarily something permanent."

"What happens if I want it to be permanent?"

"Don't, Leon. Let's stop this."

She turned her head away again, watching the island falling behind them, then stared across the glittering blue sea as if thinking of far-off things. Leon watched her, feeling furtive, a gray cloud filling his head, something ominous and darkly confusing, based on how Kate was acting. She was hesitant, rather distant, almost abstracted and too tense, the tension tightening the skin on her face and making her older. He thought of what had happened on the Mount, and of her long time in the hospital, and then, with something twisting inside him, he thought forlornly of Moshe Eitan.

"There it is," he said.

"Pardon?"

"The fjord. One of Israel's most lovely of natural wonders: Norway with sunshine."

It was indeed a majestic sight, a great bay shaped like a horseshoe, the blue water clear as glass, showing coral and exotic flora, the bay surrounded by towering mountains, all barren and sunbaked, tumbling down to sandy coves and a beach that thrust out toward the boat. Kate had seen it before, but she looked up nonetheless, tilting her glasses down her nose a little bit and then pushing them back again. The beach was clean and deserted, almost white in the dazzling sunlight, and the silence, once the engine had been turned off, was almost ethereal.

"It's beautiful," Kate said. "It will *always* be beautiful. It's places like this that make you never want to leave Israel."

Startled, Leon stared at her and took note of her expression, a combination of suppressed fear and yearning, intangibly haunting. He turned away and dropped the anchor, trying to distract himself from his thoughts, but then, straightening up, felt compelled to pursue the matter further.

"I don't believe my ears," he said. "This can't be Kate Hirschfield talking. The Kate Hirschfield I knew hated Israel and wanted to leave."

"I changed my mind," Kate replied. "I saw things differently in the hospital. And it's not that I'm too old to leave, but that I really belong here."

"What made you change your mind?"

"I can't explain that, Leon."

"Moshe Eitan?"

"No, Leon, not Moshe; it was more than just Moshe."

It was an unconscious admission, stating at least one half of the case, and Leon, after he really took it in, felt impossibly wounded. He glanced around the magnificent bay which had once overwhelmed him, but his eyes, instead of gazing at the mountains, were looking inward. There was pain to contend with, a growing desperation and need, and he began to understand that if it was possible to have Kate, he would gladly cast his future to the winds and ignore Rashid Idriss.

"Shall we eat?" he said.

"Just a little bit," Kate replied.

"This place used to make you laugh and throw your clothes off and make love; and after, you would eat like a pig, if with the grace of a lady."

"I'm just tired, Leon. I told you."

"This trip hasn't been successful."

"I'm honestly not as miserable as I look. Let me tend to the hamper."

She put the trestle table up and started unloading the hamper while Leon, not encouraged by her words, uncorked a bottle of wine. He kept glancing furtively at her, ashamed as he did so, but unable to control the temptation to read her mind from her face. She laid the table very efficiently, with a feigned enthusiasm, and he noticed that her tension had increased and was making her hands shake. He thought again of Moshe Eitan, remembered himself shouting after him, burned with shame at the recollection of his own words, but wondered if they were true or false. The table was quickly set and Kate pulled her chair up; they both sat down at the same time, then Leon poured the wine; they raised their glasses and the sun flashed off the glass as it touched in midair.

"Cheers!" Leon said.

"L'Chaim!"

He noticed the use of Hebrew, but made no comment on it, since the lunch, prepared by Kate, was certainly Jewish, if not strictly kosher: a small selection of pâtés, a roast leg of lamb, pimientos, cucumbers, fresh tomatoes and olives, a cheese spiced with paprika, another spiced with assorted vegetables, fruity yogurt and pastries and bread sticks. They both ate in a desultory manner, neither tempted by the pleasant lunch, but the first bottle of wine soon disappeared and Leon uncorked another. This bottle was soon half empty and Leon, to his surprise, did not feel even remotely at ease. He studied Kate and noticed that far from being relaxed, her tension seemed to be increasing every minute, her hands quite visibly shaking.

"Are you all right?" he asked.

"Yes," she replied.

"You keep staring at the mountains and the sea, but you don't seem impressed."

"I'm sorry," she said. "I'm not giving you a good day. I'm tired. I really am tired. I can't get used to this freedom."

"What are you thinking about?"

"Nothing. Not a thing."

"As a psychiatrist, you should know that that's impossible, so what are you thinking about?"

"I can't explain it," she said.

"The hospital?"

"Yes."

"In that case I can ask no more questions; now you'll have to start talking."

"I'm sorry. I'm truly sorry."

"So am I, but it doesn't help. Normally, by this time, we'd both be lying on that deck, but I can't see it happening today."

"No, Leon, it won't."

"Why?"

"I can't explain it."

"The hospital?"

"Yes."

"Moshe Eitan?"

"Please don't ask me that question."

The pain was unexpected and shockingly real, something shooting from his stomach to his brain and clouding his mind. He poured another glass of wine, feeling feverish and confused, put the glass to his lips and had a sip and tried to keep himself calm. Looking around him, he saw the mountains, the blazing anvil of the sun, the sea as blue as the sky high above it, very still, without shadows. He drank more wine and then looked back at Kate, trying to find recognition.

"It's Moshe," he said.

"No," she said, "not just Moshe. If you're concerned, nothing happened between us, and it isn't just him."

"I don't understand, Kate."

"I can't tell you. That's all."

"Either it's Moshe or it isn't. If not Moshe, it's something else. You've changed and you hardly recognize me, and I have to know why."

"Why?"

"Because I care."

"Not that much."

"That much."

"You never cared that much and you never will. I can't tell you. I won't."

She pushed her chair back and stood up and then sat down on the companion seat, and Leon, standing up automatically, followed her into the cockpit. She removed her sunglasses, looked up with her dark eyes, displayed fear and indecipherable yearning, then covered her face with her hands.

Leon stood there, feeling choked, torn by unfamiliar grief, unable to comprehend what was happening but desperately wanting to help her. He thought of what he had promised Rashid, of his own plan to betray her trust, and his shame, like a blade drawn from the flames, seemed to melt through his soul. Looking down at her, he was lost, his future not worth a damn, his every impulse concentrated on the need to win her over and shelter her. To betray her was inconceivable, the very negation of human reason, and he reached out and placed his hand on her head and tried to draw her back to him.

"I missed you," he said, covering his shame with a simple truth. "I really missed you more than I ever thought I could—and I hope you believe that. I thought about you a lot. I could hardly stop thinking about you. It was as if, when we were in bed together just before that terrible storm, something chained up inside me suddenly broke loose from its bonds and demanded, as it could not have done before, your complete recognition. You understand what I'm saying? I'm trying to say that I love you. I couldn't say it before because I couldn't trust myself, because my suitcase, as you so notably pointed out, was my life's shabby symbol. I thought I would move on again, another suitcase, another room, still retreating from the failures of my past, afraid of failing again. I always lacked commitment, Kate. It was something I could never give. I left my wife and family, unable to stand daily trivia, and packed the oddments of my life in a suitcase and went looking for hideaways. Thus Vietnam, Northern Ireland, international terrorism, and the Third World, my beliefs constantly switching, first the Left and then the Right, never able to make a firm stand and thus haunted by cowardice. But then, in the hotel, just before we went to bed, when you said you were only drawn to me because I didn't give a damn—because of my inability to stake a claim—it was then I suddenly realized that I might actually lose you, and that I valued you and wanted to fight for you—yes, Kate, it was then, at that precise moment, that I understood the full extent of my commitment to you and wanted to show it. But I was foiled by that storm. The storm stole you away from me. And in the days since then I've lived with the conviction that that storm had said: *Show it!* I'm trying to show it now. I'm trying to say it loud and clear. I love you, Kate. I really and truly love you. Please believe and accept that."

He stopped talking and stepped toward her, his heart pounding with tension, as if everything kept locked up for years was about to burst out of him. He saw her shuddering and leaning forward, hiding her face in her hands; and then, as he knelt down, slid his arms around her and pulled her to him, he felt her body shaking in aching spasms as she started to weep. Then burst he finally did, his suppressed emotions pouring out of him—pouring out like water from a dam and flooding all over Kate. She responded in kind, her own darkest fears exploding, and his exultation spiraled out of his pain and cleansed his deep shame. He clung to her, and she to him, and he rocked her to and fro, holding on to her as if to a child, his love seeking to heal her wounds.

"I have to tell someone," she sobbed. "I can't bear all this confusion. It's all been like a dream, or a nightmare, and I can't grab the truth of it. I have to talk to someone. Not someone who was involved. I have to talk to someone without beliefs of the kind that he represents. You have to promise not to repeat it. You have to swear to it and stick by it. If you love me, if you truly care about me, you have to give me your word on that. I want your promise! *Your promise!*"

"I promise!" Leon said, truly believing it and meaning it, his heart breaking with love and concern, no other thought in his head. "Who *is* he? Is it Moshe?"

Then she told him about Joshua, her words tumbling out like stones, forced along by the babbling brook of her confusion and falling brutally upon him. He listened, disbelieving, trying to grasp it and failing, the immensity of what she was telling him almost shattering his reason. He moved closer, staring at her, concentrating on her lips, trying to judge from their rapid, demented movement if her words added up. She kept talking, breathing harshly, letting her words cleave the air, mentioning Moshe and Paul Frankel and Joshua as if talking of dreams. Then he looked at her eyes, at their dark, haunted depths, saw fear and yearning naked as the bone, and knew her words spoke the truth. The mystery of the Mount, the descending object that did not exist, the bulldozers piling the rubble over the hole where the black obelisk had risen—all the pieces now fit.

Leon stepped away from Kate, then stepped forward and stood over her, his hands reaching out to the web of her dark, tangled hair. He pressed down with his palms, very lightly, reassuringly, then slid his fingers down along her face to dry the tears on her cheeks. He felt stunned by disbelief, rocked by terror and jubilation, and his faith, once a dried riverbed, now flowed out to embrace her. He bent low and kissed her head, his lips trembling, almost numb, and remained that way, his lips lost in her hair, for a very long time.

"It's all right," he murmured.

"I know," she said, "I know. I feel better for having released it, and now I can face it."

"*We* can face it," he said, as if the miracle had joined them. "We can go away and simply forget it and let them work it all out."

Then he realized what he had said, his own words echoing mockingly, and he drew his lips away from her head and straightened up to look down at her. She moved her head to return his gaze, her upturned eyes dark and moist, almost luminous with gratitude and relief and a terrible trust. He thought of what she had experienced, then of Joshua and what he meant, and he realized that even at World's End personal need would prevail. The Messiah, the Mahdi, the Christ of the Christians—it mattered little who Joshua might be, since his very presence was stupefying. The human mind could not grasp it and, failing to grasp it, would turn inward, rejecting the more terrifying possibilities and searching for private peace. Now Leon wanted that peace, not believing in Judgment Day, more concerned with the reality of flesh and blood and his inviolable rights. The irony was excruciating, as stupefying as Joshua's arrival; and Leon, even understanding this truth, reached again for Kate's love.

"Don't stay here," he said. "You can't take this situation. Neither of us has to be involved. It's not real. We don't need it."

"*I* need it," Kate replied.

"I don't understand, Kate."

"There was never enough between us, Leon. This is where I belong."

She raised her eyes to his face, silently begging him to understand, and Leon felt the winds of loss sweeping through him and destroying his hopes.

"You mean Joshua?"

"No, Leon, not just Joshua. I mean more than that."

And then her words came back to him, ringing out in his head, brutally forcing him to face what he had missed in the drama of Joshua: the other participant was Moshe, who had been present from the beginning, who had, either willingly or unwillingly, been drawn into the dream, and had since, in Leon's absence, been the rock upon which Kate had stood.

"You mean Moshe."

"I think so."

He turned away from her, his heart beating against his chest, his senses flying out like the wind and scattering all he had gained. He hardly knew what he was doing, saw the anchor, heard the engine, then the boat was heading out of the fjord and back into the Red Sea. The majestic mountains fell behind and the empty beach disappeared, leaving only the broad expanse of glittering water dividing Jordan from Israel. Kate was silent by his side, now calmer, perhaps resigned, and he felt his love clamping around him to crush the life out of him. He was dying, suffocating, his dreams turning to dust, and as he passed Coral Island and headed back to Eilat, he felt his hatred rising up to fortify him and give him something to cling to.

He had lost her to Moshe, completely, irrevocably, and now he was alone, his whole future in the balance, owing nothing to no one but himself, but with much to avenge. He spoke to Kate no more, but instead stared straight ahead, then looked across at the Moab mountains, at the distant town of Aqaba, and accepted that he would now betray her trust without feeling more pain.

He would sell the story of Joshua.

He dropped Kate off at the hospital and they parted in silence, his car scattering the stones as he left and drove back to Jerusalem. Kate stood there for some time, looking around her in a daze, then eventually she turned away and entered the hospital and went straight to her room. She undressed and lay down, her body rigid on the bed, her eyes dry but her heart beating fast as the darkness descended. Sleep came remarkably quickly, carrying her along a silent stream, taking her out to where the mountains and valleys offered solace and hope. The air shimmered and flashed, revealing the mirage of her dilemma, the faces of Moshe and Leon and Joshua materializing like gray clouds. She melted into the rock, became one with the parched earth, and let her pain, which before had been unbearable, drift away with the shifting sands.

The room door was pushed open and she awakened to the morning light, flooding the room and burning into her eyes as she slowly sat upright. Moshe was standing above the bed, his lips tight, his gray eyes hard, his whole body quivering with rage and possible shock. He was holding a lot of newspapers, most of them obviously foreign, and he threw them over her body one by one, as if burying her in rubbish.

"There's no by-line," he said, his voice harsh and contemptuous, "but we've no reason to doubt who blew the story. Joshua's on the front page of every paper we've received, and our telephones haven't stopped ringing. That bastard, Leon Halcomb, your good friend, has told the whole world about it. Now just watch it explode!"

He walked out and slammed the door, leaving Kate with her shame, and she rolled over to stare at the wall and try to live with her feelings. What she learned at that moment, in terrible wonder and grief, was that if the world exploded and history changed forever, she, a mere woman, would go with it thinking of only one thing: her betrayal by Leon and, because of that, her equally destructive betrayal of Moshe.

She closed her eyes and wept quietly.

26

The flashlights exploded as Moshe and Ben Eliezer emerged from the
side door of the crowded Press Room and sat down behind the long
table on the wooden dais in front of the gathered reporters. Moshe and
the prime minister sat together with Paul Frankel on Moshe's left side
and Rabbi Latinavots, obviously very uncomfortable, sat at the other
side of Ben Eliezer. Looking down at the jostling reporters, his eyes
dazzled by the flashlights, Moshe saw Leon at the very back of the
room, his face weary and thoughtful. Moshe quickly looked away,
trying to combat his instant rage, and saw Ben Eliezer leaning toward
his microphone, his face studiously bland.

"Good afternoon, ladies and gentlemen," he said, his voice modest
and untroubled. "Since Lieutenant Frankel has already given you the
unclassified facts on the discovery and subsequent investigation of the
man known as Joshua, I need only add here that this conference is to
be treated as an informal question-and-answer session, and that we
will answer, to the limits of discretion, as honestly as possible. Now
the first question, please."

Most of the reporters shot their hands up and started shouting for
attention, and Ben Eliezer, shading his eyes against the flashlights,
pointed at a female journalist in the front row and let her question
bring order back.

"Why the need for secrecy, Prime Minister? Why are certain facts
of this matter still classified?"

"I think you would agree that we should not, given the sensitivity
of this matter, release information that has not been verified or
substantiated."

"Can we assume from that statement that this man is still under
investigation?"

"You can."

"And will the full details, or results, of that investigation be released to the press?"

"At this stage any answer to that question would be extremely improper."

"Why?" Leon said, from the back of the room.

"I don't have to tell you, Mr. Halcomb, that the worldwide reportage on this subject to date has already led to a lot of wild speculation of the kind that is not particularly helpful."

"By wild speculation, do you mean—?"

"That worldwide reportage," another journalist interrupted, "was based on a syndicated article that was published without a by-line. Are we to assume that it didn't originate from one of your own sources?"

"You assume correctly."

"You didn't want that information released?"

"No. We felt it was premature. It is not our belief that a case such as this should be opened up to public discussion before a full investigation has been completed."

"Do you know who released the information?"

"We believe we know the person involved, but unfortunately we can't verify it."

"Are you suggesting by the use of the word *unfortunate*," Leon said, "that you would, if you could prove your case, take retaliatory action against the journalist involved?"

"Yes," Moshe replied, trying to keep his face controlled. "We try, as much as possible, to respect the freedom of the press, but we won't encourage journalists to abuse that freedom with such underhand methods."

"Do you know the journalist's source?" another reporter inquired.

"No," Ben Eliezer said.

"It was obviously inside information," the journalist replied. "Does that worry you much?"

"We are naturally shocked," Paul said, "that this leak came from the inside, but the matter is now being investigated."

Another journalist now picked up Leon's interrupted question: "By wild speculation, do you mean the worldwide debate on whether or not this man is some sort of messianic or Christlike figure?"

"Precisely," Ben Eliezer said.

"Such speculation should bother the Rabbinate more than the government. Why does it bother you?"

"That question, from a journalist, is almost superfluous. It is no secret that already some of the more extreme Jews, Muslims, and Christians are adopting this man as their savior. The Jews are claiming him as their Messiah, the Muslims are suggesting that he might be the returned Mahdi, and the Christians are discussing him in terms of the Second Coming of their Christ. While it is not the function of the government to involve itself in anything other than secular matters, it *is* of great concern to the government that such views are leading to dissension—increasingly violent—between Jews, Christians, and Muslims, and that thousands of people are now clamoring to come to Israel in what can only be termed a mass religious fervor."

"Reportedly thousands of Diaspora Jews are already pouring into Israel, and are having no trouble in getting in."

"Israel has always been open to those Jews who wish to come here. We cannot and will not revoke that right."

"The Christians are protesting that they're not being given the same privilege—that they are, in fact, having considerable trouble in getting into Israel."

"We simply cannot handle the numbers involved—and the Jews, in all cases, must be given first consideration."

"What about the Arabs, Prime Minister?"

"What about them?"

"Is it not true that no Arabs at all are now being allowed into this country?"

"Unfortunately we were forced to take that measure."

"Why?"

"We cannot admit Arabs whose sole interest in wishing to come into Israel is to inflame insurrection by spreading the news that this man is the returned Mahdi. Many of the recent riots in the streets of Jerusalem have in fact been caused by extremist Arabs who are claiming that we are holding their Mahdi prisoner and that his presence here is a sign that the sovereignty of the Muslim religion must now be established at any cost."

"By all-out war if necessary."

"Correct."

"But isn't it also true," Leon said, "that many of those riots were started by extremist Jews, such as the Neturei Karta zealots, who are making similar claims for your prisoner—namely, that he is the

Jewish Messiah who will inaugurate the sovereignty of Judaism and establish the true Promised Land?"

"He is not a prisoner," Moshe said, "but a man under investigation. As to your main point, yes, unfortunately that is true—but those riots would not be happening had not the news of this man been prematurely and unofficially released."

"Would the major general care to comment on the widely held belief that the Israeli government is admitting thousands of Diaspora Jews to this country—while keeping the Arabs out—because they are concerned that another Arab-Israeli war might break out and they want to build up their human resources?"

"Our intelligence sources have reported no increased signs of aggression on the part of the Arabs," Paul lied, "and it is not our belief that the violence on the streets of Jerusalem will incite those Arabs outside Israel's borders."

"The riots in the streets of Jerusalem," another journalist said, "are reaching epidemic proportions, and have already involved Jews, Arabs, and Christians. Many of the rioters, when interviewed, claimed that they were demonstrating for the release of the man you are holding. Would you care to make a comment on that?"

"What sort of comment do you want?" Moshe replied.

"Do you intend releasing the man?"

"That would depend on the results of our investigations."

"What are you trying to prove, Major General?"

"We're trying to ascertain just who, precisely, this man is."

"The man has memories of biblical days, he knows every known language, he can apparently work miracles, and according to reports his robe has been dated to approximately the time of Jesus Christ. What more do you need to know?"

"Much of that information has been exaggerated."

"That hardly answers the question, Major General."

"To answer the question would be improper before all the tests have been completed."

"And when might that be?"

"Possibly another year."

Some of the journalists laughed openly, others shook their heads cynically, and Leon, still standing at the back, merely gave a tight grin. Then he stepped forward a little and put his hand up.

"Yes, Mr. Halcomb?"

"In an official statement, the Vatican has rejected any possible theological interpretation of Joshua—"

"That is correct," Rabbi Latinavots said too quickly.

"—but unofficial sources claim that they have sent a secret communiqué to the Rabbinate asking if it would be possible for Joshua to be interrogated by the Sacred College of Cardinals in Rome. Would the chief rabbi care to comment on this?"

"You are as aware as anyone in this room," Jozsef said, "that the Rabbinate would not be able to comment on *any* secret communiqué."

"You are admitting, then, such a communiqué has been received?"

"I am not. I am saying that if such had been received, I would not be able to mention the fact."

"That sounds like an admission."

"It is not. It is simply a statement of fact."

"Let us assume, then, that the communiqué is hypothetical. If such a communiqué were received, what would be the reaction of the Rabbinate?"

"The Rabbinate has no legal or theological grounds for preventing this man from speaking to anyone."

"So you'd be willing to hand him over to the Vatican?"

"It is not a question of the Rabbinate either holding him here or handing him over to anyone. Jurisdiction over this man is in the hands of the security services."

"Regarding the riots in Jerusalem—" someone began.

"Would the chief rabbi," Leon continued stubbornly, "be willing to state the Rabbinate's view, theologically speaking, of this man?"

Jozsef looked uncomfortable, cracking his knuckles and blushing a little; and Moshe, staring directly at Leon, felt a cold, clean contempt. Jozsef managed to gain control over himself and give his statement in a calm, measured tone.

"The Rabbinate's view, as of this moment, is that this man represents a secular, rather than a religious, matter. Since the most extensive physical, psychological, and historical examinations have failed to prove conclusively that this man is anything other than a normal human being, we must reject the various claims being made on his behalf."

"It is not your view," said another journalist, "that he is the Messiah?"

"No."

"Yet the Rabbinate has not formally stated that view," Leon said.

"A surprising omission in view of the recent riots by extreme Orthodox Jews."

"The Rabbinate cannot deny what it does not recognize. Until proven otherwise, this man is a man like any other, and a formal denial would therefore be singularly superfluous."

"Would the chief rabbi not agree that such a statement is superfluous in view of the recent riots by certain members of his own Jewish community? It is, after all, the function of the Rabbinate to give moral and theological guidance to its community. Surely, then, a formal denial from the Rabbinate would put an end to the rioting."

"The Rabbinate condemns the rioting, but is in no position to offer a formal denial of a claim that it has not officially published."

"Semantics!" someone yelled.

"Exactly," Leon said. "Are you claiming that the Rabbinate has not even discussed this extraordinary event?"

"The Rabbinate has not formally discussed the event."

"But it *has* discussed it *informally*?"

"Various individual members have naturally stated their points of view."

"Hypocrites!" someone yelled.

"The Vatican and the World Council of Churches," Leon continued, "have taken a similarly cowardly stand: they refuse to make a formal declaration about the matter, but discuss that same matter in secret communiqués."

"I cannot speak for the Vatican or the World Council of Churches."

"To get back to the riots in Jerusalem," a woman said, "would either the Cabinet or the Rabbinate be willing to officially request that the Vatican and the World Council of Churches put out a statement formally condemning those rioting in Jerusalem in the name of this as yet unproven savior?"

"Since the Rabbinate has not been officially involved with this man, it cannot put out an official statement of any kind."

"And the Cabinet?"

"The Cabinet," Ben Eliezer said, "has given the army complete freedom in the curtailing of the riots and is drafting up new laws to deal with offenders. Since it is the function of the Cabinet to deal with secular rather than religious matters, it can obviously do no more than that."

"Has the prime minister any comment to make on the fact that in taking such action he has willy-nilly pitted Jew against Jew?"

"The prime minister," Ben Eliezer said, "would like to state that he deeply regrets these unfortunate events."

"What about the West Bank?" Leon said.

"What about it?" Moshe replied.

"It is a known fact that the West Bank has become an armed fortress controlled by the fanatics of Kash and Gush Emunim, and that both groups, in their determination to rid Palestine—"

"Israel," Moshe said.

"—Palestine of all Arabs, have made it clear that they would like to topple the present government and replace it with an ecclesiastical Cabinet devoted to Zionism."

"That's a statement," Moshe said, "not a question."

"Would the major general care to comment on what course of action he is likely to take now that both groups of Jewish fanatics are demanding the release of your prisoner, Joshua—"

"He is not a prisoner."

"Surely the experienced major general must be aware that his own troops have already been forced to take retaliatory action against a group of Kash fanatics when they tried to storm the Hadassah Medical Center and spirit your famous prisoner away."

"The isolated action of a group of political thugs is hardly proof of a major Jewish insurrection."

"Possibly," Leon said, "but what has the major general got to say about the fact that his troops have dramatically increased their search raids on such Jewish strongholds as Ramallah, Nablus, and Kiryat Arba—all on the West Bank—and have, during such activities, been resisted with gunfire and hand grenades?"

"We have always had trouble with the West Bank, as you know, and we believe that situation can be contained."

"You have not had armed resistance before."

"That matter," Ben Eliezer said, "is indeed of grave concern, but may not be related to this man Joshua."

"It is related to Joshua because both Kash and Gush Emunim are openly claiming that he is the Messiah."

"I do not think—"

"Could someone else get a question in here?"

"Of course," Ben Eliezer said, obviously relieved, his bland facade momentarily cracking before reinstating itself. "We're delighted to give attention to *The Observer* of London."

"Thank you, Prime Minister. I would just like to follow up the remarks of my expatriate colleague, Mr. Halcomb, by asking Lieutenant Frankel, member of Shin Beth and Orthodox Jew, what his reaction, both personal and political, is to this situation."

Paul flushed beneath his dark skin, dropped his eyes, and then looked up again, his fingers spreading out on the table as if trying to grab it.

"Since I am here as a representative of internal security and counterintelligence, I'm afraid I must keep my personal views out of it."

"And your political views?"

"My political views are the views of the serving government, since my sole function is to serve the government in office."

"Your view, then, is that this man is still something of an unknown quantity and must therefore be treated as a possible subversive or enemy agent?"

"Correct."

"Is it not true, Lieutenant Frankel, that you are an extremely Orthodox Jew with a rather strict view of Zionism?"

"I have never tried to hide my Zionist beliefs."

"Can you therefore, in the present situation, with Jew fighting Jew, keep your political and personal views apart?"

"That question," Jozsef intervened, "is already too personal and has very little bearing on this matter."

"Are you not disturbed, Rabbi Latinavots, that at a time such as this —with Jew, Muslim, and Christian all fighting together, and all over this man of unknown origin—that a member of Shin Beth, the internal security service, should hold the sort of views that have led to a lot of criticism of your own more liberal preachings as Ashkenazic chief rabbi?"

"Judaism is a coat of many colors—and hopefully will always remain so. The fact that Lieutenant Frankel has views different from my own in no way reflects upon his activities on behalf of Israel."

"Lieutenant Frankel has long been noted as one of the brighter stars in the Shin Beth firmament; nonetheless, since he is a relatively young officer, the fact that he has recently been put in charge of security regarding the man Joshua—and indeed is representing Shin Beth at this conference—has led a great number of people to think that this is a purely diplomatic move, designed to pacify the more extremist Orthodox Jews. Does the chief rabbi have any comment on that situation?"

"Such a question should not be directed at the chief rabbi," Ben Eliezer said smoothly, "but at Lieutenant Frankel's superior officers in Shin Beth."

"There are no such officers present at this conference. Perhaps Major General Eitan would care to comment."

"I'm afraid not," Moshe said. "As an officer of the IDF it is not my duty to comment on the decisions regarding the deployment of members of Shin Beth."

"If I may change the subject just a little," Leon said, his voice ringing out loud and clear. "Is it not true that the Soviet and American governments are both disturbed by the possibility that the riots in Jerusalem—whatever their reasons—could spread throughout Israel and encourage the surrounding Arab states to exploit the situation?"

"A hypothetical situation," Moshe replied.

"Not quite so hypothetical, Major General. The United Nations is already alarmed at the increasing violence in Jerusalem and is convinced that it is going to explode elsewhere. Indeed, if we may forget Israel for a second, there have also been less violent demonstrations in many other countries—notably those with a strong religious flavor—over your man Joshua—and the United Nations therefore has, according to Reuter's, stated its discomfort over the rioting in Jerusalem and demanded clarification of the situation. Ergo, it is not so hypothetical to add that the Soviets and Americans have expressed similar thoughts and are concerned about certain troop movements along the Syrian, Lebanese, and Jordanian borders."

"We cannot comment on any movement along those borders."

"Would you be willing to comment on the widely held belief that if the Israelis fail to control their more fanatical and increasingly violent Jews of the West Bank, and if, because of that, the Arabs decide that the time is ripe to sweep into a divided Israel, the Soviets and Americans—overtly to maintain peace in the Middle East, covertly to ensure the continuous flow of Arab oil—will have to take sides in the issue in a so-called war of intervention and thus subsequently carve Israel up between them?"

"No," Moshe said, "we wouldn't care to comment."

"Is the major general speaking on behalf of the prime minister and his Cabinet?" another journalist asked.

"Yes," Ben Eliezer said.

"You refuse to accept the possibility that this could all happen because of the man you are holding?"

"Let me just say this," Ben Eliezer replied. "The riots in Jerusalem are the results of religious fervor encouraged by extremely exaggerated reports of the man we are holding, but they will die away, as all such riots do, with the passing of time. The problem of the West Bank, which has been with us for years, has merely been inflamed by the same highly irresponsible articles and will doubtless be resolved in due course. As for the Arab situation, I need only point out that to date not one Arab leader has offered a formal comment regarding the man Joshua, and the movements along our borders, while not to be ignored, are certainly not as dramatic as has been suggested. Finally let me just add that there is still no absolute proof that this man is anything other than a normal human being, that time will doubtless prove him to be just that, and that this whole situation, unfortunately inflamed by the press, will gradually become much less controversial."

Ben Eliezer nodded at Moshe as if to signal that the conference was over, but Leon's voice, ringing out loud and clear, made him stay in his chair.

"Since the chief rabbi has refused to either admit or deny the existence of any communiqué between the Vatican and the Rabbinate —or indeed between the Rabbinate and the World Council of Churches—would you, Mr. Prime Minister, care to comment on the widespread rumor that both the Soviets and the Americans are demanding their own unbiased examinations of the man you are holding, particularly in view of the fact that you have consistently denied that anything solid actually crashed on the Mount of Olives?"

"We do not comment on rumors, widespread or otherwise."

"Would you state categorically that neither the Soviets nor the Americans have made any such request?"

"I would not make any comment on any rumor."

"What would your reaction be to such a request?"

"The man is of unknown origin but was found in Jerusalem, so until such time as his nationality can be ascertained, we must treat him as an Israeli citizen. There would therefore be no justification whatsoever for handing him over to any foreign power."

"Would you consider the Vatican to be a foreign power?"

"I believe we've already covered that, Mr. Halcomb."

Leon smiled but said no more, merely letting his gaze slip toward Moshe; but Moshe, determined to keep his feelings neutral, looked down at the table.

"One last question," Ben Eliezer said.

"It has been a fortnight since the news of this man's discovery was broken," a woman said, "and in that short time there have been violent clashes between the various religious sects in Jerusalem; less violent demonstrations in many other countries; an enormous upsurge of interest in numerous occult, UFO, and other quasi-mystical organizations; a mass migration of Diaspora Jews into Israel; a total blocking of most Christians—including tourists—and all Arabs into this country; and a buildup of Arab troop movements along the Syrian, Lebanese, and Jordanian borders. Do you not think, given these extraordinary events, that the man you are keeping under surveillance should be exposed to the public, at least by means of the media?"

"No," Ben Eliezer said. "I'm afraid we cannot agree with that. We cannot release this man until we are fully satisfied regarding his origin and nature, and until we understand how he got here. Violent demonstrations will not help; we simply will not release him. Ladies and gentlemen, thank you."

Moshe raised his eyes and looked along the room, but Leon had vanished.

27

The taxi driver refused to take her along Jaffa Road, but instead headed away from the smoking rooftops of the Mea She'arim quarter by driving along Agrippas and turning right into King George V Street. The normally busy street was unusually quiet, many of the windows boarded up, and the few lights bleeding into the darkness seemed bleak and forbidding. Kate glanced through the rear window and saw the smoke over Mea She'arim, red glowings fanning above the rooftops where the flames were still burning. The sound of gunfire made her twitch, and then she shivered and turned away, glancing through the left-hand window and seeing the soldiers around the heavily guarded entrance of the Plaza Hotel. There were few tourists left, but the hotels were filled with recent immigrants, most of whom were enamored with the Messiah and oblivious to the armed guards. Thinking of this, Kate shivered again, feeling haunted with guilt, then she wondered what she might say to Moshe, and the pain bit inside her. The taxi turned left at Keren Hayesod and King David Street, crossed the road, and then stopped outside the King David Hotel, directly facing the floodlit YMCA and its magnificent Oriental tower.

She paid the driver and climbed out and stood for some time on the pavement, looking up and down the broad boulevard on which the trees cast their shadows in the lamplight. The dark smoke was still billowing in the starlit sky above West Jerusalem, and the gunfire, sporadic and distant, was eerie and chilling. She could not believe that it had happened so brutally and quickly, and she shook her head sadly from side to side and walked up to the hotel. There were armed guards at the swinging doors and they checked her identification, then nodded, their young faces very solemn, and let her go through.

The enormous lobby was packed with soldiers, many on cots or in sleeping bags, the furniture pushed back against the walls beneath the large Victorian paintings, weapons glinting in the bright light of the chandeliers hanging down from the ceiling. Some of the soldiers were sleeping, others playing cards or reading books, while the women volunteers, notably all Jewish, were wending their way between the prostrate bodies, serving simple food and drinks.

Kate walked through the lobby, feeling the eyes of the soldiers upon her, and made her way to the terrace overlooking the Oriental gardens. Most of the tables were crowded, both with soldiers and determined clientele, and she saw Moshe near the edge of the room, his figure framed by the gardens. She almost turned and walked back out, the panic seizing her with startling speed, but she simply stopped very briefly, nodded at him, and then walked over to him. He was drinking a beer, the glass tiny in his large hand, and he put the glass back on the table and gave her a pained smile.

"*Shalom*, Kate."

"*Shalom*."

She did not sit down immediately, but stood there, feeling paralyzed, the guilt and shame turning her flesh to stone and draining her mind. He raised his left hand and pointed at the opposite chair, his face terribly weary, his eyes dull, his raised hand visibly shaking.

"It's all right," he said. "Sit down."

"You look completely exhausted."

"I am. I haven't slept for two days. Now please, Kate, sit down."

She slid gratefully onto the chair, placing her shoulder bag on the table, looking around her at the soldiers and civilians and thinking of how things had changed. Eventually, when his silence became unbearable, she returned her gaze to his face.

"The lobby looks like a battlefield," she said. "Are they all riot-control troops?"

"Yes," Moshe said.

"I saw the light of the burning buildings in the Mea She'arim quarter, and also heard isolated gunshots."

"The Arabs are particularly incensed at the messianic claims of the Mea She'arim quarter since those same Arabs naturally believe Joshua to be their Mahdi. In all fairness to them, the situation was doubtless exacerbated by the fact that the Jewish fanatics of Kash and Gush Emunim have been similarly terrorizing the Arabs in every major town on the West Bank."

"Do you think the situation can be handled?"

"No, I don't. I think the situation is getting out of hand. During the past few days we've had fighting in Bethlehem, Nazareth, Tel Aviv, and Netanya, and I simply can't spare enough troops to handle it."

"And you can't use your border-patrol troops?"

"No. Contrary to what we normally say, or like to believe, the mass fervor that has gripped every religion in Jerusalem is now spreading out beyond her borders. Apart from the fact that a great many Arabs, both inside and outside Israel, are convinced that the Mahdi has returned, the less religiously inclined are viewing the riots in our streets as a sign that Jerusalem is about to fall. Small wonder they're massing around our borders and getting ready for war. So, no, I can't use my border-patrol troops; and in fact I'm having to take troops from the streets to swell the thin ranks of those protecting our borders."

"You really sound weary."

"I'm weary. I don't know what to do."

He called a waiter over, ordered a beer and a gin and tonic, then sat back and rubbed his eyes with his hands, his head shaking from side to side. Kate watched him, wanting to beg his forgiveness. He sat forward and put his large hands on the table, staring at her, not smiling.

"So," he said, "how have you been?"

Kate shrugged. "Not so good," she said. "I've had a lot on my mind. I don't think I have to elaborate on that. You must know what I'm talking about."

"Why did you do it, Kate?"

"Any answer would be an excuse. At least any answer would *sound* like an excuse, which is probably the same thing."

"You must have trusted him a lot."

"Yes, I suppose I did. Although I'm not at all sure if it was that, if that even came into it. . . ." She heard her own voice trailing off, dying away to a whisper, a sibilance that arched through the air to form a large question mark. "No," she said, "it was something else. Trust didn't even come into it. What I mean is that I didn't think about it, one way or the other. I just had to tell someone—someone I hadn't experienced it with—and Leon, also the person closest to me, happened to be there at the right time. I just let it out, trying to get rid of the doubt and pressure, and remember exacting his promise not to tell anyone, as if that would absolve me."

"Then he told the whole world."

"Yes, Moshe, he did. He told the whole world and it shocked me because I was the guilty one."

"You trusted him."

"You trusted me."

"I don't think it's the same thing."

"Why? Because I'm just a silly woman and you're a sensible man?"

Moshe winced. "I didn't mean that. Why are you always so defensive? I simply meant that he was your lover and that that sort of trust is fairly different from the trust I had in you."

"Why different?"

"It's a trust based on love—and love doesn't ask questions."

Kate almost flinched with shock, feeling as if she had been slapped, then was further shocked by what she was feeling, and by its mindless intensity. What she was feeling was resentment and an almost childish hurt because Moshe, either deliberately or innocently, had disowned any such feelings for her. At this she almost laughed, feeling the hysteria in her throat, a bitter and self-mocking humor that luckily died on her lips.

"You think I loved Leon?"

"I naturally assumed so," Moshe replied.

"You mean you equated the knowledge that Leon was my lover with the fact that I had to be in love with him?"

"I would have thought that was a natural deduction, Kate. After all, it was more than a one-night stand."

"You mean a woman has to be in love to take a lover?"

"Yes, I suppose so."

She had to smile at that, her humor bubbling up through her pain, an almost maternal warmth pouring out at his impossible innocence.

"Lord," she said, "what a good Jew you are: so puritanical and moral. What does a woman do with a man like you in the twentieth century?"

She saw the trace of a smile, but he quickly disguised it by picking up his glass and having a drink. He set the glass back on the table and examined it thoughtfully.

"You think I'm old-fashioned?" he said.

"The thought's crossed my mind occasionally."

"And you, of course, are an emancipated lady of the wonderful twentieth century."

"You disapprove," Kate said.

"I am not a rabbi," Moshe replied.

"Nevertheless I can sense your disapproval and I'd like it explained."

He shrugged and looked away, gazing around the other tables, his attention obviously focused on the soldiers as they tried to relax.

"They've had a bad time," he murmured. "They're patrolling the town in shifts. They haven't had a decent sleep for days and the work isn't pleasant."

"Because they're fighting and arresting fellow Jews?"

"Yes," he said. "It eats at them." He turned his head back to look at her, his gray eyes slightly bloodshot, weary and filled with a sadness that tore at her heart. "So," he said, "the lady wants an explanation for my supposed disapproval."

"Yes," Kate said. "I do."

"I don't really disapprove. I simply don't understand. Perhaps I'm prejudiced, perhaps I simply *am* old-fashioned, but I just don't understand how a woman like you can be so casual about whom you go to bed with. Please believe me, I don't disapprove: I just find it bewildering."

She felt a flicker of anger that made her lips tighten, but the impulse to get up and slap his face was also the impulse to stroke him.

"I have physical needs," she said, "of a perfectly normal kind, and I see little value in frustrating them. As for being casual about it, I don't think that's quite true, since I felt a great deal for Leon Halcomb."

She saw the flickering of his eyes, a helpless sign that she had hurt him, and she felt an equally helpless satisfaction combined with quiet hope. She had a drink and put her glass back on the table, trying to keep her hand steady.

"So," he said, "you felt a great deal for him, but you didn't quite love him."

"That's it, Moshe. Precisely."

"You sound almost defiant."

"Why should I be?"

"Because you think I'm attacking you over this, but believe me, I'm not."

"Admit it: you disapproved."

"I found it difficult to comprehend. On the other hand, you're a very attractive woman, so perhaps I am prejudiced."

She felt her hope growing like the blossoming of a rose, but her fear, like the thorns around that rose, still threatened to strangle her.

He was so unrevealing, so hesitant and withdrawn, and her anger at his inability, or refusal, to express himself also drew her inexorably toward him and made her want to release him. It was very much a feminine attitude, but she wasn't too comfortable with it.

"Do you mind if I smoke?"

He shrugged indifferently and picked his glass up and took another sip while she lit a cigarette with nervous fingers, feeling oddly confused. She inhaled and then blew the smoke out and kept her eyes on his thoughtful face.

"Just how attractive do you think I am, Moshe?"

"*Very* attractive, Kate."

"And did you expect me to lead a celibate life?"

"Well . . ." He hesitated. "Not quite."

"So if you didn't expect me to be celibate, what did you imagine my private life was like?"

"All right, Kate, I get the message."

"No, Moshe, I don't think so. I seriously doubt that you get anything. Like most men you have a double set of standards—one for men and another for women—and your disapproval, which you pretend not to feel, simply can't be disguised."

"You're getting angry, Kate."

"Damned right I'm getting angry. Tell me this, Major General —and please give me an honest answer: How would you respond if I made it perfectly clear that I thought you a very attractive man?"

"Why? Do you?"

"Damn it, I didn't say that. I merely asked how you would react if it *were* true."

"I'm sorry," he said. "My reaction was perfectly natural. We male chauvinists are like that."

It was unmalicious mockery, offered quietly and dryly, but Kate felt an unreasonable resentment that made her want to hit back at him. Her response was automatic, purely emotional and instinctive, and she realized, with a trace of self-mockery, that she wanted to capture him. He was wary, uncertain, unable to express what he was feeling, and the irony of this was a mirror to her own hapless dilemma. He wanted her as she wanted him, but there were walls to be knocked down.

"You haven't answered my question, Moshe."

"No," he said, "I didn't answer it."

"Well?"

"I think my vanity would be touched—another natural reaction."

"And if I invited you into my bed?"

"Please, Kate, that's enough."

"I want an answer."

"I would find it hard to refuse. I think you know that damned well."

"Fine," she said. "An honest answer. We're getting somewhere at last. And do you think, Major General, that in taking me to bed, you would later disapprove of yourself?"

"No, Kate, I don't think so."

"Then why on earth disapprove of *my* private life?"

"All right, Kate, I get your message. Loud and clear, as they say. And I have, incidentally, taken note of the fact that you always call me 'Major General' when you're angry."

She looked away in disgust, or perhaps in feigned disgust, feeling more like an adolescent than a grown woman and thus resenting him even more. The soldiers were coming and going, all weary and much too young, and the smoke from their cigarettes filled the terrace, making everything hazy.

"I'm sorry," Moshe said, after a very lengthy silence. "Believe me, Kate, I really am sorry, and this time I mean it. Your point has been taken and you're absolutely correct: I disapproved of your affair with Leon Halcomb, and I'd no right to do so."

"Just my affair with Leon?"

"Yes, Kate, I'm afraid so. I'm not quite as old-fashioned as you seem to believe, and your former private life didn't interest me."

"Why Leon?"

"Various reasons, not all easy to explain. I knew about you before I met you and I was, rightly or wrongly, annoyed because you are a Jew and Leon is a notorious anti-Semite."

"He's not an anti-Semite: he's anti-Zionist."

"Perhaps, perhaps not, but it hardly made any difference: you happened to be the daughter of one of our more well-known and loyal Jews, and your very public affair with Leon was—at least in my eyes —a blatant insult to your father's work with the WZO."

"I thought my father was a hypocrite, Moshe, and I wanted to punish him. That's not why I had the affair with Leon—but it *is* why I flaunted it."

"Yes, Kate, I know. At least I came to understand it, particularly during your term in the hospital, when you were locked up with Joshua. My attitude changed then—toward you, not toward Leon

—and my disapproval, for want of a better term, became something more personal."

She wanted him to continue, but instead he looked away, obviously uncomfortable and trying to distract himself by examining his troops. She knew how exhausted he was, and how serious his problems were, and yet she could not resist her ruthless desire to make him state what he felt. Following his gaze and studying the troops, seeing their young, weary faces, she suddenly remembered, with shocking guilt, what was happening because of Joshua, and that she, in her inexcusable weakness, had been personally responsible for it. To know this was almost unbearable, a waking nightmare that refused to vanish; but much worse was the knowledge that even in her shame and guilt her feelings for Moshe were taking precedence over everything else and obliterating the terrible weight of her crime. Jerusalem was in flames, Jew was pitted against Jew, the Arabs and Christians were rampaging through the streets—and she, Kate Hirschfield, who had carelessly sparked it off, was more concerned with her feelings for the man who might suffer in her stead. Now her shame was even greater, her guilt shocking in its intensity, and yet, as Moshe turned back to face her, she couldn't resist leaning toward him.

"What are you trying to say, Moshe?"

"I don't know. I'm not sure. I think I've probably said too much already—and it makes me uncomfortable."

"Why?"

"I'm not sure what we're talking about. I don't think you know your own mind. We met under extraordinary circumstances, have shared some extraordinary experiences, and your feelings for me, like my feelings for you, might have nothing to do with anything other than the highly charged emotional atmosphere of those experiences."

"Does that matter?"

"Yes. Because I'm not as strong as you think I am. There are things in my past that have marked me in strange ways and made me mistrust my own feelings. I confess, Kate, I've wanted you, and hated Leon for having you; and now, because of Leon, because of what has been done, I can't rid myself of the feeling that in you all I'm after is vengeance."

"Do you know what you're confessing, Moshe?"

"That's what I'm not sure of."

"We're actually discussing how you care for me and how I care for you."

"I didn't want to discuss it."

"I want to be in your bed, Moshe.."

"Not now, Kate. Not at this time. We can't commit ourselves now."

"Not commitment: just bed."

"That's not enough. Not for me."

"Forget about Leon and my past, and just take me to bed."

"No, Kate. I can't do that."

She stubbed her cigarette out, feeling juvenile and defeated, humiliated by her blatant, shameless candor and wanting to walk away from him. But she knew she wouldn't do it, not now, possibly never, because what she had experienced with him, irrespective of what he said, was as binding as a ring on the finger, and possibly more so. She raised her head and stared at him, trying to read his veiled gray eyes, but he simply turned his head and looked away, surveying the crowded, smoke-filled terrace.

"Do you know where Leon is?" she asked him abruptly.

"He's vanished," Moshe said. "Like a puff of smoke. We haven't seen him for weeks."

He was staring steadily at her, taking note of her obvious discomfort, and she felt, with resentment and pleasure, that he was reading her mind.

"Yes," she said, "I still care for him. I'd be a liar to say otherwise. But it still doesn't concern you and me; in that sense it's all over."

He nodded his head thoughtfully, his eyes drooping with weariness, and she felt a resurgence of hope and helpless relief. Then he reached out for his beer glass, picked it up, set it down again, and started to run his finger lightly around the rim in a distracted fashion.

"How's Joshua?" she asked him.

He shrugged. "The same as always. Inhumanly passive and patient. He's virtually a prisoner, the whole world is crying out for him, and he sits there in his room, surrounded by guards, just waiting for something to happen. We still don't know who he is—and I don't think we'll ever find out—but Joshua, if he knows no more than us, is convinced that he is here for some purpose and that his time will be soon."

"That's why he finally let me go," Kate replied. "He said that I'd served my purpose, that I'd guided him from the darkness, and that now he was ready to face whatever was coming."

"And how did you feel about that, Kate?"

"Strange. Confused. I think I felt almost maternal. Like a mother watching her child growing away from her: both wounded and proud."

She found herself staring down at the table, embarrassed by what she had said, one part of her torn by her feelings for Leon and Joshua, the other part wanting to capture Moshe and hold him close to her.

"You two had a strange relationship."

"Yes," she replied. "It was eerie."

"You seemed to be able to read his mind."

"And he mine," she said.

She raised her eyes again, suddenly feeling remote, and saw him leaning over the table toward her, his face very intense.

"What was the blood in the Pool of Siloam?" he asked. "Joshua told you to will the blood. He told you to admit what you had previously denied, to accept the shame and then put it behind you. What did he mean by that?"

Kate stared down at the table, then looked blindly around her, seeing nothing but the agony of her past and the guilt she had buried. Joshua's words filled her mind, his voice reverberating spectrally, and she thought of the fetus spinning in its pool of blood and offering freedom. She felt that freedom now—not shame nor the former guilt —and she turned her eyes back upon him, relieved to be telling him.

"My abortion," she said. "The guilt I tried to ignore. He was telling me to free myself from guilt by accepting that guilt."

His eyes flickered with shock, but he held it in check, trying to honor the pact they had made without uttering a word. She wanted to reach across the table and take his hand, but she didn't dare do it.

"Let me explain," she said. "The great irony of my life is that my first real position was as a psychiatric consultant in a well-known New York abortion clinic. A good Jewish girl, I was relatively innocent at the time, and what I saw in that clinic—what very few men have to see—was enough to put me off men for life."

"I thought abortion was routine," Moshe said dryly. "At least in New York."

"The operation, dear Moshe, may well be routine, but the psychological repercussions, for both patients and staff, form a problem that has yet to be solved. Think of what it means to be a woman working in an abortion clinic: young and emotional, almost certainly romantic, she is brutally exposed to the real blood and marrow of sex and its impersonal, almost surgical terminology: not violins and roses and the light touch of a lover, but the pill and the diaphragm, the intrauterine device, the vaginal jellies and creams—the whole messy business coupled with the lesser known possible side effects such as benign tumors or gallbladder disease, migraine or heart disease, vaginal or cervical cancer, heavy bleeding or perforation of the uterine wall —the part of sex that few men understand or are willing to recognize. How easy for the man to have his moment of idle pleasure and then treat it as a casual encounter; not so casual for the woman who discovers she is pregnant and then pays for her moment of pleasure with menses extraction, vacuum aspiration, dilatation and curettage, hypertonic saline or intraamniotic prostaglandin abortion, dilation and evacuation or, if she's particularly unlucky, hysterotomy or hysterectomy. The aftermath of careless passion—the dilating of the cervical canal, the injection of saline solution into the amniotic sac, the uterine wall scraped and the fetus and placenta removed, either sucked out or pulled out with forceps—flesh and blood: love's reality. God, yes, it's unpleasant—and if the women survived it physically, a great many were wounded emotionally; and the nursing staff—who saw more than their patients did—often just couldn't take it. It was the late abortions that did it, that gave rise to thoughts of murder: when the fetuses had perfect shape, when the salines were born alive, and they were dumped into a bucket of formaldehyde or just left to wriggle and die on the operating tables. A lot of us couldn't take it—we had nightmares and even crackups—and for me the experience separated love from sex, making the latter seem at best a dangerous pleasure, at worst a crudely primitive physical impulse. . . . Yet ironically, once it made me feel that way, I went out and got myself pregnant."

Moshe was gazing steadily at her, neither sympathetic nor disapproving, his face, with its square, granite handsomeness, trying to conceal what he felt. Yet his eyes, gray and weary, lined with age and lack of sleep, were unable to hide his mild shock at what she was telling him.

"I had trouble sleeping," she continued. "I kept dreaming of fetuses: giant fetuses in the cupboards, at the foot of my bed, fetuses wriggling in buckets of formaldehyde or on smooth, shiny tables. I lost a lot of sleep and I wanted someone with me, but sex, as it had not been before, now seemed squalid and frightening. *Physician, heal thyself:* the good psychiatrist, I decided to do so; I decided to take a lover not to satisfy my desire, but to prove that I was still a normal woman and that sex was no nightmare. That's no way to choose a lover, much less soothe emotional stress, and the man I found was what I deserved: a stud always in heat."

Moshe visibly winced at that, and she wished she hadn't said it, not wanting to hurt him more than necessary, but not wanting to soften it. He glanced down at the table and then looked up again, obviously finding it painful to listen, but determined to do so. If not courage, it was a form of honesty that moved her immensely.

"I'm sorry," she said, "but that's the only way to describe him: a stud always in heat, an unemotional, selfish animal, a man who prided himself as a sexual athlete, but knew nothing of feelings. Perhaps I picked him because it was easy—because he made it easy for me—but whatever, the very first night we met, he ended up in my bed. If he was good, I hardly knew it—I never judged men that way—but certainly when I went to bed with him, I scarcely thought of the consequences. I had only one thought, which was to rid myself of fear, but my work in the clinic, instead of frightening me off pregnancy, had given me some peculiar aberrations: the pill made me nervous, I couldn't bear an IUD inside me, the thought of inserting a diaphragm only filled me with repugnance, and any other form of contraception seemed clinical and messy. He was angry when he found this out, but promised not to come inside me; but it was clear, shortly after he started, that he was very unhappy. I knew he was going to do it and begged him to stop, but he just called me a stupid bitch and held me down with both hands and then, hardly knowing the word *rape*, pushed even deeper inside me. He wasn't trying to excite me or make me forget myself; he was punishing me, as only men can, for trying to deprive him of the satisfaction of coming inside me. So, he came inside me—as far into me as he could get—and when he did, I knew as surely as I was breathing that I was going to be pregnant."

She kept her eyes on Moshe's face, determined not to let him go, knowing that she had to tell it all and let him take it or leave it. So far he had not averted his gaze, and his large hands were steady.

"I never saw him again," she said, "since my lack of precautions had obviously annoyed him, but he left me with a child in the womb and much inherited guilt. My father was at that time returning to Orthodox Judaism; and apart from my disgust at what I felt was his rank hypocrisy, I knew that to tell him about the baby would have made life impossible. Cowardice? Yes. And I despised myself for it, hating the man who had made me pregnant and also hating my father for unwittingly forcing me to opt for an abortion. Nonetheless I delayed it, wanting the baby, frightened of having it; until, by the time I eventually decided to go through with it, I was seventeen weeks pregnant and required a second-trimester abortion. I was given the saline infusion fairly early in the morning, spent most of the day convinced that my insides were falling out, and sometime late that evening I had a miscarriage, the fetus was expelled, and I looked down to see it lying on the bed in a large pool of blood. I didn't make a sound. I was too horrified to scream. I propped myself up on my elbows and just stared at that bloody fetus as it lay there on the bed between my legs, looking terribly alive. The nurse refused to take it away until the placenta came out—which took another thirty minutes —and during all that time, the longest nightmare of my life, I just lay there, supporting myself on my elbows, staring helplessly at what I felt I had murdered. Then when the placenta came out and they finally took the fetus away, I fainted with pure horror and shock, hardly noticing the physical pain."

She kept her eyes fixed on Moshe, refusing to let him look away, aware that what she was telling him could destroy his feelings for her, equally aware that she did not wish to have him under false pretenses. He gazed back very steadily, obviously not trying to avoid her, and she thought of their first meeting, of the black obelisk on the ruins, of the beam of light pouring down through the darkness onto Joshua's face. She and Moshe had been united then, in fear and incomprehension, but now, she was convinced, they were united by something deeper and truer. It was love of a very earthly kind—and would break or endure.

"I changed after that," she said. "I divorced my mind from my body, separating my physical desires from my emotions and thus dividing my nature. I did this because of guilt and shame, denying them both by trying to bury them, using sex as the means of obliteration; and keeping emotion, which would have reminded me of what I had lost, well clear of my various affairs. That's what I eventually found with Leon: a lack of commitment that made me feel safe; in Leon I found a remote, dry affection that never seemed threatening. It wasn't love, Moshe—at least not as you imagined it —and when Leon mistook what I felt for love, I had to let him go also. As for Joshua, he understood that I was divided and unhappy, that I would not be able to live with myself until I accepted my guilt and shame, and so he made me draw the past from my mind and face it squarely; and in facing up to it, find freedom. You understand, Moshe? I am free. And being free, I want you."

She fell silent and stared at him, her gaze focused on his lips, waiting, for what seemed like an eternity, for his reply to emerge. The eternity came and went, stretching out and then dilating, and she felt a brief fluttering of panic at what his response might be. He seemed unreal at that moment, out of focus, hazed in smoke, but his presence seemed to percolate through her and make her part of him. She waited quietly for his decision, trying to control her desperation, but then a shadow fell over him, briefly obliterating his features, and she glanced up to see a young soldier leaning over the table. He handed Moshe a written note, and Moshe read it, his lips tightening, then rubbed his forehead wearily with one hand and raised his eyes to look at her.

"I'm wanted urgently at the Hadassah Medical Center," he said, "and I think you better come with me. . . . They're going to release Joshua."

28

The jeep turned left off Keren Hayesod and went along Derekh Aza, heading away from the flaming rooftops of the besieged West Jerusalem to the quieter environs outside the city. Yet even here there were soldiers, passing their jeep in crowded trucks, the trucks all heading back toward the city and its dark, smoke-filled sky. They heard the sound of an explosion, behind them and far away, and Moshe winced, thinking of what was going on and wanting to be in control of it. He turned his head to look at Kate, saw the lamplight on her dark eyes, her long hair blowing out in the wind and exposing her angular face. She obviously sensed his attention and her eyes turned toward his, one hand brushing the hair from her forehead, the other pressed to the seat.

"What did the note say, Moshe?"

"Nothing very informative. Just that they had to release Joshua, and they wanted me up there."

"The violence is getting worse."

"That's right. Every minute. I suspect that's why they have to release Joshua: because they just can't contain it."

"And they think that will help?"

"Well, it's Joshua they're fighting over. The Jews and the Muslims and the Christians all want to lay hands on him."

"That's what I mean," Kate said. "I think what they're planning is dangerous. What are those people, now fighting each other, going to do when Joshua is let loose?"

"It might pacify them."

"Why should it pacify them? Indeed, what do they expect of him? He can't be Jesus Christ and the Messiah and the Mahdi all at once, yet those warring groups all want to lay claim to him. What happens if he picks one group over the others? I don't think they'll accept that."

Moshe studied the neck of the driver in front of him, then turned to look back on Jerusalem as it fell far behind them. He saw the towering office blocks darkly outlined against the red sky, skeins of smoke drifting across the few lit windows, isolated yellow flames flickering dimly, as pretty as candles. Joshua had prophesied it, and now it had come true: Jerusalem the Golden, his home, was being set to the torch. Moshe shuddered and turned away from the eerie sight, scarcely able to credit it.

"It's like the end of the world," he said.

"It's only Israel," Kate replied.

"Israel is the center of the world—and if it falls, the world breaks."

"You think this will spread further?"

"It's already spread, Kate. There have been demonstrations in an awful lot of countries, some of them violent."

"Not as bad as this."

"Not yet, but it might come. Joshua, whoever or whatever he is, has set the spark to men's dreams."

He covered his face with his right hand, closing his eyes and trying to think, a desperate fear churning up from his stomach and filling his mind. It was an unfamiliar fear, divorced from thoughts of physical danger, arising from an increasing feeling of helplessness before the intangible. The jeep growled and shook beneath him, slightly comforting in its reality, but it wasn't enough to shake him out of the coils of the nightmare surrounding him. He was a soldier, a man of concretes, a man who knew the rules of war; but this extraordinary situation, which had exploded around Joshua, defied every tenet of his teaching and left him adrift. He felt Kate beside him, her thigh pressed to his own, her warmth like a beacon to his senses, luring him in. He wanted her there and then—in the back of the jeep, beneath the stars—but no sooner had he felt this than his thoughts vaulted back to the real world. Death and destruction by the bullet and the bomb: would Joshua's release put an end to it or fan the flames further?

He glanced briefly at Kate, wanting to reach out and touch her, and wondering why he couldn't say the words that were perched on his lips. The wind was rushing through the jeep, blowing her hair around her face, and she raised a hand to brush it away and let it fly out behind her. He wanted to reach out and touch it, to lose his fingers in it, to wipe it like a rag across his face, cleansing himself with its softness. The desire was voluptuous, slightly decadent in its nature, and, shocked, he turned his head, stared out the front, and surveyed the dark road. The jeep was turning toward the hospital, the land dark on either side, and he glanced up at the sky and saw the stars in their remote, glittering brilliance.

"Are you all right?" Kate asked.

"Yes," he replied, "I'm fine."

"You seemed very strange there for a moment."

"I'm just tired. My mind's drifting."

It was the truth as subterfuge and he used it without guilt, simply surprised at Kate's instinctive response to what he was feeling. She knew him, and he her, and through Joshua they had been drawn together, and now they were bound up in a drama that transcended them both. He wondered if they could hold together, alone, without Joshua; and his doubt, like the dark clouds in a dream, swam around his pained love. He glanced out of the jeep, trying to let the night dissolve him, and there, at the beginning of the sloping road, was the first of the roadblocks.

"I don't believe it," Kate said.

"You'll just have to," he replied. "Now we know why they want to release Joshua: clearly they don't have a choice."

The roadblock was new and heavily guarded by armed troops, and both sides of the road winding up to the hospital were lined with a great number of similar troops. The soldiers were not facing the road but the grassy slopes on either side, their weapons pointed at the hundreds of people—Jew, Christian, and Muslim—who had obviously come to demand the release of Joshua. The people were all chanting, "We want Joshua! We want Joshua!", their clenched fists rising up and down in unison, many holding large candles. It was a great multitude, covering the fields on both sides of the road, and all of them were looking uphill toward the linear buildings of the hospital.

The driver stopped at the roadblock and a young sergeant walked up to the jeep, leaning forward and looking at Moshe and then nodding his head; he did not salute but merely glanced nervously around him before looking at Moshe again.

"Major General," he said, nodding his head in recognition, the term of address both casual and respectful, his youthful face not too happy.

"Any trouble?" Moshe asked.

"Not yet, Major General. They just refuse to leave until we release him, but more are coming each minute."

"How many are here at present?"

"We think close to a thousand. There've been a few fistfights, some of the soldiers have been abused, but apart from that they're just lighting candles and shaking their fists."

"But you think it will get worse."

"Almost definitely; they're getting angrier each minute."

"Fine, Sergeant. Let us through."

The roadblock was raised and the driver headed up toward the hospital, passing the stiffened spines of the soldiers on either side of the winding road. The massed people were still chanting, their fists rising and falling, their raised faces illuminated by the pale moon and starlight and by the hundreds of candles that flickered in a very mild breeze. The jeep kept moving uphill, past the soldiers and the chanting masses, and then drove through the car park that overlooked the series of dark hills, and finally stopped at the second roadblock near the synagogue and the hospital entrance. Here the soldiers had set up spotlights that were beaming over the crammed car park; and the soldiers themselves, heavily armed and at the ready, were grouped in front of the solid mass of trucks that filled the hospital grounds. Another sergeant approached Moshe, recognized him, and nodded; then Moshe and Kate got out of the jeep and walked into the hospital.

Moshe gazed along the reception area and saw another group of soldiers, some sitting on the seats, others sitting on the floor, women moving through them serving drink and food and handing out magazines. Some nurses and medical orderlies were present, obviously waiting for the expected trouble, and stretchers were piled up along the walls with the blankets and first-aid kits. Joshua was at the far end of the room, standing upright, wearing his white robes, anachronistic with his long hair and beard, yet undeniably dignified. Close by were Ben Eliezer, General Meshel, and Paul Frankel, the three of them in serious discussion, heads nodding, hands waving.

Moshe turned to look at Kate and saw her staring at Joshua, her dark eyes strangely luminous and intense, filled with sorrow and love. She shivered and closed her eyes and then opened them again, staring at Joshua and then turning to look at Moshe, one hand reaching out toward him. He caught her hand in its downward flight, squeezed her fingers, felt her warmth, then let the hand gently fall away while he stared at her, drowning.

"Are you all right?"

"Yes," she said, "I'm all right. I just feel that I'm losing him."

"You never really had him, Kate."

"I know that . . . but that just makes it worse."

He nodded and took her elbow and then walked her along the room, occasionally nodding at a soldier he recognized but feeling strangely divorced from them. Paul looked up when he approached, his handsome face very tense, his brown eyes moving slightly to take in Kate before sliding away again. Ben Eliezer, looking diminutive beside the broad-chested General Meshel, offered a slight, grateful smile, obviously glad to be seeing him.

"Ah, Moshe," he said quietly. "You got our message."

"Yes, Shlomo."

"And how were things in Jerusalem?"

"Terrible and getting worse."

"You should send in the tanks," General Meshel said. "You'd clear the streets in no time."

"I do not think it wise," Ben Eliezer said, "to show the world Israeli tanks blowing holes in Jerusalem. I think it wiser simply to let Joshua go."

"And you think that will stop them?" Kate asked.

"Who invited this lady here?" Ben Eliezer said, looking directly at Moshe.

"I think she could be of assistance," Moshe said, returning the direct look. "We don't know how Joshua will react, and Kate might have to talk to him."

"I doubt that, Moshe. We've already told him we're letting him go. He simply gave us a blank look and nodded his head."

"He's agreeable?"

"We assume so."

"And which group is he going to support?"

"We asked him, but he simply stared at us and offered a slight smile. I don't think he comprehends the situation, but I can't be too sure of that."

"You tried explaining the situation to him?"

"Yes, Miss Hirschfield, we tried. He simply nodded in a rather judicious manner and then turned toward the wall."

"He's looking at us now."

"Yes, Miss Hirschfield . . . perhaps because you are here."

Kate ignored the bland sarcasm and merely glanced at Joshua where he stood, as steady as a rock, with his back to the wall. He saw her staring at him and responded with a gentle smile, then turned his silvery-gray eyes on Moshe, looking at him and into him. Moshe shivered, still baffled by the man's nature, and stepped closer to Kate.

"I repeat," Kate said, speaking to the prime minister, "do you think this will stop them?"

"I take it you mean the release of Joshua?"

"Precisely."

"You have seen the riots in Jerusalem and those people massed outside. I don't think I have to elaborate on the reason: we must give them this man."

"If he sides with one group over the others, you'll have even worse riots."

"Perhaps," Ben Eliezer replied, "but we have to try something. The riots in Jerusalem have inflamed similar riots in other parts of Israel and, indeed, in various other countries. As for the Muslims, while no Arab leader has openly expressed support for the view of Joshua as the returned Mahdi, there can be little doubt that they are massing along our borders in order to exploit our internal troubles—and are just waiting for those troubles to get out of control. Nor can we ignore the fact that the United Nations, the Soviets, and the Americans are all openly discussing the necessity of military intervention should the Arabs decide to cross our borders and head for Jerusalem. So, as you can see, we have to bring order back to Jerusalem; and the only possible way of doing it—short of sending in the tanks—is to give them the man they are all clamoring for. We're not saying that it will work, but we have to try. We have no other choice."

"And what if it doesn't work?"

"Then we send in the tanks," General Meshel said.

Moshe caught Kate's frightened glance and dropped his eyes, ashamed to look at her, knowing that the tanks would be unavoidable if the rioting continued.

"Has it occurred to any of you that someone might try to kidnap him?" Kate said. "After all, a gang of Kash fanatics has already tried to do just that right here in the hospital; if they tried it when he was here, they'll almost certainly try it when he's unprotected."

"We have reason to believe that won't happen," Paul said, looking at Kate for the first time.

"What reason?"

"We believe his extraordinary powers will protect him."

"He might use his powers to protect himself from violence, but if anyone tries to spirit him away, I think he'll go with them."

"And why would he do that?" Ben Eliezer asked.

"Because he doesn't know what he's here for, nor what he's

supposed to do, so he'll simply let events take their course. The sight of a gun might well make him use his powers, but if someone, or some group, simply asks him to come with them, I think he will passively do so in the belief that it is preordained and part of his fate."

"He was not very passive with the members of Shin Beth when they tried to separate him from you for further questioning."

"That was a different matter, General Meshel. Both those soldiers were carrying guns. And at that time Joshua was convinced that I had to stay with him."

"I still don't think anyone will abduct him," Paul said, "or attempt any violence against him."

He was looking straight at Kate, but then he glanced quickly at Moshe, his brown eyes very nervous and restless, as if trying to conceal something. Moshe remembered him at the Pool of Siloam after the blood had materialized: falling down to his knees in abject worship, convinced that Joshua was the Messiah. Although he tried to conceal it, that conviction was still with him; and now, staring at him, trying to analyze his dark gaze, Moshe was certain that Paul was suppressing a dangerous fanaticism.

"Why not?" he said, keeping his voice calm and level, determined not to reveal his suspicion and latent contempt. "What Kate says seems logical to me."

"Not necessarily," Paul said, glancing at everyone in turn, then finally forcing himself to look at Moshe. "The fact that Joshua has been viewed variously as the Christ of the Christians, the Jewish Messiah, and the Muslim Mahdi is the very fact that could keep him from all harm. It is true, as Miss Hirschfield says, that should Joshua side with any one group over the others, the repudiated groups may well be outraged. On the other hand, if Joshua takes no side—and so far he has not done so—then each one of those individuals, in the conviction of his personal religion, will assume that Joshua is his own savior and consequently won't lay a hand on him. He will be sacred to each and every individual and will therefore be safe."

"The fact that some thought him their Messiah did not prevent them from attempting to storm this hospital."

"I'm aware of that, Shlomo," Paul replied. "However, interrogation of the captured Kash members revealed that they truly believed Joshua to be the Messiah and were merely going to locate him in Hebron where all believers could have contact with him, while the military, in all likelihood, could be kept out. They did not intend

holding him prisoner; on the contrary, they were simply going to keep
him there for a few days, let the news of his freedom spread
throughout Israel, and then either let him stay there—well protected
by themselves—or allow him to travel wherever he wished."

"Assuming, in both cases, that he was definitely Jewish and would
therefore either stay gladly in Hebron or go traveling to inaugurate the
sovereignty of Judaism."

"Correct."

"And the Muslims and Christians?"

"Lieutenant Frankel is right," Kate intervened. "While Joshua's
recollections suggest a peculiar mixture of Judaic and Christian
history—and could just as easily be interpreted in favor of Muslim
history—Joshua's reactions to the most famed religious sites were
nonconclusive and even contradictory; and Joshua himself has never
suggested that he is one thing or the other. Ergo, if he continues to
make no claims for himself and retains his undeniably ambiguous
form of speech—a form of speech that can be interpreted in just about
any light—then, as Paul says, each individual religion will claim him
as its own and no single individual will dare to touch him."

"Peace on Earth," Ben Eliezer said.

"It might work," Moshe added quietly.

"We simply don't have a choice," Paul said fervently. "We have no
options left."

Again Moshe found himself staring at Paul, trying to penetrate the
veils of his brown eyes and see what he was thinking. He would not
quickly forget the sight of Paul on his knees, his head bowed over the
feet of the man whom he thought was the Messiah. Paul was an
Orthodox Jew, an extremist, a true believer; and now, with a messiah
to follow, he would not be stopped easily. This bothered Moshe, but
what bothered him even more was the fact that Paul had not, since that
fateful day, made his new belief known.

"Is it not true," Moshe said, "that you, Lieutenant Frankel, believe
this man to be the Jewish Messiah?"

Paul stared at him, startled, then flushed and looked at Joshua, who
returned his stare with gray-eyed equanimity, hardly moving a
muscle. Paul shivered, licked his lips, and lowered his head, and then
turned back to Moshe.

"Yes," he said, almost whispering, "I do. By my faith, I believe
this."

"And you are willing to let him go down there with the Arabs and Christians?"

"Yes," Paul replied. "In my faith, I am willing. If, as I believe, he is the Messiah, then no harm will come to him."

"And if he is the Mahdi or Jesus Christ?"

"He is not."

"If he *is*?"

"Unless he specifically tells me otherwise, I refuse to believe otherwise. Until he specifically denies it, he *is* the Messiah."

"Fine," Ben Eliezer said. "Lieutenant Frankel is a believer. If, as we believe, the others are equally adamant, and if, as we hope, Joshua takes no particular side, we might just have the odds in our favor. It would seem, then, that our fate lies with Joshua's decision —but, alas, he's not forthcoming on that matter."

Kate immediately left the group and walked up to Joshua, who lowered his gaze to look down on her face when she stopped just in front of him. Moshe glanced at Ben Eliezer, who smiled sardonically and shrugged, then they all went and gathered around Joshua where he stood by the wall. He did not glance at any of them, but kept staring down at Kate, his gray eyes uncommonly bright and observant, his lips curved in an almost imperceptible smile that showed warmth and affection.

"You willed the blood," he said, "which took courage and faith; and now, in your eyes, is the light of redemption and hope."

"Yes," Kate replied.

"That is all you need to say. You must hold to your faith as to the root of a tree, and let the seasons bring what they will. You will not break nor fall."

"I have to talk to you about something."

"I understand there is a problem."

"Do you understand what is happening outside and what people expect of you?"

"The situation was explained to me. There is little I can do about it. If they wish to send me out, it is my time—but I cannot give reasons."

"They think of you as their savior."

"They must believe what they believe. If, by simply being, I give them faith, I might then save their souls."

That remark filled Moshe with dread, despair beating with blackened wings, but he noticed, with a hesitant hope, that Kate did not seem perturbed.

"You mean, you think you are their savior?"

"I would not presume such. I merely state that if they believe in me, that belief may redeem them."

"Redemption through you?"

"Not through me: through their faith. It matters not how they come to faith; faith itself is what matters."

"There are Muslims, Christians, and Jews."

"I do not recognize such. These are names for the religions of men, and such religions are false. There is only the one religion: the worship of the One. The religions of men divide—they do not unite —and as such debase Him."

"Some think of you as the Mahdi."

"I cannot confirm or deny it."

"Some think of you as the Messiah."

"I cannot confirm nor deny it."

"Some think of you as the resurrected Jesus Christ."

"I am Joshua and can say no more than that. I am what I am."

Kate nodded and stepped back, turning her head to look at Moshe, and he saw, in the luminous darkness of her eyes, the calm of acceptance. She looked at General Meshel, then at Paul and Ben Eliezer, and the latter, returning her gaze for some time, finally turned toward Moshe.

"Well, what do you think?"

"I think you've got your answer."

"It says neither one thing nor the other."

"That's just what we want."

Shlomo looked at him steadily, perhaps challenging him to back down, but Moshe, refusing the offer, kept his own gaze very steady until the prime minister surrendered with a gentle smile and turned his attention on Paul.

"That's it," he said. "Let's get him out of here. Let's find out what happens."

"I want to go with him," Kate said.

"So do I," said Moshe.

"We'll *all* go with him as far as the end of the car park," Ben Eliezer said. "No one goes any farther than that. *Oy vay*, let's get moving!"

At a nod from Kate, Joshua left his position near the wall and began walking along the crowded reception room, followed first by Kate, then by Moshe and Paul, with the Prime Minister and General Meshel in the rear. The nurses and medical orderlies serving food and drink stopped what they were doing as Joshua, in his white robes, walked quietly past them. Likewise, the soldiers lounging around the walls or sitting on the floor fell silent as they watched him, their eyes taking in his attire and strangely primitive, noble face, then filling up with awe and fear before sliding away to study, with the relief of familiarity, Moshe and the others coming up behind him. Moshe nodded at some of the soldiers, understanding what they were feeling, and was relieved when they finally got through the long room and stopped on the steps outside the hospital, where the darkness, if split by the raised spotlights, still offered some solace.

The troops were massed in front of the entrance, forming a cordon across the road, and the spotlights, moving back and forth slowly, were focused on the lawn behind the synagogue and the car park beyond. Army trucks were coming and going, making a roaring and clattering, but even this noise could not entirely obliterate the rhythmic chanting from the fields just below the distant car park. Joshua stared at the synagogue, then raised his eyes to look above it, as if willing himself to see the crowds who were chanting beneath the glittering star-bright sky. He glanced briefly at Kate, his lips shadowed, his eyes in moonlight, then turned away and started to walk forward without saying a word.

They all followed him around the synagogue and across the dark lawn, taking the shortcut directly to the car park above the mountainous valley. Here the sound of the trucks was weaker, the rhythmic chanting growing louder; and the spotlights, weaving back and forth eerily, illuminated the crammed cars. Moshe kept his eyes on Kate, inexorably drawn to her slim form, wanting to reach out and stroke her long hair when the wind made it shiver. She was walking beside Joshua, looking deceptively small beside him, her blue denims and suede jacket at odds with his white Arab robes. A spotlight picked them out, passed across them, leaving darkness, then they arrived at the soldiers guarding both sides of the road that wound down from the car park. Some of the soldiers stared at them, recognized them and stepped aside, allowing them to walk off the lawn and onto the road.

"We stop here," Ben Eliezer said.

From where they stood, they could look down and see the people massed on the grassy slopes at both sides of the road. They were all staring uphill, the candles flickering above their heads, those empty-handed raising and lowering their fists to the loud, rhythmic chanting.

"We want Joshua! We want Joshua!" they all chanted in unison, their joined voices forming a hollow, bass tone that reverberated ethereally. The scene was bizarre—the hundreds of flickering candles, the stars glittering above, the candlelight and starlight both illuminating the thousand faces in the darkness—and was not, in Moshe's view, made any the less bizarre by the sight of Joshua standing above it all like some biblical prophet. As if reading Moshe's mind, he turned around to look at each of them in turn, finally settling on Kate.

"I am free to go?" he said.

"Yes," Kate replied, "but please, please be careful."

"What is willed, will be done."

He walked off down the road, between the two lines of soldiers, his body erect, his white robes whipping, his feet kicking up stones. The crowds saw him and stopped chanting, their voices trailing off in confusion, their raised fists slowly sinking to their sides as they took in his presence. The sudden silence was eerie, giving life to a rising wind, and the thousand faces, illuminated by candlelight and starlight, moved slowly around as they followed the man walking down the guarded road. Joshua walked very slowly, continually looking left and right, as surprised by the watching people as they were by him and finally stopping about halfway down the road with the crowds on both sides of him. The crowds started to surge forward, instinctively impelled toward the road, ignoring the soldiers' raised weapons, pushing them away and rushing between them, until eventually they were leaving the grassy slopes en masse and reaching out to touch Joshua with their hungry hands.

Moshe felt the rising wind and then saw the dark clouds gathering, materializing impossibly from the clear, starlit sky and forming an ominous black mass directly over the road. He stared at it, startled, remembering the storm over Jerusalem, and then looked down and saw Joshua's white robes flying out in the sudden wind. The people around him had stopped moving, obviously as startled as Moshe had been, and were staring wildly from Joshua to the sky and then back again. Some fell to their knees, stretching their arms out in worship, while others stepped back even farther, moved by fear or confusion. The wind started to howl, whipping Moshe and rushing past him, moving in a circular motion that embraced all the others. He saw Kate just in front of him, her hair blowing out behind her, then bolts of lightning tore viciously through the boiling clouds and were followed by thunder. Moshe glanced up, disbelieving, waiting for the rain that didn't come, then he looked down the road and saw Joshua as a shimmering white dream. The people were still around him but had moved away from him, beaten back by both the wind and their fear of what they were witnessing. Joshua stood with his arms raised, his robes blowing out behind him, the lightning daggering out of the clouds and disappearing into a white haze that coiled down like a faucet through the darkness and surrounded his body.

Kate sobbed and turned to Moshe, pressing her face into his shoulder, and he held her in his arms and stroked her hair as the wind howled about them. Paul entered his line of vision, stepping forward as in a trance, his jaw slack and his brown eyes very large as he looked down at Joshua. Following his gaze, Moshe saw the storm, a minor tornado on the road, Joshua standing untouched in the vortex, the crowd outside the swirling dust. Kate sobbed and clung to Moshe, her warmth negating the wind's fierce cold, and he felt himself dissolving into her body as the storm raged below. The dust was swirling around Joshua, just outside the shimmering white haze, while he stood there, his arms still outstretched, his robes whipping around him. Then the thunder roared again, the lightning flashed and disappeared, the white haze around Joshua faded away into the darkness, and the wind seemed to sigh and expire to let the swirling dust settle.

Kate raised her head again, looked at Moshe, and then turned around, her spine pressed to his body as she wearily leaned against him and they both stared down the dark, silent road. Joshua was standing in the starlight, lowering his arms to his sides, his shoulders slumped as if something had been drained out of him and had now left him spent. He bowed his head for a moment, raised it again, and looked around him as the crowd, now totally silent and awed, gradually moved in to touch him. Their hands fluttered like birds, touching lightly and then departing, and Joshua straightened his shoulders, as if finding his strength again, and then, with the confidence of one accepted, moved on down the road.

Moshe watched him disappearing, being swallowed up by his flock, and then, when the last of the people had disappeared, realized that his hands were on Kate's shoulders—feeling flesh and blood, her coursing blood, and wanting it desperately. He looked at Ben Eliezer, at General Meshel and Paul; then, suddenly embarrassed, dropped his hands, knowing what would become of him.

"A reprieve," Ben Eliezer said.

29

"Peace in Israel," Jozsef said. "At least for the moment. He has given everyone a little of what they need, and they are temporarily satisfied. Regarding how long it will last, your guess is as good as mine, but for the time being each has claimed him as his own, and he has taken no sides."

They were walking along the Sea of Galilee, on the northern shore, facing Tiberias, the sun blazing down on the limpid blue water and the greenery surrounding them. Kate was wearing a pair of slacks and an open-necked blouse, her face scrubbed and healthy, her eyes clear, her long hair hanging loose. Jozsef studied her with fondness but could not forget the heat, his abundant flesh sweating too much, his breath emerging in spasms.

"I'm too old for this," he said, mopping his brow with a handkerchief. "The chief rabbi, in the responsibility of his station, rarely gets such good exercise."

"We could have driven," Kate replied.

"I thought the walk would do us good. A noble thought, if rather too ambitious, as I'm now finding out."

Kate didn't look at him, but she smiled to herself, her gaze focused on the bleached grandeur of the Golan Heights in the distant heat haze. Jozsef followed her gaze and remembered the Yom Kippur War, when the guns of the Syrians had fired from those very same mountains. He had been much younger then, without doubts, his faith a rock; now that faith, in its complexity and mystery, was being put to the test.

"Is he clever or innocent?"

"What do you mean?" Kate said.

"He moves from Jew to Christian to Muslim, and gives each what they want."

"He gives them nothing," Kate said. "He neither confirms nor denies. He simply lets them define him as they wish because he knows nothing else. Joshua is passive, an empty well to be filled; from that well they can draw what they need and depart feeling better."

"He's avoiding the issue."

"For him there is no issue: he does not know who he is or where he came from, and he thinks they can tell him."

"They all tell him he's their savior."

"He neither confirms nor denies that. Not knowing who he is, he has to listen to what they believe of him."

"Messiah, Christ, and Mahdi—all three rolled into one. He believes, at the very least, that he has been called and is one or the other."

"He believes he has been called, but certainly not in the sense you mean; he does not think of himself as Muslim or Christian or Jew, but is someone with an undefined purpose that will soon be revealed."

"It doesn't matter what Joshua thinks; what matters is what *they* think . . . and each assumes that he has come to inaugurate the sovereignty of his personal religion."

"And you think it will explode?"

"It will explode. Sooner or later, it has to."

He glanced across the blue water and saw the town of Tiberias, its white-walled buildings nestling in the lush green of the hills of Galilee. They had taken the ferry from there, stopping for lunch in the Kibbutz Ein Gev, and now, though well replenished with St. Peter's fish, Jozsef was feeling exhausted. The sun was very hot, beating out of the azure sky, and he rubbed his stinging eyes and looked at Kate, wondering what she was thinking.

"Do you want to rest?" she said.

"No," he replied. "We're nearly there. If I sit down, I'll never stand up again, so we'd better keep walking."

Kate smiled again, looking at him very briefly, then let her gaze roam across Yam Kinneret, her cheeks no longer hollow with tension, her bare arms brown and healthy. Jozsef thought of her in the hospital, her face drawn, her eyes wild, and his relief at the positive change in her made him feel slightly younger. Nonetheless he couldn't stop thinking of Joshua and the dreams he was nourishing.

"He performs miracles," he said. "At least people say he does. I have yet to meet anyone who has actually *seen* him perform a miracle, but everyone knows someone who has, which amounts to the same thing."

"What about me, Jozsef? And Moshe and the prime minister? All of us, and more, have seen just what Joshua can do."

"A form of parapsychology. I am talking about miracles: the healing of the sick and the lame and the blind, the conversion of the masses through magic: we have not witnessed that."

"His extraordinary powers, in human terms, are magic—and magic makes miracles."

Jozsef gazed across the water and looked again at Tiberias, seeing the motor launches racing back and forth, towing people on water skis. Jesus had avoided the town, but his presence was all around it —in Tabgha and Migdal and Capernaum, and right here on Yam Kinneret. Here he had gathered his followers—Simon, Andrew, James, and John—and here also he had filled the empty fishing net and walked on the waters. A Christian myth, possibly, but like most myths it was rooted in fact; and those bronzed young water-skiers, to a primitive eye, would likewise be walking on water and looking miraculous.

"Magic," Jozsef said. "I sometimes think you might be right. Joshua has been all over Israel, from Jerusalem to Netanya, from Jericho to Eilat, reportedly often in separate places at the same time —and no one knows how he gets there. Also he speaks to everyone, rich and poor, Jew and gentile, and was recently found meditating in the eastern corner of Solomon's Stables, which, according to Christian tradition, is the Pinnacle of the Temple where Jesus was brought by Satan during his final temptation."

"What's so unusual about that?"

"Because, dear Kate—and I merely repeat the widespread story —when Joshua was thus engaged, those around him in Solomon's Stables felt a dreadful, searing cold, experienced feelings of horror and dread, and heard a terrible hissing and wailing which they thought was pure evil. This was, of course, exactly what you experienced on the Mount of Temptation, and could well be some form of mesmerism. However according to other reports, all conveyed to us by those present, at precisely the same time as Joshua was supposed to be in Solomon's Stables, he was also seen by numerous worshiping Arabs at Abraham's altar in the El Haram es-Sharif; was, at the same time, observed by other Arab and Christian pilgrims studying the Rock in the Mosque of Omar—from which Muhammad is said to have ascended to Heaven—and was also simultaneously observed at the

Wailing Wall by the other worshiping Jews. I repeat, Kate: all at the same time—and with numerous witnesses."

"Has anyone asked him about this?"

"I believe Lieutenant Frankel did so. Joshua merely replied that he had been sleeping at the time mentioned, but that he had during his sleep experienced those incidents as dreams of particular intensity."

"Jew, Christian, and Arab . . ."

"An unholy trinity," Jozsef said. "He cannot unite Jew, Christian, and Muslim by being the savior to all of them."

They passed the ghostly stones of the excavated remains of Capernaum, including the ruins of the synagogue built over the one in which Jesus had preached, and then began the uphill climb to the Mount of Beatitudes. Jozsef had to stop and rest, sitting gratefully on an angled stone, mopping the sweat from his face with his handkerchief and shrugging his shoulders forlornly.

"I'll never make it," he said.

"A short rest and you'll be fine. You'll soon feel as good as you look in your sport shirt and snappy pants."

Her good humor pleased him and he smiled in return, thinking back on how she had been in the hospital and amazed at the change in her. It was based on her experience with Joshua—he knew that without a doubt—but he wondered at the nature of the faith she had obviously recaptured.

"What about you?" he said. "You've been closest to Joshua. Can it be that he's returned you to the faith that you renounced years ago?"

She smiled at him and turned away, looking back down the hill, surveying the blue water, the blue-hazed mountains, the dazzling blue of the sky. The great lake, which could be treacherous, was very still and quiet, the water-skiers now far away, their white wakes forming jigsaws.

"Faith?" Kate shrugged lazily. "Yes, a kind of faith. Not Orthodox Judaism, nor the Christianity you feared, but certainly a belief in the Almighty and His ultimate benevolence; perhaps faith in faith itself —the simple acceptance of being—the belief that no matter what His nature, He brings light to the darkness. I needed that faith, Jozsef. I think all human beings do. To live without faith, believing yourself to be ephemeral, is to live with a fear of extinction beyond what we can bear. Meaninglessness is extinction, the kiss of death to the living, and I think that in turning my back on Judaism I invited that torture. That's how Joshua brought me redemption—he gave me back faith in my own future—and in doing that he forced me to accept a very private and separate peace. Not Judaism, Jozsef, and not Christianity —for those and all the other religions are divisive and binding. What he gave me was freedom—the joys and terrors of personal choice —and now, without the strictures of a religion created by men, I can still feel that my faith is untarnished and that my life has its meaning. I don't need Judaism any longer. . . . Faith itself is enough."

Jozsef felt very moved and turned his head away, fixing his gaze on the lush vegetation at both sides of the track. If moved, he was also embarrassed, remembering his accusations of blasphemy, and now, in the shimmering light of her conviction, he hardly knew what to say. His own belief was very different, a faith based in solid roots: all the law codes and commentaries of the Talmud and its sweeping guidelines. He had faith, but it was ordered, perhaps too literal to be pure, hemmed in by the Mishnah and Gemara, bound by man's moral needs. His faith was like a rock, but his beliefs had been shaped, hammered out on the anvil of a discipline imposed from outside himself. For most men it was necessary, bringing order to moral chaos, but it did, in certain ways, remove from them the burden of personal choice. Kate had now chosen that burden, taking her faith from within herself, led into it by the man known as Joshua, but now left on her own. For that he had to admire her—if also fearing for her —and he sensed, more important, that the challenge she had faced might soon shake the roots of the three great monotheistic religions and render their laws and rituals obsolete. This possibility, given the needs of the mass of men, did not offer him comfort.

"Perhaps you're right," he said, turning back to look at her, seeing the sunlight flashing around her tall figure and blotting her face out. "Perhaps faith itself, without discipline imposed from outside, if held firmly and closely to the heart, will purify and sustain. For some this has been so, but alas not for many, and the majority needs the guidance of moral laws, no matter how imperfect those laws may be. This is the function of the theologist—in mosque, church, or synagogue—and the religions of men, the Almighty's imperfect creatures, are necessary to the mass of mankind, no matter their differences. Are the religions of man divisive, pitting brother against brother? Alas, we must accept Joshua's judgment, for indeed this is true. Yet what would we do without them and the moral laws they impose upon us? Born in ignorance, and into moral chaos, we need signposts along the way. Man's religions serve that purpose, impos-

ng order on moral confusion, and no matter how imperfect they may
e, they represent a foundation. Some don't need that foundation, but
he majority does, and until man himself becomes perfect, we cannot
et it go."

"And Joshua? Where does that leave him? Will he destroy your
oundations?"

"That question remains open and is not without its terrors, for either
he will bring us together or he will tear us apart. Is Joshua good or
evil? Is he innocent or calculating? If innocent, is his innocence as
dangerous as the forces of darkness? I admit, I feel shame, for myself
and for the Rabbinate, for the Vatican and the World Council of
Churches and our long, cowardly silence. Yet what can we say? How
can any of us survive Joshua? The Christians await their Christ, the
Jews their Messiah, the Muslims their hidden Imam, the Mahdi—but
all these are abstractions. Were they ever more than symbols, the
graven imagery of our hopes, the very necessary humanization of a
spiritual quest? We all wait for Judgment Day, for revelation and
redemption, and the bridge between man and his Creator must be
instantly recognized. The Torah is not a history—nor are the Bible
and the Koran—these works represent man's attempt to give shape to
a Deity beyond our powers of conception. How do we recognize
Judgment Day if we cannot recognize Him? We cannot, so we have to
build a bridge between the human and spiritual. That bridge is
theology, the great works of religious thought, all the words that give
shape to an abstraction and render it human. Thus Christ, the
Messiah, the Mahdi of the Muslims—the recognizable bridges
between man and his Creator, the images that shadow our lives and
reflect our poor vanity. Yet Judgment Day is in the future—it was
always in the future. Thus the image of our Savior, or the Almighty's
messenger, is in truth just as unrecognizable as the darkness of
Judgment Day. Will Judgment Day ever come? And if so, how do we
recognize it? Given this, how do we recognize a Christ or Messiah or
Mahdi? Do you understand, Kate? Do you comprehend my shame?
Neither the Rabbinate nor the Vatican nor the World Council of
Churches are equipped, whether willing or not, to pass judgment on
Joshua. How do they accept or deny him? On what grounds can they
do so? Let the rain turn to flames, let the Earth turn to dust—these are
mortal men faced with a question they simply can't answer. So they
must stay silent. The foundation must not be shaken. If our religions
are to crumble, it must not be from within, but from some force

beyond our control—the Lord's or the Devil's. So we must wait, as we have waited for centuries; as Joshua, in his innocence or wisdom, also patiently waits. Like Joshua, who knows not what he is or where he came from, we are passive and await the revelation that will not require answers."

He stood up as Kate walked toward him and stopped just in front of him. She stared at him, smiling slightly, a soft blush on her cheeks, then leaned over and kissed him on the forehead with a shy, touching tenderness. He didn't move, feeling lost, love and trepidation blinding him, then she turned without a word and walked away and he followed her uphill.

It was a long, arduous walk, made no easier by the heat, and they said no more until they reached the summit with its hospice and chapel. The chapel was baroque, eight-sided, and domed, standing more than three hundred feet above the Sea of Galilee, which, shaped like a lute and surrounded by blue-hazed mountains, glittered and reflected the glory of the dazzling azure sky. Jozsef looked down in wonder, his spirit soaring like a bird, understanding why Israel, with its violent, bloody history, could still make men cling to the dream of paradise here on Earth.

"Why did Joshua come here?" he said. "Did it mean something to him? Did he know about the Sermon on the Mount and the choosing of the Apostles?"

"No," Kate said. "Some Christians brought him here. When he got here, he seemed to recognize it and decided to stay awhile."

"He's been here for two months."

"All over Galilee," Kate said. "He's been wandering all over, collecting more and more followers, talking and listening, and, as you pointed out, healing the sick, the lame, and the blind."

"He invited them to join him?"

"No, they just remained. People seem to know where he's going to be, and they quite simply follow him."

"All kinds?"

"Jews, Christians, and Muslims—all wanting his blessing."

"Does he bless them?"

"He answers them—that's all. I think they see what they need to see, and hear what they need to hear."

They did not enter the chapel, which, inside, on the eight sides of its dome, listed the beatitudes stated by Jesus. Instead, drawn forward by the murmuring of nearby voices, they passed the Italian hospice and continued across the Mount to where the land started sloping down again. There, on the grassy slopes, the Sea of Galilee far below them, were Joshua and his large group of followers, including the Franciscan nuns from the hospice. There were more than a hundred people, some sitting, others standing, all forming a close-knit circle around the white-robed Joshua who, sitting down, his arms wrapped around his knees, was tilting his head, first left and then right, obviously listening and talking to the people who kept coming up to him. The sun, blazing out of a flawless sky, bathed the scene in a brilliant light.

Jozsef felt very strange, as if time had suddenly stopped, and the murmuring of the people—not talking—did not heighten reality. He mopped sweat from his forehead, felt the aching of his muscles, and then saw that Kate was looking down the hillside, her eyes fixed on Joshua. Jozsef thought of her in the hospital, her face tense, her eyes wild, but now as he studied her, he saw something quite different: not obsession, but an almost maternal love, a calm acceptance and trust.

"Are we going down?" he asked.

"Yes," she said, "that's what we came for. I want to hear what he has to say. I want to know if he's changed."

She started walking down the slope and Jozsef hurriedly followed her, feeling the eyes of Joshua's followers upon him and becoming strangely self-conscious. There was no antagonism—simply a quiet curiosity—but he sensed a kind of muffled hysteria behind those visionary eyes. It was almost like a dream, something vivid but unreal, and he was glad when he reached the white-robed Joshua and knelt down beside Kate. The grass was warm to the touch, its physical reality a solace, then he looked at Joshua's silvery-gray eyes and was instantly disoriented. Calm eyes—inhumanly so, their depths draining the senses. Now they stared at him, recognized him and turned away, fixed themselves steadily upon Kate, growing darker and softer.

"Kate," he said simply, his voice resonant and warm, touched with a candid affection of the most human kind. Kate did not reply, but merely offered a bashful smile, her brown eyes fixed steadily upon him, her hands on her knees. "I haven't seen you for a long time," he said, "but I'm glad that you came."

"How are you?" she said.

"As I should be," he replied. "The light blossoms in the darkness and my head fills with the knowledge of men."

"Does that knowledge make you happy?"

"I am not as I was. I talk and I listen, and by giving I receive, and what fills my head is the pain and bewilderment of man. Lost, he is bewildered; without faith, he suffers pain; and his anguish and confusion are reflected in his greed and suspicion. Now I take it into myself, experiencing men and becoming man, my strength weakening, my soul flirting with temptation, my heart breaking in silence. There is something coming toward me—something dark and destructive—a wind of desolation that will cover Jerusalem and clear away to leave me to my fate. Yes, desolation: Jerusalem's suffering and shame; the manifestation of the sickness of men, a boil bursting to heal itself. And then, only then, when the healing has begun, my penance and the suffering of Jerusalem will ordain the redemption. No, I am not what I was—but I am what I will be."

Sweating profusely, Jozsef froze, the cold coming from within, a chill that went beyond the merely physical and clutched at his heart. He glanced at Kate but couldn't focus, looked at Joshua and regained his sight, saw himself twice reflected in those gray eyes, their depths luring him in.

"Jerusalem?" he heard himself whispering, his voice as dead as a tomb. "I don't know what you mean by that."

But in truth he did know, and felt the shame of his cowardice, his refusal to accept the blinding terror that Joshua's words had encouraged. He tried to tear his eyes away, but Joshua held him, his gaze implacable, his voice frightening in the calm of its acceptance, letting truth have its day.

"Jerusalem the Golden must fall to rise again; and my blood, which will signal its shame, will also herald its redemption."

Jozsef tore himself away, hardly knowing he was doing it, and found himself heading back up the hill with his heart beating madly. He heard Kate calling his name, her voice sounding far away, but he didn't have the strength to look back and see the face of the future. She caught up with him quickly, her hand clutching his left arm, and he turned his head away to hide his fear and then saw Moshe above him. Moshe was standing by his jeep, wearing full battle dress, his hand on the pistol at his hip, his face grim and forbidding. Jozsef stopped just in front of him, feeling Kate by his side, then saw Kate and Moshe looking at one another and felt the tension between them.

"I've come to say good-bye," Moshe said. "I might be gone for quite some time. We think the Arabs are going to attack, and it might be today. It all started with the *Hajj*—the Muslim's annual pilgrimage to Mecca—and has something to do with the Black Stone that's housed in the Kaaba, the stone placed there by Abraham. The Arabs suddenly started claiming that the Black Stone in the Kaaba is made from the same substance as the black stone of our Mount of Olives obelisk. Ergo, Joshua is the Mahdi—and the Arab leaders now support that—and they've sworn to recapture the Temple Mount before the week's out. They've been massing all night along the Syrian and Jordanian borders, and we think they're ready to launch their attack, probably starting from Syria. I have to leave now."

He looked at Kate, and she at him, the tension palpable between them, and Jozsef sensed that there was something left unspoken, some question unanswered. He felt dizzy, disoriented, caught between them and Joshua, and his thoughts, dominated by his beating heart, seemed to fly to the wind. Then he heard the distant rumbling, a very faint, familiar sound, and turned around, following Moshe's startled gaze, to see the smoke on the Golan Heights. The smoke rose in separate columns, ballooning up and drifting sideways, very black against the blue of the sky before dissolving to dirty gray. Kate gasped, Moshe cursed, and Jozsef looked down the hill, and saw Joshua staring at him, his silvery-gray eyes very clear, affirming that the destruction he had prophesied was the war that was starting.

The planes suddenly screamed overhead.

30

Dearest Kate:

Already the war is over, perhaps the shortest war in history, a mere twenty-four hours from start to finish and the dust not yet settled. Is it possible that it really happened, that it could begin and end so quickly, or was it simply some mass hallucination engendered by Joshua? It might have been better had this been so—if all of us had just gone mad—but now, in the cold light of sanity, we must count up the cost: the Americans in the United Arab Republic, the Soviets in Jordan and Syria, and both "benefactors" carving up the Middle East in the name of world peace. Zion, that forlorn dream of Orthodox Jews, is now wrapped up in chains.

Have you personally survived it all? Perhaps I've no right to ask. I am staying for the time being in Damascus—possibly just to be alone and study the mirror without pride, certainly also because I would not be comfortable in Jerusalem after what has occurred. Time seems to be endless and requires a lot of filling; and my mind, once so lively with malice, has become a blancmange. I walk below the minarets, through the green trees to the desert, and too often, with a hip flask in my pocket, spend hours in the unprofitable contemplation of that implacable Nothing. Other hours are wiled away in exploring the covered "Street called Straight," looking mindlessly at silks and leather, and gold and silver filigree work, in the bazaars that cross the city from west to east. I walk and I walk, a man obviously in a trance, through the gardens and orchards along the Barada River, trying to convince myself that nothing has changed. Alas, the camel trains have been replaced with a noisy stream of trucks, the only authentic history is in the Qasr al-'Azm Museum; and in the Marjah Square, between the fashionable shops, the

government offices are filled with men who talk of Israel as if it
is lost. Only 4 percent of the population are Jews, which may
account for this view.

Is Israel lost? My head is too muddled to think about it. I walk
about Damascus with a hip flask in my pocket, and the days
dissolve slowly but surely into the dream of the evenings. The
traditional house with patio and fountain is no longer being built
(though still available in the Old City), French and Italian styles
are now very much in evidence, and my own dubiously Mediter-
ranean villa is in the al-Akrad quarter on the slopes of Jabal
Qāsiyūn—considerably less grand than the ambassadors' houses
in Abū Rummānah, but suitable to my sinking station in life and
my late drinking habits. I am rambling already, because I'm
drinking as I write, and the night, which is hotter than hell,
seems to suffocate clear thought.

I don't know quite what to tell you, but I have to tell you
something—if not for your sake, certainly for mine, since I now
sink into the well of self-pity and need my memories for comfort.
When I fled from Jerusalem (running from Moshe Eitan's
contempt?), I went traveling around Lebanon, Syria, and Jordan
with Rashid Idriss and his bunch of merry men. We sometimes
stayed in good hotels, but mostly slept in trucks and tents,
nestling down in that wilderness that only the Arabs know and
arising in the brilliant light of dawn to a crystalline silence. I
now remember the murderous heat, the merciless glare of the
sun, the silence that haunted my thoughts and made them dwell
on the Void. The desert takes what it wants and gives nothing
back in return, and in learning this I came to understand what
makes the Arabs so hard. I was not hard, and they knew it and
accepted it, either amused or contemptuous of my weakness in
their pitiless world. That world is unique, a shimmering dream
on the shifting sands, and it makes a man travel through himself
to where the truth spills its blood.

The Arabs only know black and white, truth and untruth, and
have no time for the doubt and introspection that haunts Western
man. My moral confusion amused Rashid, made him mock my
indecision, and he frequently interpreted my political grayness
as self-indulgence and cowardice. "We believe," he said,
"simply because we believe; we do not need to justify." Whether
right or wrong, the remark made me feel weaker, separated from

the inner core of my being and refusing to face myself. Anger, outrage, the lust for vengeance and domination: these are weaknesses that we in the West try to hide, while the Arabs, either wisely or ruthlessly, accept them and use them. We view this as cruelty, but the Arabs view it as truth; and after a few weeks with them, as if changing my skin, I came to view myself as a hypocrite of the most awesome kind, and my lack of commitment, both personal and political, as abdication based on cowardice and self-deceit. We do not cleanse ourselves by wiping the blood from our hands; we have to accept that there are causes and effects and make some sort of stand on that basis. I now know, and can never forget, that I refused to admit this.

Can I live with this truth? Not too well, I fear. I drink constantly—as I am drinking right now—to kill the shame that eats at me. In my moral cowardice I lost myself, and in losing myself I then lost you, and during those nights in the desert, lying awake with that awesome silence, I learned to face these facts with no little amount of pain and came to understand that they were more important to me than the possibility of Judgment Day.

Judgment Day—Joshua—the terrible challenge of revelation —all the nightmares and glories suggested by his presence on Earth. I lost you because of Joshua, because he showed us both the truth, and now Israel itself might be lost to the Americans and Russians. Intervention is a foul word, a mere excuse for expansionist greed, and now Israel, through the stupidity of threatening the Arabs with atomic weapons, is surrounded by the two superpowers who think of nothing but oil. Israel is trapped, and now the nightmare has trapped me, and here in Damascus, the crossroads of the Middle East, I slide down the tunnel of drink into the dark tomb of witchcraft.

Witchcraft—Joshua—the unexplainable in human form, the revelation that the more we discover, the less we will know. God or the Devil? Reality or unreality? Does Joshua represent the ultimate truth or the final illusion? He started this war—the war that could have been the last one—and he did it without saying a word, without raising his finger. A fantasy? No: the Arabs were also obsessed with him. Rashid Idriss refused to discuss the matter in public, but in private, throughout the Muslim world, in Bedouin tents and sheik's palaces, the Man from the Mount was an issue that grew larger each day. Did Joshua encourage it? No, he said nothing. But like the ghost horse that races through the night, his silence was everything. He neither affirmed nor denied, leaving a blank slate to be filled, and eventually, as all silence must be filled, the wind of hearsay was everything.

Joshua the Mahdi, the twelfth and last Imam, now returned to spread the word of Muhammad, but being held by the Jews. Rashid tried to control it by threatening punishment for those who discussed it, but the whispering was carried on the wind and obviously traveled to Mecca. From wishful thinking to reality —man imposes what he wills—before long there were rumors about the Black Stone in the Kaaba—rumors that would fan the flames of Islam and make Joshua the Mahdi.

It was the time of the Hajj, the annual pilgrimage to Mecca, when Muslims from all over the world flock to Saudi Arabia to share the supreme moment of their lives: to make seven circuits of the Kaaba in the Sacred Mosque and see the Black Stone once kissed by Muhammad. It is the greatest spectacle in the world —over a million and a half people in the one place—but it is no time for the spreading of rumors about the return of the Mahdi.

At first Rashid was amused, not believing the stories, but gradually even he, with his Western education, succumbed to the magic of Islam and its timeless seductions. Each day a thousand million people throughout the world turn five times in prayer toward the city of Mecca, their thoughts focused on the Kaaba, the first House of God built by Abraham and his son Ishmael. Standing in the immense courtyard of the Sacred Mosque around which Mecca was built, and covered in the kiswa—the enormous black cloth embroidered in gold with verses from the Koran—the Kaaba is also the site of the sacred Black Stone, first placed there by Abraham and later kissed by Muhammad after he drove the idolaters from the temple. The Black Stone has never been seen by any non-Muslim, but reportedly it is composed of some totally unknown substance and imbued with mysterious powers. Consequently your Joshua, possessed of his own mysterious powers, became part and parcel of a startling new story regarding the Black Stone of Mecca.

For the whole world, including the Muslims, one of the most intriguing aspects of the story of Joshua was the large black obelisk, or tomb, in which he was found. From what substance *had it been made that it could have been so completely black and then disintegrate into normal dust shortly after its appearance? Now, according to the Muslims, there were two new revelations: Joshua's tomb had been made from the same substance as the Black Stone—and the Black Stone had recently started to give off strange glowings and show holographic images from the life of Muhammad and his followers. Ergo, Joshua was the returned Mahdi, and the Black Stone was calling him to Mecca.*

Rashid's amusement turned to intrigue, and then to concern when the whisperings about Joshua and the Black Stone gradually turned into shouts. The Black Stone was calling Joshua, demanding his return to Mecca, and the Muslims, growing increasingly obsessed, wanted to do something about it. Rashid was losing control—his men wanted to capture Joshua—and eventually he decided to go to Mecca and check it out for himself. As I said, non-Muslims aren't normally allowed into the city, but Rashid, with his considerable authority, got me permission to go with him. That journey, which now seems like a dream, was a journey into the Self.

We flew from Beirut and landed at Jeddah to join the thousands of other pilgrims as they were channelled through the airport and onto the government buses that would take them to Mecca. There, in the Madinat al-hujjaj, while passing through customs, we were surrounded by the mass of pilgrims, all wearing their white ihrams, all constantly repeating, "Labbaika-Allahumma, Labbaik!—Here I am, O God, at Thy command, here I am!" The numbers were enormous and totally overwhelming: fifty thousand pilgrims a day were passing through Jeddah Airport alone, thousands more were coming by sea and overland, and even more thousands were landing at the airports of Medina and Dhahran and Riyadh and Jizan and Najran—well over a million, all to perform the Hajj, all in the state of ihram—body and soul dedicated to God—all repeating the suras from the Koran, and all, in this terrifying year, whispering feverishly about Joshua, now their very own Mahdi.

I think Rashid changed then, possibly swept up in the fervor, his Western education turning to dust in that immense, white-clad mass. He had always been a moderate, both in politics and religion, but there, in the Madinat al-hujjaj, in that extraordinary religious atmosphere, his eyes took on the gleam of a man

who has just found himself. Now he knew what he was—a true
Arab and Muslim—and in truth, as I stood there, as that mass
fervor gripped me, I felt that I was being stripped of my
Westernized modes of thought and returned to some primal state
of grace and inchoate, elemental truth. Belief or unbelief—no
gray areas in between—at last, as I studied the pilgrims
swarming all around me, I understood a little of what that meant
in its deceptive simplicity.

From Jeddah, crossing the Hejaz, we drove the forty-five
miles to Mecca, arriving in the early-morning light, just before
the Dawn Prayer. The road was filled with cars and buses,
thousands of pilgrims walked alongside it, and the dust, like the
clouds of the Apocalypse, fell over us constantly. Then Mecca
and the Sacred Mosque, more thousands gathered outside, all
preparing to pray, being guided by the muezzins whose voices
were amplified through the hundreds of unseen loudspeakers
that cover the city. It was an awesome, haunting sight, the sound
of the muezzins making it more so, their voices ringing out
above the pale blue light of dawn as the thousands of worshipers, all wearing white ihrams, knelt down on their prayer mats
on the ground around the Mosque, bowing and prostrating
themselves in unbroken chains.

In any gathering of one and a half million people there are
bound to be many deaths by natural causes. Thus, at the end of
the salaam—the salutation denoting the end of prayers—an
imam led the kneeling multitudes in the funeral prayer, the salat
al-janaza, after which it was time to enter the Sacred Mosque
through the Door of Salvation.

The experience was extraordinary, a feast for all the senses, at
once a spectacle and an intimate drama, a strange and beautiful
catharsis. The inner courtyard of the Mosque was huge,
containing half a million worshipers, its arched portals and
balconies serenely attractive above us, its eight minarets soaring
to the sky in the dawn's light blue haze. The Kaaba was in the
middle, a great cube draped in black cloth, the words from the
Koran embroidered in gold and dazzling the eyes. Bizarre,
unreal, it appeared to melt into the dawn, to be suspended rather
than sitting on the ground, its beauty springing from its very
simplicity and relative lack of adornment. Already the worshipers were moving around it, shoulder to shoulder, their heads

raised, crying, "God is great! God is great! There is no other God but God!", their hands reaching up to touch the sacred stone as they made the seven circuits that formed the circumambulation. It looked like a human whirlpool—a white whirlpool in blue light—and that half million voices, murmuring prayers or crying to God, formed into a single bass rumbling that seemed to come from the earth.

Being a non-Muslim, I was not allowed near the Black Stone, but Rashid, in the course of his circumambulation, was able to see it. He was away a long time, making his seven circuits of the Kaaba, and when he returned, the sun was high in the sky, the heat vicious and clammy. He appeared to be transformed, his brown eyes shining brightly, his expression one of helpless exultation and passionate yearning. I asked him what he had seen, but initially he refused to comment, merely filling his flask with water from the holy Zamzam well, and then leading me on the s'ay—the required walk between the hills of al-Safā and al-Marwa along the air-conditioned, marble-paved masa—during which, as we passed holy men and cripples and praying women, he spoke once before returning to the silence of his obviously exalted thoughts.

"In the Black Stone I saw only the sun's reflection," he said, "but that light, which kept changing like a prism, filled my soul with contentment. That contentment was the product of redemption and belief in our future. I thought instantly of the El Haram es-Sharif in Jerusalem, and understood that we would have to get it back to ordain the Day of Salvation. The Black Stone, if it showed me nothing else, showed me what I must do."

That's when the war started—though I wasn't to know it then —when Rashid saw whatever he saw in the Black Stone and vowed to recapture Jerusalem and the lost Temple Mount. No, I didn't know it then, though I saw the change in Rashid, who looked every minute, and in a way I can't explain, more and more an authentic, vengeful Arab born and bred in the desert; a religious leader rather than a politician-warrior, a man shedding his old skin.

This change was also manifest in the thousands of worshipers around us, most of whom, in normal circumstances, would have been quiet in reflection, but were now, after their circumambulation, unusually excited. Perhaps excitement is the wrong term: it was more than that—it was a fever. Who knows what they saw in the Black Stone—or what they imagined they saw? It only matters that they took from it what they wanted at that time, and that the images it had reflected, if existing only in their minds, were enough to fill their heads with thoughts of Joshua and his return as the Mahdi. Thus they were in a state of fervor, a million worshipers breaking loose, and as we traveled on to Arafat, through the darkness of that same evening, I was caught up in this fervor myself, and felt my old Self dissolving.

The second stage of the Hajj is the Standing at Arafat where, on the Mount of Mercy, where Muhammad preached his last sermon, the pilgrim must worship before the sun rises on the new day. Again the scene was extraordinary, almost defying the senses: a veritable city of tents, with perfectly straight streets and avenues, containing over a million people and spread across the immense plain hemmed in by the mountain range of the Taif. Both sexes were represented, all social classes and races mixed, and they covered the whole plain and the Mount of Mercy itself, packed so closely together that their ihrams and the tents formed a shifting white sea that filled the starlit darkness with murmuring. The murmuring ceased just prior to dawn as the million faces turned toward Mecca, their heads bowed in prayer and silent worship and self-abnegation. Then the sun came up, the heat resembling a furnace, and then noon came and went and the sun eventually set again, and the maghrib, the final prayer, was spoken by everyone. After that, with considerable haste, in emulation of the Prophet, the ifidah, the race to Muzdalifa, commenced.

For the pilgrim, Arafat is not the final station of his spiritual journey but the station marking the birth of the New Man—one who has been "cleansed" and is now actively committed to God. Here, by the Sacred Monument, the Mash‘ar al-Harām, he is required to remember God as He who guided the people along the "straight path," which symbolically starts from Arafat. Rashid was by this time almost certainly a New Man—suddenly stripped of his Western influences, more completely a native Arab—and as he prayed by the Sacred Monument and collected stones for the ritual at Mina, I felt that he was taking unto himself the burning rage of his people. Yes, there was anger, slowly rising from religious fervor, spreading out through that *extraordinary mass of pilgrims with their thoughts of the Mahdi. Rashid sensed it and grabbed it, taking it into himself, and as we headed for Mina, again driving through the darkness, I heard him muttering to his lieutenants about Joshua, his hands waving excitedly.*

It was a slow drive to Mina, over a rugged mountain pass, following the road the Prophet took for his Farewell Pilgrimage, passing the lights of the tents and shacks on either side, and eventually leading us to the luminous al-Khayf Mosque and the largest campsite ever witnessed by human eyes.

By now there were over two million pilgrims, their tents swamping the village of Mina, spreading across the central plain and right up the encircling hills with the pilgrims like white ants between them. Here, over a period of three days and three nights, the stones gathered at Muzdalifa would be thrown at the sacred pillars and be followed by the great Feast of Sacrifice —and here, during these rituals, the former calm of meditation would erupt into the frenzy of hatred that would lead to the war.

The Sacred Pillars are said to mark the three places where Satan appeared to Abraham and his family and attempted to dissuade them from obeying the divine command—and the ritual stoning of the pillars, or the "throwing of the pebbles," is referred to as the "stoning of Satan." There has always been an element of violence in this ritual, and the subsequent Feast of Sacrifice, for which countless animals were to be slaughtered, adds to the stoning a further element of blood and death which, in this instance—given their obsession with their captured Mahdi, Joshua—possibly led to their forthcoming cries for war.

I don't know how it happened, by what magic or osmosis, but sometime during the last of the three nights that great mass became one. One mind, one body, one eruption of blind emotion, one voice that suddenly turned into a roar that rose to the dark sky. I had seen the anger building—in the throwing of stones and the slaughtering of animals—and as accidents occurred and human blood was shed, the anger joined them together. I was on a hill with Rashid, overlooking the enormous campsite, gazing down on that swarming mass of white-clad pilgrims and their city of tents. I was no longer myself, but someone else, a naked stranger, divorced from the protective cynicisms of my past and forced to face my own failures. Rashid likewise had changed and was now a stranger to me, his cultivated Western manners obliterated and replaced with blind fervor. He was giving a speech to the Arabs around him, saying that Joshua was in Jerusalem, that he had been seen by Abraham's altar in the El Haram es-Sharif, and that his presence there was a sign that the Muslims must recapture the Temple Mount. Rashid was fiery and eloquent, his voice raging over the gathered pilgrims, and then a blazing torch appeared, and then another, and another, until eventually the dark hill had become a sea of yellow fire and the separate voices had become one voice, first chanting, then roaring, rising up from that sea of fire and from the city of tents below it, filling the darkness of the desert with the cry that set the torch to the Middle East: Jerusalem! Jerusalem!

What am I writing, Kate? Am I telling stories or asking questions? I think I'm writing this letter to myself—to make what happened seem real. It was not real at the time—or at least it never seemed real—and with each passing day, every drink, it grows more like a dream. It sprang out of whispered rumors, began and ended so quickly, and now, in the threatening silence of its aftermath, it seems never to have happened.

Were you there when they bombed Jerusalem? Did it wound you beyond repair? Or did you, intelligent lady, simply despise me for what I had done? These questions are not asked lightly, though my pen pretends to mock; for in truth, behind that pretense, is a shame that I can't seem to shake off.

I betrayed you, Kate, and in doing so betrayed myself, and now, as I write, as the bottle gradually empties, I am forced to confess that I can no longer deny my criminal guilt. I betrayed your trust and then I went with the Arabs, first to Mecca and then to the Golan Heights, for twenty-four hours of penance. A brief and bloody war, perfectly normal otherwise—the jets screaming overhead, the shells exploding in fiery patterns, men howling and dying in their own blood, the sand swirling around them —and of course I was there, thinking only of myself, sometimes hugging the earth, sometimes running for my life, now frightened, now excited, mostly just very weary, perhaps longing for the bullet that would cleanly put an end to my shame. Then suddenly it was over, the sparring partners separated, the

Soviets and Americans, the world's friends and benefactors, surrounding Israel with their guns, driving their tanks through Jerusalem, and waving the flag of truce while preparing to trade off prerogatives, getting ready to carve up the Middle East in the name of World Peace.

Jerusalem is in chains, and I, also, am in chains, imprisoned in the cell of my Christian guilt and hypocritical soul-searching. I am staying in Damascus to hide away from my sins, and to unravel the various lessons I learned on the journey to Mecca.

The Arabs are cruel, but in their cruelty is justice: the refusal to pretend that Man is more than he is; the acceptance of our logic as no more than the mask that hides the face of our still primitive emotions. We aspire to cultivation, to reasonable thought and self-control, but the Arabs, in that wisdom that was gleaned from the desert's savagery, understand that the mores of civilized men are a transparent veil. No logic explains love, nor the murderous impulses of hatred, nor that impulse, supreme above all others, for the need to have faith.

We civilized souls are lost, our sense of truth destroyed by logic, and as one of the lost, now trapped by guilt and shame, having lost myself before losing you, I assume that I am waiting, with fear and fascination, for my own, highly personal Judgment Day.

I loved you, Kate.

             Leon

31

The American tanks are moving out of Jerusalem," Kate said, standing just inside the doorway and glancing around the lounge with a mixture of curiosity and shyness. She had just arrived, unannounced and unexpected, and Moshe, both embarrassed and pleased, simply stood there and stared at her. "Well?" Kate said, still standing inside the doorway, "did you hear what I said?"

"Yes, Kate, I heard you. I'm just a little surprised to see you. I mean, I didn't expect to find you on my doorstep. Come in. Take a seat."

She smiled and walked past him, her shoulder sliding across his chest, and he closed the front door and followed her in, feeling childishly hesitant. She was standing in the middle of the lounge, wearing a loose shirt and denims, looking slim, casually elegant, and attractive, her face suntanned and healthy. She stared quickly around the room, then through the window to the patio, then turned back to face him, smiling nervously, her right hand on her shoulder bag.

"So," she said, "I'm in your house at last."

"You're very welcome," he said.

She nodded, still smiling, then removed the bag from her shoulder, draped it over the back of an armchair and looked at him again.

"You knew about the tanks?" she asked.

"Yes," he replied, "I knew. The Americans only came in to stop the fighting in Jerusalem, and now that the dust has settled down, they have no cause to stay."

"I thought once in, never out."

"I think they were hoping for that," he said, "but neither we nor the Soviets are keen to stand by and see that happen. So they're leaving Jerusalem, but the situation still stinks: the Americans are keeping their troops in the area, forming a protective flank along the United Arab Republic, and the Soviets have done likewise in Syria and

Jordan; now, with a legitimate excuse, they're starting to trade off prerogatives, the Soviets acquiescing in the American occupation of the Arab peninsula and the United States agreeing to the introduction of Soviet forces into Syria and Iraq. This, they both claim, will put them in a position to proceed along the road to a so-called 'Final Settlement' of the Arab-Israeli and Israeli-Palestinian question. It stinks, Kate—and we're bound to it."

"The prime minister should never have threatened to use our atomic weapons against the Arabs."

"Correct," Moshe replied. "That *was* a bad mistake. It was that, more than anything else, that gave them the excuse to intervene. And, of course, those bastards in the United Nations backed them up, while the governments of Japan and Europe, practically down on their hands and knees, diplomatically displayed their pleasure in the 'rescuing' of their precious Middle East oil from the vile, greedy Arabs."

Kate smiled at his anger. "Not everyone agrees," she said. "China has accused the Soviets and Americans of having engineered the whole thing for their own 'imperialist purposes,' and the governments of the predominantly Hindu countries have taken a similar stand. So, dear Moshe, you have some friends left."

"Israel has no friends," Moshe said. "It's too valuable for that. Now sit down, Kate, while I pour you a drink."

"Gin and tonic?"

"It's coming."

He went into the kitchen and poured her a gin and tonic, added ice, and then opened a bottle of beer and returned to the lounge. She was sitting in the armchair, one long leg across the other, the denims stretched tight on her thighs, the curve of her small breasts clearly visible where her shirt was unbuttoned. Desire seized him immediately, almost mindless in its intensity, and he felt the blush rising to his cheeks as he handed her the drink. Her dark eyes focused on him, looking up, very large, making him feel that he was falling toward her, into the black of her pupils. He controlled himself and straightened up, then sat down in the chair facing her, watched her put the glass of gin to her lips and take a small sip. When she put her glass down, he drank some beer and tried to keep his hand steady.

"And how long do you think the present peace will last?" Kate said.

"That's the million-dollar question," he replied. "The Soviet and American intervention was only part of the reason for the Arabs' cessation of hostility; the other reason was that various Arab representatives, such as Rashid Idriss, were guaranteed access to Israel in order to speak personally to Joshua. How long this lasts is the moot question: the Arabs still want West Jerusalem back, and we won't let them have it."

"So you think that sooner or later they'll try to take it back again."

"Yes. They obviously still view Joshua as the hidden Imam, or returned Mahdi, which means they think that the sovereignty of Islam is at hand. Sooner or later they'll want the El Haram es-Sharif, which means West Jerusalem."

Kate was staring at him thoughtfully, as if studying him rather than listening to him, and he suddenly felt that this conversation, no matter its relevance, was a subterfuge for that more personal matter that had yet to be resolved. The possibility made him uneasy, even slightly embarrassed, still foiled by his inability to accept her and forget what was haunting him. He stared at her long legs, at the curve of her small breasts, wanting to touch her and lose himself in her, but held back by the shame of his private life and the fears it had given him. Now, a mature man, but feeling more like an adolescent, he felt himself retreating behind his eyes, sinking into self-consciousness.

"It's uncanny," Kate said, "but Joshua prophesied that war—just before the bombs fell on the Golan Heights."

"Yes," Moshe replied, "and that disturbs me even more. According to Rabbi Latinavots, what Joshua actually said was that Jerusalem would have to fall to rise again, and that his blood, which would signal its shame, would also herald its redemption. Well, Jerusalem has not fallen and Joshua has shed no blood, so those parts of his prophecy haven't materialized yet. On the other hand, it's worth noting that when we escorted Joshua around the religious sites, he wept for Jerusalem, saying its enemies would surround it, and later said that the whole of Israel would be laid barren. If we are to assume, as it seems, that Joshua can foresee the future, we must then assume that the recent war, which has left Jerusalem and Israel intact, was *not* the war that Joshua has three times prophesied. That war, Kate, is the war that will come if this situation explodes again."

"It may never happen, Moshe."

"I think it will, Kate. If it doesn't start from outside—through the Muslims' lust for West Jerusalem—it could start because of the actions of our own zealots."

"You mean their attempts to set up an ecclesiastical Cabinet."

"Correct. Kash, Gush Emunim and the Neturei Karta zealots are claiming that Joshua's presence in Israel is a sign that the sovereignty of Orthodox Judaism is at hand—and that the way to ordain it is to replace Ben Eliezer's Cabinet with a purely ecclesiastical Cabinet consisting of the most Orthodox members of the community; and, much worse, with the defense forces and all other religious and political parties subordinated to a newly elected Israeli Rabbinate. So far both the government and the present Rabbinate have refused to lend their official support to any claim that Joshua is the Jewish Messiah; but if the zealots get into power, they will immediately make that very claim and use it as the reason for removing all non-Jews from Israel and inaugurating the pure Zionist State—a situation that will obviously lead to another war."

Feeling restless, he stood up, holding his glass of beer in one hand, aware that he was telling her what she already knew and knowing why he had said it. He was frightened of silence, of her thoughtful, dark gaze, aware that she had come here uninvited and understanding just why. She knew that he wanted her, as she wanted him, and her instincts, at once ruthless and honest, had made her come to him. He was hesitant, perhaps frightened, haunted by Leon's accusation, and now, remembering that night when he had taken down all his family pictures, he also remembered what had happened with the whore and quietly recoiled inside himself.

"You seem nervous, Moshe."

"Yes," he said, "I am. I keep thinking about what's happening in Israel, and it keeps me on edge."

He looked directly at her, not finding it easy, every nerve in his body reaching out to be touched by her presence. She was staring up at him, her face framed in the dark hair, the sunlight pouring over her brown eyes and making them luminous. He saw himself in those eyes, his miniaturized form twice reflected, mere ghosts in the space she was inhabiting, his real self still to follow.

"You look well," he said.

"That hardly constitutes a compliment."

"I'm very slow with compliments," he said, "but you look very nice."

"Just tell me I'm beautiful."

"That might be a lie. Beauty is in the eye of the beholder—and I can't trust myself."

"That's a beautiful compliment."

"A mere accident of speech."

"Some accidents make you feel more alive—and that's how I feel now."

He had to look away, a little shocked by her candor, beginning to feel that his inhibition was puritanical, if not based on cowardice. He stared through the glass doors, across the patio at Jerusalem, its ancient walls and modern buildings very clear on the hills in the distance. Jerusalem the Golden, the center of the world, the symbol of all that he had gained and lost in the past. Thinking this, he glanced around him, studying the walls of the room, seeing the lighter patches of white where the photographs had been before he had taken them all down and hid them away. He wanted to put the past behind him, to plant new roots in Kate, but that memory of the dead eyes staring sunward lay like ice on his beating heart.

"We know where Leon is," he said, turning back to face Kate, aware that he was staring intently at her to gauge her reaction. "He's been traveling with Rashid Idriss and is now in Damascus—apparently not too well at all, and drinking too much."

"Yes," she replied. "I know. He sent me a letter. It was a very strange letter, and he didn't sound happy."

She gazed down at the floor, obviously upset by the memory, her dark hair tumbling over her shoulders and across her white shirt. Moshe stared at her, entranced, wanting to reach out and touch her, but held back, in yearning and fear, by the words still unspoken. She raised her eyes again, smiling wearily, one hand rising and falling.

"You have to forget him, Moshe. Don't let him stand between us. We were lovers, but I never pretended to love him, and now it's all over."

The pain came and then departed, very sharp but mercifully brief, and he knew that she was speaking the truth and offering herself to him. He was shaken and very moved, filled with sad and shameful triumph, and he then knew that his love for her was, in its very strength, as selfish and possessive as the sun that drained the desert of life. His gain was Leon's loss, his joy Leon's sorrow, but he knew that with all the sympathy in the world, he would not change positions.

"Go out onto the patio," he said, "and watch the sun going down. I'll get you another drink."

She stood up and gave him her glass, smiling slightly, ambiguously, then nodded, pushed the glass doors apart, and walked onto the patio. He watched her leaning against the wall, facing Jerusalem, her back turned to him, and he wanted to press himself against her spine and her long, slender legs. The desire was voluptuous, a mixture of love and primitive lust, and he turned away, startled, suddenly flustered, and went into the kitchen. He poured the drinks automatically, hardly seeing what he was doing, his need and suppressed emotion building up and threatening to shatter him totally. Then he picked the glasses up, closed his eyes, took a deep breath, opened his eyes again and let his breath out, and left the small kitchen. He crossed the lounge slowly, seeing her spine, her long legs, then she turned around and smiled and reached out to take the glass from his hand.

"That's a lot of gin," she said.

"I'm sorry. I wasn't thinking."

"Are you trying to get me drunk?"

"No, I'm not."

"No," she said. "Not your style."

She had her back to the wall and now turned around to lean on it, the both of them facing Jerusalem and the hills all around it. Moshe thought of that first night, of how the storm had erased Jerusalem, and of how, not much later, that same storm had introduced him to Kate. Large eyes, very brown, brown hair whipping across her face, long hair thick with dust, her tanned face smeared with dust. . . . He had died when his wife was murdered, his pain numbing his senses, the later years filled with grief disguised as work, until Kate resurrected him. Now he wanted life, the pain and joy of love's commitment, but his shame, which had wrapped his flesh in thorns, still had to be exorcised.

"Do you know about my wife?" he asked.

"Yes," she replied, "I do. I read about it all in the papers, so you don't have to tell me."

"It was during the Yom Kippur War," he said, his own voice sounding distant, emerging from some dark cave in his soul and filling the air with his pain. "We were living in a kibbutz and my wife and children were working the fields, and the Arabs came out of the hills in jeeps and cut them down with machine guns. I wasn't there at the time, but I did hear the shooting, and by the time I got out of the kibbutz and reached them, the Arabs were gone. I loved my wife, Kate, and still love her in my memory, thinking only of the children she gave me and the love she showered on them. I loved them and treated them well, but my real commitment was to the army; for all my attempts at care and consideration I loved the army even more. It was ambition, certainly—but also it was dedication—I truly believed that a man without a purpose was hardly a man. My wife took a different view: She thought love was life's prime commitment—the love of a man and woman for one another, their mutual love for their children. It was our only source of disagreement, sometimes bitterly so, but always, irrespective of what she thought, the army came first and foremost. Then when they were murdered, when I found them in that dusty field, when I looked down and saw their dead eyes staring sunward, I felt a pain so deep and terribly true that the lie became manifest: no commitment to an abstraction, to an ideal or cause, should stand above the more enduring commitment between individuals."

He had another drink, not daring to look at Kate, his eyes fixed on the vast, sinking sun and the hills' shifting shadows.

"Yes," he said, "I loved them—certainly a lot more than I knew —with an intensity that I only fully understood when I saw their dead eyes. How I hated the Arabs then, thinking of all of them as bloody murderers, and hated myself even more for not protecting my family. Oh, I knew it wasn't my fault, that it could have happened anytime, but what I couldn't forget was the fact that I had put them in second place. True, I had shown them love, but it was a distant, abstract love, not as selfless as my love for the army and, in turn, Israel. And so I came to hate myself and shoulder the blame for what had happened, and then ironically, with that self-deception unique to us human beings, I then gave myself even more fully to my country and disguised my guilt and shame in patriotism: the commitment to an abstraction, to an ideal or cause, that drove me even deeper into myself, away from love's dangerous pleasures."

He had another drink of beer, wiped his lips and glanced at her, saw her profile outlined against the gray sky, her gaze fixed on Jerusalem. The top of her shirt was open, revealing her curving skin, and he wanted to touch that skin with his lips, to press his cheek to her breasts. It was physical desire and emotional need, the aching yearning to lose himself, to surrender his old self and be renewed in the well of her body. Seized by it, he shivered and turned away to fix his gaze on the distant hills.

"So," he said, "the memory haunted me—the dead eyes staring sunward—and I traveled deeper into myself and made a fortress from

hard work. The army became my life, my bed and my church, and as
the years passed, I found myself freezing in the ice of retreat. The
pain of their death had numbed me, leaving only the need to hide, a
fear of ever experiencing such pain again through the loss of a loved
one. Physical pain did not bother me, nor the possible pain of public
failure, but behind the soldier's veneer of ruthless courage was this
great fear of love. So, I retreated, refusing to involve myself
emotionally, separating my physical needs from my emotions and
making love a transaction. . . . Yes, I turned to prostitutes, paying
for purely physical release, easing the hungers of the flesh and
ignoring emotional needs. As Leon said, Kate, I had a secret life, but
that wasn't the whole of it."

He kept his eyes fixed on Jerusalem, now golden in the setting sun,
surrounded by the rolling hills and plains, the spreading shadows of
evening. It was the landscape of a dream, one that circumscribed his
being, containing joy and sorrow in equal measure, tearing the heart
and renewing it. Kate was leaning forward beside him, her bare
elbows on the wall, the light wind blowing her hair across her face
and her dark, glittering eyes. Her right shoulder was touching his, her
hair sometimes grazing his cheek, and he felt her body's warmth
seeping into him and stroking his senses.

"I never entered those women, Kate. That was something I couldn't
do. It was as if, in some lost and guarded corner of my mind, the
impulse that gave the flesh life had found a will of its own. I felt that
entering them would be a betrayal, the repudiation of my former love,
and so I only let them use their hands and lips, their expert playing on
nerve ends. A hypocritical sense of purity, a defiled moral superiority:
the point was to allay all thoughts of self-abuse and keep emotion in
check. Ridiculous? Certainly. Shameful? Even more so. I was piling
guilt on guilt, shame on shame, and calling that mess self-protection.
Oh, yes, I tried other women—they came and went in despair—but
their bodies, like my wife's prostrate body, lay like death there
beneath me. I gave up in the end, tried no more, perhaps ashamed,
and then, Kate, that night, the night of Joshua and the storm, when it
seemed like Jerusalem was falling and Judgment Day was at hand, I
found you in the ruins, your brown hair, your brown eyes, and
understood in that moment, like the flash of revelation, that my life,
which had been nailed down with guilt, could be lived once again. I
wanted you then, Kate, as I want you now and will always; but I also

want you to know and accept the truth of what I have been. . . . I don't deserve you—but I want you."

He heard her set her glass down and then felt her turning toward him, one hand reaching up, fingers outspread, to slide over his face. He pressed his lips to her palm, grabbed her wrist, kissed her fingers, then released his other fingers from the glass and let them find her dark hair. She turned her face toward that hand, licked his palm, between his fingers, and then he spread his fingers through her hair again, pulled her head back, leaned over her. She was staring up at him, her eyes large, very dark, strands of hair coiling across her unpainted lips as they opened toward him. He felt his hands around her face, her hard cheekbones, her warm skin, then closed his eyes and felt his tongue drowning in the well of her mouth. He was holding her, crushing her, his whole body pressing against her, one hand heavy on her spine, the other dividing her shoulder blades, all his senses concentrating on her belly and breasts, as if, in that extraordinary warmth and softness, he might find revelation.

Nothing mattered but her being, the flesh and bone beneath his hands, the heat that poured out from her melting loins and set his thoughts to the torch. His will had dissolved, his inhibitions had been scattered, and he felt the burning magnet of her body drawing the bonds from his flesh. Her tongue licked his eyes and nose, drew a line around his lips, then slid down between his teeth into his mouth, her breath mingling with his. He felt as if he were inside her, a beating impulse within her head, and her being, like the pale moon and stars, seemed to swim all around him. Nothing mattered but the instant, the past and future being one, his heart beating with anguished need and exultation to the rhythm of pounding blood. He was gasping, jerking his head back, sliding his hands around her rib cage, opening his eyes to see his fingers outspread on her white shirt, curling down to tear the collars apart and reveal her brown breasts. Eyes brown, breasts brown, the skin rising and falling, twin mounds that filled his hands with startling softness and sublime, heavy warmth. He saw them and lost them, his eyes closing to gaze inward, dimly aware that he was licking and sucking like a child seeking milk. Someone's fingers—in his hair. Other fingers—on his spine. He groaned and leaned forward, bending her back, stretching along her, mesmerized by her writhing pliancy and heat, his body ruling his mind.

The sun was sinking beyond the hills, a yellow fire reflected on glass, his own reflection superimposed upon it as he carried her inside. The room gray, growing darker, shadows sliding along the wall, as he felt her hands clinging to his neck, her weight pulling his arms down. He could not remember picking her up and never saw the bedroom door—only the bed, its springs squeaking in protest as he dropped her across it. He either lay or fell beside her, grabbing her hip, pulling her toward him, stripping the shirt from her body, unzipping her denims, as her spine arched and her body flowed toward him and her mouth drowned his tongue. She was gasping, kicking her legs, letting him slide the denims off, and his own clothes, removed by her hands, were soon lying with hers. They touched, their bodies met, her breasts flattening against his chest, and then she uncoiled beneath him, opening out and drawing him in, her flesh rising and falling like a river pouring endlessly over him.

He closed his eyes to gaze inward, seeing darkness and light, moving very deep inside her, letting her flesh and warmth envelop him, his every nerve reaching out to touch her and join her, becoming her and feeling what she felt as she tightened around him. She did not divide in two and survey the act from a distance, but let herself melt around his hardness and weld her flesh to him. Welded to him, she became him, her heart beating to his rhythm, their joined bodies a single river of sweat and tears that flowed into a timeless zone. She took him and let him take her, conquered him and surrendered to him, lost herself for the first time in the wonder of pure sensation, descending deep into the depths of herself to where her singing nerves scorched her. There was sound—her joyful sobbing, their synchronized gasping, his strangled groan—and then she felt the crushing weight of his flesh as the spasms whipped through her. She flew apart in that brief delirium, her senses spinning through light and heat, catapulting over the chasm of her fears and into the harbors of freedom. He felt her and she felt him, they felt each other as they collided, shuddering together in the ecstasy of release and the slow glide to peace.

The river, flowing endlessly, had not flowed very long at all, but he lay upon her body, kissing her breasts, like a man resurrected. He felt cured and purified, touched with wonder and hope, and as she ran her fingers lightly through his hair, he gave himself to her totally. His draining tension told her this, the tender sliding of his tongue, and she glanced around the room, saw the white walls in the darkness, and let the silence capture her beating heart and lay it gently upon him.

"I'm yours," he said. "Take me."

32

He was in the middle of the wilderness, a light breeze blowing his white robes, the sun beating down on his bowed head where he sat on a rock. He was motionless and silent, his face covered with his hands, apparently deaf to the sound of the jeep as it braked to a halt. Kate sat there for some time, too surprised to move immediately, one hand resting lightly on the steering wheel, the other holding the brake. Joshua looked like an apparition, a shimmering mirage, a lonely figure in the desert's vast expanse, the sand drifting around him. The silence was eerie, the heat fierce and relentless, but he sat on the rock with his head bowed as if he were sleeping.

Kate shook her head from side to side, wondering what had brought her here, yet feeling, even as she climbed down from the jeep, that the question was pointless. Joshua had brought her here, calling her out of Moshe's bed, making her drive through the pearly light of dawn as if following her instincts. She knew this as she walked toward him, her feet kicking up the sand, her yellow-tinted sunglasses easing the glare. Joshua didn't move when she approached, remaining exactly the same, his head bowed, his face covered with his hands, his hair falling about him.

"Joshua?" she said, not a statement but a question, as if, when he eventually raised his head, she might see someone else. "It's Kate. Are you all right?"

He did not immediately answer, but his posture changed slightly, his head dropping and then rising up again, his chest expanding to breathe in. His whole position suggested weariness, a massive draining of physical strength, and Kate wondered where he had been and what he had done during his month-long disappearance.

"Joshua?" she said again, and leaned forward to shake his shoulder, her fingers spreading out on the white robe to feel the firmness of flesh and bone. "It's Kate. Can you hear me?"

He suddenly shuddered and took a deep breath, held it in and let it out again, breathing deeply in a slow, regular rhythm as if exercising. His head was still bowed, his face covered with his hands, but eventually he removed his hands and glanced up, blinking against the fierce sunlight. Kate was shocked by his appearance, not prepared for what she was seeing: he looked very much older, his face gaunt, the skin lined, deep shadows under his silvery-gray eyes, his hair and beard filled with fine sand. He looked away and then looked at her again, his brow furrowed, then finally shook his head from side to side and offered a sad smile.

"I called and you came," he said. "My voice carries on the wind. In the night, in the silence of the wilderness, my own voice fills my head."

"You called me?" she replied. "I didn't know what was happening. I just woke up in the middle of the night and felt like going for a drive. I didn't plan anywhere in particular—I simply had the urge for silence —so I thought I would drive into the desert and gather my thoughts."

"What thoughts were those?"

"About Moshe and myself. About how you introduced us. I was thinking of how you drew us together and how it seemed preordained. We had made love earlier on, but I could still feel him inside me, my body closing in to take hold of him and make him a part of me. It was a very strange feeling, very beautiful, almost religious, and I realized that the night we first made love was the night that you disappeared. So, I was thinking of that, of how long you had been gone, of the fact that Moshe and I had been lovers for a month and that you hadn't been seen during that time. Then, unable to sleep, I got out of bed and drove into the desert."

He smiled again, as if at a private joke, but kept his eyes fixed upon her. "What is willed will be done," he said, "and being done has been preordained—but there was no connection between your first night with Moshe and my own disappearance."

"Why did you disappear?"

"To be alone and meditate. I am not as I was, and my heart is pained and weary, and I take unto myself the sins of man and his numerous temptations. I know that my time is coming, and feel pain and despair, but beyond it is the light of revelation and final redemption. Yet now I am weak, sorely tempted by Earth's domain, and I hope that what transpired in my isolation will return me to strength. Such strength will be needed for the time which is to come, when nation shall rise against nation and kingdom against kingdom."

His words sent a chill through her, filling her mind with trickling shadows, and she thought of the smoke over the Golan Heights the last time she had seen him.

"Are you talking about another war?" she asked him.

"The war has already begun, and you were witness to its beginning, the smoke signaling the prelude to the drama that will end after me."

"*After* you?"

"When I am gone. When Israel is devastated. When Jerusalem is desecrated and made barren and must find its redemption."

"The war you prophesied is over."

"It has begun and continues. The silence that now hangs over Jerusalem is the silence of fever. Men dream and then scheme, and their scheming brings their downfall—that defeat which offers hope or despair, good or bad, the last choice. Jerusalem must fall to rise again in its glory, radiating its light around the world of which it stands at the center. That fall has not yet come, but it will come when I am gone; and then, out of my anguish and joy, Jerusalem will sing."

The noon sun was merciless, beating out of an azure sky, making the surrounding mountains shimmer in heat waves that rose up from the burning sands. Kate glanced all around her, strangely unnerved by the silence, then wiped sweat from her forehead with a handkerchief and stared back at Joshua. He was still sitting on the rock, looking up at her, a hint of pain in his eyes.

"You disappeared for a month," she said, "and that has caused much concern: the Jews blame the Muslims, and the Muslims the Jews, and the Christians blame first one, then the other—each thinking that the other has stolen you and is keeping you hidden. If, as you say, there will be further trouble, then possibly it will be caused by your disappearance."

"I return today," he said. "You will drive me into Jerusalem. From this day forth my fate will be sealed and the fall will commence."

"The fall of Jerusalem?"

"And the beginning of man's rebirth—his transformation into that which is good or evil, redeemed or defiled."

"You don't know which?"

"No."

"You could be the instrument of either?"

"I am the instrument of revelation—no more and no less—but what will be revealed is a mystery known only to God."

"You believe you come from God?"

"I only know that I believe *in* Him. We are made manifest by His will and without Him we cannot be."

"You do not know Him?"

"He is not to be known. The mind cannot encompass His glory, but the heart must accept Him."

"Faith?"

"And love. We must give to receive. We must surrender ourselves to be whole and know the joy of redemption."

"Where does your faith come from?"

"From doubt and temptation. From the conquest of both. My faith is a light blossoming out of the darkness, as boundless as the desert to a single grain of sand, as enduring as the rock upon which I now rest my earthly body. At first I was innocent, not knowing faith or unfaith, simply watching and listening for the sign that would mean revelation. Then in watching and listening my emptiness was filled, all the vanities and weaknesses of man pouring into my nakedness. Thus humanized I knew rage, the curse of greed and ambition, the temptation to use my uncommon powers for personal gain. Then I came to the wilderness, to the purity of God's anvil, and spent thirty days and nights on a journey through the depths of my soul. I saw light and darkness, the forces of good and evil, the eternal pain of sin and the angelic song of virtue, the flame of lust and the ice of a continence that could lead to transcendence. In me they were at war —as in all men they are—and I saw that I would have to take a stand and choose the present or future."

Kate was hot, but she shivered, wrapping her arms around her body, feeling drawn to the gateway of his eyes and the cosmos beyond. He kept talking, and his voice was like a wind on a desolate planet, both frightening and beautiful.

"The present is what men have and live their lives in fear of losing: the known, the familiar, the instantly recognizable, the comfort of the illusion of Reality and the mirror of fellow men. The future is something else: the great darkness, the unknown, that which terrifies because it has no shape and might never materialize, possibly no more than the worm in the flesh—then the dust, the black Nothing. To some men it is that, but to others something worse: the bottomless pits of Hell, the blade and the fire, devils and ogres and demons beyond description; eternal damnation and torture and fear—all the horrors and terrors of their dreams and festering nightmares. This, then, is man's choice: between the known and the unknown, between reason and faith, between the satisfactions of the real present or sacrifice for an unreal future, between the weakness of his mortal human heart or the strength of his spirit. Thus, as man must choose, so I, too, was forced to choose, having taken the vices of man into myself to know doubt and temptation."

He stopped talking and glanced around him, his eyes reflecting the distant mountains, dropping down to survey the wilderness floor upon which his feet rested. In that silence Kate felt lost, torn away from the familiar, her fear rising as ethereally as smoke, with a quiet, lazy malice. She wanted Moshe to be beside her, on top of her, inside her, his flesh offering the one form of transcendence that the present could hold. She had faith but it was weak, bound with vanity and earthly love, and with Moshe, as she had found out in his bed, she could feel that faith flowing.

"Why choose the unknown?" she asked, keeping her voice level, trying hard to control her beating heart and its threat of betrayal.

"Knowledge," he replied, closing his eyes as if to pray. "The revelation that my recent unhappiness had been caused by my doubt. In the beginning I knew peace, the calm joy of not knowing, the contentment that comes from an innocence that simply accepts. Then I became as other men, learning vanity and greed, wanting so much to drink from the present that I doubted the future. Who had called me, and why? What sign had He given me? Was I child to the dazzling light or the forces of darkness? Such questions were like thorns, drawing blood from my broken flesh, biting deep into the marrow of my faith and dividing my spirit. I was tempted and turned away, tempted again and turned more slowly, tempted a third time and found myself faltering on the brink of acceptance. Mortal pleasures, power on Earth, the love of man and not his hatred, the avoidance of the pain yet to come—these rewards were at hand. So I refused, refused again with less conviction, tried to refuse a third time and went dumb, as if frightened of speaking. Yes, I was tempted, my lips drawn to forbidden fruit, and then, in the shame of doubt and weakness, I fled to this wilderness."

He opened his eyes again, raised them slowly to look at her, his face simultaneously wounded and radiant, the deep lines etching pain and joy.

"I traveled down through myself," he said, "thirty days and thirty nights, down that well of light and darkness within, to where the soul meets its source. There, in the silence, in the resonance of the beyond, I, like the mass of His children, had to make my commitment. To be, we must choose—between good and evil, belief and unbelief—between a faith that transcends our mortal fear and the rejection of hope. Knowing this, I explored my Self, surveying the forces at war within me, and realized that my worldly learning, my accumulation of greed and vanity, had brought me nothing but anguish and despair. Thus, I committed myself, casting doubt and temptation aside—and immediately felt the light blossoming out from my center to dissolve the dark forces around me and let me be Whole. Then, knowing joy, the redeeming flame of faith and hope, I ascended back up through my Self and returned to the mortal world. Here, to test my faith and the strength of my humility, I must suffer the agony that will come to force His children to Judgment Day."

Kate took a step backward, trying to retreat from his revelations, but his silvery-gray eyes, almost luminous, refused to let her go farther. He smiled at her, very gently, like a father with his child, then pressed his hands against the small rock and slowly pushed himself upright. Standing before her, he was tall, the robe falling to his feet, his face gaunt with a very human suffering, his beard and hair filled with fine sand. He smiled again and touched her cheek with his fingers in melancholic affection.

"Walk with me," he said.

They walked away from the rock, heading straight into the wilderness, toward the mountains that formed a dividing line between the white sand and blue sky. The heat hammered out of the sky, making Kate feel almost dizzy, and she saw the air shimmering before her and distorting the landscape. Joshua didn't appear to notice —neither the heat nor the desert's beauty—his gaze focused inward upon himself and the trials to come. Nevertheless he did not walk far, perhaps no more than a hundred yards, then turned around to look back at the small rock upon which he had sat.

"I am weary," he said, "my strength drained from my meditation, and now I must learn to brave my fear of the anguish to come."

"What makes you so sure it's coming?"

"My heart and mind communicate. I know because I feel it inside me, and my feelings don't lie."

"Do you know what will happen?"

"Not to me: that is hidden. I only know that I will suffer and pass on to lead the way for Jerusalem."

"Why must you suffer?"

"Because men will grieve and rage; and, in so doing, set in motion that which leads them to Judgment Day."

"Can you not avoid the suffering?"

"No. It is ordained."

"Can you not use your extraordinary powers to move men in some other way?"

"No, that would be blasphemous, going against the given way, an abuse of my faith and His trust, an admission of cowardice. I was given power to impress men, to draw them to me and make them wonder, but now that my time is coming near, I must become as they are. I cannot use my power to save myself or change events, for in doing so His word would be revoked and damnation would reign."

"But you can't always control your power," Kate said. "You could not in the hospital."

"No, I could not, because rage and fear blinded me, making me behave as normal men in the weakness of doubt. This must not happen again, no matter how I feel or think, so now, at the beginning of my trial, I must exhaust my great gift and leave myself to my fate. My power, like the wind, will dissipate and leave me as other men."

He raised his right hand, and Kate felt a deep fear, slowly rising from the knowledge of what could happen and freezing her mind. She wanted to stop him but was powerless, her muscles turned to lead, and she saw him fix his gaze upon the rock in the shimmering distance. His raised hand started shaking, then vibrated like a divining rod, and he kept his gaze fixed on the distant rock, his eyes wide in the blinding sun. Kate felt the power coming, rushing in from the elements, surrounding and then pouring through Joshua and flowing into the earth. The ground rumbled and shook, started cracking all around them, then the sand started spitting and a jagged crack appeared, racing toward them from the base of the small rock and terminating in front of them. Kate looked and was held, her mind frozen, only seeing, as the ground around the small rock started heaving and cracking, spitting clouds of sand into the air where they swirled like dark veils. Then the heaving earth exploded, showering away in languid waves, and the small rock suddenly moved, nosing up into the air like an iceberg breaking loose, growing broader at its base as the growling earth was forced away, inching higher, growing larger, one edge cutting through the sun, soil and sand falling off it, until finally, with a muffled roar, the earth stopped its convulsive heaving, and the buried mass of the original and much larger rock was exposed as a large, mud-covered hillock over which the sun flashed.

Kate's mind was frozen, admitting nothing but the visual, not open to fear or normal wonder, observing with clarity. She saw the large hillock, silhouetted against the sky, striations of brilliant sunlight flashing around it and quivering above her. The earth had stopped shaking, but Joshua was still trembling, his hand forming an arch across the sky and its few drifting white clouds. Joshua was sweating, his lips tight, his brow furrowed, and a wind, sweeping out of the former stillness, blew his hair out behind him. He leaned forward, white robes whipping, fighting against the rushing air, then the sun, one half hidden by the hillock, sank behind it and disappeared. The cold came immediately, springing out of the sudden gloom, then the sun reappeared at the opposite side of the hillock, and the heat, claustrophobic and fierce, had dominion once more.

The heat was in the wind that made the burning sand swirl, hissing around Kate as she looked at Joshua and his whipping white robes. His arched hand became a fist, trapping the elements in its grip, and then the wind, dying away to a whisper, let the sand settle down. There was silence and stillness, a frozen, brilliant clarity, and Kate looked up to see a pale moon gliding out from the white clouds. The moon seemed very large, its black craters quite distinct, and it drifted across the blue sheen of the sky toward the immense yellow sun. The light darkened, turned gray, the mountains casting enormous shadows, and the wilderness, formerly distorted in shimmering heat waves, became a colorless dream. Then the moon reached the sun, slid across it very slowly, deflecting its rays of light into space and letting the darkness roll in. The moon stopped in front of the sun, obliterating it completely, and the stars shone in glory in a blackness that embraced the whole desert.

Kate looked up and saw it, looked down and saw the same: the stars glittering above and below her in a featureless blackness. The sand and stones were stars, the desert floor a carpet of stars, and her feet, which she saw perfectly clearly, stood on vitreous starlight. She did not move at all, feeling nothing, simply observing, and then she saw a pool of light around her feet, rippling out through the blackness. In that light was her reflection, her multiplied image, countless masks of herself drifting out and fading away in the distance. She was the stem of a flower, her Self forming the petals, the petals dying and drifting away and renewing themselves. Then she sank down through the stars, through the reed of her Self, and saw the light blossoming around her and pushing the darkness back. The light brought the heat that bathed her body in sweat, became a brilliance that dazzled her eyes and erased every star. There was white haze, blue sky, a ragged mass resembling mountains, then the wilderness and sky were divided and the sun had dominion.

She stood in the wilderness, her eyes fixed on Joshua, the hillock that had formerly been a small rock soaring up just behind him. His white robes blew in the wind, the sand swirling around him, and she saw her Self standing just beside him, gazing down at the parched earth. He reached out and touched her, laying his hand upon her shoulder, and a globe of light, brighter than the sun, surrounded their bodies. She studied the large hillock, silhouetted against the sky, striations of brilliant sunlight flashing around it and quivering above her.

"I am drained," he said. "Mortal."

His white robes blew in the wind as he lowered his arms, closed his eyes, and then wearily bowed his head to let the elements retreat. The wind faded away, letting the swirling sand settle; then, in its lust to devour the silence, started growling and heaving. The large hillock shook violently, mud and sand sliding down it, then the earth around its base started sinking, sucking the hillock down with it. The hillock sank slowly, with a stark, somber majesty, sinking down as the sand subsided beneath it and dragging more sand down with it. The noise was catastrophic, the earth roaring in its hunger, and the hillock continued sinking, the sand pouring in around it, until only the peak remained, a small rock on the desolate plain, the great orb of the sun shining upon it and rendering it lifeless.

Joshua dropped to his knees and put his hands on the modest rock, spreading his fingers to explore its burning surface and then bowing his head. He was silent for a long time, breathing heavily, his body sagging, the light breeze blowing through his tangled hair and brushing sand from his white robes. Then eventually he spoke, his voice pained and yet joyous, a haunting music carried on the wind and fed lightly to Kate's ears.

"Around this rock," he said, "I will gather my Ministry—not to destroy, but to fulfill . . . for all men . . . and all time."

Kate returned to her mortal shell, to the fear and doubt of life, and felt the spasms whipping through her body and bringing her senses back. She saw Joshua on his knees, his two hands on the burning rock, his fingers outspread like a web around the globe, his head bowed in exhaustion. She wanted Moshe inside her, setting her free, beyond commitment, but her voice, as if mocking this desperate wish, whispered out over Joshua:

"What ministry?"

"The world."

PART FOUR:

Crucifixion

His blood be on us, and on our children.
—Matthew, 27:25

33

The schemes of men, Jozsef thought, *are always nurtured behind closed doors, away from the curious eyes of the world and its numerous victims*. He thought this as the closed door opened and Rashid Idriss was ushered in, his brown eyes moving from Moshe to Ben Eliezer, then to Jozsef, as the guard quietly stepped out of the room and closed the door again behind him. Rashid stood there for a moment, not pretending to be friendly, then nodded and walked across to the long table and sat down facing Moshe. They stared at one another, neither revealing what he was thinking, then the prime minister coughed into his fist and pursed his lips thoughtfully.

"We are glad you could make it, Rashid."

"I have come to see the Mahdi."

"I very seriously doubt that he's the Mahdi, but you certainly will see him."

"You assume he is your Messiah?"

"No, I do not. I merely suggest that he may not be what he seems —to you or to us."

"He is the Mahdi."

"There's no proof of that."

"He has appeared to many Muslims."

"He has also appeared to many Jews and Christians, but we can't all lay claim to him."

"I know what I feel."

"You're too educated for that, Rashid."

"My Western education is now behind me, cast off like a worthless rag."

Moshe and Ben Eliezer glanced uneasily at one another, unable to hide their surprise at the swift change in Rashid. Jozsef, too, was surprised, his gaze drawn to Rashid's brown eyes, which glittered with the bright, hard intensity of growing fanaticism. Rashid had always been approachable, moderate in politics and religion, but the Arab who now sat across the table was very much different from that. Jozsef knew about the Black Stone and how it had affected the Muslims, but he hadn't been prepared for the extent of Rashid's personal conversion. Now Rashid was staring at each of them in turn, his face stony and challenging.

"I am surprised to see no Americans here," he said.

"And why should there be Americans here?" Ben Eliezer replied. "This is Israel, not America."

"It must be difficult to admit that the Americans and Soviets are on your doorstep, with the Americans pulling the strings that manipulate Jerusalem."

"We are not puppets, Rashid."

"But you are in chains, Ben Eliezer. Right now the Americans and Soviets are deciding your fate."

"Both armies have left Israel."

"And are now massed around it, negotiating in the tents between the tanks and quietly planning your future."

"The United Nations is mediating."

"The United Nations is a joke. As usual the United Nations is impotent and merely makes empty speeches."

"Our fate is your fate, Rashid."

"Not quite," Rashid said. "The United Arab Republic has the oil; you have nothing to trade."

He was sitting up very straight, looking at each of them in turn, his eyes bright with the purity of conviction, his lips forming a thin line.

"Neither the Americans nor the Soviets are interested in trade," Ben Eliezer said. "They are interested in stealing as much as possible in the name of world peace."

"They have brought peace to Palestine."

"A temporary peace, Rashid. While it is true that the so-called peace-keeping forces have kept us from each other's throats, it is also true that that peace is very precarious indeed. The Americans and Soviets both feel that the presence of Joshua in this area remains a threat to them. As things now stand, you Muslims are convinced that Joshua is the Mahdi who will ordain the sovereignty of Islam over all the Arab states and Israel; a great many Jews are equally convinced that Joshua is their Messiah come to Earth to pave the way to the sovereignty of Judaism; and the Christians, both here and in Europe, are also convinced that Joshua is the resurrected Jesus Christ who will inaugurate the conversion of the Jews and, presumably, you Muslims. No matter what Joshua is, no matter his nature, the three great monotheistic religions are equally convinced that Joshua is theirs, and are ready to move Heaven and Hell to establish their individual supremacy under his banner. The current peace in Israel is therefore very precarious indeed, and further outbursts of violence between Jews, Arabs, and Christians are already occurring."

"The Christians have little bearing on the problems of Palestine. I am only concerned with Zionists and Muslims."

"Unfortunately the Christians, if having little effect within Israel, might soon be affecting Israel from outside."

"I don't know what you're talking about."

"I am talking, Rashid, about the speech the pope broadcast worldwide yesterday—the speech proclaiming Joshua as the Christian's Son of God and announcing the unification of the Roman Catholic and Protestant Churches into the one, once more united, Christian Church. In other words, the Christian world has been united by what they are claiming is the Second Coming of Christ."

Jozsef put his head down, feeling ashamed and humiliated, still shocked by what had happened and unable to reconcile himself to it. He was a rabbi, a Jew, and therefore not personally involved, but when he thought of the pope's speech, and of the motives behind it, he also thought of what he had said to Kate on the walk to the Mount of Beatitudes and wondered if he had been deceiving himself. In defending the silence of the Christian and Jewish religious bodies, he had claimed—as he had then thought, or perhaps wanted to believe —that their silence had been based on their inability to give an honestly objective judgment of Joshua; but now, given what had transpired in Europe, he was not at all sure of that.

"The claims of the Christian Church are of no interest to me," Rashid said. "The Christian Church has little influence over Palestine."

"I think you may be wrong there," Ben Eliezer said. "The Christian

Church, if not directly involved in Israel, is certainly involved with the Soviets."

"The Vatican diplomatically kisses the hand of the Soviets, but that hardly has any bearing on their claim that the Mahdi is Jesus Christ."

"On the contrary, Rashid, we have reason to believe that the two are very intimately connected."

"Your reasons, Ben Eliezer, if I may say so, are probably all in your head."

At this point Moshe pulled his chair closer to the table and looked down at the papers between his large hands. His eyes scanned them very quickly and then looked up, fixed directly on Rashid.

"Before you talk, Major General," Rashid said with a flickering smile, "please let me congratulate you on your recent marriage. I hope it brings you considerable joy."

It was the first sign of humor that Rashid had shown, and Moshe, obviously wary, responded with a hesitant grin.

"Thank you," he said. "I, too, hope it brings me joy. I appreciate your interest in my affairs, and accept it with gratitude."

The mockery was gentle, but not without its point, and Rashid, clearly accepting it in good spirit, smiled again and shrugged slightly.

"So," he said, "let me hear about the Vatican and how it relates to the Palestinians."

"Let me give you some background details," Moshe said, looking down at his papers. "The pope, a Pole, is only the second non-Italian pope in four and a half centuries, and as such has a particular interest in his own country and Eastern Europe in general. It is now clear that he was elected to the papacy as a sign that the Church was reasserting Eastern Europe's place in the religion of the West and, by implication, condemning Soviet influence in Eastern Europe. However in doing this, as the pope well knows, the Church was deliberately confronting the Soviets with the unenviable choice between either surrendering its influence to that of the Church or embarking on the task of eroding the Church completely in Eastern Europe. In short it was a very specific conflict, engineered by the Vatican."

"Those facts are hardly secret," Rashid said.

"Wait," Moshe replied, "I'm not finished yet. . . . Prior to the advent of the man known as Joshua, this conflict had been coming to a head—with the pope finding himself under increasing pressure from the Soviets to pull in his horns and remove the Church from the political arena lest the Soviets reassert their authority by intensifying religious suppression—and possibly crushing the influence of the Church, once and for all—throughout Eastern Europe. However, with the advent of Joshua—and the widespread Christian belief in him as the resurrected Jesus Christ—the pope's dilemma became even more acute."

"This has no relevance to Palestine," Rashid said.

"You must know of the increasing religious anarchy in Europe," Ben Eliezer said. "Many of the most bizarre and dangerous religious cults have adopted Joshua as their leader; there have been violent demonstrations by Jews, Muslims, and Christians in every European capital; and along with the mass conversions, many based on hysteria, there has been a public outcry against the silence of religious leaders, to the extent of the Vatican having to call in riot troops to St. Peter's Square."

"I still don't see the relevance," Rashid said.

"It has relevance," Moshe replied. "The growing religious anarchy in Europe had been caused, in most cases, by the widespread Christian belief that Joshua is the Christ and that the Church had refused to either support or deny that view. The Church, however, had a problem: It knew that a denial of Joshua as the Christ would simply lead to hysterical outrage, further religious anarchy, and a widespread rejection of the Church itself—a situation disastrous for the Church and beneficial to the Soviets. If, on the other hand, the Church had officially supported Joshua as the Christ, the Soviets would have been convinced that it was merely doing so in order to reinforce Christianity and strengthen its own bargaining position —and that would almost certainly have led to Soviet suppression of the Church throughout Eastern Europe. That dilemma, apparently insoluble, was what caused the Vatican and the World Council of Churches to remain silent about Joshua for so long."

"A silence that was broken yesterday," Rashid said.

"Correct," Moshe replied. "As the prime minister said, yesterday the Roman Catholic and Protestant Churches were formally united —and together proclaimed the Second Coming of Christ."

"United, they become twice as powerful."

"That, also, is correct." Moshe flicked his eyes toward Jozsef and he felt himself flushing, unnerved by the recent events and his own confused thoughts. "The chief rabbi," Moshe continued, "has just returned from a trip to Rome, and I think he should fill in from here."

Jozsef leaned across the table, staring at Rashid with some reluctance, scarcely able to formulate the words that now had to be said. He thought of his trip to Europe, of what he had witnessed there, and the ice of an insidious, relentless fear filled the blood in his veins. Joshua's influence was contagious, causing exultation and dread, driving some into religion, driving others into madness, giving rise to joy and guilt and confusion, cementing beliefs or blowing them apart, leaving very few unchanged. The Son of God to some, the Devil to others, he had, just by being, drawn out of the mass subconscious, all the passions, both noble and murderous, that had been kept buried. In England there were thousands of suicides, the normally empty churches were packed, orthodox religions and occult sects were flourishing side by side, and on hills and in valleys, by day and by night, thousands were waiting for the coming of Joshua's fellow extraterrestrials or, in equally fearful surrender, for the fire and brimstone of Judgment Day. It was the same all over Europe, and not much better in Rome, where, west of the Tiber, behind the walls of Vatican City, beneath the statues of the saints atop the balustrade of St. Peter's Square, the worshipers had turned into rioters at war with the police. Jozsef thought of it with woe and a great deal of moral confusion, having to accept that his very own Rabbinate had been equally silent about Joshua.

"There were various reasons for the Vatican's compromise," he said, "and compromise, unfortunately, it has to be termed." He found himself glancing at Moshe and Ben Eliezer, as if seeking approval. "As Moshe has already explained," he continued, "the pope's main consideration was his fear of possible Soviet suppression in Eastern Europe. On the one hand fearful of outraging his congregation by denying that Joshua was the Christ, he was, on the other hand, equally concerned that the Church could not, if it supported Joshua, stand alone against the full onslaught of Soviet suppression. Torn between these two equally dire possibilities the pope simply could not decide what to do, and therefore continued his official silence. Alas, with the pressure mounting—from the outrage of his own flock on the one side and, on the other side, the Soviet insistence that he take no formal stand on the matter—he succumbed, with the encouragement of the World Council of Churches, to the Christian Church's ancient fear of the Jews."

Jozsef closed his eyes a moment, feeling weary and sick at heart, understanding that even though he was Jewish, he was not without sin. The Rabbinate, like the members of the Holy See in Rome, had made its own dubious compromises.

"For its entire history," he continued, opening his eyes again, "the Church has worked for the conversion of the Jews. Indeed, in its Good Friday liturgy, the Roman Catholic Church made a special point of praying for the so-called perfidious Jews—*pro perfidis Judeis:* 'That our God and Lord will remove the veil from their hearts, so that they, too, may acknowledge our Lord Jesus Christ . . .' This was the only passage during which the faithful did not kneel—though they knelt when they prayed for heretics, schismatics, and pagans. This passage was altered by Pope John the twenty-third, but the sentiment remains—and for the Christians, unfortunately, the Second Coming of Christ is closely connected with the expected conversion of the Jews. How ironic, then, that the supposed Second Coming of their Christ should have taken place on the Jewish soil of the Holy Land."

"On *Palestinian* soil," Rashid said firmly.

Jozsef heard the remark clearly and, strangely, felt embarrassed, as if he had been caught in the act of stealing, his hand still in the till. Startled, confused, suddenly doubting his Zionist principles, he found that he could not look at Rashid, and dropped his gaze to the table.

"A mortal man," he continued, "with mortal man's weaknesses, the pope unfortunately surrendered to his Church's fear of the Jews; in this case the fear of what might happen to Christianity should the Jews of Israel—where Joshua had, of course, been discovered—manage to convince the Christian world that Joshua was not the Son of the Almighty, but His Messenger as heralded in Judaism—fearful, in fact, of mass conversion and the threat of a dominant World Jewry."

"What about Islam?" Rashid asked.

"I don't think they considered it."

He glanced up at Rashid, sympathizing with his anger, aware that he was thinking of all white men's religions as being riddled with racialist superiority and arrogant self-righteousness. Then, unable to brave Rashid's gaze, he dropped his eyes again to the table.

"It is possible," he continued, "that had it not been for this old fear, the pope might have maintained his official silence. Alas, this fear, combined with his fear of ostracizing his congregation, drove him closer—irrespective of his own views, which remain ambiguous—to an official recognition of Joshua as the Christ of the Christians."

"Which would, in turn, have antagonized the Soviets," Rashid said, "and led to their suppression of his own, much beloved Eastern Europe."

"Correct," Jozsef replied. "Fearful for the religious freedom of Eastern Europe, but more frightened of ostracizing the majority of his congregation, he decided that he would have to risk the wrath of the Soviets, but desperately searched for a means of discouraging them from their intended acts of religious suppression. A possible solution was then suggested by the representatives of the World Council of Churches—who were, of course, equally anxious about the threat of mass conversion to Judaism and wished to strengthen the whole Christian world. So it was that in a secret meeting between the representatives of the Holy See and the World Council of Churches, the decision was taken to unify the Roman Catholic and Protestant Churches, using the Second Coming of Christ as the reason for so doing, irrespective of what a proper theological examination of Joshua might reveal. The point was to unite both Churches into one, more powerful Church, which would, at least in theory, frighten the Soviets into keeping their hands off Eastern Europe."

Jozsef sighed and sat back, feeling obliquely defeated, unable to feel morally superior to the Christian delegates, no matter how obviously shameful their recent actions. His Rabbinate, after all, in a similar surrender to political expediency, had retained an equally shameful silence on matters pertaining to Joshua.

"So," Rashid said, "it might work and it might not—but either way, at least from where I sit, it has little bearing on Palestine."

"Unfortunately," Moshe replied, speaking quietly and calmly, "our intelligence reports indicate that the plan is already backfiring. Initial indications are that the pope's speech has aroused the wrath of those Christians who do not believe in Joshua as the resurrected Christ, encouraged the lunatic fringe in their view of Joshua as the first of an imminent invasion of extraterrestrials or the Devil come to inaugurate the Age of Darkness; and, more important, has *not* scared off the

Soviets, but on the contrary has made them more anxious to suppress the Church completely in Eastern Europe. Their intentions have been conveyed to the Vatican, and it seems that nothing will stop them."

"Never bend over in front of a goat," Rashid said. "And the Soviet mind is a goat's mind." He smiled at his own joke, but the smile contained steel, convincing Jozsef that he would not be persuaded easily to work against his own interests. "So," he said, raising his hands in mock bewilderment, "the Soviets are about to suppress the Church in Eastern Europe. . . . How does this affect Palestine?"

Ben Eliezer had been sitting quietly with his chin resting on his folded hands, his elbows propped up on the table, and now he waved his hands and shrugged his shoulders in a rabbinical gesture, his round face deceptively innocent.

"The Soviets are in Syria and Jordan," he said, "so surely any move they make should be of concern to you."

"I am not concerned with their movements in Christian Europe."

"Well," Ben Eliezer said, "*we* are. The Americans will almost certainly view the suppression of the Christian Church in Eastern Europe as a flagrant act of aggression, a warning to the Christian world—which of course includes America—that the Soviets will not be intimidated by Joshua, the supposed Son of the Almighty. This might, in turn, encourage the Americans to set their own example by taking so-called preventive military actions in the Middle East, naturally using Israel and the United Arab Republic as their playground. In short, they might conceivably move their troops back into Israel to protect it from any possible Soviet religious suppression of the kind so brutally demonstrated in Eastern Europe—as the Americans will, after the Soviets have obliterated the Church, diplomatically phrase it."

Jozsef looked carefully at Rashid, intrigued by his face, which was, paradoxically, poetically delicate and hard with intelligence. His brown eyes moved left and right, from Ben Eliezer to Moshe, and eventually came to settle on Moshe, whose rugged face revealed little. Now married to Kate, Moshe had changed and was less remote, but in political matters he remained, as Jozsef had noted, reserved and difficult to analyze. Now he was staring directly at Rashid, his gray eyes calm and veiled.

"What exactly do you want from me?" Rashid asked.

"If the Americans are given an excuse for moving back into Israel, it is unlikely that we will get them out again. Should that happen, all of us will lose, Jew and Muslim alike."

"If the Americans use potential Soviet aggression as an excuse for moving back into Palestine, we Arabs could do little to prevent it. We are not in a position, Moshe, to take action against the Americans or Soviets."

"You miss the point, Rashid: we don't want it to get that far. The religious suppression of Eastern Europe will scare the Americans into action, but it will not, politically speaking, be an acceptable *reason* for such action. No, our intelligence indicates that the Americans are already viewing the Soviet intention with alarm, but are themselves intending to use the resurgence of violence between Arabs and Jews as their excuse for moving strategically back into Israel. Once that happens, both the Jews and the Arabs will lose control of their own fate."

"You wish me to form an unofficial alliance with the Jews, and stop my Arabs from further acts of violence?"

"Precisely."

"But your own zealots are responsible for that violence."

"I don't think that's wholly true," Jozsef intervened, speaking out automatically. "The Muslims are fighting because Joshua is here and they think he's their Mahdi. They are fighting to get Jerusalem back and ordain the sovereignty of Islam."

"The majority of Arabs, Chief Rabbi, were willing to stop fighting on the condition that they be granted access to their Mahdi. However your own zealots have made it perfectly clear that they think of the Mahdi as their Messiah, that the sovereignty of Judaism must now be implemented, and that they intend throwing the present government out of the Knesset and forming an ecclesiastical Cabinet with their own flagrantly Arab-hating members. As they have also made clear, they intend, once they are in power, to inaugurate the Zionist State and remove all non-Jews from Palestine. Such ambitions would be acceptable from a few powerless zealots, but now they are being supported by some of your most influential politicians and military leaders, and that means that they could possibly succeed in doing just what they want. My fighting Arabs are very aware of this—and of what it could mean to them."

"I think you exaggerate the situation, Rashid."

"It cannot be an exaggeration when one of the strongest supporters of the zealots, namely Lieutenant Paul Frankel, is not only a leading member of Shin Beth, but the man formerly placed in charge of our Mahdi."

"I insist," Jozsef said, refusing to think of Paul Frankel, "that there are no grounds for calling Joshua the Mahdi."

"Yet your Jews call him their Messiah."

"The Rabbinate has not supported that claim."

"Nor has it denied it."

Jozsef felt trapped by that statement, almost shrinking inside himself, knowing full well that he had no defense and suffering a harsh, shameful guilt. He was the acting chief rabbi, a leading member of the Rabbinate, and he had tolerated, in timidity and humiliation, his Rabbinate's cowardly silence. There was a valid reason for it—human doubt and fear of error—but behind that, inexcusably, was the ignoble wedding of religion to politics, that sordid bed in which moral judgments were clouded and values subtly changed. Joshua's discovery in Israel had drawn the veils from that bed, forcing Jozsef, and others in his position, to examine themselves. Mortal men, indeed, and with mortal men's weaknesses; and he now knew that religion, which gave men moral guidelines, could itself form the slippery path into sin and dishonesty.

"You have no answer, Chief Rabbi?"

"Yes, Rashid, I have: We abdicated our responsibilities in order to protect our faith, and neither Joshua nor what men tried to make of him can excuse what we did."

He felt better for having said it, no less guilty but less ashamed, relieved to have unburdened himself of the self-deceit and cleared the way for forgiveness. He would pray for the Lord's guidance and strength and let events take their course. Like Joshua, he would listen and watch, and hope to find revelation.

"Well, Rashid," Moshe said, "we are waiting for your answer. Are you willing to cooperate with us to keep the Americans out?"

"Joshua is the Mahdi."

"You are welcome to that belief."

"I wish to see the Mahdi, to speak with him, and will let his words guide me."

"He will not advise you, Rashid. He won't confirm that he's your Mahdi. He does not know who he is or where he came from, and he never takes sides."

"The true saint rarely recognizes himself, nor takes credit for being one of the blessed; and if the Mahdi, in his humility, says little, I will know what he means."

Jozsef caught his passing glance, the mosque challenging the synagogue, and decided to modestly turn his gaze away and discuss the matter no further. He looked at Moshe and Ben Eliezer, the former thoughtful, the latter bland, saw them staring at one another, communicating with their eyes, before Moshe shrugged and turned toward Rashid, a slight smile on his lips.

"All right," he said. "We have Joshua waiting outside. We'll bring him in and then you can decide."

He picked up the phone and spoke to the guard outside the room, then put the phone down and sat back, his hands flat on the table. Jozsef looked at Rashid's brown eyes as his head turned toward the door, saw the light of an electric anticipation before the head turned away. The brief silence was deceptive, seeming longer than it actually was, and Jozsef looked down at the floor between his feet, feeling tense and unreal. He thought of Joshua, one man, his presence on Earth dividing the world, and realized that the fate of whole nations could hinge on his utterances. Joshua was passive, letting events take shape around him, and his innocence, or ignorance, was the living blank slate upon which the world's future was being written. He did not know who he was, nor where he had come from, but he had, simply by being, forced the world to reap the whirlwind, and the future, still obscured in the winds of chance, was yet to reveal itself.

He looked up when the door opened and saw Joshua walking in, his long hair, ascetic face, and white robes making him look like a prophet. The guard closed the door behind him and he walked up to the table, and stopped as Rashid climbed to his feet and stepped forward to greet him. He studied Rashid for some time, with a calm, detached interest, his silvery-gray eyes hardly moving at all and yet strangely appealing. Rashid seemed to be hypnotized, then he suddenly turned away, glanced at Moshe and Ben Eliezer and Jozsef in turn; then, his brown eyes bright with either panic or exultation, looked again at Joshua and licked his lips, his spine straight, his hands shaking.

"You wished to see me?" Joshua asked, his voice level and almost gentle, reaching out to caress and soothe Rashid, understanding his tension.

"Yes," Rashid replied. "I have been haunted by your presence. It is said that you are the hidden Imam, the Mahdi, and I wish to confirm this."

"I cannot confirm or deny it."

"You are He. I can see it."

"We only see what we want to see, which for most is enough."

"You do not know who you are or why you are here?"

"I am that I am—this I know. No more and no less."

"Do you know what these men want of me?"

"They do not know themselves. They speak out of the fear of the moment, and see little beyond it."

"Palestine is the center of the world, and the whole world now wants it. Who shall have Palestine?"

"The East and the West is God's: therefore, whichever way you turn, there is the face of God. There is no piety in turning your own face towards the East or the West; but he is pious who believes in God, the Scriptures, and the Last Day. Bear only this in mind: No one is a believer until he loves for his brother what he loves for himself; do not be envious of each other, and do not outbid each other, and do not hate each other; do not oppose each other and do not undersell each other. The dominion of the heavens and of the Earth is God's; and you have neither patron nor helper, save God."

Rashid obviously recognized the words, and in his exultation was terror: the knowledge that the answer he had been given had left a question mark over him. He licked his lips and glanced around him, knowing that help would not be offered, that Joshua, or the Mahdi, had left him with nothing but faith. Jozsef watched him, sympathizing, understanding what he was feeling: he was being challenged to accept the will of God and let events take their course. No bartering, no intrigue, no hatred, no opposing; no dependence on aid or patronage, political or spiritual; no looking east or west, neither to the Soviets nor the Americans—only love for his fellow man and trust in God, who alone had dominion. Truth or untruth, belief or unbelief:

Israel, the land Rashid knew as Palestine, would stand or fall by his faith.

Jozsef leaned across the table, his every thought focused on Rashid, his whole being flowing out to the space into which Rashid's words would fall. Rashid and Joshua were face-to-face, very close, neither moving, and the silence, like a song in a deaf man's ears, seemed to quiver and breathe. Rashid took a step backward, turned his head and stared at Jozsef, let his gaze roam to Moshe and Ben Eliezer and then back to Joshua. He stared at Joshua for some time, his eyes bright and intense, and then shivered, as if casting off a ghost, and dropped down to his knees, his head bowed before Joshua.

"In you, I have faith," he said. "For me, you are the Mahdi. I do not need confirmation or proof; in my faith, I believe it. I will not look east or west, nor harbor envy or hatred, but will love for my brother what he loves for himself, and await the final judgment of our Lord. Upon this I swear, and by this I stand: As long as you are safe, as long as you walk the land of Palestine, I will not take up arms against my brothers or incite them to war."

He reached out for Joshua's hand, pulled it toward him and kissed it, then stood up and walked across the room, opened the door, and walked out. Jozsef looked at Ben Eliezer, saw him raising his eyebrows; looked at Moshe and saw him visibly sighing, sinking into his chair. Then he looked at Joshua, drawn inexorably toward him, and saw, instead of the silvery-gray eyes, the shadowed hint of a smile.

A *Mona Lisa* smile. Ambiguity and mystery. Whether a smile or a grimace of despair, it chilled Jozsef to the bone.

34

Kate drove up the Mount of Olives to the Intercontinental Hotel, and parked near the small amphitheater overlooking Jerusalem. It was daylight, very bright, the domes and minarets impressive, and she sat for some time in the car, her eyes fixed on the Old City. Staring at it, she hardly saw it, her thoughts imprisoned by her flesh, by the life that was growing within her and making her whole. She desperately wanted the child, for herself and for Moshe, yet even as she thought of this with joy, an uneasiness passed through her. She thought of when she had last been here—when she had last made love to Leon, the extraordinary storm had materialized, the black obelisk had emerged from the ruins of the chapel; when she had first met Moshe and then found the robed Joshua in the blackness that defied definition and made the heart leap—and, in remembering, felt even more uneasy, wondering why she had agreed to see Leon even against Moshe's wishes.

She climbed out of the car, locked the door, and breathed deeply, then looked at the modern hotel above the green, sloping gardens. The sky was very blue, the sun very bright, sending down a fierce heat, yet she shivered at the touch of the breeze, as if totally naked. There were tourists in the amphitheater, taking photographs of Jerusalem, and their voices drove her forward, past the parked, dusty taxis, toward the steps that led up through the gardens and into the hotel.

She wished that Leon hadn't phoned her, was glad he had, felt confused, remembering the eagerness and trepidation with which she had taken his call; and, with more clarity, Moshe's anger when she had told him where she was going. His anger had not surprised her, but the violence of it had, and now, with her love for him rippling up through her flesh, she wondered if she was doing the right thing in paying Leon this visit.

The hotel lobby was deserted, the restaurant still and silent, and she thought of all the drinks she had shared with Leon beneath those large windows. Memory was a curse, nostalgia a seductive trap, and as she walked up the stairs, very aware of her extra weight, she wondered if Leon had deliberately picked this place to make her feel more defenseless. The air was cooler inside, erasing sweat and soothing tension, but when she stopped at the door of Leon's room, she was already exhausted.

She stood there for some time, wanting to see him, wanting to leave, trying to work out just why she had come and what she expected. There was no use denying it: She had felt deeply for him —not love, but certainly something close to it—sexual attraction, camaraderie, simple warmth, a good-humored affection. Love? Not really. What it had lacked was love's commitment. Her love flowed like a river to Moshe and did not suffer doubt. So why had she come? Perhaps the letter from Damascus: that atypical, if mildly sardonic, cry of pain and unexpected bewilderment. The letter had moved her deeply, making her cast off his betrayal, goading her gently into the shallows of a helpless, slightly protective concern. She owed him something, possibly that, a hand to hold in his despair, but as she stood there at his door, her hand raised, her fist clenched, she could only think of how Moshe had looked when she walked from the house.

Her fist knocked on Leon's door, first lightly, then harder, and the sound seemed very loud in the silence of the long, empty corridor. She did not wait very long—he had obviously been waiting for her —but even as the door opened and Leon's face swam into view, she remembered, with gratitude, how Moshe had relented—not easily, but attempting to understand, stifling his anger and pain. Her love, like a river flowing endlessly, went toward him for that.

Leon stood there before her, unshaven, grinning crookedly, his hair disheveled and his clothes extremely wrinkled, the room behind him too dark. She was shocked by his appearance—but when he lowered his head and raised his eyes toward her, his grin seemed more familiar.

"You came!" he said, slurring. *"Wunderbar!"*

"You're drunk already," she replied.

"I am seeing the world through rose-colored glasses—it's more acceptable that way."

He stepped aside to let her in, bowing slightly and mockingly, his left hand on the door, his right holding a large glass of whiskey. She walked past him too quickly, her shoulder brushing his bowed head, and immediately smelled the staleness of a room that had not had much fresh air. The windows were shuttered and most of the room was in semidarkness, illuminated only with a small bedside lamp that covered the unmade bed in yellow light. Leon's clothes, and a lot of magazines and newspapers, were strewn all over the place.

"You haven't been looking after yourself," she said. "This place is a mess."

"No," he said, shutting the door, his voice coming from behind her. "I decided to dispense with the chambermaid, but it's not working out."

She sat down at the table, just beneath the shuttered windows, and looked up as Leon walked toward her, the ghost of his former self. He moved out of the semidarkness and into the pale yellow light, the light making him look drawn and ill, emphasizing his frailty.

"You haven't been eating," she said, feeling claustrophobic and nervous.

"When not drinking whiskey, I drink brandy, which I hear contains vitamins." He stood in front of her, grinning crookedly, looking older than his age, then nodded at the bottles on the table, his eyes bloodshot and sleepy. "Can I offer the distinguished lady a drink? Or is it too early for that?"

"It's too early, Leon."

"A coffee?"

"No, thanks."

"You're a woman of strong moral fiber, which I hope Moshe appreciates." He had a drink of whiskey, drinking it as if it were water, then wiped his lips with the back of his free hand and sat down on the bed. His eyes in the pale yellow light were shadowed and baggy. "And what's it like, my little pacifist," he said, "being married to the new minister of defense?"

"It's fine," Kate said, not amused by his mockery, "but I don't think we should talk about that right now."

"Why not?"

"It's my private life."

"That sounds terribly prim and proper."

"I didn't come here to listen to your cynicism."

"Why *did* you come, Kate?"

She closed her eyes and lowered her head, thinking of the phone call he had made, remembering the intensity of his voice when he asked her to see him. Now she felt angry, feeling as if she had been violated, that his question, quite deliberately offered, was a singular impertinence. She opened her eyes and stared directly at him, wondering what he was after.

"I came because you asked me to come," she said, "and you sounded quite desperate."

"I was drunk."

"That's true . . . but you insisted that you had to see me. In fact, you said it was very important—so, here I am."

He had another drink, lowered the glass, and grinned at her, his thin lips curving slowly and unsurely toward the humor of bitterness.

"Did you tell Moshe you were coming?"

"Yes, Leon. Naturally."

"And how did the minister of defense react to that?"

"He didn't forbid me to come."

"That was decent of him."

"Yes, Leon, it was."

"I can tell that this conversation is making you angry, and I didn't intend that."

"I'm not amused by your sarcasm."

"I'm not amused that you married Moshe."

"I wanted him, I married him, and now I'm pregnant—and I don't regret anything."

The shock made him visibly flinch, as if he had been whipped, and he glanced aimlessly around the untidy room to avoid looking at her. He was not the Leon she knew, but someone else, a haunted man; and the room, in its squalor and semidarkness, reflected the change in him. Kate smelled the stale air, saw the shadows in the corners, and had the urge to get up and open the windows to let light and air in.

"I'm surprised they let you back into Israel."

"So am I," he replied. "Nonetheless I was simply waved through, so I must be forgiven." He managed to look at her again, but his eyes were not pretty, bloodshot and terribly weary, deep shadows beneath them. "You should know," he said. "You're married to Moshe."

She glanced at the magazines and newspapers spread haphazardly around the room, at the clothes strewn over the furniture and floor, at the bottles and ashtrays. "You were always a very neat man," she said. "Why are you living like this?"

He shrugged with weary indifference, had a drink and licked his lips, lowered his head and stared at the floor, his shoulders slumped in exhaustion.

"Why not?" he said. "The point is simply to pass the day. I have very few friends, none at all in Jerusalem, so I drink, occasionally eat, sleep a lot, usually alone, and spend hours studying the walls of this room in which we once made grand love."

"Studying the walls won't bring it back. You won't solve anything that way. The only thing you're going to find in a bottle of whiskey is the cork of another."

"You always *were* sharp with your tongue, Kate."

"You didn't do too badly yourself."

"And now, alas, my tongue has been lathered by too many whiskeys."

"You said it."

"I did."

"You could pull yourself out of it. It's not pleasant seeing you like this, and I can no longer help you."

"No, you're a married woman."

"Yes, Leon, that's right. I still feel a great deal of concern for you, but it stretches no farther than that. I came here to see you—because I still happen to care for you—but I also came to find out what you wanted, and you still haven't told me."

"Don't rush me, Kate. Please."

"I'm simply trying to keep you awake."

"I'm awake. I'm simply dead on my feet . . . my new natural condition."

Kate felt herself breaking, her defenses washed away, pouring out on the tide of a compassion that sprang from old memories. She had truly cared for Leon—not with love, but with deep affection—and now, hearing his words, seeing the frailty of his pose, she understood that her concern, now most painfully resurrected, was based on the emotions they had shared and could never forget. She was not betraying Moshe or holding on to Leon's love, but rather recognizing what could not be denied, affirming her genuine concern over what he was suffering.

"I received your letter," she said.

"I very vaguely remember writing it."

"It was a very eloquent letter, very passionate, filled with wonder and despair."

"Really?"

"You remember. Don't pretend that you've forgotten. The Arabs filled you with wonder, with the enchantment of their conviction, but you ended on a note of despair over what you had lost."

"I lost you."

"You didn't mean that. Perhaps that, but not that alone. More important than me, more destructive than your feelings for me, was the revelation that your lack of commitment had left you nothing to cling to. You envied the Arabs, Leon: their code of truth or untruth, their passionate belief in black and white, their refusal to recognize any gray area between, any emotion that left them in doubt or without the will to take action. Yes, Leon, you envied them, and felt smaller in their presence, convinced that in abdicating from commitment you had lost every value. All of that was in your letter—in the lines, not between them—it was there with the shame and the guilt that brought you back to this room."

"I loved you and lost you, Kate. It was no more than that. I was filled with self-pity, perhaps feeling humiliated, and swept along in the extraordinary fever of the *Hajj*, with the chanting and the singing and those thousands massed together, I naturally became somewhat melodramatic and put my hot pen to paper."

"Are you denying what you wrote?"

"I might as well have been drunk."

"Drunk, you couldn't have written as you did—and damn well you know it."

"Please, Kate, this is painful."

"You're inflicting the pain on yourself. You had the sense to recognize your own weakness, and now you're denying it."

Leon sighed and stood up, looking haunted in the baleful light, went to the table and refilled his glass and immediately had a long drink. He sighed again and licked his lips, scratched his chest with his free hand, then walked over to the bed and just stood there, his back turned toward her.

"My weakness?" he said. "My lack of commitment? What has commitment ever brought anyone except disillusionment? Politics, religion, art, and romantic love: all these things, changing constantly, are as ephemeral as a flickering candle. All men dream of tomorrow —the tomorrow that never comes—and from dreaming comes scheming, all the plans and ambitions, the pitiful belief in a future much improved on the present. How else would we survive it—life's constant deceit—and how else could we suffer our children and the crime of their birth? To be born is to be convicted, doomed to pain and certain death, and no belief or commitment of any kind can help us forget that. No, Kate, I don't believe—not in Joshua and not in Judgment Day—and so, lacking any belief, I can feel no commitment."

"You're lying to yourself, Leon, and trying to kill your true feelings. You committed yourself to me—let's say it: to love—and now, having lost me, you're trying to convince yourself it never happened. It won't work, Leon. You can't live with that sort of lie. The fact that there may be no tomorrow has nothing to do with it. Don't use life's disillusionments. We are born, and being born we must make choices, one way or the other. You made at least one choice—right or wrong, you chose me—and now, having lost me, you're reneging on even that small commitment. That's always been your problem: you could never accept loss or failure. It's not that you don't believe in anything, but that you can't stand to lose it."

"I refuse to accept that."

"You refuse to accept the truth."

"The truth is what gets you through the night."

"Is the truth in that whiskey?"

The remark made him visibly flinch, but he didn't turn around, remaining where he was near the bed, his back turned toward her. He was silent for a long time, breathing deeply and harshly, and when finally he spoke, his voice was filled with self-wounding bitterness.

"Yes, you're right," he said. "That's why I betrayed your trust. I couldn't stand to lose you, I was angry more than hurt, and like a child smashing his toys in frustration, I betrayed you to punish you. You didn't deserve that, and I don't feel proud of it, even less when I examine what I felt for you and come up with the truth. The truth is that I lied—to myself more than to you—that my love for you, though based on a very genuine affection, was at heart the cowardly hope that in committing myself to you, I might be able to pretend that I did at least have one thing to believe in. That isn't real love—it's self-deception and the abuse of love—and so, understanding that, having to finally face up to it, realizing that I couldn't even honestly commit myself to you, I had to accept that I was incapable of truly giving myself to anything, that I couldn't take a stand on any issue or trust my own feelings. No, Kate, I didn't love you—not as much as I pretended—and that fact in itself is an eloquent testimony to the self-deceptive cowardice of my nature. I was using you to hide from my sins, and that can't be called love."

"It's love of a kind, Leon."

"It's a halfway kind of love: it's a love that only goes so far, stopping short at commitment."

"Is that why you left your wife and children?"

"Yes, I think so. At the time I laid the blame on political disillusionment, but in truth what I was hiding was the knowledge that I just didn't care enough."

"Why don't you go back to them?"

"It was years ago, Kate. Even if I cared, if I now felt for them, it would be too late for that. In the event, such a gesture would be pointless, since I still can't feel anything."

He turned around to face her, grinning bleakly, without cynicism, then sighed and sat down on the bed, his eyes fixed on the floor. Kate wanted to help, to touch him and reassure him, but she sensed that he had gone beyond that and had to find his own way out. Staring at him, she thought him frail, a mere ghost of his former self, his skin sickly and his body undernourished, shoulders slumped in defeat. The glass of whiskey, almost empty, reflected light from the web of his fingers.

"When did you leave Damascus?" she asked him, gently changing the subject.

"About six weeks ago."

"You mean, you've been in this hotel for six weeks?"

"No, Kate, I've been here a week. I spent four weeks in Europe. I was writing about the riots and hysterical conversions, about the ritualistic murders by the new Devil worshipers, about the thousands at Stonehenge and other mystic sites who stand, in the silence of the night, and gaze up at the stars. Joshua is Jesus Christ. He is also the Devil. He is also an extraterrestrial whose presence here on Earth is a sign that the Super Race is coming to protect or enslave us. The Europe I knew has gone and will never return, all its values—its culture and history—made redundant by Joshua. Every religious organization and cult, good and evil, is flourishing; people are refusing to go to work and instead are demonstrating in the streets, chanting their demand to see Joshua the Christ; industry and commerce are grinding to a halt in the face of the new antimaterialist ethos; and the great new Christian Church, in the fifth week of its life, is under pressure from every government in Europe to do something about it."

"Their plan backfired," Kate said, "and then blew up in their faces. They united the Churches and hailed Joshua as Christ to broaden the base of Christianity and protect the religious freedom of Eastern Europe. Unfortunately, in their panic, they forgot to consider the possible effects, both personal and public, on society in general. Now Western Europe is breaking down, the Church is being held responsible, and ironically, considering why all this came about, the Soviets have still made no move against Eastern Europe."

"*Why* have the Soviets made no move, Kate? Have you thought about that?"

He raised his eyes and stared at her, not grinning, his gaze steady, the pale yellow light falling across him and shadowing his face. He was obviously very serious, very concerned, and that made her shake slightly.

"No," she said, "I hadn't thought about it. Why? Have you heard something new?"

He nodded, stood up and walked across to the window, raised his hand as if about to open the shutters, changed his mind, dropped his hand again. He stood there, looking down at the table, swirling the drink in his glass.

"I owe you one," he said. "In my anger I betrayed your trust. If I believe in nothing else, I believe in personal trust, so perhaps, in giving you this, I'll make amends, both to you and to Moshe. I could not, in all honesty and with the best will in the world, give the information personally to your husband—so, I'm going to tell you what I learned, whether or not it is helpful."

He looked at her very briefly, with a pained, tentative longing, then stared down at the table again, speaking quietly and evenly.

"I learned this from a disillusioned Vatican source," he said, "and knowing him well, I can guarantee that he speaks the truth. The Soviets have made no move because the pope has agreed to a new deal that will get him off the hot seat and hopefully solve all his problems. Appalled by the unexpected results of his machinations with the World Council of Churches—including his confirmation of Joshua as the Christian Christ—and torn between his desire to preserve the moral fabric of Western Europe and his desire to save his beloved Eastern Europe from the threatened Soviet suppression, the pope was left with no alternative but to offer the Soviets—unofficially and secretly—his second, and more shameful compromise."

Kate leaned forward and placed her elbows on the table and

covered her face with her hands. She stared down through her finger
seeing nothing, concentrating on Leon's words.

"Shortly after the unification of the two great Churches and the
proclaiming of Joshua as their Christ, the Soviets made it clear to th
Vatican that they would not be intimidated and that they intende
within a fortnight, to proceed with their plans for the obliteration
the Christian Church in Eastern Europe. The pope was given tw
weeks' grace to enable him either to dissolve the unification of th
Roman Catholic and Protestant Churches or to come up with som
suitable alternative. The Soviets, further, made it clear that they we
more concerned with the Church's official acceptance of Joshua
Christ—with its far-reaching implications—than they were about th
unification of the two Churches. Knowing this, and aware that th
unification of the Churches could not be amended, the pope had
choice but to accept from the Soviets their own, highly diabolic
suggestion: Joshua would be brought to Rome, interrogated by th
Sacred College of Cardinals, and then, irrespective of their individu
assessments, publicly be proclaimed as a false messiah and not t
Son of God, as formerly announced."

"I don't believe it," Kate murmured.

"Believe it," Leon replied.

She didn't want to believe it, but she knew it must be true, and s
felt a faint nausea and dread spreading out deep inside her. She look
up and saw Leon staring at her, his face weary and solemn.

"So," she said, "they not only save themselves, but wash th
hands of what happens in the Middle East: in renouncing Joshua th
return the whole issue to the Jews and the Muslims."

"That's correct," Leon said.

"Ben Eliezer won't stand for it. He'll understand what's going c
He'll simply ignore their communiqué—as he has all the others."

"He won't be able to," Leon replied. "They won't use a comm
niqué. This time it won't be secret—the pope needs a public dra
—so the request will be made, sometime next week, through a high
publicized worldwide broadcast."

Kate glanced around the room, at the semidarkness and squal
and suddenly felt very unreal, as if locked in a dream. She thought
Joshua and what he had become—to the individual and the world
general—and a fear as relentless as a tidal wave swept through her a
shook her. Men dreamed and schemed, and in their scheming wroug
destruction; and now Joshua, in his ambiguity, was the pivot arou

which those schemes moved. She felt that Joshua was in danger, that the tide was moving against him, and the fear, now like ice around her heart, seemed to close in to crush it. Looking up, she saw Leon looking down, a ghost standing in shadow.

"Why did you want to tell me this?" she asked. "Surely it can't, one way or the other, affect things in Israel."

"I think Moshe should know," he said, "and, in turn, Ben Eliezer, because the Americans are bound to view it as a victory for the Soviets in Europe. Viewing it thus, they will also view it as a deliberate attempt to isolate Joshua's influence to the Middle East. That brings it down to Jew and Muslim, both trying to claim Joshua, and it still leaves the question of who will finally have that dubious honor. The fate of the Middle East could be decided by a word from Joshua, and the Americans, viewing the Soviets across Israel, won't forget Joshua's presence. They will, indeed, view him as the innocent instrument of Soviet intentions."

"You mean they might want to use him before the Soviets attempt to do so."

"I mean that the Vatican, once allowing the pope to speak, will most likely have left them little choice—and Israel, whether she likes it or not, will have to deal with the Americans."

He picked up one of the bottles and poured himself another drink, his hand shaking and letting the whiskey splash all over the table. Kate watched him, feeling troubled, frightened for Joshua, sad for Leon, then she lowered her eyes, trying to shut it out, feeling sweat on her face.

"That's it," Leon said. "That's my favor. You can take your leave now."

She looked up at him, startled, aware of his sudden harshness, and watched him walking away from the window and going back to the bed. He placed his tumbler on the bedside cabinet, kicked his shoes off, and lay down, covering his closed eyes with his hands and taking very slow, deep breaths. The yellow light fell on his body, but his face was in shadow, and his voice, coming out of that darkness, was the voice of a broken man.

"You heard me, Kate: I said you could leave. You've no reason for staying here."

Kate stood up, feeling wounded, silently grieving for his suffering, but understanding that there was nothing she could do except leave him alone. She walked away from the table, the papers rustling

around her feet, and stopped when she came to the door, turning back
to look at him. He was still lying on the bed, his face hidden in the
shadows, the yellow light illuminating the disheveled shirt that fell off
his white body. He did not make a sound, and appeared not to be
breathing, but eventually his hand emerged to the light and reached
out for the glass of whiskey on the bedside cabinet.

"Open the shutters," Kate said. "Let some light and air in. Admit
the world and stop killing yourself with your pathetic self-pity."

His hand disappeared into the darkness, taking the glass of whiskey
with it, and she knew he was having a drink while still flat on his
back. Shaken, feeling lost, she placed her hand on her own stomach,
checked the life stirring within her, felt, if not joyous, at least
hopeful, and then walked from the room.

35

Looking out of the window of the roaring helicopter, shading his eyes to combat the dazzling brilliance of the sun, Moshe saw the wastelands of the Sinai Desert moving slowly far below and giving way to the incandescent blue of the Gulf of Suez. He looked down for some time, feeling himself drawn toward it, as if, were he not strapped into his seat, he would have thrown himself out. He loved the emptiness of the desert, was seduced by its dangerous beauty, and now, feeling trapped, hemmed in by the mounting pressures, he wanted to be standing on his own feet on that hot, burning sand.

"So they know," Ben Eliezer said.

"Yes, Shlomo, they know. When I rang them to give them Leon's news, they said they'd just picked it up."

"Then that's what they want to talk about."

"I would think so. Almost certainly."

"We're in for a very interesting talk, but it may not be pleasant."

Pleasant it would not be, as Moshe well understood, but as he looked down at the Gulf of Suez, at that ribbon of water dividing the deserts, he was thinking of Kate's meeting with Leon and feeling resentful. His resentment was ridiculous, almost childishly stupid, and when he thought of Kate, pregnant and proud, he was ashamed of himself. She had been sad when she returned from seeing him, obviously shocked by his appearance, and in telling him how Leon had changed, she had not minced her words. Moshe had felt better then, less suspicious of her motives, but still, like acid lying in the stomach, a faint resentment remained.

The helicopter was dropping lower, casting its shadow on the blue water, and then the edge of the Eastern Desert, looking white through the shimmering haze, moved forward as the Gulf slid past below and gradually disappeared. Moshe looked down at Egypt, at the Arab Republic, saw the rippling sand dunes sweeping away to low

mountains, a single road snaking like a black line through the
burnished lowlands. The mountains moved forward quickly, becoming higher, three-dimensional, then they suddenly spread around the
helicopter and blocked out the sky. The helicopter started climbing,
moving up the face of the cliffs, then flew over the summit, across the
parched, barren rock, until the desert opened out at the other side and
seemed to go on forever.

"There they are," Ben Eliezer said.

The American tanks were on the desert, spread out in long lines,
forming a protective flank along a makeshift airstrip on which the
aircraft sat in neat rows, their wings reflecting the sun. There were
also trucks and jeeps, gun emplacements and supply dumps, and the
hundreds of tents, forming white, linear patterns, housed the thousands of men who for now resembled black ants moving in columns
through a pool of liquid gold.

"Yankee Doodle Dandy," Ben Eliezer said blandly. "They sure
know how to put on a show and make an impression."

The remark didn't amuse Moshe who, looking down, felt nothing
but the dryness in his throat and a strange, fearful nausea. What he
saw down there was power, military might and its need to strike, and
as the helicopter dropped lower and the tanks seemed to spread out
farther, he thought of the Russians in Syria and Jordan and understood
the position.

"They mean business," he said.

"Most assuredly," Ben Eliezer replied.

"These people aren't here to protect anyone: they're here to take
over."

The helicopter dropped lower, roaring louder and rocking slightly,
coming down above the tanks, then heading west across the tents,
starting to whip the sand up as the land spread out around it and
eventually hovering just above the airstrip, beyond the last row of
aircraft. There were soldiers around the landing pad, their weapons at
the ready, and behind them, in two well-guarded jeeps, were the
high-ranking officers. The sand was blowing across them, swirling
away above their heads, as the helicopter dropped lower, bobbed up
and down a little, and finally, with a mild, thudding sound, settled
down on the ground.

Moshe unclipped his seat belt as the rotors slowed down, stood up
as they petered into silence and came to a halt. He glanced through the
window and saw some soldiers breaking ranks, moving apart to let the

two jeeps drive forward and stop nearer the landing pad. The door of the helicopter was opened, making a shrill, grinding sound, then the ladder, clanging brutally, was dropped down through the in-pouring sunlight. Ben Eliezer sighed wearily, his moon-shaped face composing itself, then he moved toward the door and reached out to take hold of the engineer. The young man responded, helping Ben Eliezer down the ladder, then Moshe followed him down and placed his feet on the soil of Egypt, turning around to see the Americans walking toward him through the shimmering heat haze.

General Kernan was in the lead, stretching his hand out to Ben Eliezer, flanked by two lieutenants and another two men wearing plainclothes. The general shook hands with Ben Eliezer, then did the same with Moshe, nodding his head and offering a formal smile that did not reach his eyes. The other officers were introduced, Lieutenants Green and Schonfield, then the two men in plainclothes, Cohn and Thompson, who belonged to the CIA. The general apologized for the lack of formality, pointing out that it was Arab territory, making a joke about the delicacy of the situation as they walked to the jeeps. Moshe and Ben Eliezer shared the first jeep with the general, and they were driven along the airstrip, past the rows of gleaming planes, turned left past jeeps and trucks and the ominous gun emplacements, the jeep churning up the sand and hurling it across the countless soldiers before stopping at a particularly large tent at the hub of the camp.

"Home sweet home," the general said, climbing down and breathing too harshly. "It's not quite the Pentagon, Shlomo, but at least there are chairs inside."

The tent was cool and spacious, the chairs surrounding a large table, lamps wired to generators shedding light on the numerous papers that lay between the ashtrays and glasses and field telephones. The general indicated two chairs and Moshe sat down beside Ben Eliezer as the other four men entered the tent and spread themselves around the table. The general, facing Moshe and Ben Eliezer, mopped his brow with a kerchief.

"A drink, Shlomo?"

"Just water."

"Moshe?"

"I'll have a beer."

"Let's settle for cans of beer and jugs of water. Okay, Corporal, get to it."

The corporal did as he was told, using the assistance of two privates, setting the water and beer on the table before being dismissed. When he had gone, they all helped themselves to drinks —only Moshe and the CIA men drinking beer, the others settling for water. Their thirst slaked, they prepared themselves, lighting cigarettes, studying each other, then General Kernan leaned across the table, his eyes fixed on Ben Eliezer.

"This talk is off the record, Shlomo."

"I *had* assumed so, Ralph."

"If this leaks out, we'll make a firm denial."

"We'll do exactly the same, Ralph."

The general nodded and sat back, mopped his forehead with the kerchief, glanced uneasily at the two men in plainclothes, and then leaned forward again. He had gray hair, a broken nose, a brick-shaped chin; and his eyes, slightly baggy, webbed with lines, were opaque with cold logic.

"Our information confirms what you picked up from that lush," he said. "The Vatican is going to deal with the Soviets to keep them off Eastern Europe."

"Quite," Ben Eliezer said.

"I don't think I have to emphasize how we feel about this projected move except to say that it's a clear defeat for the Vatican in the face of Soviet aggression."

"But the Vatican is stepping down to *prevent* Soviet suppression in Eastern Europe."

"Right," General Kernan said. "Which is in itself a clear victory for the Soviets, weakening the authority of the Vatican and strengthening that of the Soviets throughout Eastern Europe—by implication without the use of physical force."

"I fail to see how the Soviets, in agreeing to keep their hands *off* the Church in Eastern Europe, will actually *strengthen* their authority in that area."

"Don't act naive with me, Shlomo. You know as well as I do that in forcing the Church to back down, the Soviets will have won an enormous psychological victory and reaffirmed—to the world and the people of Eastern Europe in particular—that their control, in political *and* religious matters, is still absolute. All the Vatican has done, Shlomo, is walk right into the Soviet trap: giving them the opportunity to increase their authority throughout Eastern Europe without the embarrassment of having to use physical force—and willy-nilly demonstrating to Western Europe that even the Vatican, with all its power and prestige, can't stand up to the Kremlin."

"I think you're reading too much into this," Ben Eliezer said.

"We know how the Soviet mind thinks," the general replied, "and if they think they've scored a victory, that's enough—they'll try it again."

"You mean here, in the Middle East?"

"Precisely."

"Ah," Ben Eliezer said. He folded his hands on the table, turned them over, examined his fingernails, furrowed his brow as if trying to think, his face impossibly innocent.

"It is our belief," the general continued, "that the Soviets, having won so easily over Eastern Europe, will now try to exploit their moral victory by taking similar steps in this area. It is also our belief that part of their strategy concerning the Vatican was to confine your man Joshua to the Middle East and the Jewish-Arab claims for him."

"And how would that benefit the Soviets?"

"They will wait until Joshua leans one way or the other—and then move accordingly."

"I don't think I understand, Ralph."

The general glanced at the men around him, clearly exasperated by Ben Eliezer's coyness; then one of the men in plainclothes leaned forward, his face flat as a stone.

"I think you know what we're talking about," he said. "The mystery of this Joshua—whoever he is—has stirred the imagination of the whole world, causing chaos in Europe and America, inflaming the Middle East situation, and encouraging the Soviets and Chinese, and the predominantly Hindu and Buddhist countries, to accuse us of having used him to manufacture the recent Arab-Israeli war."

"A war you certainly appreciated," Moshe said, unable to let the point pass.

"We are here to protect our interests in the Middle East," the general said, "and to ensure that Israel doesn't drop an atomic weapon on the heads of our Arab friends. We are here, in short, to prevent a Third World War."

The statement was marginally true, but not nearly true enough, and Moshe felt the acid of rage in his stomach, the flush on his cheeks.

"We did not manufacture the recent war," the man in plainclothes said. "It came about because of your man Joshua—and that's my whole point."

"What point?" Ben Eliezer asked.

"The point, Mr. Prime Minister, is that the man known as Joshua has become a danger to everyone with interests in this sensitive area —not only we Americans, but the Soviets, the Muslims, and you Jews. Already he has led to one war; he could soon lead to another. The Arabs think of him as their Mahdi, most Jews think of him as their Messiah, and now, with the Vatican about to disown him completely, the claims upon him are about to be narrowed down to the Jews and Arabs alone. We happen to believe that the Soviets, in forcing the Vatican to disown Joshua, have deliberately returned the problem to where it started: right here in the Middle East."

"Why?"

"The Soviets are now massed along the borders of Jordan and Syria, their tanks and guns facing Israel. By reducing the question of who or what Joshua is to a running conflict between the Jews and Arabs alone, they are hoping that the conflict will erupt into another war, which would—due to your former threat to use your atomic weapons—give them an excuse for crossing the border into Israel as a so-called peace-keeping force. Such an action would be taken without prior warning—and once in, as it was with Afghanistan, you won't get them out."

Ben Eliezer looked up, spreading his hands on the table, his bland eyes scanning everyone in turn, his moon face totally blank.

"I don't think the Soviets will do that," he said, "unless Joshua takes a definite stand, one way or the other."

"Right," the general replied. "If Joshua claims to be the Messiah, the Jews will attempt to inaugurate the pure Zionist State, the remaining Arabs in Israel will all be thrown out, and the Arab world, understandably incensed, will retaliate with war. If, on the other hand, Joshua claims to be the Mahdi, then the Arabs will be impelled to inaugurate the sovereignty of Islam and, again, will embark on a war against Israel. Either way, sooner or later, something will break —and neither we nor the Soviets can let that happen."

"Our experience convinces us that Joshua will take no side, and that events, at least as you envisage them, simply will not materialize."

"That's the whole point," said the man in plainclothes. "You err in thinking that Joshua would have to pick one side over the other in order to start another war; unfortunately the facts seem to suggest otherwise: Joshua's presence in Israel—just his presence—is enough and current events, all springing out of his presence, are already leading to war."

Moshe caught Ben Eliezer's glance, the merest flicker of movement, and knew that he was less bland than he looked—and was in fact terribly worried. Moshe likewise was worried, but his anxiety was tinged with anger, a cold fury that the Americans and Soviets, in the arrogance of their might, could maneuver through such squalid intrigues to settle the fate of the Holy Land.

"I admit to bewilderment," Ben Eliezer said, "but do, pray, continue."

The other man in plainclothes, the one known as Cohn, lit a cigarette, inhaled, blew the smoke out, and then leaned forward slightly.

"We are talking about your own zealots," he said, "and their obsession with Joshua." He stared hard at Ben Eliezer but received no visible response, glanced briefly at General Kernan and his two lieutenants, and then shrugged his shoulders. "Okay," he continued, "I'll spell it out for you: Your zealots, believing in Joshua as the Jewish Messiah, are determined to inaugurate the Zionist State and throw out all the Arabs. They always wanted that, of course, but their intention didn't bother us, since they were at most a minority group without any great influence. However now, with the advent of Joshua, they've picked up some powerful supporters and can no longer be safely ignored. They want to oust your government and install their own Cabinet—a Cabinet consisting of hand-picked, fanatical Zionists—and, having done that, they intend making good all their promises."

"They will not get me out," Ben Eliezer said.

"I'm sorry, Mr. Prime Minister, but I'm afraid that they will. Our intelligence reports reveal that the widespread belief in Joshua as the Jewish Messiah will ensure that eighty percent of your population will vote for the zealots. It is also worth noting, if painful to accept, that the Soviets are supporting the zealots with secret supplies of arms and money—because they know that when the zealots get in, they'll have the war that they need."

Ben Eliezer, for the first time, failed to maintain his bland facade, his cheeks flushing, his eyes widening, his fist clenching on the table, as the shock of what he was hearing cut through him and destroyed his defenses. It only lasted a brief moment, perhaps one or two seconds, but it was enough to make Moshe understand just how badly he felt.

Moshe was feeling a similar shock, as if a trapdoor had been opened beneath him, as if he were falling down through a darkness that would never show light again. The world was closing in on Israel, wanting to bury it to gain the Middle East, and Moshe, in his fear and despair, had to fight to control himself.

"Presuming that what you say is true," Moshe said, "what are you after?"

Cohn glanced at the other agent, nervously seeking his approval, received a nod, and returned his gaze to the front, his eyes roaming back and forth between Moshe and Ben Eliezer as if he wasn't sure whom he was addressing. His voice, like the information he was conveying, had a funereal ring.

"Please try to bear in mind that whatever you desire, the zealots, as things stand at the moment, will soon be running your country. If that is allowed to happen, there will be another Arab-Israeli war, and the zealots, already supported by the Soviets, will turn to them for aid. The Soviets will agree to help them, but the price will be high —notably the inclusion of their 'advisers' in the reconstructed Israeli government and the acceptance of a long-term Soviet peace-keeping army in Israel. This will effectively give the Soviets dominance over the Middle East, with their military forces controlling Syria, Jordan and, surreptitiously, Israel. We cannot, and will not, allow such a disaster to happen."

"So," Moshe said, "you want to get in first."

"Right," Cohn replied, looking even more uneasy. "No matter how distasteful to you, you simply have to accept the fact that sooner or later you're going to have to make a deal with either the Soviets or us. If you decide to do nothing, the zealots will deal with the Soviets anyway—and the fate of Israel will be out of your hands. If, on the other hand, you accept our proposal, we can guarantee the survival of your present government and the freedom of Israel."

"Wonderful," Ben Eliezer said quietly. "Now just what are you after?"

General Kernan coughed into his fist and then studied his hands at length, while Cohn, glancing again at his partner, laid his cards on the table.

"We have two concerns," he said, now staring directly at Ben Eliezer. "The first is to abort the Soviets' expected triumph in Eastern Europe, and the second is to find a final solution to the problem of Palestine."

"Israel," Ben Eliezer said.

"Sorry," Cohn replied.

"And by a final solution, you also mean a formal agreement concerning Soviet and American containment of this area."

"I'm afraid so," Cohn said.

Moshe looked down at the table, feeling despair and increasing anger, silently cursing his fellow Jews for their disparate religious passions and their inability to live with one another. Israel, which had once been divided between Jew and Arab, was now, more ironically, divided because of Jew fighting Jew. It was meat for the Americans and Soviets, a dinner set down on a plate, and the Jews, their heads bowed, their thoughts focused on Judgment Day, would still be worshiping when their country was gobbled up by those more realistic. The thought of it made Moshe sick to his stomach, but it also stirred rage.

"So," he said bitterly, finally unable to conceal it, looking directly at the man in plainclothes, the American called Cohn, "what's your proposal?"

"Our proposal," Cohn replied, turning his eyes toward Ben Eliezer, "is that Joshua be removed from the scene before he reaches the Vatican."

There was a very long silence, letting the shock settle down, and then Moshe, coughing into his fist, heard the sound of his own voice:

"Are you talking about kidnaping?" he asked.

"Termination," Cohn said.

Moshe stared at Ben Eliezer, but his stare was not returned; Ben Eliezer was gazing down at the table, his head in his hands. He stayed like that for some time, not moving, perfectly silent, but eventually, with an audible sigh, he looked up once more. His eyes roamed from Moshe to General Kernan and his two lieutenants, then finally came to rest on the CIA men, particularly Cohn. He kept looking at Cohn for a long time, not saying a word, until Cohn, obviously getting the message, finished off his proposal.

"To remove Joshua from the scene," he said, "before the pope can make his request will, in preventing the pope from publicly disowning him, ensure that the authority of the Church is not undermined by the Soviets—and, incidentally, since the Vatican won't be responsible, leave the Soviets with no excuse for suppressing the Church in Eastern Europe."

"So," Ben Eliezer said, "you deny the Soviets that particular

victory, and, in making it impossible for the Church to deny Joshua
ensure that the conflict about his nature is not confined to the Middle
East."

"That, as far as it goes, is correct."

"And the rest?"

"Please remember, Mr. Prime Minister, that if you reject the
proposal, the zealots will take over Israel, there will be an Arab
Israeli war, and the Soviets will end up controlling Jerusalem."

"Please, Mr. Cohn, get it over with."

Cohn sat up very straight in his chair and tried to keep his gaze
steady. "Our proposal is that Joshua be terminated, by pistol shot, in
some area where his body is certain to be found. Once his body is
discovered, the news of his murder will spread like wildfire, with the
Jews blaming the Arabs and the Arabs blaming the Jews for the crime.
The shock and anger engendered by this—particularly throughout the
whole Arab world—will give us an excuse for embarking on further
preventive action right here in the Arab Republic, but also entailing
base from which to expand our military presence into the Arab oil
states of the Persian Gulf. Having done that, we will be in a stronger
strategic position when it comes to negotiating with the Soviets as we
orchestrate, with them, final settlement of the Arab-Israeli and
Israeli-Palestinian problem. As part of that settlement—and negotiating from a position of strength—we will offer the return of the
Egyptian, Jordanian, and Syrian territories, but insist, in return, for
the fulfillment of the Israelis' dream of statehood, and ensure, during
this process, that certain Israeli laws be amended to reduce to the
barest minimum level the political freedoms of the zealots. Your own
Cabinet, along with Israel's freedom, will thus be ensured—and the
United States will be able to guarantee the security of your borders
from a position of much greater military strength."

"The United States, Mr. Cohn, will be able to guarantee the
security of our borders because they will, to all intents and purposes,
rule most of the Arab world."

"Better the United States than the Soviets, as I'm sure you'll
agree."

Moshe looked at Ben Eliezer and saw the flickering of his eyes, his
cheeks flushed as he tried to control his emotions over what he was
hearing. For Moshe it was a nightmare, something chilling and final,
God's punishment for an Israel divided within itself and torn by the
passionate religious differences that made Jew fight Jew. He glanced

quickly around the table, seeing the faces of normal men, and wondering, with a suffocating bitterness, at their suspicion and greed. He wanted to hate them, but failed, since their duplicities were not uncommon, since they were in fact endemic to Israel and its religious dissension. As for himself, he was no better—and now he realized it —because even as he accepted the horror of what was being proposed, he knew that he was going to agree because there was no other choice.

Ben Eliezer was staring at him, his moon-shaped face haggard, and Moshe knew, from the flickering of his eyes, that they were thinking the same thing.

"Let's assume for the moment that we agree," Ben Eliezer said. "If, as you propose, we are to assassinate Joshua, who's to be responsible for pulling the trigger? I can't think, offhand, of one Jew or Arab who'd be willing to put a gun to Joshua's head."

"Not at the moment," Cohn replied. "But it can be arranged."

He nodded at his partner, the other plain-clothed man called Schonfield, and the latter, putting on a pair of spectacles, leaned over his papers.

"Obviously," he said, "the United States cannot be involved in this, so one of our own men is out of the question. The assassination, therefore, will have to be arranged by yourselves and carried out by one of your Israelis. Assuming that this would be the case, we then reasoned that in the unlikely event of the assassin's identity being uncovered, a religious zealot with a grudge would make it easier, diplomatically speaking, to absolve the Jews in general of the crime. Ideally, then, what we were after was a military-trained religious zealot who would either keep his silence after the assassination or could be dispensed with shortly after the event."

"A religious zealot," Moshe said, hardly believing his own calmness, "would be the last person to consent to murdering Joshua, the so-called Jewish Messiah."

"A fanatic is a fanatic," Schonfield replied levelly, "and fanaticism in a human being simply makes him into an instrument that can be turned, if handled with care, in any direction."

"You have someone in mind?"

"Yes, Major General, we have. He's Lieutenant Paul Frankel. Lieutenant Frankel is a zealot, he's been supporting the overthrow of your government, he's passionately devoted to Joshua, whom he thinks is the Messiah, and we think that if properly handled, he will turn on his Master."

Moshe took a deep breath, feeling as if he had just been slapped, and then glanced across at Ben Eliezer to check his reaction. The prime minister, no longer able to feign indifference, was staring at Schonfield with wide eyes. Moshe, disoriented, wanting to get up and walk out, expelled his breath and gazed down at the table, thinking of Paul with pure hatred.

"Paul Frankel," he said, "may well have supported the zealots, but he certainly wouldn't support them to the extent of overthrowing this government."

"On the contrary," Schonfield said, not looking up from his papers, "Lieutenant Frankel is something other than a run-of-the-mill zealot: he believes that Joshua is the Messiah, that Judgment Day is at hand, and that his duty as a Jew—above all other moral commitments—is to ensure, at any cost, that the present government be overthrown and a new, purely ecclesiastical Cabinet installed in the Knesset. Lieutenant Frankel, therefore, did not only support the zealots: he arranged for the bombing of the Mea She'arim quarter to kill one of his religious rivals; he passed secret information to foreign journalists like Leon Halcomb; and finally, most important, in order to incite the Arabs and weaken the credibility of your government—thus giving the zealots their first chance to replace you—he personally revealed the secret of Joshua to a worldwide syndication agency. It was not, we can assure you, Leon Halcomb, but Lieutenant Frankel of Shin Beth."

Moshe stared in a daze at Schonfield, not believing what he was hearing, believing it and reeling with the shock and a pure, violent hatred. He stared at Ben Eliezer, at General Kernan and his two lieutenants, then forced himself to concentrate on Schonfield, who was finally raising his head. Schonfield removed his glasses, wiped them distractedly with a paper napkin, placed them gently on the papers before him, and then spoke very calmly.

"Lieutenant Frankel is a fanatic, a man of immense frustration, and if we can turn that frustration in another direction, we can make it work for us. Fanatically devoted to Joshua, he will be just as fanatically against him if you convince him that Joshua, during his meeting with Rashid Idriss, confirmed that he was the Mahdi of the Muslims and said he would make it public knowledge by taking up residence in Mecca and spreading the gospel of Muhammad. Fanatically devoted to Zionism, he will do as you wish if you point out that

Joshua, the Mahdi, if allowed to stay alive, will incite the Arab world to a Holy War designed to get back Jerusalem. Finally, Lieutenant Frankel, who exposed Joshua to the world, will—if informed how his crime could benefit the Arabs and humiliate his fellow zealots —perform his military duty and keep his mouth shut as long as you maintain your silence about his crime. Given these facts, I think we can all safely assume that Lieutenant Frankel will assassinate Joshua —Messiah or Mahdi."

Moshe stared at Ben Eliezer and saw him staring back blindly, his moon-shaped face haggard and old, his eyes bigger than normal. Moshe didn't know what to say and could scarcely formulate his thoughts, his head swimming with images of Leon and Kate and Paul Frankel and Joshua, of the web of love and pain and betrayal that now bound them together. He felt lost and ineffectual, totally drained and empty, and then, out of the silence of the wilderness inside him, he heard the sound of his own much altered voice, whispering rather than talking:

"So be it," he said.

36

Paul entered the office tentatively, his lips aggressive, his brown eye
cool, obviously aware that the request to see him was not routine an
wondering what it could mean. He closed the door carefully behin
him, keeping his back to it, facing the desk, looked at Moshe and Be
Eliezer in turn, and then walked toward them. Ben Eliezer nodded a
the chair, saying nothing, his face blank, and Paul sat down, foldin
his hands in his lap and keeping his uniformed spine straight. Be
Eliezer was behind the desk and Moshe was standing in the corne
near him, his arms folded, his eyes sliding across Paul and the
surveying the room. Paul lowered his head and coughed into his righ
hand, and then raised his eyes again.

"I'm sorry to have brought you over here at such short notice," Be
Eliezer said, "but the matter is particularly important and urgent." H
looked steadily at Paul, his hands cupped beneath his chin, but Pau
merely blinking and licking his lips, made no reply. "Before gettin
on to the main subject," Ben Eliezer continued, "I would just like t
say that I am extremely unhappy about your public support of th
Zealots, including Kash and Gush Emunim."

"I am a Zionist," Paul replied, raising his chin and looking defian
"Such a belief is not forbidden in Israel—though you may disapprov
of it."

"I disapprove," Ben Eliezer said, "and would be a liar to sa
otherwise, but it has not been my practice to try to suppress the view
of the Zionists. The point in your case, Lieutenant Frankel, is that yo
are a member of the defense forces, and as such are committed t
serving the government in office, keeping your political differences t
yourself except when conversing with friends or at the polling booth."

"I have only gone against this government by expressing m
religious views and publicly supporting those groups who share thos
views."

"Those groups who share your views are very active politically, and your support of them must therefore be interpreted as political activity."

"You cannot suppress free speech."

"Your activities have gone beyond that."

"This government has betrayed Zionism and does not deserve office; only the zealots, as you call them, have the will and belief to lead Israel away from compromise and into pure Zionism, undiluted by your diplomatic considerations and opportunistic internationalism."

"Israel cannot stand alone or ignore events outside its borders; it has to deal with the international community and make certain compromises. Your friends, with their religious ideals, are politically naive."

"You are betraying Judaism."

"This is the twentieth century, Paul. We cannot turn our back on the rest of the world and hope to survive."

"Your kind of compromise is blasphemous. The Holy Land belongs to the Jews. The Muslims and Christians have no place here and must be removed. That time is now coming. The Messiah has arrived. His presence here on Earth is a sign that the sovereignty of Judaism is at hand. The Messiah is the sign, but under him we are the instruments: we must inaugurate the pure Zionist State and await Judgment Day."

Moshe studied Paul's eyes, very brown, very bright, and understood that the intensity of his belief had indeed made him fanatical. He belonged to the Mea She'arim quarter, to the gun emplacements of the West Bank, and sooner or later, if left alone, he would unleash his fury. The CIA man was right—that fanaticism had to be directed elsewhere—but Moshe, in the knowledge of what was happening, still felt sick to his soul. He glanced at Ben Eliezer and wondered if he felt the same, but the prime minister, with his chin in his hands, was showing nothing at all.

"Can I take it," he said, keeping his eyes fixed on Paul, "that you are refusing to cooperate with us by keeping your views to yourself?"

"I will not give up my freedom of speech or change the company I keep."

His specific crimes had not been mentioned, and would not be until necessary; for the moment Ben Eliezer's only intention was to lead him gently to Joshua.

"Your own beliefs," Ben Eliezer said, "and the beliefs of your friends, are clearly based on the assumption that Joshua is the Jewish Messiah."

"Yes," Paul said, "of course."

"But Joshua has never made such a claim."

"Nor did he deny it."

"A lack of denial is hardly confirmation, as I'm sure you would agree."

"He does not have to know who he is to be what he is. I have listened to his words and been witness to his miracles, and I know, from what I have seen and heard, that he is the Messiah. Do you need to know more? Is your lack of faith so gross? He came down from the Mount of Olives the night the Golden Gate was opened, he is a man of flesh and blood, but one with supernatural abilities, and his ignorance about himself has not blinded him to the knowledge that he is here on the Earth for some purpose, which must be the Redemption. As surely as the Golden Gate has been opened, he *is* the Messiah."

Ben Eliezer had what he wanted—confirmation of Paul's fanaticism—and he leaned back in his chair, removing his hands from his chin and letting them rest on the desk. He stared flatly at Paul, revealing nothing of his thoughts, and Paul finally looked away and glanced at Moshe, his dark eyes more confused. Moshe felt very uncomfortable, very guilty, almost criminal, understanding that what he was involved in was, if necessary, undoubtedly sordid. As a soldier Moshe was used to making unpleasant decisions, hardened to the necessity of political and military intrigue, conditioned in the acceptance of sacrifice as a means to an end, yet now he felt vile, his palms sweaty, his stomach churning, convinced that what they were doing was pure treachery and murder, and that his own hands, which would soon be dipped in blood, would never be clean again. When Paul looked up at him, he did not avoid his gaze—but he was glad when Paul returned his attention to the calm Ben Eliezer.

"To support the Zionists is one thing," Ben Eliezer said quietly, "but to proclaim Joshua as the Messiah—irrespective of the government's official silence—is something we simply cannot tolerate. It was bad enough before, but will now be more embarrassing, since Joshua will personally soon be proclaiming that he is not the Messiah but is, indeed, the Mahdi of the Muslims."

Paul visibly stiffened, his eyes widening in disbelief, then the hands that had been folded in his lap came apart and moved restlessly.

"That is nonsense," he said.

"I wish it were," Ben Eliezer replied, "because it means bad trouble for us—but unfortunately it is absolutely true and we just have to face it."

Paul glanced up at Moshe and then back to Ben Eliezer, his hands opening and closing on his thighs as if wanting to grab something.

"I don't believe you," he said, his voice different, sounding strained, emerging from his lips with reluctance and dying slowly in silence.

Ben Eliezer broke the silence: "Don't accuse me of lying," he said, his face convincingly angry and offended, his fists visibly clenching. "As you know, Rashid Idriss had a meeting with Joshua—here, in this very office, a few weeks ago. Rashid came at Joshua's request, because Joshua wanted to speak to him, and when they met, in my presence, the first thing Joshua said was that he was the Mahdi and needed Rashid's protection when he traveled to Mecca. That's what the meeting was for—to arrange Joshua's journey to Mecca—and once there, as he explained, he was going to take up residence and thereafter preach the gospel of Muhammad. He will be making that journey within the next few days—and once he does, the messiah theory will be finished and the Muslims will own him."

"*No!*" Paul exclaimed, the word sounding like a pistol shot, a denial and a cry of fear at once, whipping Moshe with its violence. "It's not true! *It's not true!*"

Ben Eliezer stood up quickly, seizing the drama of the moment, hurried around his desk, grabbed Paul's shoulder, and then shook him vigorously.

"Damn you," he hissed, "it's true! The man is going to Mecca! He is going to proclaim himself as the Mahdi and gain the allegiance of the Arabs! Do you want to check it out? Then go see him—right this minute. Right this minute, he is in the El-Aqsa mosque with Rashid Idriss! Do you think the Jewish Messiah would worship Muhammad? Go and ask him, Paul! *Ask him!*"

He actually bawled the last words, his face very close to Paul's, and then shook him one last time and let him go and walked back around his desk. Sighing loudly, despairingly, shaking his head in a weary gesture, he sank down into his chair and then leaned forward, keeping his gaze fixed on Paul. Paul was sitting up very straight, his fingers digging into his thighs, his brown eyes very large, roaming back and forth restlessly, as if in this movement he might find something hopeful to cling to. Eventually, with a shudder, after trying to speak and failing, he wiped his lips with an agitated hand and managed to get the words out:

"It is true?"

"It is true. Right now Joshua is with Rashid. He has been staying with Rashid for quite a few days now, and soon he will go with him to Mecca to spread the gospel of Islam."

What Ben Eliezer said was true—or at least based on truth—since Joshua, currently staying with some Arabs in Silwan, had been visited that very day by Rashid Idriss. However there the truth ended and the fiction began: Joshua alternated between Jew and Muslim, between Muslim and Christian; but he listened more than talked, and, when he talked, couched his words in a studied ambiguity that avoided commitment. If he had been seen in the El-Aqsa mosque, he had also been seen at the Wailing Wall; and his conversations with Rashid, all instigated by Rashid, had so far produced no clarification of what Joshua might be. Ben Eliezer had lied with skill, basing his lies on certain facts, and now Paul, if he checked out those facts, could think only the worst.

"Do you know what this means?" Ben Eliezer now said dramatically. "If Joshua goes to Mecca to be hailed as the Mahdi, the Arabs will be compelled to go to war and recapture Jerusalem." He paused to let his words sink in, not removing his eyes from Paul, not flinching at the sight of Paul's anguish and shocked disbelief. "Do you understand?" he continued. "We simply cannot let that happen. If Joshua proclaims himself as the Mahdi, he will unite the whole Arab world, and the Arabs, once united, will sweep in on Israel from all sides." Paul was now leaning forward, his elbows resting on his knees, his hands clasped and his head hanging down, his body wracked by slight spasms. "We will be surrounded," Ben Eliezer said. "Every Arab state will attack us. From Saudi Arabia, from Jordan and Syria, from Lebanon and the Arab Republic of Egypt—they will all want Jerusalem." Paul choked back a sob and wiped his eyes with one hand, while Ben Eliezer, histrionically intense, leaned over his desk. "Jerusalem will fall," he said. "We will not be able to prevent it. Inflamed with thoughts of the Mahdi and Judgment Day, the Arabs will wipe out the Jews."

"The Soviets won't allow it!" Paul exclaimed.

"I'm afraid they will," Ben Eliezer said. "Informed by Rashid of Joshua's statement, they are already negotiating the return of the Arab territories and their share in the future division of Israel."

"They can't do this! We agreed!"

"We know about your agreement, Paul. Unfortunately, at least for you, that agreement only had relevance while the Jews could claim Joshua as their messiah. Now, with Joshua turning to the Arabs, the Soviets must deal with the Arabs."

Paul raised his head again, his brown eyes large and glittering, as if they were no longer looking outward, but inward to himself. The thought of the Messiah had given him new life, illuminating the dream of Zion, and now, as Moshe could see in every line of his face, in the anguish of his expression, he was seeing that dream fall apart, his illusions in pieces. Moshe disliked him but sympathized; indeed, he felt a terrible shame: for Ben Eliezer, for himself, for the Americans and the Israelis, and, most of all, for the despicable thing they were planning in order, rightly or wrongly, to preserve the precious freedom of Israel. At that moment he despised himself, wanting to find some other way, but he knew, even as he heard Ben Eliezer's voice, that he would follow it through.

"This cannot happen," Ben Eliezer said. "We simply cannot let it happen. If Joshua is allowed to go to Mecca, if he proclaims himself as the Mahdi, then nothing on earth will stop the Arabs from overrunning Jerusalem. When that happens, neither the zealots nor my own Cabinet will be able to stop the dismantling of Israel: Jerusalem will become the new Mecca, and Islam will reign."

The words were spoken with quiet brutality, calmly hammering the lies home, and Moshe, having to listen to them, aware that he was a collaborator, lowered his head to avoid Paul's stricken gaze and begged the floor to devour him. He looked up again, his eyes drawn against their will, when Ben Eliezer, with his gently murderous skill, slipped the blade between Paul's ribs.

"Joshua has to be removed," he said. "We cannot let him reach Mecca. We cannot have this man—whom most of the Jews think is the Messiah—turning around and proclaiming himself as the Mahdi. We would not survive psychologically—nor would we survive the ensuing conflict—so Joshua, this man claiming to be the Mahdi, must never reach Mecca."

"We can't stop him," Paul whispered.

"We can," Ben Eliezer said.

"We can't stop him from proclaiming himself as the Mahdi."

"He can disappear," Ben Eliezer said.

Paul stared at him, shocked, understanding the implication, and his eyes, which had been glittering with despair, now dissolved into panic.

"Disappear . . . ?"

"He must be terminated."

"No!"

"We have to do it. We can stop him from going to Mecca, but we can't stop him talking, and once he proclaims himself as the Mahdi, Israel is lost."

Now Paul knew what Ben Eliezer meant, and the horror, sinking in, made him sit up very straight in the chair, his spine curved, in retreat. He glanced at Moshe, his eyes blind, looking inward upon himself, then his head turned in a slow, distracted motion, until it faced Ben Eliezer.

"No," he said, shaking his head, "not me . . . I can't do it. . . . No, not that, even now. . . . I just can't . . . *I won't do it!*"

Ben Eliezer was calm, his saintly patience an indecency, as he waited for Paul to settle down and stop shaking his head. Then he leaned across the table, touching the edge with his chest, pressed his hands down and spread his thin fingers and turned the blade in Paul's flesh.

"Yes," he said, "you will do it. Your own beliefs will make you do it. You have supported the zealots, you proclaimed Joshua as the Messiah, and now, if your messiah proclaims himself as the Muslim's Mahdi, the zealots representing your beliefs will be totally humiliated. You understand, Paul? The dream of Zion will dissolve. You will be dishonorably discharged for having released that information, your zealots will reject you for having made them look like fools, and the possibility of a true Zionist State will dissolve into dust. So you will do it, Paul—for yourself and your ideals—and, having done it, you will never mention the deed, in return for which we will never mention the fact that you, and not Leon Halcomb, blew the story of Joshua."

Paul gasped and took a deep breath, covered his face with his hands, bent forward as if he were praying, and then straightened up again. He removed his hands slowly, opening his eyes as he did so, glanced at Moshe, licked his lips, turned away, and finally faced Ben Eliezer. Ben Eliezer let the silence flay him alive, and then gave his instructions.

"Every night," he said, "Joshua walks to Gethsemane to meditate, alone, in the garden of the Basilica of the Agony. No one knows that he goes there—and at that time the garden is deserted—so tomorrow night, precisely at midnight, you will be there to greet him. We want you to use a pistol. We also want you to use a silencer. When you have finished, you will simply walk away and let us do the rest. Now is that understood?"

Paul looked at Ben Eliezer for a very long time, and then, in a silence utterly damning, the tears rolled down his cheeks. Moshe stared at him, revolted, then feeling only pity, his revulsion reserved for himself and his part in this vile plot. Paul wept silently and helplessly, not moving, his tears glistening, and Moshe felt that everything he had personally believed in was turning to mud. Paul's tears were like rain, falling mournfully for Zion. Moshe thought about Kate, about the child she was carrying, about Joshua, who had resurrected belief from the deserts of hopelessness. Joshua had given him Kate, another child, a new life, and now, as Paul's tears signified, Joshua had outlived his usefulness. Feeling sick, his soul streaming with guilt and shame, Moshe turned his face to the wall.

"Yes," Paul sobbed. "I understand."

37

Moshe drove into the carport of the small house in Talpiot, feeling like one of the damned, his soul lost in despair. He turned the ignition off, switched the lights out, and just sat there, looking over the darkened flatlands and hills to the distant lights of Jerusalem. In two hours Paul would be leaving, wearing plainclothes, carrying a pistol, to hide himself in the garden of the Basilica of the Agony and await the arrival of Joshua, who had shattered his dreams. Moshe thought of their terrible deception, of the plotting and intrigue, and shivered, feeling feverish and haunted, confused between right and wrong.

He climbed out of the car, locked the door and glanced around him, glad that it was dark, his fugitive heart needing that cloak, and then walked around to the front of the house and opened the door. The light was on in the lounge, beaming into the short hallway, and he hung his jacket up and then walked in to find Kate on the couch.

She was showing her pregnancy, her body heavy and maternal, but her skin glowed with vitality, an inner radiance and contentment, and her dark hair, still long and hanging loose, framed her calm, lovely face.

He leaned over and kissed her, pressing his lips to her forehead, sliding one hand through the softness of her hair and pulling her toward him. He sensed that she was smiling, pulled his head back and confirmed it, was simultaneously touched and terrified, unable to forget what was happening. Right now, in Jerusalem, Paul Frankel was preparing to kill Joshua—and Kate, as Moshe knew too well, was devoted to Joshua.

He straightened up and looked down at her, his heart beating unusually fast, various emotions conflicting within him, some warm, some ice cold. Kate patted her stomach, still smiling, obviously happy, nodding to affirm that her body was giving its blessing.

"A girl," she said. "I know it. She's as stubborn as her mother. Do you want another woman in the house, or would that be too much for you?"

"Two Kates are better than one. I'll be spoiled beyond repair. No man, if he has any sense at all, could complain about that."

"I could be wrong," she said. "It might even be a boy. The competition won't do you any harm—and I *will* be appreciated."

"You're appreciated now."

"I'm pampered," she said. "Really."

"Let me pamper you by giving you a drink. A glass of wine can't be dangerous."

He went into the kitchen, her face floating through his mind, her quiet radiance merely increasing his guilt and shame over what was to happen. He poured the drinks automatically, wine for Kate, beer for himself, only noticing that his hands were shaking slightly as he picked up the glasses. He tried to erase the image from his mind, but failed, his imagination running riot, seeing the Basilica of the Agony, the garden silent and dark, Paul emerging from behind an olive tree, his pistol pointing at Joshua. The image shook him badly, made him almost nauseated with guilt, and as he walked back out to Kate, carrying the drinks in his unsteady hands, he was haunted not only by his personal part in the affair, but by the sudden realization of how Kate would feel when she heard of the murder.

He gave her the drink and watched her sipping it, looking lovely, at peace, and he wanted to reach down and embrace her and tell her the truth. That thought alone was enough to chill him, conjuring an image of her reaction; he could visualize, with shocking clarity, the horror in her expression, the disbelief at his complicity in the matter and her subsequent revulsion. Disturbed, he turned away and faced the glass doors of the patio, looking beyond the patio to Jerusalem, twinkling high on the hills.

"How are things working out?" Kate asked.

"What things?"

"The current intrigues . . . the Vatican and the Soviets, the pope's forthcoming announcement . . . whether or not you'll let Joshua go . . . all those humdrum affairs."

"Nothing's changed," he lied, feeling the flush on his cheeks. "The pope will make his speech in a week or so, and we'll have to let Joshua go."

"I think you should talk him out of going."

"Joshua can't be talked out of anything. As well you know, he'll simply accept the Vatican summons as having been preordained."

"Then what happens, Moshe?"

"Then anything can happen, Kate. There's not a damned thing we can do about it, so we'll just have to wait and see."

He despised himself for lying, for the political expediency that made him do so, and, most of all, for the fact that it was a betrayal of Kate.

"How *is* Joshua?" Kate asked.

"As far as I know, he's fine. He moves from Jew to Muslim, from Muslim to Christian, from Christian back to Jew, giving everyone a little of what they need and making no firm commitment. He's still passive, an observer, responding, never initiating, still ignorant, I think, of what he is and where he came from."

"He may still be ignorant," Kate said, "about who he is or where he came from, but he is at least convinced that his resurrection is a sign that he is on the Earth for a specific purpose."

"That conviction, if anything, is now stronger."

Kate frowned and dropped her eyes, as if disturbed by what she was thinking, then her hands, in a gesture of hope, came to rest on her stomach.

"Don't think about it," Moshe said.

"I can't *stop* thinking about it. He's not sure of what is coming—at least not in the details—but he's convinced that his own blood will be shed, and that Jerusalem, or Israel, will then fall in order to rise again."

Moshe immediately thought of Paul, now preparing to kill Joshua. He drank, trying to deaden his churning emotions, and then looked down at Kate.

"He prophesied the recent war," she said, looking up, her dark eyes anxious. "He implied that that war hadn't really ended at all, and that his blood, when it was shed, would signal the coming downfall of Israel. I'm worried, Moshe. I think I know what he meant: His death, which will come soon, will lead to another war—and this time it won't be a minor war, but something quite catastrophic. I'm worried about Joshua, Moshe, and I'm worried about the future of Israel."

He sat down in the chair facing her, not wanting to be too close to her, afraid that her proximity and warmth would break his resolve. He had a long drink of his beer, wanting to soothe his ravaged nerves, then put his glass down on the small table, not feeling much better.

"You worry too much," he said.

"I can't help it," she replied. "I've got Joshua in my blood. As long as I live, I won't be able to shake the feeling that Joshua and you and myself and our child are all connected in some mysterious way. That storm, that strange star, meeting you, then finding Joshua, the conviction, even before we found him, that someone was calling me —all of it, Moshe, all of it, including those weeks in the hospital with him, the feeling that he was feeding off me, taking energy and life from me, the conviction that he was coming alive in my mind as, in fact, he then *came* alive—all of it, Moshe, all of it ties me to him in a bond I can't break. You understand what I'm saying? It's some kind of love, Moshe. Not like my love for you, not like the love for the child I'm carrying, but something even more abstract, something spiritual, beyond myself, a feeling that his fate and our fates are intertwined and that we, in a manner I can't explain, are responsible for him. I guided him into the world, Moshe—yes, and you too —together we looked after him and allowed him to develop, and now, though he's on his own, and with the whole world trying to claim him, I feel that he's in danger, that something terrible is about to happen, and that whether or not he knows about it, I just can't let it happen."

Moshe leaned forward in his chair and placed his clasped hands to his lips, feeling that he was slipping into a nightmare and floundering in darkness. His love for Kate had released him, giving him new life and commitment, but now that very love, in its need for truth and honesty, was making him feel even more strongly the imprisoning guilt of duplicity. What he had sanctioned was a terrible thing, lacerating him with shame, but much worse was the thought of how he would feel when Joshua's body was found. She would not know that Moshe was part of it, but her ignorance would hardly help her: the pain that she would suffer over his death would almost certainly be terrible. Moshe didn't want to think about it—he wanted to pretend it would not happen—and so, in desperately wanting to change the subject, he took an equally dangerous road.

"I've something to tell you," he said.

"About Joshua?"

"No."

"You've got that serious look on your face."

"It's about Leon," he said.

Her cheeks reddened a little, with embarrassment and anxiety, but

she kept her eyes squarely upon him, not hiding from anything. He n
longer felt jealous or suspicious of her feelings, but he knew that th
mention of Leon's name still made her uncomfortable.

"This information is bona fide," he said. "It comes from America
intelligence. Leon didn't blow the story of Joshua . . . he ha
nothing to do with it."

She stared at him for some time, saying nothing, not moving
letting the words sink into her consciousness and obviously fighting to
hold them. Then her eyes moved to the side, almost furtively, wit
guilt, sliding back to focus directly on Moshe, her face registerin
confusion.

"He had nothing to do with it?"

"No, Kate, not a thing."

"Then why . . . ?"

"I have no idea, Kate. You'd better ask him."

She stared blindly around the room, her cheeks flushed, her bod
shivering, and he knew that she was struggling with guilt and a grea
deal of confusion. Looking at her, he felt wounded, his heart breakin
for her pain, understanding that the joy her pregnancy had heightene
was now being demolished by her anxiety over Joshua and Leor
Every second he felt worse, accepting the responsibility for her pain
having to face the fact that what he had implemented was going t
make that pain greater.

"Why?" Kate said. "*Why?* He never once tried to deny it. Why di
he take the blame for all that? I just don't understand it!"

Moshe stood up and went to her, bent down and embraced her
pulling her head into his chest and stroking her hair as she tremble
against him. She held him tight and sobbed quietly—her quiverin
body told him that—and then she pushed him very gently away an
stood up, her cheeks wet. She smiled painfully, biting her lower lip
and wiped the tears from her eyes, then shook her head slowly fro
side to side in self-mocking despair.

"This is all too much," she said. "First Joshua and now Leon.
can't take any more for tonight, so I'm going to bed. Do you mind?

"Of course not."

She nodded her head distractedly, still smiling, if painfully, the
slid her arms around him and clung to him, her head on his chest.

"Joshua and Leon," she murmured. "The other two men in my life
Leon very much of the Earth, and Joshua out of my dreams. The
both managed to change me, Moshe, to make me view myself clearl

Leon by making me face the self-deception of my emotional life;
Joshua by making me see that there were things *beyond* this life. It's a
form of faith, Moshe—I think that's what they both taught me—faith
in myself, in the commitment of love; faith in my future here in Israel
where I rightfully belong. I owe them both and love them both,
Moshe—but not in the way I love you."

She held him very tightly, trying to glue herself to him, making
him feel the swelling expanse of her belly as she pressed herself to
him. He kissed the top of her head, stroked her shoulders, squeezed
her waist, then again she pushed him gently away, her eyes closing
and opening.

"Come to bed," she said. "*Soon.*"

She turned away and went into the bedroom, leaving the door
slightly open, and he stood there until the light, once turned on, had
been turned off again. Hoping she would sleep well, undisturbed by
thoughts of Joshua, he went into the kitchen and poured another beer
and then returned to the lounge. He looked out across the patio, at the
distant lights of Jerusalem, then sat down in the chair behind the table
and drank the beer much too quickly. The alcohol didn't soothe him,
but in fact had the opposite effect: snapping the stretched threads of
his control and letting his fear take command. He thought of Kate and
her love for Joshua, of what she had just said about him, and
immediately, very vividly, imagined Paul aiming his pistol, his hand
jerking and Joshua falling to the ground, his heart stopped by the
bullet. The feeling of horror was overwhelming, almost freezing him
to the chair; but then when he heard Kate screaming, when that sound
slashed through his reverie, the room around him poured back into his
consciousness as if resurrecting him.

He jumped up and rushed through the door with his heart pounding
wildly.

Kate was sitting up on the bed, her knees raised, her arms around
them, holding herself and rocking back and forth, her dark eyes filled
with panic. A beam of moonlight was pouring in, cutting a line across
her face, and that light, in its thin, wavering brilliance, made her skin
look like marble.

"*Joshua!*" she hissed. "Something's happening! I know it! *I feel
it!*"

He sat down on the edge of the bed, hardly knowing what he was
doing, twisted sideways, and then leaned toward her and pulled her
close to him. She was sobbing, her body quivering, and he rocked her

back and forth, pressing her head to his chest, feeling her hair against his lips, guilt and a lacerating dread whipping through him in spasms. Paul would now be on his way, wearing plainclothes, carrying a pistol, emotionally blackmailed into carrying out a deed that could never be rectified. He was doing it for Israel—for that abstraction that ruled them all—but now, as Moshe rocked Kate, as she sobbed in his arms, he felt that the assassination was of a vileness that could never be justified. To let it happen would be a sin, against Kate, against God, and as he felt Kate's warmth thawing his frozen soul, he knew what he must do.

He kept rocking her back and forth, stroking her hair, murmuring to her, until eventually she stopped sobbing, sniffed her tears back and was silent, and then, emotionally drained and exhausted, fell asleep on his shoulder. He eased her back onto the bed, tucked the blankets around her, kissed her gently on the forehead, stared at her for some time, and then, feeling the urgency of his heartbeat, walked out of the house.

It was cold and very dark, and he backed the car out quietly, then headed as fast as safety would allow back down to Jerusalem. His lights beamed through the darkness, illuminating the rushing road, and it seemed as if that road were moving endlessly and leading him nowhere. His thoughts scattered and spun, weaving arabesques of panic, his heart beating to the rhythm of the car as it raced down the winding road. The lights shone on the distant hills, fewer now as Jerusalem slept, seeming to slide in majestic splendor across the sky as the road curved away from them. He cursed quietly, checking his watch, seeing the hand creep toward midnight, thinking of Joshua meditating in the garden, unaware of Paul's coming. He tried to blot it out, to retain his objectivity, but that vision of faith and destructive doubt wrapped his tight head in thorns.

The road leveled out, unveiling the outskirts of Jerusalem, darkened houses and synagogues whipping past while streetlamps dazzled his eyes. He drove blindly, automatically, the world outside but a dream, his head filled and tortured with the vision of Paul walking toward Joshua. A crossroad—another car—the Old City sliding past; the final leg of the journey was composed of fragmented images, the familiar sights that in the darkness, in his dread, seemed singularly unreal. Only the Golden Gate distracted him, drawing his eyes to the gaping hole, and he shivered and followed the road to the right, in the direction of the lower slopes of the Mount of Olives. I was dark and deserted here, the Kidron Valley black as pitch, and he braked below the Basilica of the Agony, and turned the ignition off. The sudden silence was shocking, rushing into his head; and he sat there, feeling stunned, looking over the dark slopes, and then suddenly jumped out and slammed the door and headed up toward the walls of the basilica.

He hardly knew what he was doing and looked neither left nor right, his every impulse and thought concentrating on what he might find. He thought of Kate in her bed, of her dreaming thoughts streaming outward, traveling over the distance he had journeyed and spreading out through the garden. She was living and breathing Joshua, her nerves tuned to his every impulse, and Moshe dreaded the effect it would have upon her if that shot had been fired. He entered the garden at a trot, kicking up twigs and leaves, saw the splashing of moonlight on bougainvillaea and cacti, emphasizing the shadows that shifted and changed in the silence.

Not silence: someone sobbing. There was no sign of Joshua. He saw Paul on the ground, resting against an olive tree, bent forward with his head on his knees, his hands clasped on his neck. He was rocking back and forth—as Kate had rocked back and forth—and his sobbing, like Kate's sobbing, held an anguish that cut to the bone.

Moshe froze where he was standing, suddenly confused and disoriented, stared at Paul, and then looked all around him in a vain search for Joshua. The bougainvillaea whispered, dripping moonlight, casting shadows, but Joshua was nowhere to be seen and Paul sobbed all alone. His lower spine was against the tree, his huddled body forming an arch, and his sobbing lacerated the crooning breeze with a choked, ragged hollowness.

Moshe went to him, feeling embarrassed, no longer fearful for Joshua, and stopped a few feet away from him, wondering what had occurred. Paul heard him and raised his head, letting his hands fall away, looking up with his brown eyes very large and glistening with tears. Moonlight fell through the tree, spraying over his face, illuminating his dark, handsome face and a terrible anguish.

"I couldn't do it," he sobbed. "He was here, but I couldn't do it. I tried to, but I couldn't press the trigger when I looked at his eyes. He was staring straight at me, not frightened, just smiling, and I knew, when I looked into his eyes, that I just couldn't do it. 'Not yet,' he said. 'Not yet, and not you. It is coming, but not by your hand and not in this garden.' Hearing that, I was terrified. Seeing his smile, I was in torment. I knew then that he could not be the Mahdi, but was indeed our Messiah. 'Is this what you want?' he said. 'Can you truly betray yourself? Is your faith of the kind that can be shaken by the whisperings of mortal men?' My heart broke when he said that. My shame destroyed my will. In his eyes, and in his smile, I saw reflected my weakness and doubt. Then he raised his right hand, brushed the pistol aside, touched my cheek with the tips of his fingers and said, 'Don't be frightened.' Only that. Nothing else. He turned away and walked out. I was left in the silence of this garden with my shame and self-hatred."

He turned his head away from Moshe, his body heaving as he sobbed, the moonlight falling over his shaking shoulders and splashing on green grass. Moshe watched him, feeling stricken, not knowing what to do, his cheeks burning with the shame of his duplicity and evil intentions. He thought of Kate in the safety of her sleep, but the thought brought no comfort.

"We betrayed him," Paul sobbed. "In our weakness we doubted him. We dreamed and schemed for the Holy Land, committing our crimes in the name of faith, and in the end, forgetting the nature of our faith, we let our vanity rule us. We betrayed him by betraying ourselves, refusing to wait for His sign, and then, in our impatience and greed, we were corrupted by doubt. He looked at me and smiled. I will never forget that sight. Whether a smile or a grimace of despair, it chilled me and frightened me. We betrayed him—you and I, Ben Eliezer, the Holy Land—and I knew, when he walked from this garden, that I would never forget it."

He started weeping again, his head still turned away, the moonlight beaming through the olive tree and falling over his shoulders.

"It's all right," Moshe said. "It's all over. You can forget it. Nothing happened, so there's nothing to worry about. Just go home and relax."

He turned and walked away, unable to listen anymore to Paul sobbing, wanting to get out of the garden as quickly as possible and lie down beside Kate. He did not get very far before he heard the single shot, loud and clear in the stillness of the night, briefly blotting his senses out. Horrified, he spun around and saw the shivering olive tree, the moonlight filtering through its gnarled branches and falling on Paul. He lay on his side, his legs bent, one arm outstretched, the other bent under his face in the tree trunk's dark shadow.

Moshe walked back and looked down, but there was nothing he could do: Paul had placed the barrel of the pistol in his mouth and blown his own head off.

38

The small house was in Silwan, overlooking the Kidron Valley, its door open and shedding light into the darkness. Moshe stood quietly outside, watching the visitors coming and going, a constant stream of Muslims, Jews, and Christians, all solemn and awed. He felt sweaty and unclean, thinking of Paul in the garden, and his shame, which before had been acute, turned into horror. He wanted to see Joshua alone, wanted to warn him about the plot, knowing full well that the disaster of Paul's suicide would not put an end to it. Too much was at stake—for the Americans and the Israelis—and Moshe, his love for Kate at odds with his love for Israel, had decided, once Paul had killed himself, that enough was enough. He loved Israel, the Holy Land, the land dominated by Jerusalem, but he now felt that nothing worth having could spring out of their vile scheme. What Paul had said was right—in a bid to preserve Israel they were betraying what Israel stood for—and now Moshe, in his despair, in his horror at what had happened, was convinced that no matter the importance of their cause, the murder of Joshua would be a crime beyond forgiveness, bringing nothing but infamy.

He waited a long time, feeling the cold eating at him, hearing the murmuring from inside the house, watching the people emerging, silhouetted very briefly in the outpouring light before being swallowed up by the darkness as they headed for home. They seemed to come and go forever, as if none of them ever slept, but eventually, in the early hours of the morning, the endless flow tapered off. An Arab materialized in the doorway, silhouetted in the bright light, reached up to close the door for the night, and then noticed Moshe standing there. He stared at Moshe with curiosity, then glanced back into the house, then turned toward Moshe again, smiling gently, and motioned him inside.

Moshe stepped in, stooping low, feeling sweaty and slightly

feverish, unable to shake off the nightmare of Paul's suicide, and aware that what he was doing would not please Ben Eliezer or the Americans. The house was small and Spartan, the stone walls unpainted, and Joshua was sitting behind a crude wooden table, still dressed in his white robes. The only source of illumination was a few hanging oil lamps, and their light, very dim and pale yellow, shadowed his silvery-gray eyes. He looked up at Moshe, a faint smile on his lips, then he nodded at the old Arab, who lowered his head and then backed out, closing the door quietly when he went and offering them privacy.

"So," Joshua said, "you came."

"You sound as if you were expecting me."

"I knew that you could not let transpire what was not meant to be."

"You mean Paul?"

"Yes."

"Did you know what you were doing to him? When you left, he put the pistol in his mouth and blew his own head off."

Joshua's response was minimal, a mere flickering of his eyelids, but he kept his gaze squarely on Moshe, his hands flat on the table.

"I did nothing to him," he said. "I merely made him question himself. If he took his own life, it was preordained, and not without meaning."

Moshe studied Joshua carefully, feeling chilled by his response, which, with its tone of calm acceptance, seemed utterly inhuman. Who, or what, was Joshua? They had never found that out. Now, looking at him, at the smile that was not a smile, Moshe wondered if Joshua was good or evil, on the side of God or the Devil. They had all assumed his goodness, his affinity with the Almighty, but sometimes, though he never mentioned it to Kate, Moshe wondered about that.

"You feel nothing?" he said.

"Love and sorrow," Joshua replied. "But such feelings are not for Paul alone; they embrace all of mankind."

"What about individuals?"

"I could not prevent Paul's suicide. My powers, once formidable, are gone, and like you I am mortal."

"The people who come here hardly think so."

"They take from me what they need. They speak to unravel themselves, and I listen to learn."

"What are you learning?"

"That the time for change has come. That my own time, so brief, will soon be over, and revelation will come."

He was gazing steadily at Moshe, his lips curved ambiguously in a manner that suggested a smile that was not actually visible. Moshe felt even more unreal, as if locked in a waking dream, unable to comprehend Joshua's nature or feel any warmth for him. Kate loved him and felt part of him, her nerves tuned to his every impulse, yet Moshe, staring into those silvery-gray eyes, felt only confusion. Joshua was a cipher, his mysterious nature seducing men, but Moshe, in his presence, saw nothing but his remote, unrevealing face. Did Joshua feel love and sorrow? His eyes belied the possibility. Those eyes, like the dark side of the moon, had the chilling beauty of lifelessness.

"You doubt me," Joshua said. "Your face cannot hide that truth. In thinking of your wife and her feelings, you wonder why you feel differently."

"We don't know who you are. You claim not to know, yourself. You claim to feel love for mankind, but you don't show your feelings. Are you good or evil? Did you come to help us or destroy us? Your face is a closed book, a mask, concealing what you might be."

"My face conceals nothing, but merely displays my own ignorance. I do not know who I am, or whether I am good or evil, but only that I am here for a purpose that will soon be revealed. I believe in the Almighty who is Himself unknowable, and, given the mystery of His nature, I must stand on my faith. Is the Almighty good or evil? Can either exist without Him? Is it possible that good and evil—both concepts of Man—are in fact the two sides of the Almighty's face? These questions cannot be answered—not by me and not by you—but I have to accept what I feel and know to be true. I am here to serve a purpose, and only this do I know about it: Jerusalem, now tarnished, must fall to rise again, and I am the instrument of that change. Will it rise again to glory? Will it inaugurate the Dark Age? I am not here to answer such questions, but to make men face up to them. These are my feelings—the only feelings I know—and if, as you say, I do not show my feelings, perhaps there is nothing to show beyond curiosity. I am here to watch and listen, and to wait for my sign—and you, coming here to this house, are revealed as that sign."

"I came here to warn you."

"That Paul was just the beginning? Yes, you came to warn me

—you have the need to save my life—and that, in itself, is the sign that I have patiently waited for."

"You have to leave Jerusalem."

"I belong to Jerusalem."

"You'll probably have to leave Israel entirely. If you don't, they will kill you."

"What is willed, will be done. Your coming here is the sign. That which will be done is now beginning—and cannot be stopped."

"You won't leave?"

"I will not."

"Don't martyr yourself."

"I do not. I simply orchestrate the events that will lead you to Judgment Day."

"I don't believe in Judgment Day."

"That's why you see nothing in me. You look at me and wonder why your Kate has such deep feelings for me. Her feelings come from faith—or, more accurately, from belief—and your Kate, like the others who come here, takes what she needs from me. Think of me as a mirror: I reflect what the viewer seeks: faith, hope, confirmation of the hereafter, the promise of forgiveness and mercy through the joy of redemption. You do not believe in such—at least you question their validity—and so, when you look to me for meaning, your own doubts are reflected."

"I have doubts about your nature, about whether it's good or bad, and it worries me that people assume that you represent goodness."

"Then why try to save me?"

"Because I can't condone murder, because I think that your murder will do more harm than good, and because I don't want to be instrumental in causing pain to my wife."

"Those are public and private reasons."

"There can be no other reasons."

"You have not denied me—you have simply held on to natural doubt—and in doing so, you have admitted to yourself that all things are possible."

At that point he smiled—a genuine, gentle smile—and Moshe felt himself responding automatically, with helpless warmth and respect. He tried to fight it and failed, gradually losing himself, his antagonism and doubt disappearing and leaving him stronger. He looked at Joshua and thought of Kate, felt her love and passed it on, and Joshua's silvery-gray eyes, in response, became much more human.

He was doomed and knew it, his eyes reflecting joy and anguish, and Moshe, even knowing that it was useless, felt compelled to press on.

"You just can't let them kill you."

"That they want to means I must."

"I can't stand aside and let it happen."

"Your own gun is the instrument."

Moshe reached for his pistol instinctively, hardly knowing he was doing it, and then, when his fingers curved around it, he felt a fierce chill. He started to speak but failed to do so, his mouth opening and shutting dumbly, and a fear such as he had never known before took hold of his senses. More than fear: horror—a cold and clammy revulsion, rising up as he looked at Joshua's eyes and understood what he meant.

"You must go through with it," Joshua said. "You must end what you have begun. My presence on Earth has changed the world, and the fate of Israel will change it further—and whatever that fate, good or bad, it cannot be avoided. I know what is being planned—that certain men wish to deny me—and I cannot, whatever the cost, let that denial be uttered. I am here as a beacon, to light the path to Judgment Day, and it is imperative that that light is not diminished by those who would fear me. For this reason I must depart, leaving my name on the lips of men, and you, who came to me as the sign, must remain as the instrument."

Moshe felt the butt of his pistol, fitted snugly between his fingers, and he jerked his hand away, feeling scorched, his will dissolving in Joshua's eyes.

"The instrument?" he whispered, hardly recognizing his own voice, a sound that divided the silence like a knife shredding paper.

"Yes," Joshua replied. "By your pistol I will die. And you, being the instrument of my departure, must come with me tomorrow."

"Tomorrow?"

"In the evening. When the moon dissolves the sun. You will drive me along the road I need to take and ensure that the end comes."

"No, I can't do it!"

"You tried to make Paul do it."

"And then went to stop him!"

"And then he killed himself because of what you had almost forced him to do. You are guilty; now pay for it."

The words cut Moshe to the soul, leaving no room for pride, opening him out to let hatred rush in and offer protection. He stared at

Joshua with fear and loathing, seeing his logic as the road to Hell, his blunt honesty as a weapon more final than the pistol in Paul's hand. Joshua's eyes were prismatic, reflecting all things to all men, and now, focused intently on Moshe, reflecting all things to him. Life and death were in those eyes, the vaults of Heaven and the flames of Hell, and below the eyes, rich with ambiguity, was a smile that was not a smile. He was gentle—and gently murderous, offering no respite from truth, his words, spoken softly, offering nothing but cold, moral logic. Human beings could not contain him, or cleave to what he valued; and Moshe, feeling human and therefore powerless, had to bend to his will.

"Why me?" he asked.

"Because you came to this house. Because you and Kate found me, and through me became one; and because, having come to this house from Kate, you are completing the circle. Let the circle be unbroken. Let my passing fill men's minds. When your child comes, and the dust of the apocalypse reigns, you will look to the future."

"I feel nothing but hatred for you."

"You did not feel it before."

"I feel it now."

"You feel that hatred for yourself—and I reflect it back to you."

The door behind Moshe opened and the cold air rushed in, caressing his neck with icy fingers that caused him to shiver. He looked back over his shoulder, expecting to see the old Arab, and instead, with a shock, saw Leon Halcomb, his blue eyes flecked with crimson. Leon closed the door behind him, obviously drunk but in control, then bowed mockingly, his grin less than assured, his cheeks flushed and unshaven.

"So sorry to have intruded," he said. "I didn't expect to find you here, Moshe."

Moshe didn't reply, but stepped sideways, automatically, leaving the space between Leon and Joshua free, feeling vaguely embarrassed. Leon stared at him, still grinning, his eyes wavering in the dim light, then walked forward a little, very steadily, and looked down at Joshua.

"I'm Leon Halcomb," he said.

"I have heard of you," Joshua replied.

"As a good journalist, I have a leading question: When do you sleep?"

"You are inebriated," Joshua said.

"That is true, Messiah or Mahdi. But your observation doesn't answer my question: When do you sleep?"

"I admit, your question baffles me."

"Because sleep itself baffles you. I came here at this time because I've heard that you see people anytime."

"My time on Earth is short."

"Anytime and anywhere."

"People see me when they need to feel my presence—wherever they are."

"You don't sleep?"

"It is natural."

"When?"

"When it is needed."

"Then you move through time and space like a ghost—or like a god seeking shelter."

"No, I am not a god."

"Then what?"

"I am mortal."

"If mortal, how do you explain yourself?"

"I am here to be witnessed."

Moshe noticed the change in Leon, his subtle slide back to sobriety, his shoulders straightening and his grin disappearing as the fear cleared his drunken eyes. He rubbed his eyes with his fingertips, his head bowed in apparent weariness, then pressed his fingers into his cheeks and opened his eyes again. He studied Joshua for some time, his face thoughtful, no longer cynical, while the wan yellow light from the oil lamps made him look like a dying man.

"Why did you come here?" Joshua asked.

"Curiosity," Leon said. "I couldn't bring myself to leave the Holy Land without seeing its savior."

"You are leaving?"

"Tomorrow."

"As was written," Joshua said.

"Nothing was written," Leon replied. "I just decided to leave."

"Why?"

"My time is up."

"Time runs out for us all."

"I think we're talking on two different wave lengths; what I mean is, I'm finished here." Moshe caught his brief glance, at once uneasy and challenging, as if, still surprised to find him here, he didn't know what to do. Perhaps realizing this himself, he quickly turned back to Joshua. "You've obviously heard of me," he said, "but you talk as if you know me—know me, shall we say, in an intimate manner, which certainly surprises me."

He was trying to be flippant, but was no longer grinning, and his eyes, starkly shadowed by the yellow light, revealed a strange, muted fear. Moshe looked at him with sympathy, no longer capable of despising him, feeling for him, much to his surprise, an almost tender regard.

"I know you," Joshua said. "You were called, but not chosen. Like the majority of men you feel rejected and diminished in stature."

"I'm not sure I understand."

"You have not been chosen to lead. Needing to be blessed, you were blessed but not called, destined to swim in the tide that makes most men as one. Unrecognized, you felt bitter—refusing to accept your fate—and in anger you turned away from Him, embracing sin and self-hatred."

"The thirteenth Apostle?"

"The one called but not chosen. The one representing the mass of men in their tragedy and hope."

Leon took a step backward, as if someone had slapped him, his hands slipping away from his face and sliding down to his chest. At that moment he seemed haunted, his face drawn, his lips shivering, his skin, in the flickering yellow light, like some pale, ancient parchment.

"This is nonsense," he said.

"You did not come here for nonsense. You came here in search of suitable punishment before burying yourself."

"I'm not a masochist," Leon said. "Nor do I intend burying myself. I'm leaving Israel for no other reason than that I've been here too long."

"You lie," Joshua replied calmly. "To me and to yourself. You are leaving because of failure—both in life and in love—and because you were called but not chosen, and now feel rejected. Your cynicism was a mask, hiding your need for the faith you lost, and my presence here in Israel, which has focused your attention, has made you look deeply in the mirror and see your weak self-betrayal. No, you are not a masochist, but you valued yourself too highly, putting yourself above other men and expecting His grace. An idealist, you asked too much, wanting more than His blessing, wanting not only to be called as the

mass of men are, but to be chosen and separated from the mass of
men, as very few are. Yet why did you feel rejected? To be called is
enough. Those who are called by being born, are the salt of the Earth.
The Earth abides and is abundant, nurturing His flock through their
trial, and they who are called but not chosen are a bridge to the
heavenly vaults. Those chosen are but His messengers, spreading his
gospel throughout the earth, but they are not held in greater esteem for
it, since He sees all as equal. You were called but not chosen, one
blessed but not a saint, and in your arrogance you felt as one rejected
and thus turned away from Him. Now you come here in shame,
hiding your shame in cynicism, but you come like a child in trembling
guilt, in search of punishment and cleansing."

"No!" Leon gasped.

"Yes," Joshua said. "You came here as you were destined to come
—to purge yourself with self-sacrifice."

He stood up very slowly, as if wearied by his own words, then
walked around the table and approached Leon, placing his hands on
his shoulders.

"This man, Moshe, is your brother," he said, "as all men are your
brothers, and like you he suffers doubt and confusion through the
weakening of faith. He was called and then chosen, but does not yet
accept it, but tomorrow, when the moon dissolves the sun, he will
have understanding. You leave Israel tomorrow. You go to bury
yourself. Bring your suitcase to this house and come with us before
you finally leave. Be a witness to understanding. Support your brother
in his hour of need. Do this and you will come to self-sacrifice and
purification."

His eyes were fierce and commanding, almost mesmeric in their
brilliance, and his hands, arched across Leon's shoulders, now dug
deeper to shake him. Leon stared back like a blind man, licking his
lips and breathing harshly, the wan yellow light washing over his
features and making him ghostlike. He glanced briefly at Moshe, at
once embarrassed and fearful, then tore himself away from Joshua's
hands and turned his face toward the door. He stood there for a very
long time, breathing harshly and shuddering.

Moshe stepped forward, wanting to say something, then stopped,
unable to speak, feeling his eyes turning inexorably toward Joshua,
who was staring straight at him. Joshua's eyes were very large, their
brilliance cutting through the dim light, his beard and hair tangled and
dusty, his face fiercely ascetic. Moshe felt himself floating, drifting

out of his body, his essence, the reality, spreading out above Joshua and Leon. He looked down on them with pity, understanding what was to come, then his pity changed to love and compassion and a flickering of terror. There was beauty in that terror, the recognition of necessity, and his essence, the reality, having observed and accepted, drifted back to the mortal shell of his body and witnessed Leon's decision.

"Damn you," Leon said. "Yes!"

Joshua looked at him and smiled, without malice, with warmth, and then closed his eyes and lowered his head, having no more to say.

39

Kate slept after lunch, her bloated body exhausting her, and awakened in the hot, sunlit bedroom, feeling very depressed. She climbed off the bed slowly, blinking her eyes and gazing around her, still held in the web of the dream about death and destruction. Fiery skies and drifting smoke, the earth exploding around Jerusalem: in her dream she had seen it, an apocalyptic rain, but had also seen Joshua, his white robes red with blood, sinking down with his hands to his head, his eyes raised to the heavens. Now she felt haunted, convinced that something was wrong, and when she heard the front door slamming, then the roar of Moshe's car, she went to the window of the room, more fearful than ever.

He had said he was going to the Knesset and would be there until the late evening, but now as she watched him drive off, the dust billowing up behind the car, she was more sure than ever that something unpleasant was in the wind. Feeling almost deserted, she watched his car disappearing, then looked down at her considerably enlarged abdomen and took comfort from it. She spread her fingers to feel the child, imagined its movement and felt better, held her face up to the sun pouring in through the window, letting the heat bring some warmth to her skin and make her feel healthier.

"I want this child," she said, taking comfort from her own voice. "A boy or a girl—it doesn't matter—as long as it's healthy."

Turning away, she went downstairs, into the silence of the empty lounge, and glanced across the patio to Jerusalem, sitting high on the sunlit hills. The domes and minarets were clearly visible, separated from the modern buildings, thin white clouds drifting across the blue sky, looking almost artificial. It was a beautiful sight, very peaceful and bright, and yet Kate could not shake off her feeling that something was wrong.

She went into the kitchen, drank some water, and then just stood

there, feeling lonely and terribly isolated, but not knowing why. It
was something to do with Moshe—he had changed since visiting the
Americans—and now, thinking about him, her eyes focused on the
wall facing her, she knew that he had become embroiled in something
that he could not discuss. He had been moody since seeing the
Americans—still loving but more distracted, his brow constantly
furrowed with anxiety, his lips pursed in a tight line. And that
morning he had been worse, hardly eating, talking less, only
managing to vaguely mumble that he had arrived home so late
because of an emergency meeting in the Knesset. Kate hadn't
believed his story—although she believed it was security business
—and now, staring blankly at the kitchen wall, she felt the strain of
her ignorance.

Still sleepy, she closed her eyes, let her senses float in darkness,
trying to imagine her child, the years passing, the child growing, and
then seeing, instead of a mature child, the shimmering white robes of
Joshua. The white robes were covered in blood, fluttering down upon
the sand, falling away to reveal Joshua's face, his dead eyes staring
sunward. She felt fear and terrible grief—suddenly aware of what was
wrong—and then, before she could open her eyes again, saw Moshe
and Leon together. They were standing in the wilderness, their eyes
fixed upon one another, the body of Joshua lying between them, the
sand covering his drying blood. Kate gasped and opened her eyes,
saw the kitchen wall in front of her, then twitched when the doorbell
started ringing, sounding louder than usual.

She hurried out of the kitchen, feeling nervous and confused,
wondering who could be visiting at this hour and not feeling like
talking. The doorbell stopped ringing, leaving a sudden, shocking
silence, and she knew from the way she was reacting, that her nerves
were on edge. The caller was still outside, silhouetted by the frosted
glass, and she went along the hall, feeling sluggish, and opened the
door.

It was Leon. His eyes were sleepless and shadowed, his face pale
and terribly thin, and when he shrugged, without offering his usual
grin, his whole body quivered.

"Well, can I come in?"

She was startled to see him—not only because of his ill appearance,
but because she had not expected him to come to Moshe's house. She
just stood there, staring at him, slightly embarrassed and confused,

and then, managing to get her senses back, smiled and waved him inside.

He sat down immediately, sinking gratefully into the deep chair, his back turned to the hills around Jerusalem, the sun pouring in over him. He glanced around him automatically, his journalist's eyes still not at peace, but then very quickly returned his gaze to her, staring up with great weariness. In fact he looked awful, his eyes baggy, his cheeks hollow, the skin of his face almost yellow, pulled tight on his bones. He looked thin and seemed fragile, his jacket and trousers too loose, and his former ebullience, his witty cynicism, was no longer in evidence. She felt truly shocked, unable to accept the change in him, and she sank into the chair directly facing him, feeling weak and forlorn. He shrugged and waved one hand in a desultory fashion, tried to grin, and failed dismally.

"So," he said, "I've finally seen your new home. I feel very privileged."

"I didn't think you'd ever come here."

"Nor did I, Kate."

"Why did you?"

"I've come to say good-bye—and that's it: short and sweet."

It was a sharp, unpleasant shock, surprising in its intensity, and she understood immediately, and without the slightest doubt, that she was seeing him for the very last time. There was pain in this knowledge, but also something chilling, as if, in awakening to her depression, she had sensed what was coming.

"You're leaving Israel?"

"For good."

"When?"

"This very evening. I'd have told you a lot sooner if I'd known, but I just didn't know."

"A last-minute decision?"

"Something like that."

"You're packing the oddments of your life in a suitcase and just taking off again."

"That's it, Kate. Exactly."

He ran his fingers through his hair, shaking his head from side to side, then abstractedly massaged the back of his neck. Kate felt a terrible sadness, the first intimations of loss, and her pain wasn't eased by the conviction that he was seriously ill.

"Are you all right?" she asked him.

"Yes," he said, "I'm fine."

"You look terrible."

"Too much drink, too little food . . . maybe that's why I'm leaving."

"Why, Leon?"

"Different reasons."

"Am I one of them?"

"Absolutely."

"I'm not worth it."

"Alas, you are, Kate—which I learned far too late."

She didn't know what to say to that, but found herself blushing slightly, a strange reaction considering their former relationship, perhaps because of her pregnancy. She was very conscious of her own appearance, her extra weight and swelling belly, and she let her eyes fall to the floor, feeling senselessly shy.

"You're looking forward to being a mother?"

"Yes, Leon, I am."

"Then why are you looking so anxious?"

"It's not because of my pregnancy."

She raised her eyes again, trying to beat her depression, but the ominous feeling was still with her, darkening her mind. She looked at Leon and thought of Moshe, and thinking of Moshe, thought of Joshua—and the three faces, merging in her mind, merely heightened her fear. Yes, it was fear, a premonition of pain and grief; and as she studied Leon's face, and saw the skin on the bone, she felt that his departure was merely the beginning of some much greater tragedy.

"So why are you anxious?"

"Why are you leaving, Leon?"

"Is that why you're anxious? Because I'm leaving?"

"It's a shock—and you know it."

He smiled bleakly at that, his eyes wandering around her face, always focused on some point just beyond her, never meeting her gaze.

"You're one of the reasons," he said. "I'd be a liar to say otherwise. I learned too late just how much you meant to me—and having learned it, I lost you. So you're a reason for going—I think we'll both benefit from my absence—but there are, I must confess, other reasons, most of which I learned through you."

"Through me?"

"Through your honesty. Your refusal to accept a lie. The lie, for instance, that you loved me—a lie you never breathed once."

"I didn't feel good about hurting you."

"No, Kate, you wouldn't. I think that telling me hurt you as well, and I respect you for that."

"And still hate me a little?"

"No, Kate, I still love you. I value nothing else in my life, but I *do* value that."

She tried to keep her eyes on him, but failed and looked away, warmed and embarrassed by his revelation, knowing how she had wounded him.

"And the other reasons?" she asked.

"Too many to discuss," he said. "Feelings of failure, feelings of shame, too many glances in the mirror, too many mornings coming out of sleep wondering how to get through the day. What am I doing here? I don't really belong here. I'm an Englishman working for an American paper from a hotel in Israel. Schizophrenia, dear Kate. The utter loss of myself. I am leaving for a complex of reasons that sum up my lost Self."

She studied him very carefully, trying to read between his words, believing what he said, but believing, even more, that the reasons he was offering were a subterfuge for something much greater. He refused to meet her gaze, but instead examined the space around her, as if, in looking at her, he was drawn to a presence over her shoulder. She shivered, feeling haunted, sensing that Leon was also haunted, his flight from Israel motivated by something that he could not divulge. Leon and Moshe: two haunted men, both hiding within themselves; she remembered Moshe arriving home in the early hours of the morning, his troubled face when he lay her down to sleep before leaving for work. . . . Troubled, secretive, pretending to be lighthearted, yet emanating fear and despair from every pore in his body. Leon and Moshe: the men divided by Joshua's presence; the men joined by their commitment to herself, both now plunged into misery. . . . She thought about it and felt confused, wondering if she was to blame, and then saw Leon moving very slowly, standing up like an old man. He shrugged, grinning bleakly, much too frail to be healthy, then rubbed his wasted face with one hand, his fingers visibly shaking.

"Where will you go?"

"Back to England—to home."

"To your family."

"No, I don't think so. It's too late for that now."

He would not meet her gaze, but instead looked over her shoulder, in search of that distracting, ghostly presence that she felt might be real. Joshua? Imagination? The hidden fear of her pregnancy? She shivered and tried to cast such thoughts aside, concentrating on Leon. He felt her gaze and glanced down, examining his dusty brown shoes, rubbed his eyes like a man going blind, and took a long, painful breath. At that moment she sensed it—his fear and despair—and what she felt emanating from him suddenly gripped her like ice.

"What's the matter, Leon?"

"It's nothing. . . . I'd better go."

"There's something else, Leon—not your leaving—and it's tearing you up."

"You're imagining things, Kate."

"No, Leon, I'm not. I know you—as well as anyone can—and there's something disturbing you."

He made a move toward the hall, stepping forward as if dragging chains, beads of sweat on the pale skin of his face, one hand rubbing his forehead. She watched him, feeling frightened, contaminated by his behavior, remembering her dream, the blood splashed on Joshua's robe, Leon and Moshe standing over his body, the sand swirling around them. A dream—no more than that: subconscious fears in search of meaning. She tried to rationalize the dream, to put her fears in proper perspective, but her feelings defied rationality and left her nerves dangling. Leon turned back at the hallway, his lips pursed in thought, and then, for the first time since he had arrived, managed to look in her eyes.

"You deserve Moshe," he said. "He's a lot stronger than me. I think that if I'd won you, I'd have dragged you down to my sorry level, whereas Moshe, a much better man than I, will keep you where you belong. He's still not my favorite man—moral rectitude is not my forte—but he is at least a man of strong convictions, so you're clearly well matched. Be considerate to him, Kate. He may be in for an unpleasant time. Certain things could be happening that you won't quite understand, so try to keep yourself from blaming Moshe—in fact, he'll need your support."

He walked along the narrow hall, turned the handle, and opened the front door, and she followed him with her heart beating uncomfortably at what he had said. She reached out and grabbed his shoulder,

making him turn back to face her, his eyes once more refusing to look
directly at her but wandering restlessly around her. She felt the ghost
over her shoulder, that emanation of despair and fear, and she
shivered, as if touched by an icy wind, and heard the hiss of her own
voice.

"*What things?*" she said.

"I don't know, Kate—not the details. I only know that there's a lot
going on, and that Moshe is involved in it."

"The Americans?"

"That's right."

"And the Soviets?"

"Correct."

"And does Joshua fit into this somewhere? Tell the truth, Leon! *Tell
me!*"

She shook him hysterically, almost pulling him toward her, and he
pulled away from her, opened the door wider, stepped outside, and
then turned back to face her. For the second time he looked directly at
her, his face pale and sweaty.

"Yes," he said, "Joshua's involved. At least I think he's involved. I
honestly don't know precisely how, but I'm sure something's
coming."

She immediately thought of her dream—of the flame and smoke
around Jerusalem, of Joshua lying between Moshe and Leon—and
then the fear, which before had been like an ominous fog, became a
blade that cut straight through her senses and left her in disarray. She
reached out for the door, feeling dizzy and weak, and then placed her
other hand on her belly, trying to find reassurance.

"I'm sorry," Leon said. "This is no way to say good-bye. I wanted
to warn you, but perhaps I shouldn't have mentioned it, since it might
make it worse for you. Who knows? It may not happen. The wind
might blow it away. Have faith, Kate, and be a good mother—the
world won't end with this."

He made a move toward his car, but she stepped out and grabbed
him again, feeling grief at the finality of his departure, her senses
drowning in hopelessness. He stared at her, trying to smile and still
failing, then reached out for her hand.

"Yes, Kate?"

"One last thing. I have to know before you go. *Why*, Leon? Why
did you take the blame for releasing the news about Joshua?"

He was looking directly at her, no longer trying to avoid her eyes,

eal feeling of loss and sadness in his face, giving life to his
weariness. She felt deeply for him then, remembering what they had
shared together, and it struck her, perhaps for the first time, that she
might never see him again.

"Self-punishment," he said. "The punishment I deserved. I be-
rayed you in planning to expose Joshua—and I meant it as vengeance. Yes, it's true I didn't do it, that someone else beat me to it,
but if they hadn't, if I'd managed to get in first, then certainly I would
ave. It was the intention, Kate: that vicious need to make you suffer.
You rejected me, and I wanted to pay you back by betraying your
rust. Someone saved me from doing it—Paul Frankel, I believe—but
e only did what I had planned to do, which hardly lessens my guilt.
Would I have done it in the end? Perhaps, perhaps not. Now I'll never
now—and neither will you—and that, by itself, is enough to prove
hat I was guilty. Do you understand, Kate? I took the blame because I
eserved it. If I believed in nothing else, I believed in my love for
ou, and I hope that I shouldered the blame to reaffirm that belief. I
oved you and love you. I have kept my faith in that. And I want you
o remember it and keep it with you always—not in the hope that it
will make you suffer guilt, but in the hope that you'll think of me with
ondness and not with contempt."

Kate felt her eyes weeping, the tears rolling down her cheeks, and
he stepped forward, shaking with emotion, and let his arms slide
round her. He held her very tightly, pressing his lips to her head, and
is body, also shaking, seemed as light as a reed in the wind. He was
ading away, killing himself with drink and guilt, and she knew that
whatever she said, he would never return. She pressed her hands
gainst his spine, digging her fingers into his jacket, feeling no sense
f betrayal, no guilt over Moshe, as she tried to let him know that she
till cared and that her heart still beat for him. He responded with a
groan, a muffled cry of loss and yearning, and then pushed her away,
gently, with great tenderness, and walked back to his car.

He drove off far too quickly, the car churning up clouds of dust, his
ree hand thrusting out through the window, waving slowly and
weakly. Then he was gone, the dust settling back on the road, and she
tood there in the silence, the tears still on her cheeks, her grief
attling with the clammy, relentless fear that was creeping back over
er. After a long time, feeling haunted and heartbroken, she returned
o the empty house.

40

Moshe drove straight through Hebron, continued south to Beersheba, then followed the asphalt road past the remaining fertile stretches and into the desolate grandeur of the Negev Desert. Leon saw very little, feeling trapped inside his head, his thoughts swirling like a murky, dangerous whirlpool that was sucking him down. He felt ill and extremely weak, broken up at seeing Kate, and now, in the jeep, sitting beside the silent Joshua, he wondered just where they were going and what was to happen.

He glanced at Moshe, studying that harshly handsome profile, and noticed what could only be fear in the lines of his brown skin. That fear was what united them, binding them together in speechless wonder, neither willing nor able to speak for fear of what might be said. He kept his eyes on Moshe, saw the sweat on his forehead, sensed his revulsion and despair, but didn't know what was causing it. Did Moshe know what was going to happen? If he did, it could not be pleasant: what Leon sensed in him was a horror that rose out of his soul.

Leon tried to forget it, sinking down through himself, trying to will the past to rise up around him and blot out the present. He saw the fires of Con Thien, the smoking streets of Londonderry, the other nameless villages lost in flames in nameless countries where he had, in his weakness and self-duplicity, lost the will to go on. Then his wife and two children, if not nameless now faceless—how old were they now?—mere ghosts that occasionally crossed his mind and touched his soul with mild guilt. Beyond that there was no past—only Israel and Kate—or, at least, an Israel in transition since the arrival of Joshua. The whole world had changed since then—as Kate had changed and he had changed—and he now felt divorced from all the strands that had woven reality. He was a dreamer, a sleepwalker impelled by intangible forces, neither knowing in what direction he was moving nor what he would waken to.

He glanced briefly out of the jeep, blinking his eyes against the glare, seeing the desert sweeping out to the mountains and their harsh, primal beauty. The sun was melting as it sank, the heat distorting its crimson brilliance, making it look like an enormous pomegranate with its blood-red juice flowing. Leon blinked and looked away, his eyes falling on Joshua, his profile made unearthly and mysterious in that darkening crimson glow.

He shuddered, feeling frightened, wondering just who Joshua was, whether a saint or a sinner, God's child or the Devil's, the incarnation of man's most valiant dreams or his most monstrous desires. The world had changed because of Joshua—and was going to change more—and yet Joshua, the most passive of living creatures, had done nothing at all. He had simply materialized, emerging mysteriously out of time, and had since that moment offered nothing but his seductive ambiguity. He had changed the world just by being, affirming nothing, denying nothing, simply waiting, with inhuman patience and dignity, for the world to reveal itself. And that the world had done, removing its mask and showing its real face, every impulse, good and bad, pouring out to create a new countenance. So Joshua had changed the world—not by living, by merely existing—and now as Leon accepted this fact, he felt his fear growing stronger.

"I have to catch a plane," he said.

"Patience," Joshua replied.

"It'll take hours to get back to Tel Aviv, so I want to know where we're going."

"Where the end begins," Joshua said.

"What end? What does that mean?"

"It is not very far," Joshua said. "I will know when we get there."

Leon glanced across at Moshe, but saw no change in his face, the beads of sweat glistening on his forehead, his lips forming a tight line. He knew that Moshe was not himself, that some imminent horror had engaged his mind, and realizing that, his own fear no help at all, he remembered the light of terror in Kate's eyes and wondered what she had sensed.

"There's nothing here," he said. "We're in the middle of the Negev. Apart from the Bedouin, there's nothing but desert and mountains."

"Here the end begins," Joshua said.

"You still haven't explained that. You couch everything you say in ambiguity, as if frightened of truth."

"Do you know what truth is?"

"Do you?"

"I seek to find it. The end begins where truth reveals itself and forces wise men to stutter."

He decided not to reply, his fear of Joshua sealing his lips, and instead he glanced across the burning plain at the immense, ochre cliffs. The sun was lower in the sky, an enormous orb in the shimmering heat waves, its lower half dissolving and spreading out as twin streams of red lava. The cliff peaks started bleeding—or at least appeared to bleed—the jagged peaks turning pink, then crimson, then blood-red, the blood dripping down the scarred face of the rock and filling its dark, pockmarked surface.

Leon shivered, feeling cold, aware that he should be burning, and tore his eyes away from the bleeding cliffs to look into himself. He saw darkness and light, the light shrinking in the darkness, his soul retreating before the advancing unknown and what it might represent. The unknown was the darkness, the challenge in Joshua's smile, and the light was the flickering of his own will at the doors of oblivion. Why had he come with them? What had he hoped to find? He had come because that light, the final flickering of his will, had been challenged by the mystery of Joshua's smile to flare up in defiance.

"I can't fight you," he said, and then heard his own voice speaking. "I no longer have the will to believe—and belief requires will."

"Open your eyes," Joshua replied. "Don't be frightened of looking at me. I am mortal, I bleed, I have known the sin of pride; and you, because you feel that sin acutely, are no less than I am. You spoke before knowing that you had spoken—which requires some belief."

Leon opened his eyes and saw the blood on the nearby cliffs, the sun melting and pouring away to dissolve in the shimmering heat haze. A pale moon was materializing, very faint in the still bright sky, and Leon felt, more than ever, that he was living the events of a dream.

"What can you possibly show me?"

"What do you wish to see?"

"Riddles, enigmas, conundrums—I didn't come here for that."

"You wanted something specific?"

"You promised some sort of revelation."

"I promised only self-sacrifice and purification—and you obviously wanted it."

Leon flinched from that truth, remembering what had been said, accepting the accuracy of the statement, but appalled by its heartlessness. The Messiah or the Mahdi—possibly even the Christian Christ —Joshua lived by the breath of every word and would not let one pass. Was it heartlessness or faith, the stern belief in ultimate truth? Leon shivered in his ignorance of the answer, looking down at his hands. Flesh. Blood and bone. The only reality was himself. The only truth was the love he had felt and let slip through his fingers. He thought of Kate and felt despair, the terrible grief of his last farewell, realizing that in her, through her honesty and strength, he had understood the fallacy of cynicism and lack of commitment. She and Joshua were the same, the two sides of a glittering coin; and Joshua, in his heartlessness, in his calm hold on truth, was the embodiment of an honesty and commitment that defied normal men.

"Why did I come?" he murmured, his voice emerging after the thought. "We're just driving like lunatics through this desert—with no fixed destination."

"You came for revelation." Joshua's voice was like the wind. "And what is a fixed destination when the Earth shifts so much?"

"I want to know where we're going."

"You are frightened of your future."

"I won't find any future in this desert."

"You will. When the end begins."

He looked at Leon and smiled, a strange smile, filled with anguish, a smile contradicting itself by binding joy to its opposite. Leon shivered, feeling lost, no longer able to trust his own judgment, wondering where anguish ended and joy began, if one supported the other. He glanced at Moshe and saw only anguish, the pain of dreadful anticipation, and then knew that the terror in Kate's eyes had been based on sound instincts. Moshe was caught in some sort of trap, his face reflecting a secret nightmare, and Leon knew, with a horrible sinking sensation, that it was bound up with Joshua.

"Are we close?" he asked Joshua.

"Yes, I think we are."

"You don't know?"

"I only know what I feel—and I feel we are close."

"Stop the car," Leon said.

"Why should we stop?"

"Because I don't want to go any farther; I want to turn back right now."

"You are frightened?"

"Yes."

"Why?"

"I don't know. I only know that I won't go any farther, and I want to turn back."

"You will never turn back again."

"Moshe, stop the car."

"If you insist, we will stop," Joshua said, "because this must be the place."

Moshe slowed down and stopped, applied the hand brake and then just sat there, leaning slightly forward over the steering wheel, his eyes fixed straight ahead. He had not said a word throughout the whole journey, and now, in his silence, there was a tension that Leon felt he could touch. Disturbed, he glanced around him at the darkening crimson sunset, saw the top edge of the sun sinking down behind the cliffs, and the blood, which was the light of the sun, turning black on the barren rock. A pale moon was in the sky, its light seeming to dissolve the sunlight, and then Leon, in remembering what Joshua had said, felt fearful and unreal.

"Here," Joshua murmured. "It ends here. This is where it begins."

The contradiction had a resonance that filled Leon's head with horror, and as he turned to stare at Joshua and saw him climbing down from the jeep, he felt himself beginning to shake as if with some fever. He glanced at Moshe in desperation, wanting a sign about what was coming, but Moshe, as he also climbed out of the jeep, kept his gaze well averted. Leon felt himself freezing, his body paralyzed with indecision, only his eyes still alive, flicking repeatedly from Moshe to Joshua, ascertaining with the clarity and unreality of a dream that they were standing about six feet apart, directly facing each other.

Moshe's face was ravaged by fear and doubt, his left hand wiping the sweat from his furrowed brow, then falling away like a wounded bird. Leon started climbing down, feeling ill and slightly dizzy, his eyes still moving from Joshua to Moshe and then back again. The pale moon had dissolved the sun—that phrase echoed in Leon's head—and as he placed his feet unsteadily on the ground, the crimson twilight enveloped him. The rippling sand dunes were red, the red mountains darkly shadowed, and that red light, falling over Moshe and Joshua, made them both look demonic.

"What is it?" Leon heard his own voice. "What's happening? Why are we—?"

The question died on his lips when he saw Moshe suddenly quivering, his head shaking from side to side in protest as he unclipped his pistol. He just stared at Moshe, horrified, suddenly realizing what was happening, and then, in the desperate hope that it would not be true, turned his head toward Joshua. The silvery-gray eyes were staring at him, ignoring the pistol in Moshe's hand, glittering brilliantly, with calm, ruthless challenge, through the dark crimson haze.

"No," Joshua said. "Not Moshe. It was never him. It is *you*."

Leon stepped back in confusion, then with slowly mounting terror, understanding what Joshua was implying and unable to face it. Self-sacrifice and purification—now he knew what was meant by that —and the darkness, briefly obliterating the crimson sky, was his wavering right hand. He felt fear and despair, a terrible revulsion and nausea, and as his hand dropped away, letting the crimson sky rush back, he saw the shock on Moshe's face, the pistol dangling from his fingers, and realized that Moshe was merely to be the witness to his ultimate transgression. The horror of this was catastrophic, whipping his nerves and stabbing his soul: he, Leon Halcomb, the one called but not chosen, was, in the end, being chosen to test his faith in the flames.

Leon lost his senses then, finding faith in delirium, stepping forward into that swimming crimson haze, his hand outstretched and searching.

Kate dreamed of Moshe and Leon, of Joshua stretched out between them, and awakened in the crimson haze of sunset with her heart beating wildly. She opened her eyes and saw the room, its white walls pink-tinged, a bloody womb in which her soul was being contained, well away from the living world. There was no wind outside, allowing the silence to have dominion, and she heard, in the completeness of that silence, her own slow, painful breathing.

She climbed off the bed slowly, one hand resting on her swollen belly, stood up, feeling weaker than expected, and then put on her dressing gown. Her terrible lonesomeness had not abated—had in fact been exacerbated by Leon's farewell—and as she slid her feet into her slippers, she wished that Moshe would come home.

Leon had gone for good and this knowledge clung to her mind. The sadness overwhelmed her, but was mixed with a clinging fear, mainly caused by the fact that the morning's dream had been repeated that afternoon. She felt haunted and almost crazy, unable to grasp what was happening to her, convinced that the dream, with its blood and death, was a sign to the future.

The crimson haze filled the room, making her feel that she was still dreaming, and she walked much too quickly into the lounge, feeling less claustrophobic. It was brighter here, less threatening, the crimson haze not so prevalent, and she walked to the sliding doors of the patio and looked across at Jerusalem. It sat high on the hills, its gold and silver domes gleaming, its modern buildings silhouetted against the clear, fiery sky of the twilight.

Leon's departure had wounded her. Moshe's secrecy had caused concern. The dream about Joshua had dragged him back into her thoughts, his image spiraling constantly in her mind to form a large question mark. She and Joshua were bound together, her nerves tuned to his every impulse, and now, as she gazed upon Jerusalem the Golden, she thought about him with anxiety—and then felt a very sharp, stabbing pain that briefly numbed her whole body.

She cried out and grabbed her stomach, shocked and terrified by the pain, then heard the roaring of thunder and glanced up to see lightning daggering impossibly across the cloudless, crimson sky. Stunned, not believing it, she stepped forward to look again, then realized that she could not feel her legs and fell to her knees. Pain exploded in her left shoulder, stabbing down her flailing arm, and she cried out as her body twisted sideways as if punched by an invisible fist. The thunder roared and the lightning flashed, and she looked up, amazed, seeing no trace of a cloud in the crimson sky and wondering if she was imagining things. Pain exploded again—this time in her left hip—and she shrieked and fell onto her right shoulder, then rolled onto her back.

She closed her eyes and breathed deeply, trying to get her senses back, feeling the life returning to her limbs as the numbness wore off. A roll of thunder killed her thoughts, then she heard the crackling lightning, and the floor beneath her started to shake as if in an earthquake. The fear was luminous within her, forcing her eyes wide open, and she looked up to see the cracks appearing in the ceiling above.

Dust and plaster rained down as she slithered across the floor, moving backward, stretched out on her spine, the child pressing upon her. Thinking of this, her fear increased, almost turning into panic, and she reached out for the edge of a chair and pulled herself to her knees. She shook her head from side to side, trying to clear it, trying to think straight, but then the thunder rolled again, quickly followed by the crackling lightning, and she turned around, still on her knees, to look out at the patio.

Joshua was standing there, his arms raised, fingers outspread. He was motionless, but his white robe blew dementedly in a sudden, fierce wind. He was there and not there. His white robe was translucent. Through his white robe she could see the low wall and the distant domes of Jerusalem.

The fear grabbed Kate like a vise—not love, but pure fear—and she blinked and looked again to see his white robe blowing out from his raised arms. Now the robe was opaque, revealing nothing but his outlined form, the fierce wind sweeping across the small patio and pressing the cloth to his body.

The thunder roared and the lightning flashed, daggering across the cloudless sky, darting fingers of silver in the crimson haze of the darkening twilight. The wind howled across the patio, sweeping pots and plants away, making Joshua's white robe billow crazily and blowing his hair about. Then a bolt of lightning struck him, exploded blindingly around him, and he burst into flames, became a floating ball of fire, and then the fire became a dark cloud of smoke which the wind quickly scattered.

Kate heard herself screaming, the sound reverberating through her head, and she threw her hands over her ears and turned away from the patio. The thunder roared, the floor shook, the chair beside her slid away, the carpet beneath her started rippling and the bedroom door slammed shut. That sound sent a chill through her, froze the scream on her lips, and she glanced around the room in a panic as the cracked walls spat powder. The room was bathed in the crimson haze, growing darker and hotter, and the carpet, rippling beneath her like sand, had a will of its own.

Then death. The grave's darkness. She felt a terrible, icy wind. The room was silent and the floor had stopped shaking and she heard her own breathing. She thought of death and then heard it, creaking lightly like a rusty hinge, turned her head and saw the bedroom door opening, very slowly and quietly. The terror froze her where she crouched, in that darkening, bloody haze, but refused to let her move her eyes away from that opening door. A beam of yellow light emanated, creeping across the floor toward her, coming closer as the door opened wider to let more light out. Then a shadow materialized, thin at first but growing wider, stretching along the rectangular strip of light to reach out and touch her. She tried to pull her hand away, her fingers stung by the ice of death, but the shadow grew wider and longer and finally stopped at her knees. She looked down at the shadow, her mind paralyzed with fear, then her eyes, against her will, traveled back along the shadow to where it ended, parallel to the door frame, at two white, sandaled feet.

Joshua was standing there, silhouetted in the yellow light, his silvery-gray eyes piercing through to her soul.

She stared at him, terrified, looking through him to the room beyond, his body fading in and out like a light growing weaker and stronger. He faded away and then returned, his white robe clearly visible, and his eyes, which had the brightness of polished stones, revealed nothing at all.

She sobbed and struggled backward, moving along on her hands and knees, tugged between the seductive horror of death and the life kicking inside her. The living child gave her life, encouraging fear and the urge to flee, and she turned away from Joshua, trying to stand, feeling the cold at her back. The glass doors were the color of blood, reflecting Joshua's white-robed form, and she screamed her defiance, a single word of denial, as his image disappeared from the glass to let her look at Jerusalem.

Freedom. The patio. She had to get out of the room. She saw the darkening sky, the pale moon in ascendance, and stumbled forward to reach for the handle and pull the doors open. Her hand reached the door handle, and she shrieked, her fingers burning, then looked down to see the ice on the glass, illuminated by lightning. She straightened up, her senses scattering, feeling the frost on her skin, then looked out at the patio and saw Joshua, clouds of sand sweeping over him.

She was drawn to the wintry depths of his eyes and felt them melting around her. Inside him, she became him, her nerves tuned to his every impulse, feeling death coming closer every second, bringing horror or glory. She let it come and was not afraid, knowing Joshua as light and darkness, his nature as mysterious as good and evil, perhaps embracing them both. She felt the nearness of death, let it touch her and surround her, its whispering silence seductive and sly, offering peace everlasting.

A dream. Or not a dream. An experience of the night. The fear limned the edge of the experience and then cast her back out. She heard sobbing—her own sobbing—and then opened her eyes again, the tears streaming down her cheeks as grief came to lay its hands on her heart. She saw the lights of Jerusalem, the red sky turning darker, a cloud of sand drifting mysteriously off the patio, the frost melting in warm air. She knew then, with no doubt whatsoever, that Joshua was dying.

The cloud materialized out of nothing, not too high up in the sky, first a dark spot, then what looked like a globe of smoke growing larger each second. It was dark and very dense, boiling out of itself, mushrooming and spreading across the sky and blotting out the pale moon. Kate watched it, mesmerized, remembering the first night, the discovery, as the cloud, growing larger, descended and drifted over the house. The first tendrils caressed the patio, spiraling lazily, draping the wall, then more cloud, like gray smoke, drifted down and obscured the whole patio.

The languid silence of death. The slow descent of death's darkness. She watched the moon disappearing, then the stars, then Jerusalem, and finally, when the lights of Jerusalem vanished, her heart cried out for Moshe. In this pain was humanity, the refusal to surrender, and she stepped back, her eyes fixed on the door, the child kicking inside her.

She saw Joshua on the patio. His head was bowed and he was weeping. He raised his head, his eyes glittering through the gray cloud, and she saw his tears streaming. The child kicked in her stomach. The thunder roared and the lightning flashed. She felt love and fear at once—for her child and for Joshua, for Moshe and Leon, for Jerusalem and the promise of a future, no matter its nature—and then she screamed her defiance, that single word of denial, and the lightning came down, hissing through the swirling cloud, turning Joshua to flame and shimmering light, and signifying the end.

Kate knew it was over—that Joshua's death had come—and her grief and exultation came together and fused her child to her. The gray cloud flashed and crackled, hissed and glowed in electric splendor, and then the thunder rolled again, the lightning daggered from the sky, and the glass doors containing Joshua's image exploded into the room.

Thrown back, she was saved, falling under the flying glass, but she screamed for her child, her stomach pounded by the sliding table, and then pain, or perhaps implacable horror, plunged her into unconsciousness.

The rolling thunder awakened Moshe, jerking him out of his freezing horror, and he looked up to see a bolt of lightning daggering out of the cloudless sky. Startled, hardly believing it, he dropped his eyes and looked at Joshua, saw him bathed in the darkening crimson haze as he stepped toward Leon. Moshe felt lost, his senses in disarray, but he suddenly understood what was happening, and he glanced wildly around him, at the desert and its nearby cliffs, and then forced his gaze back to Joshua and Leon where they stood in that fiery light. Joshua was reaching out to Leon, placing his hands on his shoulders, and Leon, at the touch of those hands, seemed to break deep inside himself.

"Not Moshe," Joshua said. "It was never him. Now you know it was you."

The horror returned to Moshe immediately, making him tremble where he stood, the weight of the pistol dragging his hand down as it had not done before. What was happening was unreal, too bizarre to be true, and he wondered, with a bitter, self-wounding humor, if he was going insane. Yet Joshua and Leon were there, the one calm, the other trembling, and then he saw the glittering delirium in Leon's eyes as he grabbed hold of Joshua's wrists. "No!" he said. "I won't do it! You can't ask me to do it! I won't sacrifice myself for your madness! I won't do it! You're crazy!" The thunder rolled and the lightning flashed, daggering out of a cloudless sky, illuminating Leon's eyes as he clenched Joshua's wrists and tore his hands off his trembling shoulders. Joshua stepped back, smiling slightly, love and anguish in his face, and kept his eyes fixed firmly on Leon, refusing to pardon him.

"You claim to believe in nothing. That belief can now be tested. If, as you say, you believe in nothing, then you have nothing to lose. You must pull the trigger for me. Believing in nothing, you cannot sin. You will pull the trigger, Leon. You have left yourself no choice. You were called but not chosen, and let bitterness destroy your faith, and now, with neither faith nor belief, you have nothing to live for. My death will release you, Leon. It will bring you revelation. Whether exalted or debased, good or bad, right or wrong, that revelation, whatever it reveals, is all you have left. Now find out. Pull the trigger."

Leon sobbed and turned away, his shoulders stooped, his body quivering, and Moshe felt a terrible wonder and grief that almost swept him away. The thunder rolled and the lightning flashed, daggering through the darkening sky, and the pale moon, like an eye slowly closing, was obscured by a passing cloud. The crimson haze started fading, letting the cliffs sink into darkness, and Moshe felt the wind tugging at his clothes, then saw it sweeping the sand up. Leon sobbed and quivered helplessly, his back still turned toward them, and the sand, carried up on the growing wind, started swirling around him.

Moshe raised the pistol slowly, feeling lost and demented, only aware that it was he who had started this bleak affair and that he could not, no matter what Joshua said, allow Leon to finish it. The pistol wavered in his hand, being whipped by the hissing wind, and he saw Joshua's head, the noble profile, the blowing hair, and then saw Kate's face floating before him, her dark eyes filled with anguish. That anguish lanced through him, lacerating his resolve, and he tried to think of Israel, the Middle East, the whole world, willing himself to believe that salvation could lie in one shot. He tried, but did not succeed, feeling embarrassed by his vanity, unable to accept that the future could depend on his action. Who was Joshua, after all? No one knew, nor ever would. He was a man of unusual talents, of seductive and mesmeric powers, but for all that he was still a normal man, flesh and blood, very mortal. Let the world decide its own fate, let the sands of time take charge: it was vanity and possible hysteria that had led to this moment.

"Don't be frightened," Joshua said. "Death will not have dominion. I go to my death to bring life to the wounded and lost. What is asked is necessary. Beyond death is revelation. And revelation, its horror or glory, is all we can hope for."

Moshe started lowering the pistol, feeling lost and defeated, now aware that no matter what Joshua said, he could not pull the trigger. The thunder rolled and the lightning flashed, and he looked up, disbelieving, and saw the enormous black cloud descending as the sand spiraled skyward. The desert was in revolt, either attacking or defending Joshua, and Moshe lowered his eyes and saw Leon turning into the swirling sand. He stared bitterly at Joshua, rubbed his lips with one hand, let the tears trickle over his knuckles, and then turned toward Moshe.

Moshe stepped back automatically, hardly aware that he was doing

it, as Leon stumbled toward him out of the swirling sand, his eyes
haunted and anguished. Joshua watched him, saying nothing, then
raised his eyes to the sky. Leon reached out and snatched the pistol
from Moshe and then turned away from him. Moshe stood there,
briefly frozen, looking down at his empty hand, then looked up to see
Leon pointing the pistol directly at Joshua. The pistol wavered in his
hand, being whipped by the howling wind, and Moshe stood there,
paralyzed, unable to accept what he was witnessing, and then found
his hands clawing at Leon, trying to snatch back the pistol.

Leon sobbed and jerked away, then turned back, his right hand
swinging, and the pistol, smashing into Moshe's head, made him
stumble and fall. He managed to stay on his knees, his head reeling,
filled with pain, and the blood, pouring over his eyes, seemed to pour
over Joshua. He jerked and stumbled backward—only then did Moshe
hear the shot—and then raised his hands to shoulder level, his fingers
curved downward. Leon sobbed and fired again, without skill, his arm
jerking, and Joshua twitched and took another step back, his white
robe splashed with blood. The thunder rolled and the lightning
flashed, then the third shot rang out, and Leon sobbed as Joshua fell to
his knees, the sand swirling about him. He raised his arms in entreaty,
his dangling fingers dripping blood, and then the wind, after the
fourth and fifth shots, made him fall gently sideways. Leon sobbed
and ran forward, aimed the pistol, fired the last shot, and Joshua, his
white robes flapping wildly, quivered once and was still.

Moshe climbed to his feet, feeling dizzy, swaying slightly, then
looked through the dark, swirling sand, trying to focus his eyes. He
saw the huddled form of Joshua, his white robe like a fallen flag, the
pistol thudding into the sand by his head as Leon turned away from
him. Moshe walked forward, moving slowly, feeling nauseated and
weak, and reached out to take hold of Leon's shoulder and pull him
toward him. His hand found the wind-whipped air, the sand biting his
dangling fingers, then he saw Leon walking past the jeep and heading
into the wilderness. Leon was still sobbing—Moshe could hear it
from where he stood—and that sound, replacing the thunder and
lightning, was the cry of a dying man.

Moshe ran forward, calling out to him, trying to bring Leon back,
but then he stopped, the blood blinding him, the dizziness defeating
him, and sank to his knees in the sand, feeling drained and exhausted.
The wind suddenly died away, the swirling sand settled down, and the
cloud that had obscured the moon and stars was no longer in view. He

wiped the blood from his eyes, raised his head and looked at Leon, saw him shrinking and eventually disappearing in the immense, starlit wilderness. Only then, feeling broken, the full horror sweeping through him, did he turn back and look at that huddled form in the shivering white robe.

Joshua was dead.

PART FIVE:

Resurrection

"Touch me not; for I am not yet ascended to my Father: but go to my brethren, and say unto them, I ascend unto my Father, and your Father; and *to* my God, and your God."

— John, 20:17

"The end begins where truth reveals itself and forces wise men to stutter."

— Joshua

41

Every corridor in the hospital was being guarded by soldiers, all of them armed to the teeth and exceptionally experienced. Moshe nodded at them as he passed, taking no pleasure from their presence, too aware of the reason for their being here and disturbed by that reason. He still felt that he was dreaming, that Joshua's death had not occurred, but the news of that death had been broadcast two days ago, and already the repercussions were beginning to shake the whole Middle East.

Kate was in a private ward, propped up against some pillows, her long hair piled up on her head, shadows under her dark eyes. He stood in the doorway, looking at her, hardly able to walk in, his guilt and shame more than he could bear, his deception lying upon him like chains and draining his spirit. She smiled when she saw him, but her pain was clearly visible, etching fine lines around her eyes and making her lips shiver slightly.

"*Shalom*, Kate."

"*Shalom*. Don't just stand there: come in. You look almost as ill as I feel; we should change positions."

He walked up to the bed and kissed her, appreciating her attempt at humor, but knowing, with his cheeks burning shamefully, that her smile hid real anguish. Moving back, he saw her dark eyes, luminous with grief and fear—grief at Joshua's death and fear for her child, still convinced that the blow to her abdomen had caused her some damage. He pulled the wooden chair closer, sat down, and held her hand, trying to keep the guilt from his face, feeling furtive and criminal.

"So, how do you feel?"

She shrugged. "Not too good. I have the same dreams every night, and during the day I'm depressed. I'm trying not to give in to it —honestly, I'm trying—but the tears come before I can control them, and I feel like a child."

"It's Joshua," he said, ashamed to even speak his name. "You still haven't recovered from his death; it's been a very bad shock to you."

She closed her eyes and turned her head away, shielding her face with a cupped hand, obviously about to weep and trying to hide it, her body trembling in spasms.

"Why?" she said. "*Why?* And what was he doing out there? Someone must have taken him out there for that very purpose."

"We'll probably never know," Moshe lied, his cheeks burning, his eyes lowered. "He was found by some wandering Bedouins—two days after it happened."

"Maybe they did it."

"No," Moshe said, "they didn't. We have witnesses who saw them in the camel market in Beersheba at approximately the same time as Joshua was killed. The Bedouins stayed in Beersheba until late that evening, and found Joshua on their way back to the Negev; that, plus the fact that they had no weapons, makes it clear that they were innocent."

He stared at the back of her head, wanting to reach out and stroke her hair, but his guilt at the deception he was practicing made the thought seem indecent.

"Where is he now?"

"Right here—in the morgue. We thought it best to keep him in Jerusalem until we decide where to bury him. He'll probably be buried near here, on the Mount of Olives, more or less where we found him."

Kate quivered and started sobbing, her back still turned toward him, her chin on her chest, her spine curved, her hands covering her face. Sunlight poured through the window, falling obliquely on the bed, and Moshe felt it on his already burning cheeks as he leaned over toward her. She had pulled her hand from his in order to cover her face, but he tugged at her elbow, gently coaxing her hand back, and when finally it slid into his, he drew it close to his chest. She leaned back against the pillows, sniffing mournfully, her eyes fixed on the ceiling.

"You'll forget it," Moshe said, "sooner or later. . . . The pain won't last forever."

His own words cut a hole in him, letting the pain rush in, the awful hypocrisy of his remark carrying shame and remorse. Joshua was dead—and he had planned it and witnessed it—and now, weaving his web of deceit, he wanted to walk out and throw up. He had lied to her, betrayed her, and was still lying to her—and would, to his shame and dismay, have to lie in the future. His love turned to lead inside him, weighing him down and draining his spirit, and he raised her hand and pressed his lips to it, trying to blot out his guilt.

"I'm always frightened," Kate said. "I feel frightened and confused. I'm haunted by the conviction that he's not really dead, that his presence, at least, is still around me, refusing to leave. The dreams are very vivid—the sort of dreams you don't forget—and sometimes, when I sleep during the day, I'm not sure that they're dreams. I'm often convinced that I'm awake—I check the room, pinch myself —and then, if I blink and look again, I can still see him standing there. He's always standing in front of the door, right there, where you stood, saying nothing, his hands by his sides, smiling very ambiguously. Sometimes I call his name. When I do, he smiles and nods. When he does that, I usually feel comforted and drift into sleep. . . ."

She blinked her eyes and licked her lips, obviously foiled by her own thoughts, trying to reconcile reality with the dream and find some solid ground.

"I can't forget what happened," she said. "I mean what happened the night he died. When I saw him, when the world turned upside down, I felt nothing but fear. I loved him, but he frightened me —whether in my mind or not—as if, instead of the warmth I had felt in him, there was nothing but malice. It was evil, pure and simple, radiating from his image; and I wondered then, and still wonder now, if it came from myself."

"No," Moshe said, squeezing her hand gently, "it was not in yourself. It was death, Kate—you sensed that he was dying—and what you felt was just fear."

Moshe could not meet her gaze, feeling defiled by his own actions, and he studied the tanned skin of her wrist, very smooth, highly sensual. He thought of Leon in the desert, his eyes bright with delirium, being lured into Hell's fiery portals to find revelation. Glory or horror; salvation or damnation: just as he would never know Joshua's true nature, so, too, would he never come to know what Leon had found. Death, almost certainly, and beyond that, the unknowable: the peace of eternal sleep or the nightmare of life ever after. Moshe shuddered to think of it, wanting only the one life, and then bent down and kissed Kate's tanned wrist, taking hope from her flesh.

"You're very affectionate today, Moshe."

"I feel lonely without you."

"I feel frightened without you—unprotected—and I want to get out of here."

"You have to stay a few more days. The doctors want to keep their eyes on you. They don't think the blow caused any damage, but they want to be sure."

It was the wrong thing to say, and he knew it as soon as he said it, silently cursing himself for his stupidity when she turned away from him. She covered her face with her right hand, her body shaking as she wept, obviously trying to stop the tears from coming but unable to do so.

"Damn him!" she sobbed. "It was Joshua—I didn't imagine it. He was there, materializing wherever I looked, and he caused all that havoc. What was he trying to do? Was he deliberately trying to hurt me? He destroyed the room and nearly destroyed me and might have damaged our child. It was Joshua! I know it! When he smiled, I was terrified. He made all those things happen, tried to frighten me and hurt me, as if he was seeking revenge for something I'd done. What did I do? Was he after our child? Damn him! He tried to hurt our child, and I'll never forget that."

She shook her head from side to side, still sobbing, her body shuddering, and Moshe just held her hand, feeling humiliated and guilty, not able to forget what he had done, letting it eat at his heart.

"No," he said, "I think you're wrong. I think it was all a sort of accident. You were very close to him—you seemed to be tuned to his every impulse—and I think that when he was dying, perhaps just before death, the emotions he went through, rage or fear, grief or pity, were made manifest through you, in the house, with particular force. Joshua must have thought about you—you were the person who gave him life—and, in thinking about you, caused the manifestations that occurred about the same time as his death. Not evil or malicious, Kate—possibly not good *or* evil—perhaps simply a paraphysical manifestation of conflicting emotions. You were there, Kate, and felt what he felt at the moment of death."

In saying this, he accused himself, since he had sanctioned the original plot; and now knowing it, unable to forget it, his humiliation was total. He felt haunted and debased, pursued by his own shadow, unable to look in the mirror that reflected his soul. He had planned it for Israel, even knowing how Kate felt, and in doing so had made a clear choice between his country and Kate. He was loath to admit that, but the truth of it stuck, and his only consolation was the fact that he had changed his mind, stopping out of fear or his love for Kate —though he would never know which.

"We'll never know," Kate said despairingly. "That's what haunts me more than anything. We'll never know if he was good or evil, malicious or concerned, and because of that, if anything happens to my baby, I'll never forgive myself."

"Yourself or Joshua?"

"Not Joshua—myself. For having given myself to Joshua. For believing, without proof, on faith, that Joshua was good. I should never have done that—it was romantic and immature—and now, even suffering as I am for his death, I can't resist a certain hatred of him —for endangering my baby."

"The baby is in no danger."

"Damn you, we don't know that! You're a man, you're not pregnant, and you can't know what I feel—so don't sit there and tell me there's no danger—you don't know a damned thing!"

He recoiled from her sudden anger, almost stunned by her vehemence, and felt the blush rising to his cheeks as the hurt made his heart leap. He saw her turning her head away, obviously shocked by her own words, and then her body, again, started shaking as she choked back her sobs.

"Oh, damn it," she said. "I didn't mean to say that. Really, Moshe, I didn't, I didn't—I didn't mean to say that. I'm behaving like a bitch, trying to take it out on someone. I'm frightened for our baby, I'm convinced something is wrong, and so, even knowing that it's your child as well, I'm trying to make you suffer in my stead, as all bitches do. Yes, I'm a bitch—I'm being thoughtless and selfish—but I just can't get it out of my head that something is wrong."

Sniffing the tears back, wiping her eyes, she turned to face him once more, and he stood up and leaned across the bed to pull her into his arms. She came to him like a child, her strength and courage briefly weakened; and he embraced her and kissed her tangled hair, his love rendering him desolate. He deserved what she had said for the damage he had done—to Joshua, Leon, Paul Frankel, and her—and, accepting this, feeling her warmth in his arms, he let his brimming pain be the punishment that might never end.

"The baby's fine," he murmured. "There's no need to worry. I've talked to the doctors and they said that nothing's wrong, that you're just suffering from a form of mild hysteria that will soon go away. You've got to try to forget Joshua—to forget what happened in the house—and just try to remember that both you and the baby are fine. You'll soon be a mother, Kate—a mother—and nothing else matters."

"You spoil me."

"You deserve it."

"You deserve more than me."

"Having you, I'm worth more than I was. I want our child . . . I want you."

He pressed his lips into her hair, holding her tight, feeling her warmth, and then she raised her face and kissed him on the lips, clinging to him, her eyes closed. He then closed his own eyes, kissing her cheeks, her neck and shoulders, traveling down through himself, through his crippling guilt and shame, and taking hope from the magic of her flesh with its promise of permanence. Their child would be an anchor, holding them steady in the storm, and he knew, as he gently released her, that she sensed that as well.

"I have to go now," he said. "I'm wanted urgently at the Knesset. There's a lot of Arab movement along the borders, and we have to get ready."

"Because of Joshua?"

"I'm afraid so. They're convinced that the Jews murdered him. Certain Jews, of course, are equally convinced that he was murdered by Arabs."

"You think there'll be more trouble?"

"I don't think—I'm certain. The Arabs think we've murdered their Mahdi, and they're set for a Holy War."

He didn't want to discuss it further, so he leaned over and kissed her, then hurried to the door and glanced back, trying to seem unconcerned. She was sitting up on the bed, her spine pressed to the pillows, and her dark hair, being piled upon her head, made her face look too thin. She smiled, but her eyes, dark and luminous, did not show the same humor.

"*Shalom*," he said.

"Come back soon," she replied. "It doesn't matter what we say or believe—I only know what I feel—and I'm frightened for my child, my body telling me something's wrong, and also because the dreams are so vivid, they seem almost real. Joshua's presence . . . I feel it."

He nodded and walked away, feeling as if he was deserting her, shivering a little as her parting words clung to him like a lingering bad dream. The armed soldiers were in the corridors, nodding respectfully as he passed, contrasting darkly with the white-smocked medics and nurses who were moving about with an air of quiet efficiency. The windows framed a bright day, the sun high in the sky, beaming down on the lower slopes of the Mount of Olives, where this hospital was situated.

Moshe longed to be outside, in open space and fresh air, but he forced himself to enter the chilled gloom of the well-guarded morgue. Joshua was stretched out on a table, still draped in his white robe, his eyes closed, his hands folded on his stomach, his feet bare and washed clean. Rabbi Latinavots, wearing a plain shirt and slacks, was silently looking down at him; he looked up when Moshe entered, and shook his head from side to side, a gesture of weary bewilderment, if not actually of sadness.

"*Shalom*, Moshe."

"*Shalom*, Jozsef."

"Well, he's back where he came from. A mortal man, he died like a mortal man and can be buried as such."

"Let's hope so," Moshe said.

He walked across to the table and looked down at Joshua, wondering what he expected to find and feeling shocked when he found it: the same mask of inhuman composure and impossible serenity. Joshua's face was the light, drawing it in and reflecting it, turning it back upon Moshe and making him burn. The face was innocent and wise, very young and very old, too blank to be real, too vivid to be forgotten, defying, in its terrible beauty and repose, definition and logic.

Shocked, Moshe stepped away, touching his dry lips with his fingers, blinking and then staring at Jozsef as if seeing a ghost. Jozsef smiled and spread his hands in the air to suggest wry defeat.

"Who was Joshua?" Jozsef sighed. "That mystery remains unsolved. It will haunt me for the rest of my days, frustrating my faith."

He dropped his hands and stared at Joshua, shivered slightly and looked away, his gaze roaming around the gloomy, windowless morgue before returning to Moshe.

"You saw Kate?"

"Yes."

"And how was she?"

"Not too good. She's still convinced that that blow to her stomach might have damaged the baby. The doctors think so too, but I didn't tell her that, since, as the doctors also said, her other fears aren't helping her condition."

"What other fears?"

"Joshua," Moshe said, keeping his eyes off the table. "She's having very vivid dreams—so vivid they seem real—to the point where she's no longer sure if she's awake or still dreaming. She sees him constantly, just standing there, smiling, his hands by his sides."

He noticed Jozsef's startled expression, his eyes widening, his cheeks flushing, and the fear that had recently become too familiar slithered back through his soul.

"What's the matter, Jozsef?"

"What you said . . . about what Kate saw . . . A great number of people—Jew, Arab, and Christian—are reporting the very same phenomenon."

"Dreams of Joshua?"

"More like visions. They also see him when awake: he has been seen in broad daylight, by more than one person at a time—at the Wailing Wall, in the Haram es-Sharif, by the Garden Tomb, and in the Garden of Gethsemane—and even in the Church of the Holy Sepulchre, reportedly standing by the Sepulchre itself, gazing down at the shelf that was cut out of the rock of Golgotha. Of course it could be mass hysteria—very common in religious matters—but some of the sightings have been remarkable . . . and have been reported by very reliable people."

Moshe glanced briefly at Joshua, felt cold and looked away, wondering about the nature of reality, if the mind knew a separate world.

"It's not helping us," Jozsef said. "It's merely increasing speculation. The obsession with Joshua, always acute, now seems even greater."

"I know," Moshe replied. "And it's contaminating the Arabs. Rashid Idriss is claiming that Joshua was the Mahdi, that the Jews arranged his murder, and that the Muslims are now honor-bound to take his body to Mecca."

"We cannot concede to that?"

"No," Moshe said, "we can't . . . and that's why Rashid is talking about a Holy War—to capture Joshua's body."

"Do you think that's likely to happen?"

"Yes, Jozsef, I do. The whole Arab world is obsessed with the idea of Joshua as the Mahdi, and because of that, for the very first time, they've put their differences aside. They don't care about the Americans and Soviets—they only care about their Mahdi—and the possibility of dying in a Holy War is a song in their hearts. They're massing along all our borders, defying the Americans and Soviets, and I think their one thought is for Jerusalem and Joshua's body."

"Is Joshua's corpse worth a war? I'm not at all sure that it is. If Jerusalem is threatened, it might be best to hand the body over."

"We can't do that, Jozsef, for more than one reason. As you know only too well, too many Jews think of Joshua as the Messiah; consequently, if we handed him over to the Muslims, we would be accused of blasphemy and find ourselves fighting our own Jews. Likewise, the Christian world has adopted him as the Christ of the Christians, and would therefore be similarly outraged if we surrendered his body. No, Jozsef, we're hemmed in on both sides, so we have to keep hold of him."

He felt the burning of his cheeks and turned his face away from Jozsef, not wanting him to see the guilt and shame that his words had encouraged. What he had said was perfectly true, but not the most important truth: the fact that Joshua's body had to stay here in Israel to inflame the Arabs into the war that the Americans needed. The plan formulated in the desert now had to proceed, in order that the Americans could intervene—to their benefit and Israel's. Moshe had sanctioned that plan, in shame and humiliation, but now, unable to meet Jozsef's gaze, he wondered what he had started.

"Joshua," Jozsef said, letting the word hang in a brief silence. "He came, he saw, and he conquered—and he hasn't left yet."

They both looked at Joshua's body, both frightened and fascinated, and at that very moment, as if Joshua had responded, the floor shook and they heard a dull rumbling sound that seemed not too far off.

Moshe knew the sound well and felt the dread lancing through him, seeing nothing but Jozsef's widening eyes as his head jerked around. The floor shook again and the rumbling noise repeated itself, and then Moshe headed straight for the door, pushed forward by instinct. He heard Jozsef calling his name, but ignored him and heard his footsteps, following him as he rushed out of the morgue and turned into the corridor. The armed soldiers were alert, checking their weapons, shouting remarks, while the medics and nurses were frozen, as if trying to see through the walls. The rumbling sound came again, making the floor beneath him shake, and then he heard another sound, the muffled roar of an explosion, and a jet plane shrieked low across the hospital, heading south toward the Negev.

Moshe started to run, hearing the soldiers shouting around him, their voices drowned out by another plane, then a third and a fourth. The walls shook and trolleys rattled, bolts were slamming home in rifles, and then another explosion, obviously very close by, reverberated along the corridor and was followed by the growling of tumbling walls. There was bawling, a single scream, and Moshe raced into the reception area to see the swirling clouds of dust and smoke where part of the wall had been blown away. He stopped and took it in—the bloody bodies in smoldering debris—and then turned in the direction of the reception office, wanting a telephone. More jets screamed overhead, another explosion came from Jerusalem, and then an army lieutenant, very young and bathed in sweat, emerged from a dust-covered doorway and stopped just in front of him.

"HQ has just called," he said, speaking breathlessly and informally. "The whole Arab world seems to be on the move and heading straight for our borders. They're already crossing at Lebanon and still advancing from Syria—and their aircraft are heading toward us from Jordan and Egypt. They're obviously defying the Americans and Soviets—neither of whom have made any move yet—and the attacks appear to have been synchronized with the bombs that have just exploded all over Jerusalem. Right now, on the West Bank, and in certain areas of Jerusalem, there are an awful lot of Arabs on the loose, all carrying weapons. In short, we have a war in Jerusalem —and at all of our borders."

Jozsef raced up to Moshe, breathing heavily, sweating profusely, his dazed eyes taking in the swirling smoke and the bodies lying in rubble. He stared at Moshe, obviously shocked, and Moshe had to turn away, unable to believe that he had sanctioned what was now just beginning.

42

It was a slow descent into Hell. At first, from the summit of Mount Tabor, it looked almost pretty, the sun shining on the hills of Galilee, reflecting off the lake itself, beyond which, the smoke of war no longer visible, were the lost Golan Heights. It was also pretty in the other direction, looking across the Plain of Jezreel, where the Israeli tanks, forming a wall in front of Megiddo, were moving forward into mushrooms of purple smoke and darting fingers of yellow flame. The Lebanese guns were beyond the plain, south of Nazareth and Haifa, and their shells, exploding between the advancing tanks, soon started darkening the clear air. Moshe looked back in the other direction, the binoculars straining his eyes, and saw the Syrians advancing, a mass of ants on the rolling hills, spread out between Tiberias and Zefat, a thin smoke hovering over them.

Most of Galilee was gone and he couldn't hold the plain much longer, so he stood up in the jeep, feeling weary and bitter, and waved his right hand, very slowly and methodically, to indicate that the evacuation of the Mount should commence. The trucks and jeeps moved out quickly, trundling down the dusty road, the sun flashing off mirrors and weapons, a strong wind whipping parched grass. The dust soon filled the air, forming a single, boiling cloud, and Moshe had to use his binoculars again to see the plain just below him. The tanks were still advancing, moving left and right sluggishly, trying to avoid the explosions of flame and spewing earth, crawling forward into the darkening smoke, the soldiers spread out behind them.

"We need more aircraft," Sergeant Aranow said. "We can't hold out without them. Those tanks won't hold anything back if we don't get more air support."

"We won't get it," Moshe replied. "We have to let this area go. Most of the aircraft are being used to stop the Arab advance in Sinai, the few remaining to keep the Jordanians back, though that can't be for long."

"We're pulling out of the Jezreel Valley?"

"We don't have much choice. The Syrians have captured most of Galilee, the Lebanese have captured Haifa, and so we have to pull back to north of Samaria and hope that something will break."

"That leaves a lot unprotected."

"I repeat: we have no choice. Anything north of Nablus will simply have to go, including all the coastal towns north of Netanya. We've got to try to hold Tel Aviv and Nablus, and keep them out of Samaria. If they manage to get Samaria, they'll get Jerusalem, and we can call it a day."

The scenario, a nightmare, was not much worse than the reality: the Jordanians were advancing toward the River Jordan, the Egyptians were advancing across Sinai and would soon be in the Negev, and in and around Jerusalem, where army strength was minimal, there were bombings, ambushes, and minor battles every hour of the day. Moshe despaired when he thought about it, and felt fear when he thought of Kate, wondering if she was safe in the hospital, guarded or not.

"It's hopeless," the sergeant said, scratching his nose in a desultory fashion, his eyes scanning the Plain of Jezreel below, where the tanks advanced slowly. "We can't hold them off on all sides without some kind of help; we don't have enough men, enough tanks, enough aircraft, enough anything. We need the intervention of the Americans or Soviets, whether we like it or not."

Moshe looked down on the Plain of Jezreel, which seemed a lot closer now, and saw the smoke swirling across the tanks and over the men massed behind them. The Lebanese guns were firing constantly, the shells hissing and then shrieking, exploding with a terrible roaring between the tanks, black smoke boiling from balls of fire.

"They're already moving," Moshe said. "They were just taken unawares. They didn't think the Arabs would ignore them, they didn't expect them to be coordinated, and they certainly weren't prepared for the sheer number of Arabs involved."

He thought of it with bitterness—not forgetting his own part in it —now faced with the fact that the situation was out of control, and that neither the Americans nor the Soviets could put a stop to it. The Americans had miscalculated, underestimating the Arab fervor, and had, in rerouting their forces to the Arab oil states of the Persian Gulf, depleted their forces in the Arab Republic of Egypt and opened the door for the invasion of Sinai. This situation, bleak at best, had degenerated further when the Soviets, outraged at the "imperialist aggression" of the Americans, used the major portion of their forces in Syria and Jordan for a "defensive" invasion of northern Iraq, thus weakening the line dividing the Syrians and Jordanians from Israel and allowing them to quickly conquer all of Galilee. Both the Soviets and the Americans were now rushing in fresh forces, but the likelihood of them stopping the Arab advances seemed very remote. Indeed, Jerusalem could fall before the Americans managed to reach it; and Moshe, when he thought of this possibility, knew what the damned suffered.

The road ahead was leveling out, curving toward the Plain of Jezreel, and Moshe gazed across the flat expanse of earth at the smoke in the distance. The tanks looked like large stones, the troops like ants in the rear, and the shells were raining down at a terrible rate, the noise now a lot louder. The earth roared and erupted, spewing soil and jagged flames, the flames forming into brilliant balls of fire that spun crazily in the air and then spiraled away as black smoke. The tanks moved left and right, lumbering through the inferno, and then the soldiers, suddenly within range of the guns, started zigzagging furiously. The shells shrieked and then exploded, fire and earth swirled and soared; then one tank was hit, slewing sideways, vomiting smoke, and then a series of explosions ripped viciously through the soldiers, throwing them into the air like broken dolls and then hurling them down again.

Moshe tore his eyes away and looked at the trucks ahead, the column now following the road across the plain toward the ruins of Megiddo. The army was scattered around Megiddo, the tents flapping in the wind, more tanks and half-tracks and men moving out every minute. From here Megiddo was a small mound on the skyline, rising above the army massed around it, its modest ruins overgrown. Megiddo: *Har Megiddo*. Armageddon: the ultimate battlefield . . . Now the battle had come, very possibly the final battle, and Moshe suddenly smelled the smoke and cordite as the trucks raced ahead.

The trucks growled, the guns roared, the shells shrieked and exploded, and the smoke, swirling crazily above the tanks, was carried back on the wind. The air suddenly turned dark, became a gray, choking cloud, and then the trucks up ahead started scattering left and right, driving around the outlying tents and braking near the big guns. Men were running back and forth, reduced to shadows in the murk, while the big guns, roaring awesomely, rocking violently to and fro, made the very earth shake beneath them as they belched smoke and flame. Moshe's jeep braked to a halt, its wheels shrieking in the soil, and he stood up and jumped out immediately, the smoke making his eyes sting.

General Meshel was in the command tent, jabbing his fingers at some officers, all of them grouped around a trestle table that was covered in maps. He looked up when Moshe approached, not smiling, his eyes bloodshot, but his hand reached out to touch Moshe on the shoulder in a gesture of sympathy.

"We have to pull back," Moshe said. "The Syrians have nearly reached Mount Tabor. When we left, their southernmost flank was closing in on Sharona, so it's only a matter of time before they get here."

"And the Lebanese?"

"Their guns are close, and their army's advanced to Yoqne'am; another arm has advanced through Haifa and is moving down the coast, and should shortly be reaching the outskirts of Caesarea."

"What about air support?"

"It's not possible," Moshe said flatly. "We need all our remaining aircraft down south, for the Sinai and Jordan."

The guns roared and the ground shook, the Lebanese shells kept falling, and more tanks and half-tracks were pulling out, churning up the dried earth. He glanced across the Plain of Jezreel, saw the flames and soil erupting, the black smoke swirling across the weaving tanks and zigzagging men. It was a nightmarish scene, extraordinarily violent and surrealistic, the soldiers looking like specters in the dark, streaming smoke, the tanks resembling weird prehistoric monsters, some broken and dying.

"We're being slaughtered," General Meshel said.

"Pull them back," Moshe replied. "We can't hold the Galilee any longer, so there's no point in staying here."

The general reached for the field phone and Moshe stared across the plain and saw the Syrian jets glinting above Mount Tabor, heading straight for the camp. He opened his mouth to warn the officers, automatically, hardly thinking, but before the words were out of his mouth the jets were diving straight at him. He saw the smoke trail of the rockets, heard the jets screaming past, and then the ground ahead erupted, geysering up through the tents, forming monstrous umbrellas of spewing soil and smoke, immense balls of brilliant fire spreading

ut and soaring upward and then splashing back down again. The
ents disintegrated in a second, became smoldering rags in flight,
apping furiously and falling on the human torches who were
creaming dementedly. The jets returned, shrieking hideously, the
ockets howling, then the hell began again, the flames devouring men
nd tents, a tank outlined in flames, a truck coughing and then
xploding, the smoke and dust swirling across the camp with the force
f a hurricane.

General Meshel was bawling, his mouth close to the field phone,
rdering his tank commanders to pull back, his voice barely audible.
he ground spasmed and erupted, making a catastrophic din, and a
loud of dust was swept through the tent on a wave of fierce heat.
Moshe turned and saw light, was sucked into it, somersaulting, fell
own through a tunnel of scorching heat and found himself on his
ack. Dust and soil rained upon him, pouring out of an oily black
moke, and he kicked his feet, rolled onto his belly, and then stood up
gain. General Meshel was slamming the phone down, smacking his
emple with his free hand, then he blinked, stared at Moshe, and
odded vigorously, his lips set in a tight line.

"Right," he said, "they're coming back. They can actually see the
Lebanese. You men"—he turned to the officers around him—"start
evacuating the camp."

The officers scattered in different directions, zigzagging around the
erupting earth, and Moshe looked above the flames of the burning
camp to see the jets flying off. Blackened men were screaming
terribly, all blistered, some still smoldering, and the medics were
racing frantically through the smoke, carrying stretchers and field
packs. He saw blazing trucks and tanks, the skeleton frames of burned
tents, a blind man wandering aimlessly about, his hands clawing his
bloody face. Then he looked the other way, across the ancient Plain of
Jezreel, saw the first of the soldiers racing back out of the smoke, the
tanks rattling and rocking behind them, some smoking, some burning.

Another telephone rang and General Meshel picked it up, his free
hand reaching up to stop the blood that was pouring out of one ear. He
shook his head and listened intently, trying to hear above the
exploding shells, while behind him, like phantoms in a nightmare, his
men ran from the swirling smoke. The shells were still falling, tearing
the retreating men to pieces, the flames illuminating the smoke and
seeming to push the earth ahead of them, after which the earth rained
back through the smoke in great looping waves. Moshe stared at it,

mesmerized, his guilt and shame freezing thought, and then General Meshel tugged at his arm and held the phone out toward him.

"It's the prime minister," he said. "He wants to talk to you. He sounds very agitated."

Moshe took the telephone, covering one ear with his hand, trying to hear above the roaring of the guns and the cataclysmic explosions.

"Shlomo?"

"How are things?"

"Terrible," Moshe said honestly. "I'm afraid we've lost the whole of the Galilee, and we'll have to pull back."

"Where are the Syrians?"

"Right here."

"And the Lebanese?"

"Practically here. They're also moving south along the coast, clearly heading for Tel Aviv."

Ben Eliezer was silent, obviously shocked by what he was hearing, and Moshe looked straight ahead to see the men pouring out of the streaming smoke. They were running and falling, catapulting and spinning, mere puppets in a maelstrom of daggering flames and dark, swirling soil. A tank shuddered and exploded, its barrel snapping and flying away, its turret lid falling back to reveal a man's head and shoulders, briefly silhouetted in a tongue of yellow flame that fanned over the tank.

"I need you back here," Ben Eliezer said. "I want you personally to take charge of Joshua. I want his body removed from the morgue and taken out of Jerusalem to our temporary HQ in the New Hebrew University, where we'll keep it until this situation is resolved. We can't afford to lose him, Moshe—it would have catastrophic results—and Jerusalem is now practically in a state of siege, with Arabs running all over the place. I'm talking about professional fighters, men well trained and rehearsed; they've bombed the Central Post Office and the Hebrew Union College, the Jewish Agency, half a dozen synagogues, and various parts of Mea She'arim. We caught some of them at it and tugged their tongues for information: they belong to Rashid Idriss, parachuted into the Negev, and now we've reason to believe that Rashid is here himself, making his way to Jerusalem with a group of skilled commandos, determined to get to the Augusta Victoria Hospital and take Joshua out of there."

"That's where Kate is," Moshe said.

"I know, Moshe. I know. You can collect her as well and bring her here to the university; we'll then transfer her from here to the Hadassah Medical Center, where you'll be able to keep a closer eye on her. I want you to do it immediately, Moshe. We can't afford to lose Joshua's body. Joshua might be the only card we have left: we might need him for bartering."

"Bartering?"

"With the Arabs. I don't think the Americans can help us. In their greed for the Arab oil states, they left it too late, and now, even though they're trying to get here, I don't think they've a hope. The Arabs will get here before them—I don't think we can pretend otherwise—and the only thing that might keep them out is the offer of Joshua."

"What about the Jews and Christians?"

"We can't worry about that now. Let the Christian world protest —we can handle that when it comes—but an Israel filled with any kind of Jew is better than no Israel at all."

"All right," Moshe said. "I'll do it."

Ben Eliezer hung up and Moshe slammed the phone down as the retreating men poured in around the tent, covered in filth and exhausted. The falling shells were moving closer, the explosions making the tent shake, the dust and soil pouring in on waves that lashed his skin like a whip. He heard the growling of the tanks, the frantic roaring of trucks and half-tracks, and looked around to see them all moving off, heading back toward Samaria. General Meshel was staring at him, suppressed anguish in his bloodshot eyes, then he turned away and watched his men retreating, his shoulders stooped in dejection. Moshe walked up beside him and gripped his shoulder, wondering how it could come to this.

"They want me in Jerusalem," he said. "I've got to go immediately. Don't hang around here longer than you have to; we'll need you down south."

The general nodded, but said nothing, his eyes fixed on the retreating soldiers, then he suddenly stepped forward, straightening his shoulders as he walked, bawling orders and waving his hands as the column moved off.

Sergeant Aranow was in the jeep, the earth erupting all around him, and he glanced around when Moshe waved his hand and told him to move. The jeep was moving as Moshe climbed in, reversing sharply in clouds of dust, and then it roared and wound its way through the retreating soldiers, passing trucks and half-tracks. Moshe caught a glimpse of General Meshel, standing upright in another jeep, but then a cloud of smoke obscured him, Sergeant Aranow put his foot down, and when Moshe next looked the general was gone, far behind with the marching men.

They soon left the column behind, traveling an empty road to Jenīn, then turning onto the road to Nablus and Ramallah, racing past the fields of olive trees and grapevines and wheat, the sun blazing out of a sky free of smoke, the wheat bending in waves. Moshe saw little of the scenery, his senses numbed by defeat, his one thought to get Kate out of the hospital before it was too late. He felt drained and exhausted, letting time pass in a dream, but then Sergeant Aranow shouted, his finger jabbing straight ahead, and when Moshe looked up, he saw a column of dust spiraling over the road ahead.

Moshe reached for his Uzi gun as Sergeant Aranow slowed down, one hand still on the steering wheel, the other sliding toward his pistol. They came closer to the column of dust, saw one civilian, then another, a great mass of civilians tramping the road to Jerusalem, all fleeing from the direction of Netanya, in fear of the Lebanese. Some were walking, some cycling, some empty-handed, some carrying suitcases, others pushing carts piled with furniture, their children sitting on top. The column was moving very slowly, the wheels of the carts creaking loudly, and occasionally a car would push through, its horn honking dementedly.

"Go through them," Moshe said. "Just go through them. We've got to get to Jerusalem."

The sergeant did as he was told, advancing slowly through the shuffling people, honking his horn when they didn't move quickly enough, ignoring their pleas for a lift. They seemed desolate and lost, a cloud of dust hovering over them, the wind whipping frocks and baggy trousers and racing on through the wheat fields. The line stretched right down to Nablus, the town chaotic with refugees, but thinned out at the other side, letting the jeep race on ahead, the road rising and falling and bending on the way to Ramallah.

There were more refugees at Ramallah, snaking a mile back from the town, and Moshe felt a mixture of grief and frustration when Sergeant Aranow slowed down again. His grief was for Israel, for the homeless and the dead, and his frustration sprang out of his fear for Kate and what might already be happening. He was terrified of being too late—of marauding Arabs getting there before him—and when the jeep's horn started honking, when they parted the refugees, when they

rawled at a snail's pace through the crammed streets of Ramallah, he
elt the fear swirling like a tide that was sucking him under.

They broke through at last and headed straight for Jerusalem, the
ergeant pressing the gas pedal flat until the jeep roared and shook.
They soon reached the outskirts, passing apartment blocks and hotels,
and Moshe noticed how the streets were unusually empty, how the air
tank of smoke. He heard shots in the distance, an explosion, more
shots, saw some Jews running across the road ahead, crouched low,
carrying rifles. Sergeant Aranow didn't stop and Moshe raised his Uzi
gun, holding it level with his chest as he looked left and right, his eyes
earching for the glint of an assassin's weapon as the buildings rushed
past.

He saw nothing but the smoke, a constant gray gauze over the
streets, rising and falling like a wave, curving gently and spiraling.
There was the smell of conflagration—burning wood and smoldering
rubble—and then he saw the buildings reduced to ash, blue and
yellow flames flickering. An explosion, geysering sparks, a great
mushroom of black smoke—and then the jeep turned a corner and
some Arabs were firing at it, crouched low behind the rubble of
someone's home, their weapons making a chattering din. Sergeant
Aranow cursed, lowered his head, and put his foot down, and as the
jeep raced ahead, bouncing over the street's debris, Moshe twisted to
the side and aimed his Uzi gun and then pressed the trigger. The gun
bucked in his hands, making a horrible, metallic noise, and he saw the
rubble spitting pulverized limestone as he raked the whole area. The
Arabs dropped out of sight, jumped up again as he passed them, and
their guns started screeching and rattling as they dropped far behind.
Moshe fell across the seat, letting the bullets whine overhead, then sat
up and saw the walls of the Old City, also covered in drifting smoke.

The jeep bounced over more rubble, careened around a corner, and
was then racing alongside the Old City through another gray pall of
smoke. There were corpses by the roadside, the Arabs' robes flapping
frantically, the black coats of the Orthodox Jews almost brown from
the dust.

Moshe looked away, revolted, fixing his eyes on the Mount of
Olives, its summit rising above the pall of smoke and made bright by
the dazzling sun. Some jet planes shrieked overhead, speeding south
toward Sinai, and some Israelis, armed to the teeth, passed them by in
a truck. The lower slopes were free of smoke, the air crisp and very
clear, but then, when they neared the hospital, the smell of smoke

returned, and Moshe, to his horror, heard gunshots and another explosion.

"Hurry up!" he hissed. *"Hurry!"*

The sergeant took no precautions, but rushed into the hospital grounds, slamming on the brakes, sliding into a minor skid and then stopping in clouds of dust. Moshe jumped out without a word, seeing dark smoke streaming skyward, his heart pounding as he raced toward the entrance, thinking only of Kate. The smoke was coming from the far end, from an explosion around the corner, but some of the windows in the front wall were shattered, the walls pockmarked with bullet holes. The medical director was in the lobby, broken glass beneath his feet, shaking his head wearily from side to side as some nurses surrounded him; seeing Moshe, he quickly raised his right thumb and gave him a positive smile.

"Kate's out of it," he said. "I took the liberty of moving her earlier. You'll find her in the Hadassah Medical Center, probably under sedation. There's something wrong with her, Moshe, but we don't know yet what it is—in the meantime, however, she's safer there than she would be down here. Arabs shot us up, and they may not be the last; they also planted a bomb at the far wing and blew half the wall away. Luckily there's nothing down there but the morgue—and those patients don't hurt."

Moshe turned away and started running, closely followed by Sergeant Aranow, the sergeant unclipping his pistol as he ran, Moshe still holding his Uzi gun. Smoke was drifting along the corridor, growing darker the farther they went, until finally, by the time they reached the morgue, they could scarcely see anything. Moshe ran straight into the morgue, not concerned with lingering Arabs, and was met with a solid mass of smoke beyond which he saw nothing. Sergeant Aranow crashed into him, grabbed his shoulder, steadied himself, and then they both stumbled forward through the smoke and looked down at the table.

Joshua's body was gone.

43

The pain in his head was fierce, dragging Jozsef from unconsciousness, and he opened his eyes and looked all around him, thinking he was still in the morgue. The reality came soon enough, the truck growling and shaking beneath him, the canvas top shivering and shadowing the watchful eyes of Rashid Idriss and his Arab commandos, most of whom were sitting on the wooden seats on either side, their weapons clattering together as the truck bounced over holes in the road. Jozsef sat up very slowly, feeling dizzy, his head aching, and then gingerly touched the lump on his head where Rashid's pistol had felled him. He licked his lips and blinked repeatedly, trying to focus his watery eyes, and then looked beyond his feet to see Joshua stretched out on the floor. He stared at Joshua for a very long time, feeling worse every second.

Rashid was kneeling on the floor of the truck, holding on to the wooden seat, directly facing Jozef and right beside Joshua's prostrate body. He leaned forward, a slight smile on his face, looking at him without malice.

"How do you feel?" he asked.

"You knocked me unconscious, Rashid."

"I didn't want you running off to tell your men that we were taking the Mahdi."

"You mean stealing him," Jozsef said.

"I mean *taking* him," Rashid replied. "Joshua, as the Mahdi of the Muslims, must be buried in Mecca."

He smiled with his lips, but his eyes were brightly feverish, afire with the conviction of the belief that had inflamed the whole Arab world. Jozsef glanced down at Joshua, shivered briefly at the sight of him, then glanced around the back of the truck, at the faces of the young Arabs, most of whom were exhausted and filthy, their clothes reeking of cordite. They stared back at him, merely curious, their dark eyes without enmity, but still he felt uncomfortable and slightly frightened, wondering what would become of him.

"Why did you bring me along?" he asked.

"You might be useful as protection. Presumably the Jews value their chief rabbi and won't want us to harm him."

"Where are we going?"

"The Negev."

"And then?"

"We'll meet our brothers. Right now, the Arabs are advancing across the Sinai and will soon reach the Negev."

"You will never take Jerusalem."

"I think we will, Rabbi. The presence of the Mahdi has united us at last—and now nothing can stop us."

"The Americans or Soviets might stop you."

"That seems very unlikely. Their mutual suspicion and greed has greatly reduced their chances of stopping us. Most of the Soviets are in Iraq, most of the Americans are in the Persian Gulf, and now, though they are both rushing more men to Palestine, those men will arrive far too late to be of much use to them. We will capture Jerusalem, and, having captured it, will keep the Muslim world united around it, once and for all."

Jozsef held his aching head and examined the floor of the speeding truck, understanding that what Rashid had said could be true and deeply, bitterly shocked by the thought of it. *Yerushalayim,* the Holy City, the sacred center of Jewish belief, might indeed fall to the Arabs, taking Israel down with it, thus tearing the very heart out of Judaism and rendering it prostrate. The possibility was monstrous, too horrible to contemplate, and he tried to blot it out of his mind, feeling pain when he failed.

"You will not help the Muslims by claiming that Joshua is the Mahdi when half the world thinks of him otherwise. Joshua, whoever he is, has become all things to all men, and your insistence that he is the Mahdi will only turn the Christians and Jews against you."

"The Christians can do nothing—and the Jews will no longer hold Palestine."

"And what do you intend doing with the Jews once you have Israel?"

"We will treat the Jews as successive Jews have treated the Arabs: Palestine will be open to those Jews who obey Palestinian law."

The irony was not lost on Jozsef, but he found it difficult to smile,

his heart breaking at the thought of the possible fall of Israel and the
equally likely dispersal of the Jewish nation. He glanced out of the
back of the truck, saw the road racing away, lonely houses and
hamlets whipping past and then receding, bathed in the brilliant light
of the sun beyond the cloud of dust being thrown up by the wheels of
the truck. It was his land, his home, the very roots of his being, and
losing it, he now realized, would be tantamount to losing his soul.

"The Jews will not bend and accept Arab law," he said. "You know
that as you know, as surely as you are sitting there, that you will
eventually remove them completely from Israel."

"The choice will be theirs," Rashid replied, his dark eyes glittering.
"We will do unto them as they have done unto us—dispersing them, if
they resist, as the Arabs have been dispersed, and letting them enjoy
the refugee camps we will no longer need. Try not to be upset, Rabbi;
think of it as natural justice. The Jews will simply learn to taste what
they have made the Arabs taste: every Arab village demolished to
make way for new Jewish homes will be rebuilt over the ruins of those
Jewish homes; every Arab farmer exiled to make way for Jewish
settlers will return during the exodus of those settlers to the refugee
camps. I call it natural justice, but it is not even that harsh: we will
merely return to the Arabs what the Jews callously stole from them."

"There were injustices, certainly."

"It was deliberate exploitation."

"We are talking of the mistakes that men make when they fight for
their lives."

"The Jews were not fighting for their lives—they were fighting to
steal this land—and now, having had the land stolen from us, we are
fighting to get it back."

"And what if you do? Do you think it will bring you peace? There
will be no peace in Israel as long as the land is divided."

"Before the Jews it was not divided. Before the Jews it was not at
war. The Jews divided the land as they also divided Jerusalem,
robbing the Arabs not only of their homes, but of their houses of
worship. The Jews, in the self-righteousness of their obscene religion, tried to spit on Muhammad."

"Certain Jews, not all. You also have your extremists. The actions
of such people, on both sides, have not always been helpful."

"And that is your excuse? That only the extremist Jews are guilty?
Is the chief rabbi absolving himself from sin by denying his
responsibility for Jewish actions?"

"I am not denying my sin nor the sins of the Rabbinate; I am merely pointing out that both sides have their extremists, and that both sides, Jew and Arab, have been guilty of similar crimes."

"Our only sin, Chief Rabbi, is that we let the Jews deprive us of our Homeland. We did not steal from the Jews, but they from us, and that crime was one-sided."

"The Jews also needed a Homeland and it had to be Israel. In coming here, we simply returned to our original source."

"We let the Jews settle here. We gave them all the land they needed. When they had what they needed, they wanted more and began stealing from us. They proliferated like lice, taking more and more from us, casting us out of our own homes, murdering those of us who resisted, and eventually setting their sights on the whole of Palestine, irrespective of Arab rights. Don't mention original sources to me: you came here and stole from us."

Jozsef didn't reply, knowing the argument would go in circles, both of them right, both of them wrong, neither capable of answers. He looked out of the speeding truck, saw the hamlets and small holdings, the land rising and falling on either side, turning increasingly barren. The driver was using the back roads, avoiding the main towns, and the army truck, having been stolen from the Israelis, passed on unmolested. Jozsef recognized the area and knew they had just passed Beersheba, were heading south into the Negev Desert, where the war would soon rage.

He stared at Joshua, fascinated, thinking of what his presence had wrought—plots, counterplots, religious squabbles and political intrigues, a world divided in the name of God, the Holy Land once more in flames—and then imagined a dark, devouring mass closing in on Jerusalem. The Galilee had already fallen, the Jordanians were heading for the Jordan River, and right now, farther south, their hearts and minds inflamed by Joshua, thousands of Arabs were swarming across the Sinai Desert and approaching the Negev. The picture was terrifying, more so in his mind, his imagination, overwrought with grief and despair, turning it into a nightmarish reconstruction of the portals of Hell. It was, indeed, Armageddon, that final, most terrible battle, and Israel, if it managed to survive at all, would never be the same again. Jozsef wondered if he would live to see it, or if the Arabs would let him return, and the possibility that he had seen it for the last time sent a chill through his soul. He looked at Joshua and then at Rashid, the dead more alive than the living, and wondered at the

mystery of belief that had bound them together. Rashid, staring back
with brown eyes, was no longer smiling.

"What will you do with me?" Jozsef asked.

"When we get there?"

"Yes."

"We can hardly leave you to the mercy of the desert, so you'll have
to come with us."

"To the Arab Republic?"

"Of course."

"And then?"

"Wherever you wish."

"Including Israel?"

"No, I'm afraid not. Once in power, we will not permit the return
of the exiled chief rabbi."

"You mean you'll make an example of me."

"That is more or less the case. Your absence will emphasize that
Jerusalem is no longer Judaic, that the Rabbinate has little authority,
and that the new rulers, the Muslims, will not be intimidated by
protests from even the most illustrious of Jews. I will repeat what I
said before and would ask you to remember it: Palestine will be open
to those Jews who obey Arab law—but certain Jews, such as Ben
Eliezer and Major General Moshe Eitan, will be deported as an
example to Jewish citizens that we Arabs mean business. No Jew of
major importance will be allowed to remain, but the nameless, as long
as they obey our laws, will be treated respectfully."

"You will, in short, remove all possible resistance."

"We will ensure peaceful sovereignty."

Jozsef lowered his head, closed his eyes, and gave a sigh, the truck
growling and shaking all around him as it carried him far away. He
thought longingly of Jerusalem, as if years had already passed, as if
the shock of his abduction had disoriented him completely and was
eroding his sense of time and place. He thought of Kate and Moshe,
of Ben Eliezer and his fellow rabbis, and they seemed as remote as the
faces from his childhood, conjured out of some impossibly distant era
that could never return. He was traveling into the wilderness, across
God's scorching anvil, and he felt that he was making his final
journey into the void of the unknown.

"It was strange," Rashid said, "to blow the wall of that morgue
way and walk in and find you standing there."

"Why strange?"

"Unexpected. What did you want in there? We know from our sources that you have gone there every day—alone and for no apparent reason, just to stare down upon him. What were you looking for, Rabbi? What were you thinking? You have consistently refused to acknowledge him as either Messiah or Mahdi, so why were you so obsessed with him?"

Jozsef looked around the truck, at the faces of the Arab commandos, then looked out at the road as it unwound behind him, becoming a black line in the distance, snaking back through the desert. They were now deep in the Negev—the word itself meant "south"—and he felt that they were traveling south forever, to the world's hidden base. He saw the rippling sand dunes, the ochre cliffs tearing the blue sky, and his thoughts journeyed down to that point where man's logic meets truth. Why indeed had he gone to the morgue? What had drawn him there every day? One: The fact that Joshua's body had refused to decompose. Two: What the law courts would call "irresistible impulse," a need beyond personal belief or logic, an inane fascination. What had he hoped to find? Had he imagined that the dead would speak? Now, thinking about it, trying to avoid Rashid's brown eyes, glancing constantly, repeatedly at Joshua, he had to face the hard truth: He had gone there in expectation, waiting for something, wanting something, knowing only that Joshua had haunted his dreams with a startling reality.

"I don't know," he said.

"I think you do," Rashid replied. "I think that you were looking for the answer to your own brimming doubts."

"What doubts?"

"About Joshua's nature. About who or what he was. About whether he was the Messiah or Mahdi or the Christ of the Christians."

"I do not believe he was any."

"Then what?"

"I refuse to contemplate."

"You contemplated when you went to the morgue every day he was lying there."

"I was curious, of course."

"One day is curiosity. *Every* day is more like obsession, an irresistible impulse."

Jozsef stared at him, startled, the fear rippling through his flesh, not believing that Rashid could have used that particular phrase by accident.

"Yes," Rashid continued. "You may not have known why—you may have refused to admit it—but you went to that morgue, every day without fail, because you felt that you could find revelation in Joshua's dead eyes."

"What revelation?"

"The secret. *That* secret! The truth that lurks in sleep. The one mystery that has challenged all men, irrespective of creed: the secret, the unanswerable riddle of the nature of being. Yes, Rabbi, you went —in fear and trembling and expectation—or, rather than going, you were drawn because Joshua had called you. Messiah or Mahdi? The Christ of the Christians? Did such questions, in the end, really matter in the presence of Joshua? You said it yourself, Rabbi—he has become all things to all men—and that, in the end, is all that matters as the world spins in panic. *Of course* Joshua is the Mahdi! What else can he be to us? If Joshua is all things to all men, then he *must* be our Mahdi. You want him. We want him. The whole Christian world wants him. We all want him and need him, for reasons both good and bad; and, this being so, no matter what the rights or wrongs, someone must eventually claim him and loudly proclaim him. Jew, Christian, or Muslim? What known logic can resolve this issue? The truth, my Jewish friend, my searching rabbi, is in irresistible impulse. You were called as I was called. We were both called to that morgue. We were called, Jew and Arab, to journey south to where the desert brings silence."

"Silence?"

"The unanswerable. The only thing that unites all men. In my dreams he came to me, my eyes open or closed, and spoke, his robes white and radiant, of the need to believe. Truth or untruth. A clear choice between two opposites. Black or white, no gray areas in between, only hard, pure commitment. Come to me, he said. Either come or turn away. If you come, you must come for your brothers, who are all things and all men. And so, Rabbi, I came—to the morgue and to you—and there, at that moment, with the sound of the bomb still ringing, I saw you leaning over his body and knew that you, too, had been called. No, Rabbi, you are not protection. You are not here for that. You are here because he called and you answered, and now we are brothers. Will I take you to the Republic? Will I leave you in the desert? These are questions that are written on the wind as it blows toward Judgment Day."

Jozsef felt an electric shock, the sudden light of revelation, looking deep into Rashid's brown eyes and seeing himself twice reflected. What, indeed, was Joshua, if not all things to all men: the Messiah, the Mahdi, and the Christ all rolled into one. Did it matter who held Jerusalem? Did it matter who claimed Joshua? Joshua, being all things to all men, would join opposites together. Jerusalem would still stand, singing the gospel of the One, and life, being all things and all men, would continue evolving. Jerusalem the Golden, if nothing else, was an abstraction, a symbol of the brotherhood of man, built on disparate creeds. It did not matter who held Jerusalem—nor who held the body of Joshua—what mattered was that Joshua, in the wisdom of his silence, had forced men to examine themselves and acknowledge their frailty. Jew, Muslim, and Christian—all were one and the same —and Armageddon, that final, most terrible battle, would resolve their sad differences.

"Leave me in the desert," Jozsef said. "I want to die here in Israel."

"We will see what is written," Rashid replied. "Let Joshua decide."

What was it?—the end—an exploding hell of noise and heat, the truck screeching and careening sideways and leaping up and rolling over as its canvas top burst into flames and the men screamed and burned. First the sky, then the mountains, then the desert spinning over, a wall of flame rushing at him and around him, then the ground smashing into him. *Aircraft*—one thought, a spark of consciousness quickly fading—then sinking down through the noise, the screaming men, the crackling flames, through parting curtains of pain to a darkness that swept over him soothingly, offering oblivion.

The wilderness.

Silence.

44

The doctor was waiting for Moshe when he arrived at the Hadassah Medical Center, the light flashing off his rimless glasses and concealing his eyes. Moshe glanced quickly around the lobby, unable to ignore the weeping and wailing, seeing the floor covered in stretchers, the young soldiers covered in blood, parents and relatives grouped around them, murmuring soothing words, weeping. He looked away again quickly, returning his gaze to the doctor, and knew immediately, from the expression on his face, that the situation was serious.

"I'm sorry to drag you away at a time like this," the doctor said, "but I thought I should talk to you personally, before you talk to Kate." He nodded toward the corridor at the end of the chaotic lobby, then lightly touched Moshe on the elbow and walked him away. "Let's go to my office," he said. "It's a lot quieter there. These kids were all butchered in the battle just outside Netanya, and we don't have any room left in the wards."

They walked across the lobby, weaving their way through the wounded, sometimes having to step over the stretchers and their pitiful burdens. Moshe was glad when they reached the corridor, leaving the grief and pain behind, the stench of cordite and urine and sweat being replaced by the disinfected air of the hospital proper. The doctor said nothing as they walked, his Lithuanian face composed, and Moshe felt his heart fluttering with panic at what was to come. They soon turned into the doctor's office, a small room, Spartan and clean, and the doctor thoughtfully closed the door behind him before looking at Moshe.

"Do you want a drink?" he asked.

"No," Moshe replied, "I don't. I want to know what's wrong with Kate, and I haven't much time."

"She's in a dangerous condition, Moshe, and getting worse every hour. Having this baby could kill her, so we want to abort it."

The pain was cold and clean, cutting through his exhaustion, slicing the cobwebs out of his mind and reawakening his senses.

"What kind of condition? Something other than hysteria? Are you saying that the blow from that table somehow damaged the baby?"

"No, Moshe, I'm not saying that—the table didn't harm her at all —she's suffering from acute toxemia or, more accurately, eclampsia."

"And what might that be?"

"The toxemias are disorders occurring spontaneously only in human females and only during pregnancy or the puerperium, and they can, when severe, lead to numerous complications, including kidney, heart, pulmonary, and gastrointestinal disturbances."

"What causes it?"

"The factors producing it are still unknown: what *is* known is that there is a generalized spasm of the minute arteries, with associated severe circulatory effects. The term *eclampsia* is reserved for those instances in which there are convulsions or coma—both of which Kate has been intermittently suffering—and really severe eclampsia can lead to death."

The pain was clean no longer, but was now inducing nausea, a combination of fear and revulsion that made him start sweating.

"And you say that the causes are unknown?"

"That's right, Moshe: totally unknown."

Moshe looked down at the floor and closed his eyes, trying to think, trying to feel what Kate was feeling, doubtless fear and despair, still convinced that her affliction was caused by Joshua for some obscure reason. What could he now say that would make her think differently? It was a disease of unknown factors—without rational explanation —and that in itself would be enough to convince her that Joshua, still haunting her, had cursed her. He raised his eyes again, trying to keep his face controlled, determined to do the right thing by his wife, no matter what befell Israel.

"Are you absolutely sure it's this eclampsia thing?"

"Yes, Moshe," the doctor replied. "Kate's displaying all of the symptoms. She's excreting more than six grams of protein in the urine every twenty-four hours, she's suffering from pulmonary edema, or cyanosis—which is a bluish or purplish color of the skin—and, as I said, she is also suffering minor convulsions and brief comas—all of which indicate a rapidly deteriorating situation in which the toxemia is seriously affecting her cardiorespiratory apparatus. If we allow the pregnancy to come to term, she could end up with fluid in the lungs, which would in turn lead to heart failure. We therefore feel that her pregnancy should be terminated by cesarean section."

Moshe covered his face with his hands, pressing his eyelids with his fingers, observing the white spots in the darkness while his grief stripped him bare. For a moment he drifted away, seeing the advancing hordes of Arabs—now marching through Netanya, approaching the outskirts of Nablus, swarming down the Mountains of Moab toward the glittering Dead Sea, stretching across the Sinai Desert and inexorably heading for the Negev to begin the encirclement of Jerusalem—but even this nightmare, totally horrifying and final, could not for very long erase the pain he felt at what he was hearing. He knew what Kate felt—how much she wanted their child —and even as he looked up and heard his own words tumbling out, he knew what the answer to his question was going to be.

"You've told her all this?"

"Yes, we've told her—but she refuses, absolutely, no matter the risk, to have an abortion. She insists on bringing the pregnancy to term, and we can't talk her out of it. You understand, Moshe? It's up to you. If Kate sees this pregnancy out, if she insists on having the baby, we can't be responsible for her life. You have to talk to her, Moshe."

Moshe turned without a word and walked out of the office, heading for Kate's room as the blood pounded fiercely at his temples. The corridors were also full, the soldiers lining up for treatment, some leaning against the walls, their heads thrown back, their eyes closed, others grimly supporting one another, blood and filth on their uniforms. The doctor rushed up behind him, breathing heavily, his white coat flapping, and together they entered Kate's room and walked up to the bed.

Moshe looked down at her, shocked, pain and fear washing through him, knowing that he would never forget this day as long as he lived. She was lying back on the bed, her face thin, her skin blue, her eyes deeply shadowed and too large, filled with glittering dread. She smiled feebly when she saw him, her right hand rising weakly, and he took that hand and felt that he was holding a frail, wounded bird.

"*Shalom*, Kate."

"My Moshe."

"I've just heard the bad news. There's no doubt about it at all: you have to have the abortion."

"No, Moshe."

"You might die."

"No, Moshe, I won't do it. I'm going to have our baby—I *will* have it—and you won't talk me out of it."

"Kate, it's too *dangerous*! I simply can't let you do it! It's not that important—we can try again—but you can't have this baby."

She stared up at him, smiling, her lips parched and cracked, her eyes almost luminous with the fear that she refused to accept.

"I can't have my baby? Is that what you're trying to tell me? That having already killed one, I should kill another and go back to the start of it? No, Moshe, I won't do it. They can't be certain of what will happen. They *think* it might harm me—they don't know—and that isn't enough for me. Joshua didn't curse me, Moshe; he just put me to the test. He made me will the blood and face the truth, and having faced it, know faith. Now he's testing that faith—and my faith in our future—and I'm not going to let my fear destroy me for the rest of my life. How could I do it, Moshe? Could I then live with myself? Could I live with the possibility—after losing my baby—that the doctors had been wrong, and that I could have given birth to the baby without harming myself? We can't answer that question—not until the baby comes—and as long as there's the possibility that I'll survive, I can't let them destroy my child."

Her eyes glittered with fear, and with the need to have faith, and he sat down on the bed and leaned across her and placed his hand on her forehead. She was feverish and sweaty, her dark hair a tangled mess, but her face, with its strange, suppressed beauty, drew him in through its light.

"I'm worried for you," he said. "I want the child, but not that much. I don't want you doing this for me, because the risk is too great. It's not worth it, Kate. In giving birth you might die. I don't want to live without you, Kate—and I don't want this gamble."

"Have faith, my Moshe. I won't give up that easily. I see Joshua in my dreams, and when my eyes are wide open, and I know that what happened in our house was not the product of malice. He soothes my pain, Moshe, and eases my fear when he is here, and I know that what is happening is a test of my faith, and that whether I live or die, I can't sacrifice a child for the second time. He is kicking me right now—him or her, I can't tell—and as long as I feel that movement inside me, I won't have an abortion. Don't ask me again, Moshe. Don't force me to refuse you. I love you—very deeply and truly—but I won't kill my baby."

Her weak smile stole his will, her glittering eyes his resolve, and he leaned down, disguising his own fear, and pressed his lips to hers. Her free hand fell on his head, her fingers wandering through his hair, and he shuddered, feeling despair and terrible yearning, his heart breaking in two.

"My Moshe," she said. "Trust me."

He pulled his head back and sat upright, watching her hand fall away, then squeezed her other hand and stood up, his smile hiding his fear.

"All right," he said. "Fine."

"No, Moshe!" the doctor said.

"It's her child," Moshe said, "and her life . . . and I can't take that from her."

The doctor threw his hands up, rolling his eyes at the ceiling, then turned and walked out of the room, his white coat flapping behind him. Moshe looked down at Kate, feeling helpless, wrapped in pain, afraid that if he reached down and touched her he would break into pieces.

"I have to go now," he said.

"The war?"

"It's getting worse. I'll try to keep in touch as much as possible, but it might not be easy."

"Be careful."

"*You* be careful."

"I'll be all right—I know it."

"If I don't get back, I'll ring you this evening. *Shalom*, Kate."

"*Shalom*."

He turned around and walked out, hearing a plane screaming overhead, not daring to look back but averting his eyes from the soldiers who were filling all the corridors with blood and misery as they waited for treatment. He stepped outside, feeling broken, taking lungfuls of fresh air, glancing around him at the hills that were bathed in brilliant sunlight, not yet ravaged by the gray smoke of war and its multiple horrors. They would come soon enough, filling the silent air with screaming, and as he climbed into the jeep, and drove himself to the university, he shook with the anguish of his fears both for Israel and Kate.

The green fields of the university were swarming with troops, filled with trucks and half-tracks and big guns and portable canteens. More trucks were coming and going, bringing more troops into the area, swelling the ranks of the battalions around the nearby Knesset and the Shrine of the Book. Moshe went straight to the new HQ, in the heart of the university, passing hundreds of troops in the corridors of the main building, some sleeping, some reading, others eating and drinking, and eventually entering the assembly hall that had been transformed overnight into the center of defensive operations. Ben Eliezer was waiting for him, his moon-shaped face terribly anxious, surrounded by various high-ranking officers, none looking too happy. They were standing around a table, looking down at maps and grids, jabbing fingers and arguing heatedly with one another as Moshe approached Ben Eliezer.

"How's Kate?" Ben Eliezer said.

"Not too good," Moshe said honestly. "They wanted to perform a cesarean, but she wouldn't let them, so things could be tricky."

"I'm sorry, Moshe. Truly."

"Bad days all around," Moshe said. "They can't be sure when it's going to happen, but they'll ring through to here."

"I'll make sure you get the message."

"What's happening?"

"It looks like we're finished."

Ben Eliezer rubbed his eyes, his shoulders slumped in exhaustion, then raised his head and looked straight at Moshe, trying to keep his voice steady.

"The situation is this," he said. "The Lebanese have taken Netanya and are now moving south toward Tel Aviv. The Syrians have taken Nablus and are now heading across Samaria to Ramallah. The Jordanians are entrenched along the base of the Moab Mountains and are preparing to launch themselves across the Dead Sea. In short, it's only a matter of hours before they march into Jerusalem."

"We can't let that happen," Moshe said.

"No, Moshe, we can't." Ben Eliezer glanced around him, obviously feeling ill-at-ease, then reluctantly brought his gaze back to Moshe, trying to show no emotion. "We're going to have to use our atomic weapons," he said. "There's no other way out of it."

Moshe felt himself retreating, trying to hide deep in himself, not wanting to accept what he was hearing, unwilling to sanction it. Ben Eliezer kept staring at him, his gaze steady and ruthless, refusing to let sentiment intervene, his shame wrapped up in ice.

"It's *Jerusalem*," he finally said.

"I know," Moshe replied.

"We simply cannot let them take Jerusalem—if they do, it's the end for us."

Moshe put his head down and thought of Kate in the hospital, imagining an Arab shell screaming down and tearing into her room. He shuddered with revulsion, but also felt shame, realizing that her safety was, at least for him, more important than what they were contemplating in all of its horror. Eventually, feeling defeated and dirty, he looked up again.

"The Lebanese, the Syrians, and the Jordanians are too close," he said, "so presumably you're thinking of the Egyptians."

Ben Eliezer sighed, his head nodding. "Correct," he said. "And if we do it, we do it now. The Egyptians are approximately halfway across the Sinai Desert, still advancing toward our army in the Negev. We will use an atomic warhead to decimate that army, and then, when the world knows about it, and is reeling from the shock, make it clear that we will do the same, suicidal or not, to any army still advancing from north of Jerusalem."

He was staring steadily at Moshe, not letting him off the hook, but Moshe knew, with a terrible shame, that he would have made exactly the same decision.

"We think it will work," Ben Eliezer said. "It will be interpreted as desperation. One bomb—just one dropped on the Sinai—will put a stop to the rest of them."

"And the Americans and Soviets?"

"They're moving in very fast, but unfortunately they won't get here on time. That atomic missile will buy us the time—putting a stop to the Arabs around us—and by the time they decide whether to advance again or not, the Americans and the Soviets will be in a position for more positive intervention."

"Where are the Soviets now?"

"Following the Arabs into the Galilee."

"And the Americans?"

"Spread out between Suez and Sharm el Sheikh, in hot pursuit of the Egyptians."

"They won't do much good behind them."

"Exactly my sentiments. And it means that the salvation of Jerusalem might rest with the Soviets."

"And our threat could also keep the Soviets out."

"Correct. So let's do it."

He started to turn away from Moshe, but Moshe reached out and grabbed him, taking him too firmly by the elbow and making him turn back.

"How long to launch the missile?"

"Thirty minutes," Ben Eliezer said.

"I want a helicopter to take me to the Negev—I should be with my men."

"Keep in touch," Ben Eliezer said.

Moshe hurried away, feeling driven and possessed, wanting to be there when the light of the desert turned to mushrooming smoke. He was doing it for Israel, for Kate, for their future, but these reasons, important though they were, could not diminish his shame. It was the survival of the fittest, the law of the jungle, and that law, in all its bloody permutations, had come to dominate Israel. Was anything worth it? Did Israel need it to survive? He was starting to doubt it, feeling revolted when he thought of it, and as he left the university, and drove off in the jeep, he wondered how his soul could still breathe in the swamp of its guilt.

The helicopter was nearby and was always ready for takeoff, the crew being rotated in shifts and condemned to wait inside. The men were there when he climbed in, and they took their places automatically, and before he had managed to strap himself in, the rotors roared into action. He glanced around as they took off, again surprised at how young the crew was, then looked out as the helicopter started climbing and the ground fell below. He saw the buildings of the university, then the Shrine of the Book, then the Knesset in its setting of green lawns and strategically placed trees. The helicopter kept climbing, then moved south across Jerusalem, and he looked down at the domes and minarets, the maze of *souks* in the Old City. Then the wilderness of Judea, starkly beautiful and desolate, rolling on to the northern edge of the Negev with its raw, rippling grandeur; looking down there, at that stillness and silence, he felt the weight of his sorrow.

He put his head back on the seat, closing his eyes, trying to relax, hoping to find some dark corner of himself that was not webbed with guilt. He did not find such a place, and felt his sweat breaking out, the physical manifestation of the tension that now seemed to be part of him. He thought of Joshua and Kate, of the night he had found them both, and was filled with a strange, childish wonder at the changes since then. Joshua's face floated before him, very vivid, very real, his smile as mysterious as the dark side of the moon, his gaze as enigmatic as the *Mona Lisa*, drawing light to its darkness. Yet Joshua was dead, a suicide by assassination, and Moshe felt a sudden chill passing through him when he thought about Leon. First Joshua and Kate, then Kate and Leon, then Leon and Joshua in the desert, finally putting an end to it. Moshe would never forget that—he dreamed about it every night—and now, as he opened his eyes, as he looked down at the Negev, he wondered how far Leon had gone before the sun cut him down.

The helicopter was dropping lower, letting the mountains reveal their features, and Moshe saw the shadowed rock, the jagged peaks bathed in sunlight, and then, in the rippling sand of the desert floor, the tanks and men of the army. They were spread out a great distance, between Tel Sharuhen and Mitzpeh Ramon, facing the burning hell of the Sinai Desert and the Arab advance.

The helicopter dropped lower, coming down south of Shivta, and Moshe soon saw the tents of the command post with the big guns around them. He glanced across toward the Sinai, his eyes dazzled by the burning wastelands, then looked around the gloomy helicopter, his thoughts wandering to Kate. The fear gripped him immediately, tearing savagely at his nerves, and he knew, with a sudden, fierce conviction, that Kate was in labor. His nerves started to fall to pieces, letting the fear have dominion, but then the helicopter touched down, rocking lightly from side to side, and he managed to regain control of himself as he unclipped his safety belt.

The door slid back with a screech, the ladder clattered to the ground, and the crew members moved to the side to let Moshe make his exit. He climbed down to the burning sand, felt the heat and turned around, putting his sunglasses on as he did so, and then looking ahead. Major Steinberg was waiting for him, silhouetted in the dazzling light, his face only regaining its features when he stepped aside and waved Moshe ahead.

"We're still waiting," he said.

"Five more minutes," Moshe replied.

"I still can't believe we're really going to do it."

"Nor can I, Saul. Not really."

He entered the command tent and shook hands with the assembled officers, noticing that none of them were smiling and that few met his gaze. There was tension in the air—an almost palpable manifestation

—and he turned away, trying to ignore it, and picked up some binoculars.

"How far away are they?"

"Thirty miles," Major Steinberg said. "They're advancing across a very broad front—and they're coming right at us."

Moshe stepped out of the tent and placed the binoculars to his eyes, surveying the vast expanse of the Sinai Desert and seeing nothing at all. He turned north and surveyed the Negev, seeing his own tanks and planes, stretching back in separate groups to the horizon, the sun beating upon them. Feeling dazed, he lowered the binoculars, rubbed his eyes, and shook his head, then looked at the unlined face of Major Steinberg, whose hazel eyes seemed bewildered.

"I'm sorry, Saul, but it's going to happen."

"I know, Moshe, I know. I know, but I just can't believe it: I keep thinking I'm dreaming."

They joined the other officers at the far side of the tent, all facing the spectacular immensity of the Sinai Desert, all holding binoculars. Moshe checked his watch. There was one minute to go. He put the binoculars to his eyes, saw the sky, the rippling sand dunes, a dazzling whiteness rolling away to a brighter whiteness in a shimmering heat haze. He looked at it and became it, dissolving into its deathly stillness, letting the silence surround him and seduce him until the moment of impact.

Nothing happened. Not a thing. Moshe checked his watch and looked again. Nothing happened and he stared at the other officers and saw them shaking their heads. They kept looking at the Sinai, at the sky, at one another, until two minutes had passed, and then three and then five, and only then, looking stunned, obviously as stunned as Moshe felt, did they realize that nothing was going to happen and they were wasting their time.

After that it became unreal, a dream without solid substance, sliding down over Moshe like an invisible curtain that transformed the whole world. He tried to clear it away, to take a hold on reality, but the events, too bizarre to be real, were too real to be handled. The news came over the radio, one message after the other, destroying logical thought as the hours continued passing and the Arabs materialized on the horizon like a line of black ants. The first missile had vanished, inexplicably, illogically, disappearing at the apex of its arc somewhere up in the stratosphere. A second missile had been launched, had disappeared just as mysteriously; and a third, launched approximately two hours later, had suffered the same fate. More hours passed in chilled silence, the radio crackling with static, the black ants on the horizon growing bigger, spreading out, moving forward. Another voice on the radio, almost strangled with disbelief, conveying further information that made human logic redundant. More missiles had been launched. All had disappeared in the stratosphere. Mossad had talked to London, and London to Washington, and Washington had talked to the Kremlin and received the same news: the nuclear world was dying out, the computers no longer functioning, the atomic reactors and missile silos malfunctioning and surrendering to silence. Moshe believed and did not believe. He no longer needed the binoculars. He saw the black ants on the Sinai as Arabs, moving forward inexorably. The hours passed and they still advanced. He wondered why there were no aircraft. He passed the order for his own planes to take off, but their engines malfunctioned. The planes stayed on the ground, their engines silent, their pilots baffled, and the tanks, when Moshe ordered them out, likewise stuttered and died. Moshe dissolved into the dream, his thoughts circling like smoke, being drawn in ever-decreasing rings to the crackling radio. A new shift, another voice, equally strangled and hysterical, trying to wrap itself around the impossible and make it coherent. Information from Mossad: the nuclear age had just ended; every satellite in the stratosphere, defensive or offensive, Russian and American, British and Chinese, had blinked out on every known radar screen and was no longer traceable. The nuclear age had ended. The great silos were silent. The darkness was descending and Moshe looked across the Negev and saw the Arab tanks slowing down and finally stopping. The Arab soldiers kept marching. The night took command abruptly. Then a terrible crimson light, materializing out of the darkness, illuminated the thousands of soldiers in the rich hue of blood.

The sky was on fire.

45

The Arabs started running toward the Jews. It was, perhaps, panic rather than aggression, since the terrible crimson light, turning the darkness to streaming blood, was emanating from no fixed direction and seemed part of the atmosphere. Moshe turned and bawled his orders, hearing his words before he thought them, and the officers hurriedly grabbed the field phones to pass on his commands. The crimson light was very eerie, turning everyone into a gargoyle, and Moshe had to turn away, feeling fear, and again saw the Arabs. They were coming at him in their thousands, making strange wailing sounds, looking ghostly and unreal in the crimson darkness as they swarmed down the sand dunes. A few rifles started firing—they at least, he thought, were working—and then the big guns, also working, suddenly roared from the flat earth behind him. The sand between the Arabs erupted, geysering high in graceful arcs, forced up on spreading fans of yellow flame and black, boiling smoke. The Arab guns replied in kind, sounding muffled in the distance, and then the first shells exploded nearby, catastrophically violent. More explosions, heat and light, the quavering anguish of human screaming; then the machine guns and rifles, the big guns roaring again—and Moshe stepped out of the tent, into that terrible crimson darkness, looked straight ahead at the thousands of Arabs racing toward him, and then, feeling certain that the end was unavoidable, suddenly thinking of Kate with a fierce, bitter longing, looked up at the sky and saw the star, growing bigger, descending.

Stunned, he just stood there, the guns roaring all around him, the cries of the advancing Arabs in his ears as the bright star descended. Not a star: a brilliant light, illuminating the crimson darkness, spreading out and becoming immense and defying his senses. He tried to see where it ended, wanting to know its shape and size, but it wasn't as he had thought, actually spreading across the sky, but materializing out of the very atmosphere and swallowing the crimson light. The night sky became a white haze, a protoplasmic, boiling mass, the white turning almost silvery, brilliantly luminous and dazzling, lighting up the desert with a clarity even greater than daylight.

The running Arabs slowed down, looking above them in confusion, shading their eyes as the night turned to day and a fierce heat poured down. The new sky was a living thing, something terrible in its beauty, a boiling silvery mass that stretched from horizon to horizon and descended inexorably upon them, as if to devour them. The Arabs started to scatter wildly. Some fell to their knees and prayed. Moshe looked around and saw his fellow Jews doing exactly the same thing. The big guns had ceased firing, the rifles stuttered into silence, and then, as the pulsating sky dropped down like an immense ceiling, all the men, Jew and Arab alike, started bawling and screaming.

They were kneeling to pray, jabbing their fingers at the descending sky, running wildly to and fro or staring quietly, filled with wonder or stunned. Rifles thudded into the sand, caps and helmets were thrown away, and the fierce heat, coming down with the lowering sky, made some rip off their jackets.

The sky continued falling upon them, a pulsating silvery mass, still stretching from horizon to horizon like shivering jelly. The panic spread through the ranks, gripping Jew and Arab alike, and some men started screaming dementedly as their sanity crumbled. Moshe looked up, his fear freezing him, his eyes dazzled by the silvery light, and then, as it dropped lower, as it covered the whole world, he felt himself escaping from his fear and filling up with pure wonder. He thought of what Kate had witnessed, of the light that had introduced him, and his love, rising up to greet the light, set him free from all fear. His sense of wonder blossomed forth, a child's wonder, pursuing magic, and he stepped out beneath the descending sky in the expectation of goodness.

The sky suddenly stopped falling, about two hundred meters up, shivering and pulsating like protoplasm, a shimmering white filled with silver. That low it was awesome, stretched across the visible spectrum, its fierce light and heat pouring down on the thousands below it. The men were weeping and praying, screaming dementedly and staring in silence, but Moshe, hardly aware of them, his head back, his eyes wide open, was looking at the whirlpool of darkness that was growing bigger above him.

It was a gray-streaked black hole, swirling slowly and growing larger, descending through the brilliance of the pulsating sky and taking the shape of a funnel. The funnel was very wide, its dimensions impossible to calculate, and it was spinning at an incredible rate, silvery sparks shooting through it. The funnel created the wind, first mild and then violent, a hot wind that raced in great circles and swept the sand up. The sand hissed and swirled wildly, started roaring and became a storm, and then it turned into a raging tornado that obscured the whole desert.

Moshe was picked up and hurled down, smacked across the shifting sand, crashed into the wheel of a truck and then slithered beneath it. He lay there, gripping the wheel, feeling the wind tearing at him, rubbing the sand from his eyes and looking out as the storm roared and raged. The noise was appalling, threatening to split his head in two, and he saw waving arms and spinning bodies in the dark, swirling sand. He thought of Kate, that first night, the storm raging across Jerusalem, and his love, like an anchor on his sanity, kept the fear well away from him.

The storm scattered the opposing armies, causing panic and havoc, throwing men into the air like rag dolls and then casting them down again. Moshe looked and understood—Armageddon; the final battle —and in understanding this he was released from the shame of his actions. What was willed had been done, changing the Earth for all time, and as the storm died away, having lasted only a short time, he knew that the future, if unknown, was nonetheless guaranteed. Joshua had come and gone, his spirit breathing on the Earth, and life, as men had known it and lived it, would march on down a new path.

The storm died away, the swirling sand settling down, falling lazily on the men who were scattered on flat earth and sand dunes. The whirling black hole had disappeared, shrinking back up through the new sky, then that sky, like a white fog illuminated from within, vaporized to let the darkness return and reveal the real stars.

The Arabs were scattered over the sand dunes. The Jews covered the rippling flatland. The thousands of men, Jew and Arab alike, were too dazed to do anything. Time passed and brought life back. A million eyes turned toward the stars. Eventually, standing up, the Jews and Arabs moved toward one another. They were silent and without weapons, covered in sand, their bodies shaking, and they walked through the starlit darkness, approaching each other in a dream, and then mingled together, some sobbing, some smiling, sharing water and cigarettes and food, and crossing the barrier of race. Their murmuring words, rising out of the silence, webbed the darkness with peace.

Moshe sighed and rubbed his eyes, at once weary and filled with wonder, thinking of Kate and Joshua and Leon and Jozsef, of the events that in tearing them apart had bound them together. He knew that Kate was in labor—this conviction refused to die—and as he looked at the men around him, Jews and Arabs intermingling, he knew with even greater conviction that child and mother would live.

He rubbed his eyes, turned around, and stared back across the Negev, unconsciously attempting to do the impossible: to view Jerusalem the Golden. Instead he saw another light, about forty miles away, boiling out of some space in the empty sky above the plain and emitting great striations of silvery light that fell obliquely to earth. Moshe kept staring, entranced, thinking of Joshua and Kate, of the child that Kate would have, and seeing, in that triangular column of light, a sign of hope for the future. The light fell obliquely to earth, pouring down from a greater light, an immense, dazzling, spherical mass that sank lower each second. It seemed to drop below the mountains, illuminating their jagged peaks, and then it almost touched the earth, its light setting the ground on fire, and then it flared up to an abrupt, blinding flash and just as suddenly winked out.

First the light.

Then the darkness.

Jozsef opened his eyes, saw the stars, the velvet sky, transported to beauty and wonder before the pain flayed him. He groaned aloud and bit his lip, suffering the agony of blistered flesh, and raised his right hand to affirm that his body was living. The hand hung in the air, clearly visible in the starlight, the flesh shredded and terribly burned, exposing soot-blackened bone. He shuddered with horror, hardly able to believe it, then let the hand fall to the sand, forgetting the pain it would cause him.

When it came, that pain was terrible, daggering right up his arm, and he heard his own strangled, sobbing groan as his body twitched helplessly. Settling down, he just lay there, breathing deeply but not easily, distracting himself by looking at the stars and surrendering to them. The heavenly vault seemed like a dark pool, now below him, now above him, reflecting the light of the stars and couched in dead silence. He lay there, unwilling to move, and then slowly remembered.

The scream of the jet plane, the sudden sibilance of the rocket, the truck bursting into flames and turning over and throwing him out . . . Recalling this, he remembered Rashid, the other Arabs around him; and, unforgettably, by Rashid's booted feet, stretched out on the floor in his white robe, the cold, lifeless Joshua.

Jozsef closed his eyes a moment, trying to control his beating heart, feeling the sand drifting lazily over him as if trying to cover him. A pure pain encased his body, sharpening its teeth on every nerve, and he felt the tears trickling down his cheeks with a will of their own. He tried to ignore it, and failing this, to join it, sinking down through the hell of his blistered body and becoming part of it. Eventually, still aware of it, but more able to bear it, he slowly rolled his head to the left and looked across at the truck.

The truck was lying on its side, its ribs blackened, no longer smoldering, the wheels covered in hardening, melted rubber, the engine blown off completely. The driver was hanging out of his cabin, his head resembling a pomegranate, and in the rear, beneath the remaining strips of canvas, was a pile of dead bodies. Other men lay scattered about, spread-eagled, their bodies broken, their dead eyes staring up at the stars and shining like marbles. A white flag fluttered weakly, very clear in the starlight, then became a white robe, the sand drifting lazily over it, the robe fluttering on the body of Joshua, who lay flat on his back. His eyes, unlike the eyes of the other men, were closed and at peace.

Jozsef studied him a long time, letting Joshua draw his pain, sinking into a reverie so complete it made him feel he was dreaming. He saw Kate in the hospital—*Is this your form of conversion?*—then Joshua, his smile enigmatic, preparing for Judgment Day. Conversion had come, taking many shapes and colors, for Kate, very possibly for Leon, for himself in a different way. When had that happened? What form of conversion was it? A Jew and a rabbi, he still believed, but in something quite different. . . . Kate, by the Sea of Galilee. They had walked side by side. He had cursed her conversion as blasphemy before understanding it. Understanding came later, by the waters of Yam Kinneret, the revelation tripping off his own tongue as he gazed at Kate's brown eyes. *Perhaps faith itself, without discipline imposed from outside, if held firmly and close to the heart, will purify and sustain.* . . . So there it was: a very personal and private faith, not

bound by literal theology or dogma, but springing out of the heart
. . . Jozsef smiled and saw Joshua, starlight falling on his face, then
he rolled his head and looked the other way and saw the sand-covered
mound.

There was a globe-shaped, modest rock, the only rock on the flat
plain, and resting against it, shaped like a human being, was a
sand-covered mound. Jozsef stared at it, mesmerized, feeling as if it
was calling to him, speaking out of the silence of the wilderness with
a soft, anguished eloquence. He blinked and licked his lips, kept
looking, his eyes straining, heard the wind crooning lightly around
him and saw it blowing the sand away. The sand spiraled off the
mound, forming dark, drifting tendrils, grew thinner on the mound to
reveal a hand, then a shoulder, kept spiraling away to reveal dead eyes
and lips, the squatting form of a human being, fell away from the
head, dropping down and then drifting away, and then he saw the
hands and feet, the lips and staring eyes, the thin, sun-scorched and
anguished face of the dead Leon Halcomb.

Jozsef's fear, as if surrendering to his grief, slipped away and left
sorrow. Leon was staring straight at him, his dead eyes reflecting the
moon, while his hands, palms turned upward on his thighs, suggested
entreaty. Jozsef felt that he was dreaming, that his senses were flying
away, but the pain that gnawed away at his body let him know
otherwise. He kept staring at Leon, wondering what he had been
seeking, his back pressed to the modest rock on the flat plain, his eyes
surveying the wilderness.

A mystery. No answers. Jozsef shuddered and closed his eyes. In
his mind he saw that lone rock in the wilderness, drawing Leon
toward it. He opened his eyes again, his attention drawn by a groaning
sound, and then rolled his head slowly in the opposite direction and
saw Rashid Idriss.

The Arab was still alive, crawling forward on his belly, his face
blistered and shredded down one side, his eyes bright and determined.
He looked at Jozsef, staring blankly, obviously trying to recognize
him, failed, and then crawled forward again, his fingers clawing the
sand. He was crawling toward Joshua, gritting his teeth and whimper-
ing weakly, but his eyes, flaring out of that broken face, were refusing
to give in.

Jozsef watched him, feeling pity, then compassion and even love,
wanting to help as he crawled toward Joshua, but unable to move.
Rashid reached out to Joshua, tried to touch him, and failed. He

groaned and tried to pull himself forward but his strength finally failed him. The wind crooned as Rashid sobbed, his hands scrabbling in front of Joshua, and then Jozsef, unable to bear his brother's pain, suffered his own pain with gladness. The pain lashed him when he moved, ripped his flesh when he rolled over, tried to skin him alive as he crawled forward, pouring sweat and fresh blood. It took a very long time, an eternity in Hell, but eventually he made it, almost swooning with the pain, and reached out to turn Rashid's hand upward and place Joshua's hand in it.

They lay there together—Jozsef, Joshua, and Rashid—their three hands clasped tightly in the sand as the light filled the darkness.

Jozsef saw the light and felt it, a fierce heat pouring down, and he managed to twist around and look up as that brilliance descended. The light formed an enormous circle, dazzlingly bright, almost magical, growing larger as it descended upon him over a very great area. He stared at Rashid and Joshua, turned his head to look at Leon, saw the light reaching out to embrace Leon and the small rock behind him. Leon turned into marble, reflecting the light and devouring it, and the shadow of something larger than the light moved away from the modest rock. Jozsef turned his head again, looking at Joshua and Rashid, saw Rashid staring up at the light as if begging for blindness. Tears were rolling down his cheeks, then the light erased his features, becoming so bright that it made Joshua shimmer and eventually disappear. Jozsef closed his eyes and prayed. He felt a wondrous exultation. Sighing, he rolled onto his back and opened his eyes to the heavens.

First the darkness.

Then light.

Not darkness, but light—a brilliant light in her mind—offering the triumph of transcendence and dissolving her fear. Kate bit her lower lip, embracing the pain in order to crush it, determined to give birth to her child no matter how great the risk. She was alone in the dark room, the silence pressing in upon her, and the sound of her own breathing, asphyxiated and irregular, confirmed that her circulation was failing as the doctors had prophesied.

Her time had not yet come, but she knew that it was close, feeling the child kicking inside her as she labored to free it. Her lungs seemed to be on fire, her body filled with wracking pains, but she saw that light growing in the darkness and giving birth to the future. She cried aloud and gripped the bed, trying to fight the clawing pain, her thoughts slipping in and out of reality as the drugs took command.

The light grew out of the darkness, illuminating the desert sands, and she suddenly saw Leon and the rabbi in that fierce luminescence. Leon was sitting against a rock, staring blindly at the rabbi; and Jozsef was stretched out on his back, holding the hand of an Arab. The light was a brilliant star, descending slowly, growing larger, and then it suddenly flared up into a stark, blinding radiance, making Leon and Jozsef and the Arab dissolve, and then abruptly shrinking back into darkness.

Kate opened her eyes and saw the darkness of the room, moonlight pouring through the window on her right and falling onto the bed. Was she awake or still dreaming? What had happened to Leon and Jozsef? She glanced wildly around her, feeling the pain, trying to breathe, and understood that she was very much awake, her body fighting to live. The child struggled inside her, wanting to spring forth to the world, but her womb, now contracting spasmodically, refused to release it. Kate groaned, her body arching, then reached out toward the bell, tempted to call the doctors and nurses, but still reluctant to do so. Her hand wavered and dropped away, landing lightly on her swollen stomach, then she closed her eyes and sobbed, wanting Moshe, remembering what he had told her.

The nuclear age had ended. The great silos were silent. Every satellite in the stratosphere, defensive and offensive, had blinked out on every known radar screen and was no longer traceable. The tanks and aircraft were also silent, no longer capable of moving; and in the Sinai, facing each other in the darkness, the Arabs and Jews had stopped fighting. The balance of terror had ended. Armageddon had been averted. Or at least Armageddon, that final and most terrible battle, had been fought around the ruins of Megiddo before the missiles were fired. Now the missiles were no more—they had vanished in midflight—and the possibility of nuclear destruction was no longer a worry. Judgment Day had come, bringing a brief reconciliation—between Jew and Arab, between the two great Christian Churches—and the future, for good or evil, would be built from the eerie silence of a transient peace.

Kate sobbed as her body quivered—out of pain, for the world —realizing that Israel had been saved and that Moshe had survived. She closed her eyes and embraced the pain, traveling down through herself, sinking into the dark well of her own womb and becoming one with her child. All around her was darkness, a black painted on black, closing in and retreating and then closing in again, until a pinprick of light, growing larger, flared up and revealed him.

Did she dream of him or see him? It hardly mattered at that moment. He raised his arms and let his white robes fill the darkness in fluttering grandiloquence. His face was the light, drawing it in and reflecting it, turning it back upon Kate and making her bleed. A mature man. A child. One dissolved into the other. His silvery-gray eyes, luminous even in the darkness, drew the pain from her shivering limbs.

"It is over," he said. "What was willed has been done. My time on Earth has passed and has served its cleansing purpose: the gates before the road to Judgment Day have finally been opened. Man must enter or turn away. The choice lies with him alone. The gates lead to where the sun reflects his image in the shape of a question mark. Will the future be good or evil? Will there be regeneration or degeneration? Will man, in his wisdom or folly, even walk through the gates? He can enter or turn away. The decision remains with him. He must decide in the silence of this transient peace and be marked by his choice."

Joshua was the light, drawing it in and reflecting it, letting it fall obliquely through the darkness to the wilderness floor. Kate saw Leon and Jozsef, the former dead, the latter blind, and then both of them —and the Arab between them—dissolved in the brilliant light. Joshua drew that light to him, sucked it up in the shape of a funnel, himself changing and becoming a star that ascended and winked out. Then she saw the nocturnal desert. Leon and Jozsef were still there. Leon sat against the rock, his dead eyes like two stones, and Jozsef lay on his back on the ground, holding the hand of the Arab. He died slowly and peacefully, fading away with the Arab, both blinded by the radiance of revelation, death freezing their smiling lips. The sand whispered and drifted and slowly covered their outspread limbs, as eventually it covered Leon and the rock against which he was leaning—until, when the light of dawn appeared, they were buried completely. The vision faded as Joshua materialized, his hands raised in the white robes.

"They have passed on," he said. "Like the wind, they are here and gone. They joined hands at the moment of revelation and have now become one. Do not grieve for them, Kate, nor for me nor my brothers; feared by man, death is merely transmutation to Redemption's eternal light. We are here, though we are gone. We will always be with you. The bodies being covered by the desert sands are no more than our broken shells. Think about us and we will live. Recall us and we will come. We are with you now as we always were with you—and always will be."

Kate went tumbling back through the darkness, away from Joshua, real or imagined, sinking again into a coma, fighting desperately to breathe, but determined to defeat the pain and affirm her faith by giving life to her child. In the depths she thought of Moshe, world's end, the new world's silence; and her heart, breaking in two, was renewed because Israel still stood. Her child's future was in that fact. What was it that Moshe had said? *Israel is the center of the world —and if it falls, the world breaks. . . .* Well, Israel still stood, as did Jerusalem in its glory, and Kate, who for so long had rejected it, was now, in fighting to give life to her child, affirming her faith and accepting it. She belonged to Israel—and Israel to the world—and the survival of her country was a sign that the world would be saved. Kate knew this in her bones, in her love and determination, and she struggled back up through the darkness, past accumulating layers of pain, and saw the light spreading out through the room to let Joshua materialize. Whether real or imagined, he filled her vision with a crystalline brilliance.

"No," he said, "there are no answers. I settle the matter before you raise it. I emerged from a fragmented history and am fading back into it. Where did I come from and where do I go? This mystery is as real to me as it has been to you; and revelation, if it comes, will only come when it is too late to speak. I was that I might be. I only knew what I learned from you. My purpose was to draw men toward me and let them see their own souls. Think of me as a reflection, man's conscience and hope, the manifestation of his glory and shame, the question mark drawn before his future that he might learn to brave it. I materialized and disappeared. I have left no evidence of my existence. Men will search for the proof of my being and find only frustration. Did I ever exist? Was I real or merely myth? In time, as the new world, good or evil, takes shape, what I was or might have been will be colored by man's yearnings and hopes. I was that I might be. Having been, I will remain. My signature shall be written across the sky as the Earth slowly spins. I belong to you, Kate, and to your brothers and to your child, and my presence, whether real or imagined, shall live on in your hearts. For your child, as for you, I will endure as a light in the darkness. . . . Will the light. Let it shine."

He had confirmed that her child would live, and Kate felt a great joy, rising out of her pain as a light mushrooming up through her soul. She called to Moshe, wanting him with her, wanting to share her joy with him, and then, remembering that he was still in the desert, reached out for the bell. She opened her eyes and saw the dark room, heard the song of the morning's silence, looked for Joshua and noticed nothing but the moonlight fading slowly as dawn broke. She pressed the bell to call the nurses, her body arching, pushing down; embraced the pain and willed her weakening lungs to work as the contractions increased. She heard the footsteps coming closer. The door opened and light poured in. The breath rushed from her lungs, there was pain and sudden nausea, then the blood pounded violently in her head and sent her into unconsciousness.

No light.

Just the darkness.

The cry of a child. Behind closed eyes was the darkness. Kate opened her eyes to the light and saw the child in her arms. Not a child, but a baby, wrapped warmly in swaddling clothes, its face pinched and ugly, eyes closed, lips tight and determined. A tender love filled her soul, defeating the pain still in her body, and she held the baby close to her breast and felt its softness against her. She lived and had life, and would not let it go; and when Moshe walked into the room, his face filthy, his eyes luminous, she held the baby up on her trembling hands and let her smile tell him everything. He stopped and stared at her, at the child, at the floor, then he walked up to the bed and gazed down at the gift she had given him. He wanted to touch it but was frightened—not of death, but of new life—and then his tears, pouring out of the deep well of his relief, rolled down his cheeks and fell on the child as he leaned over to kiss it. He said nothing to Kate, and she had nothing to say to him. They just stared at one another, gazing across the crying child, looking into each other's eyes to that future which love might make whole: *shielded and lifted by its precepts as a dove by its wings.*

UNHOLY MOURNING

DAVID LIPPINCOTT

All her life, Angie Psalter felt she was buried alive in the sleepy town tucked obscurely into a corner of Northern Michigan. Nothing ever happens—until Angie meets handsome, brilliant Jorbie Tenniel. His love, so overwhelming that it exceeds her wildest dreams, ignites her life with passion and excitement.

And then, one by one, people begin dying, mourning for their lost loved ones. Angie's dreams change to nightmares as she is led to the abyss of unnameable terror. The agonizing horror begins!

A DELL BOOK   19224-2 $3.50

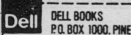

Dell Bestsellers

Who is Baby? A gift from God? Or a hoax? Whoever—or whatever—Baby is, she has changed the lives of those who know her. Doris, her mother: a fifty nine year old "virgin" who thinks she is dying, gives birth to a child who sings. Shockley: an aging professor, feels it is his mission to spread the word of Baby's gift—at any price. Jacobsen: the hustler's hustler, will manage the child's "career." Irina, beautiful but desperate, will kidnap the child for a huge ransom. Will Baby's song remain angelic after all this foul play? BABY is powerful, moving—and the story of a haunting and rampant greed.

"Astounding. An unconventional novel by a spellbinding storyteller."—ALA Booklist

A DELL BOOK   10432-7   ($3.50)

BABY

by Robert Lieberman